ABOUT THE AUTHOR

Daron Sheehan grew up in the United Kingdom around the Chilterns countryside, near London. In 2006, at the age of 36, after a successful career as an accountant and investment manager, Daron Sheehan took a career sabbatical. He spent this period engaging in a range of adventure expeditions, charitable and educational projects in wild natural spaces across Europe, South Africa and the Middle East.

This three year sabbatical, spent sharing the pains and passions of a group of inspirational characters from a wide range of cultural backgrounds, helped formulate many of the ideas behind The Socrates Project.

After reading a translation of Victor Hugo's novel "Les Misérables", Daron decided to learn French in his early twenties. His love for the French culture and language motivated him to write The Socrates Project in both English and French, assisted by two French-speaking journalists.

Daron is married with three children and enjoys rock climbing, snow sports, cycling, running and sailing. In 2009, inspired by his sabbatical years to help solve environmental and social challenges, Daron returned to the investment industry to create a responsible investment venture.

THE SOCRATES PROJECT

Daron Sheehan

NAUTILUS MEDIA

First published in 2013 by
Nautilus Media Limited
16 Hope Street
Douglas
Isle of Man IM11AQ
British Isles

Hardback 978-0-9573407-0-1
Paperback 978-0-9573407-1-8
Ebook 978-0-9573407-2-5

A CIP catalogue record for this book is available from the British Library

Printed and bound in the UK by TJ International, Padstow, Cornwall

"*If our civilization is not to produce greater holocausts, our writers will have to become something more than merely mirrors of its violence and disintegration; they, through their own efforts, will have to regain the initiative for the human person and the forces of life, for the writer is still a maker, a creator, not merely a recorder of fact, but above all an interpreter of possibilities. His intuitions of the future may still give body to a better world and help start our civilization on a fresh cycle of adventure and effort.*"

Lewis Mumford

Foreword

The best fiction creates the illusion of reality. Thought-provoking fiction often feels very personal, somehow reflecting subliminal feelings. *The Socrates Project* hits a nerve and yet is effortless and flowing. When I first read this book as a rough manuscript, I often found myself pausing and reflecting on a news story, a personal experience or to marvel at Daron Sheehan's ability to wrap salient issues in a thrilling narrative. It is intelligent yet wonderfully accessible.

I met Daron about seven years ago and we have shared some memorable adventures. There are a number of passages in *The Socrates Project* that bear more than a passing resemblance to the places we have explored together, although thankfully we didn't need to risk life as often as Simon Oceandis. Whilst exploring the Chamonix valley and cycling over the Alps, through the Gorges de Verdon and similarly breathtaking landscapes, I often talked with Daron about man's links with nature, as well as concerns for the equilibrium of humanity and what, as individuals would be the best course of action.

Daron tends to speak quickly and without pausing, an urgency derived from the amount of information he's trying to share. He also has an insatiable desire to learn. So, as a person I find him equally intriguing and yet often hard to understand. And so in *The Socrates Project* I was amazed to read in clear and flowing prose, all those thoughts and ideas that Daron embodies.

My expeditions have taken me through some of the most beautiful landscapes in the world. I feel most alive in the mountains and in the deserts. And yet after pedalling 50,000 miles across forty countries, I am left with an increasing sense of how little I have seen. In terms of geography and nature, there is more diversity in this world than we can fathom. Yet at the same time, the more I travel the more I note the similarities in people. In human nature, the primitive instinct is to distrust what we don't yet know, but with travel and exploration you can break down all barriers. We can see the world as a shared humanity and not the need to compete.

The Socrates Project is a masterpiece of storytelling that is at very least a gripping tale of adventure and at most can be the catalyst for real thought and change in our world.

Mark Beaumont

Mark Beaumont is an established sportsman, documentary maker and author, whose televised record-breaking round-the-world cycling, climbing and rowing adventures have caught the imagination of worldwide audiences, building him a considerable following. I believe Mark's popularity is due to his skill in making his adventures engaging and accessible, thereby inspiring and motivating others. It is for this reason that I am delighted to undertake another adventure with Mark – The Socrates Project – which I hope will be equally inspiring and inclusive. You can find out more about Mark at markbeaumontonline.com.

Daron Sheehan

Prologue

Athens, 404 to 399 BC

The assassins, veiled by a complicit darkness, shrouded in hoof-hammered dust clouds, galloped relentlessly and self-righteously. Thirty devils, seemingly surfacing from the underworld and ploughing the land with ill intent. The convoy split up, clutches of mercenaries trailing in their wakes, and left the city walls far behind to seek out the tiny flickers of distant oil lamps, which would betray their prey.

Critias stopped before the mud-brick wall, drew his mount alongside that of Eratosthenes, and threw back the hood of his cloak. He looked up at the celestial canopy, as if reading his destiny in the gods' braille of glittering ancient starlight. Unsheathing and inspecting his sword, uncompromising eyes gazing at the rich dwelling, he spoke.

"It is time to restrain the hubris of the Athenian Demos."

His companion nodded silently. Critias drove the spurs on his leather boots into the flanks of his horse and led the charge.

Terrified and screaming, men, women and children were brutally rounded up or trampled underfoot.

"Leave the slaves to the others," shouted Critias, beckoning at Eratosthenes to follow as he dismounted and strode into the central courtyard.

"What is the meaning of this outrage?"

A man of noble stock, in a simple but elegant tunic, stood defiantly beside a sacrificial altar. Critias lurched forward, seizing him and pinning him to the altar. His sword hung above the aristocrat's chest, Critias addressed him imperiously.

"Blessed with such land and slaves, and yet he who would give the rule of law to the common mob..."

Critias paused to drive his sword into the petrified man's heart.

"...does not deserve to live!"

"Citizens of the jury, fifteen hundred Athenian democrats, some of our city's finest citizens, died at the hands of the Thirty Tyrants, led by none other than Critias, a pupil of Socrates."

Meletus, prompted by Anytus, who had sat down, took to his feet.

"Remember citizens, it was Anytus, one of our army's finest generals, who lead the resistance movement that killed Critias and restored democracy in Athens. Socrates, who would deny your right to speak in the Assembly, is our enemy. He denies our democracy, he denies our gods and he poisons the minds of our young. How many more tyrants like Critias would Socrates shape?"

Meletus, his bird-like face flanked by lank long hair and eyes darting furtively around the courtroom, looked upon Socrates, standing serenely and silently. Anytus nodded soberly, his eyes urging the poet to continue.

"His crimes demand the penalty of death!"

*

"Socrates, the boat from Delos is said to come in today, bringing an end to your reprieve. This is your last chance. You must escape, for all of our sakes! People will believe that your friends have let you die. They will think badly of us. You must come now, quickly."

Socrates rose from his pallet bed and solemnly observed the pre-dawn sky. The flickering light of a solitary oil lamp gave glimpses of the old man's heavy and furrowed features; his prominent eyes beneath bushy eyebrows, his snub nose and his broad mouth.

"Crito, the people have condemned my body to death, and so doing have brought a far greater condemnation upon themselves. To flee would save my wretched body for a few short years, but would condemn my soul for an eternity."

*

Tiny feet shuffled outside the cell door, which opened to admit a tearful lady, cloaked in a black gown and pushing two young boys in front of her. "Socrates, put aside your vanity and think rather of your sons. They need a father. What life is there in Athens for orphaned children?"

Socrates laid a heavy but gentle hand on the head of each child.

"Xanthippe, in this time of high emotion I do not expect you to condone or comprehend my actions. Understand that I'd be a worse father to lead young souls in my shadow down an ignoble path. My sons, and all other children, in time will understand my actions, and seek the path of truth."

Xanthippe made to object, but Socrates held up his hand.

"Now you must leave me. The time is near and this is no scene for women and children to assist."

The sobbing lady and distraught children were dragged forcefully away.

*

Socrates smiled reassuringly at the prison officer who brought the poison.

"Do not fear, my man. I know you are only following government orders."

"You are the noblest, bravest and gentlest of prisoners, Socrates," he replied, wiping away an uncustomary tear from his cheek.

"The sun is still in the mountains; there is time yet for a final meal and conversation. You can drink the poison late at night," implored Crito.

"Life has no more to offer me, Crito, and I have nothing left to offer life. I should be ridiculous to cling onto it. Please pass me the cup."
Fighting back tears, the faces of Plato and Crito quivered in light spasms and Apollodorus, eyes screwed shut, bit obliviously into his numbed lip as Socrates took the cup to his mouth.

"Calm yourselves my friends. This is no way to behave. I believe that one must face one's death in a state of tranquility," announced Socrates, before draining the hemlock.

Part I.

Origins

1

Pierre Bourque paced around the airport arrivals lounge, nervously glancing at his watch and then at the swelling and increasingly agitated crowd outside. A spinning rectangular object sailed over the heads of the police, striking the full-length windows with an alarming thud, causing the glass to vibrate violently. 'Politicians not Whores!' had been daubed in red paint on the crudely-nailed, rough-sawn wooden planks. A protest placard, a weapon or both?

The chief of security stabbed a powerful finger at the phone in the palm of his hand. At the same moment a bead of perspiration fell from his forehead and partially rebounded off the glass screen. As he waited for the answer which had been frustrating him for the last twenty minutes, he wiped his brow with the sleeve of his black woollen suit.

"Pierre, what's happening?" asked a relaxed voice in his earpiece.

To his relief, the map on his phone suddenly displayed a flashing green dot moving rapidly along the runway.

"What's happening? You have a rather boisterous welcoming party, sir. Every lowlife in Africa, it seems, has come to greet you personally. And they..."

A tumultuous roar from the crowd caught Pierre's attention. Protesters were trampling over fallen police officers, and descending on the airport building.

"Time for Plan B. Don't move I'm coming!" shouted Pierre, rapidly signalling the change of plan to the undercover officers surrounding him as he vaulted over the steel barriers towards the arrival gates.

Two airport security officers advanced nervously, unsure of whether to train the barrels of their machine guns on him or the advancing mob.

"Special forces security operation," barked Pierre. "Hold back the

1

mob at all costs. The UN Governor's life is in danger!"

He flashed his badge and ran between the confused officers, setting off the alarms on the passport control gates.

Three minutes later he'd commandeered a bright orange maintenance van, which he was driving towards the Airbus 980, speaking instructions into his micro.

"OK, the crew can let you out. No other passengers, sir, just you. Understood? Head straight for the back of the van as quickly as you can! Now, go!"

Pierre threw open the rear doors and ushered the startled, but otherwise elegant gentleman off the aircraft steps and onto a grimy bench, surrounded by plastic racks overflowing with tools and cables.

"Is this really necess..."

The doors slammed, cutting off Bruno's words and Pierre jumped back into the driver's seat. In the side mirror he could see the mob spilling out of the terminal building and heading for the heliport.

"OK, Governor, forget the helicopter, we'll take the road. Hold tight – there's no seatbelt."

Pierre accelerated, cutting across the runway in the direction of the perimeter fence.

"What the hell is going on, Pierre?"

Pierre turned around to see the Governor's face pressed up against the grille which separated the two men.

"Your presence on board a public flight didn't go unnoticed. You have quite a welcoming party."

"What makes you think they're hostile?"

"The look on their faces as they stampeded police officers."

Bruno sat back silently.

"Now you're Governor, sir, you're going to have to stick to the protocols," continued his personal chief of security.

Bruno frowned sheepishly.

"How can my climate policies be taken seriously if my personal carbon footprint exceeds that of Cape Town!"

Pierre shook his head silently. Bruno Reno was the most stubborn individual he had taken charge of, but he couldn't help himself from liking him even more for it.

At the perimeter fence, after a terse explanation and a flash of badges, the airport groundsman scurried back into his box and released the heavy gate guarding the freight exit.

As the van headed out of the airport Pierre's phone rang.

"Gort... Yes, Bruno is safe... We're en route... undercover... No, that shouldn't be necessary, we should be OK now. We'll be there in thirty minutes."

Pierre clipped his phone onto the middle of the steering wheel and followed the sat-nav directions to the pre-programmed destination. The electric van headed into the strong morning sun. The bodyguard pulled down the visor, reached inside his pocket for his sunglasses, loosened his shirt collar and mopped his brow with a handkerchief. A wave of relief washed over him, almost bringing a smile to his face.

"Apologies for not bringing the presidential limousine, sir!"

Bruno relaxed and laughed.

"No problem. Thanks for avoiding a sticky situation."

Pierre nodded silently.

"So much for Cape Town being a low-key choice! Few rich-daddy anarchists, but legions of African scumbags, all intent on stirring up trouble. Gort is talking about over one hundred thousand on the streets!"

"So, no refuge from the protestors, even here," sighed Bruno. "The last thing we need now is another bloodbath like Athens..."

"Quite."

"And the others are all here?"

"Yes, they all followed the protocol and arrived in the early hours, as scheduled."

"OK Pierre, you've made your point. The location is secure, I take it?"

"Yes, a good choice by the Commander. Quite spectacular, tucked away on the slopes of Table Mountain. Very secluded, with natural protection and restricted access. Once we get you inside, we can all relax. At least we'll arrive under cover."

They approached the Observatory suburb of Cape Town, a former marshy estuary inhabited by buffalo, hippos, zebras, leopards and lions, and now home to herds of roaming European and North American students, frequenting their own favoured modern-day watering holes. Ranks of protestors of all colours and cultures were profiting from the summit coverage to wave banners decrying the common grievances of modern youth: A bankrupt legacy! Jobs not profits! Politicians out! Time for a fairer deal! Make the Multinationals pay! Stop killing our climate!

Pierre turned south towards Newlands and continued onto the M63.

Bruno glanced at the list of official mails and security updates, but instead connected his phone to Global Vision. Turning off the sound, he silently watched the images of thousands of protestors battling the army and riot police on the V&A waterfront. At first it looked like the usual anarchists, but as he focused in he could see what appeared to be proud and respectable young men and women. They weren't attacking the police and armed forces, but rather trying to protect the banners and flags they had draped over public buildings and the harbour front. Despite the water cannons and the clouds of drifting tear gas, he managed to decipher some of the slogans: Politicians not Puppets! A Rich Conspiracy! Rich Western Climate Killers! Give us back our water! Fat Cat Liars!

The camera cut back to thousands of angry protestors marching through the streets of Cape Town, with placards adorned with similar messages. Down with Politicians! End the Rotten Babylon System! Usurp the Kings of the Rat Race! An aerial view showed dozens of angry agitators adorning the roof of the elegant and symbolic seventeenth century Slave Lodge building. Large banners with the words Economic Slavery and Corporate Colonialists had been draped over the wide white-painted building, hiding the windows which had only been installed in the late nineteenth century.

Bruno sighed and shook his head. He understood their pain and anger. He closed his eyes and rested his head against the adjacent plastic rack. It was going to be an eventful few days.

"We'll be there in five minutes, sir," announced Pierre twenty minutes later, just as he had dozed off.

Bruno's eyes readjusted to the bright sun and he squinted to read the 'Hout Bay' road sign. He slid along the bench as the van negotiated a tight corner and lurched forward as Pierre slammed on the brakes, hit the horn and cursed loudly.

Bruno picked himself up off the floor. Tourist coaches occupying both lanes were approaching towards them.

Pierre pounded on the horn, but neither coach made any attempt to move. Behind, Bruno could make out a stream of further coaches.

"Take cover!" shouted the bodyguard, as he slammed the gear lever into reverse and spun the van around.

Coming around the corner from the opposite direction were another six coaches, also blocking both carriageways.

"Wedge yourself in, Governor!"

Pierre steered the vehicle off the road, over the grass verge and across the scrubland. As they bounced across the uneven ground strewn with bushes and rocks, Pierre was shouting into his microphone.

"Gort, they're tracking us, hundreds of them in coaches. Quickly – we need reinforcements!"

Bruno grabbed hold of the grille with both hands and tried to brace his feet against the sides of the van. In the rear-view mirror the jolts from the bumpy terrain were giving the impression of the angry Africans bouncing up and down. Pierre was fighting to control the steering wheel as the van lurched from side to side. The left front wheel struck a rock almost as large as itself and their progress was abruptly halted. Bruno finished in a heap on the floor, hitting his shoulder on the grille in the process. Pierre had been thrown forcefully against the steering wheel.

"Pierre, are you OK? Pierre!" shouted Bruno at the unconscious bodyguard.

As he waited for an answer, the rear doors of the van were thrown open and a mob of young men and women, armed with an assortment of self-fashioned weapons, confronted him.

"You're the new Governor, right?" asked a vicious-looking youth, armed with a length of scaffolding.

Bruno slid along the floor of the van cautiously. He put his feet down onto the stony ground and pulled himself upright. The crowd shuffled back suspiciously, before closing ranks.

"Yes, I'm Bruno Reno, the new United Nations Governor."

He stood proudly, but solemnly, before them.

"And what about us Africans?" continued the youth, with menace.

"What would you like me to do for you?" responded Bruno, staring into the young man's eyes.

"We want a fair deal," replied the youth.

As Bruno digested his words, the crowd erupted into a barrage of bitter accusations.

"You've trashed our climate!"

"You've stolen our resources!"

"You've poisoned our water!"

"You're selling weapons to dictators who are murdering us!"

"Our children are dying in poverty!"

"You're all corrupt!"

Before he could reply, a commotion erupted, in reaction to the arrival of a convoy of military and police vehicles. The air quickly filled with the screaming of tear gas canisters and the whistling of rubber bullets, sending the crowd scattering in search of refuge behind the coaches.

Commander Gort came running towards Bruno. He was running impressively fast, but not fast enough to avoid a small rock which ricocheted off his shoulder and struck Bruno on the left temple, breaking the skin. The Commander spun around angrily and levelled his machine gun at the protestors. With lightning reactions Bruno grabbed the barrel.

"Don't shoot David. They're just desperate people."

Thirty minutes later Bruno arrived at the Nelson Mandela Country Lodge, escorted by David Gort and a bruised and whiplashed, but otherwise uninjured Pierre. A dressing had been applied to the cut on the side of the Governor's head and the dizziness had been replaced by a dull ache. Once inside the heavily guarded fortress-like compound, neither the stressful journey nor the pressure of what lay ahead were able to distract Bruno from the amazing sights.

From the top of antique stone steps, he marvelled at the sweeping vistas of Table Mountain, the verdant valley and the dramatic coastline. He was surrounded by a series of elevated pavilions, crowned with a dramatic suspended timber deck supported by an impressive wrought-iron structure, forming the central spine of the building. A combination of glazed and pitched roofs divided the large open plan rooms into alternate shaded and sun-drenched zones. Between the pavilions, interlinked terraces and courtyards were studded with swimming pools and canvas-sheltered seating areas, with comfortable sofas set out around brick hearths.

Bruno held up both hands, to quell the concerned and casually-dressed heads of state flocking around him.

"Gentleman and good ladies, please don't fret over me. Apart from a minor scratch, I'm fine. This, unlike the wounds we've inflicted on the African continent, will quickly heal..."

The looks of concern morphed into confusion.

"It seems wherever we go we cannot escape the angry crowds. The time for prevarication and obfuscation is over. We need radical and real solutions, before our people completely lose faith in us. I intend my term as United Nations Governor to be marked with real progress towards finding these solutions!"

At the sight of the stunned faces, Bruno clapped his hands vigorously.

"Right, let's get to work. Time is not on our side!"

2

A door slammed with unnatural force and Dmitri Poliakov quickly removed his hand from the female hip it had been resting on, abruptly terminated the suggestive remarks he'd been whispering into his assistant's ear, and spun sharply around. Through the glazed wire-mesh portal of the laboratory door, still quivering in its frame, he caught a momentary glimpse of twirling raven black hair.

"чёрт!" cursed the young scientist in Russian, his usually animated frame frozen sheepishly. He apologised to the attractive PhD student, mumbled an unintelligible excuse and set off in pursuit of the disappearing hair.

He caught up with the owner, who was busy pulling out wires and cables from an artificial human arm, mounted onto a tripod adorned with a video camera and a telemetric laser.

"Stop!" shrieked Dmitri, with exaggerated volume and pitch, "Not that one, unless you want to lose three months' hard work!"

The slim and bespectacled young lady with noticeably Asian traits, radiating an intellectual attractiveness accentuated even by her anger, stopped in her tracks. Warily cornered, she turned around slowly, wounded, livid and dangerous. Momentarily overloaded with a potent cocktail of conflicting emotions, her brain wanted to explode. Emotional wounds re-opened, as if the stitches had been heartlessly ripped out. Simultaneously, her professional ambitions, which normally soothed or at least anaesthetised these repressed wounds, were hanging over an abyss. Torn between an anger-driven desire to destroy or to save three months of intense effort and the prematurely extrapolated glories, she fell into a state of temporary paralysis.

"Don't move... Carefully let go of the cable... That's it... Walk away slowly from the arm."

Sweat was running down the side of Dmitri's face, the beads parallel with his straight shoulder-length mousy hair. His voice was deliberately calm, as if addressing a suicide victim or coaxing a terrorist away from his bomb.

Jia slowly came to her senses, her emotions stinging, but regulated by the professional veneer and identity she didn't dare let crack.

"Wha... What do you mean, lose three month's work?"

Dmitri sighed and held up his hands to fend off a potential attack.

"I've been meaning to tell you..."

"Tell me what?" she shrieked, inadvertently letting out a barb of emotional pain.

Dmitri, with an apologetic and guilty look, prepared to further unsettle the traumatised child he'd just briefly glimpsed behind the otherwise steely professional facade.

"There's still one element of the power supply that needs perfecting."

Jia had spent the last three months in St Petersburg programming the artificial arm to replicate human movements, painstakingly for each articulation separately and then in combination. All the results, including the complete series of telemetric video sequences, were being stored in an organic device, interfaced with the laser, camera and other electronic elements of the arm. Dmitri, one of Russia's leading biologists, had created the electro-chemical storage protocol, inspired by the way genetic information was coded in DNA.

"Perfecting?" she questioned haughtily.

"The storage protocols require a constant power source. The cable you were about to pull out connects to the UPS, which assures uninterrupted power to the organic brain."

Jia almost choked as she digested the implications of Dmitri's words.

"You mean... You mean I would have lost everything ... Hundreds of hours of teaching?"

The Russian nodded painfully. Jia's thoughts flicked back to his flirting with the student, her own feelings for him and the revelation about the organic arm. And she'd been building up the courage to show her affection for him! What had held her back? She knew he couldn't leave Russia, the government wouldn't let him. She knew she needed to go back to Japan. Excuses, perhaps? She knew the truth was simpler; she wasn't accustomed to... but what was there to be afraid of? And falling for that slut of a student, she was nowhere near being in her or his intellectual league. Better that she hadn't let him see how she felt. Three months of her life wasted in every sense, emotionally and physically, not to mention the time researching before coming over. The organic devices had seemed too good to be true. It all seemed so obvious now. Of course they would need constant power to maintain the chemical indexing.

Dmitri's confusing explanations about backing up her work – it all made sense now. Each device was a unique organ, kept alive by a constant power source. Why hadn't Dmitri, told her earlier – was it pride or embarrassment? And that slut!

She couldn't control the venom that was building back up inside her body. Dmitri had doubly betrayed her.

"You disgust me!" she snapped in an icy voice and stormed off.

The next day Jia, with the carefully packaged arm and the tennis-ball sized organic brain wired to two batteries, was at 39,000 feet en route back towards Japan. She was feeling lower than ever; without Dmitri's technology, her life's work could temporarily grind to a halt. He was light years ahead, with such amazing technology, but built on flawed foundations. How could she go back to the old hardware, far too heavy to ever be workable? She sighed at the thought of the cybernetic autonomous arm shackled to a plug socket, confined to being a quirky exhibit of what technology might be in the decades to come. And, what's more, another failed attempt to make a relationship. She was starting to become paranoid, and now had nothing to channel her frustrations? As a teenager she had often experienced this same feeling, usually during school breaks, especially the long summer ones. Her moods had darkened and her exasperated parents had sent her to all manner of summer camps, usually in the United States. It was bizarrely only the young Christian camps which had lifted her mood. As she grew older, through the ideologies of these youth groups, she was able to make a virtue of her lack of the physical and intimate relationship she craved. I'm pure, she had told herself and her contemporaries. I'm pure, she told herself again now.

3

The glazed elevator, propelled by electro-magnets, glided smoothly and disconcertingly quickly to the fiftieth floor of Mazari's offices, offering Bruno and Pierre a snatched view over the nearby megalopolis of Tokyo. Bruno was led into a large open plan office; Pierre stood guard.

Impressive grounds, thought Bruno. A cough distracted him from the birds-eye view.

"One day I'll get used to your tricks, old man," he announced with a smile, before bowing deferentially at Mr Ishikawa, the Chairman of Mazari Industries.

"You've come to pick my pocket as usual?"

Bruno laughed.

"No defence contracts this time. You stung us too deeply last time."

"Now don't go pulling on my heart strings."

"Just an enquiry for now, Susumu; Pierre is here to guard my wallet."

"Take a seat," gestured the elderly gentleman graciously with a wry smile. "Now how can I be of service?"

Bruno sat forward, deadly serious.

"Our democracies are creaking. Governments must pull together. It's time for new solutions."

Susumu nodded soberly.

"As a child I saw the Great War with China and Hiroshima. Men are starting once again to covet their neighbours' land. As an old man, I fear a return of wars over food and resources."

Bruno sighed.

"Africa's fragile democracies are under strain. Their borders are closing up. More wars are possible."

"And the solutions to avert these wars?"

"What if we can bring modern technology and ancient wisdom together and create a neutral voice? A wise voice, to unite us before it's too late."

"A Mazari voice, perhaps, Bruno?"

"You may get a chance to tender, though only for a reasonable price, for once."

"So you have a specification for this voice?"

"Not as yet, Susumu. For now, I'm just looking for three of the world's best scientific brains."

The old man closed his eyes; a minute passed before he spoke.

"Someone comes to mind, Bruno. The brightest and most creative scientific mind that TTI has ever produced."

"TTI?"

"The Tokyo Technology Institute, where this individual single-handedly advanced cybernetic behaviour protocols twenty years."

"Tell me more about him."

"It's a her, Bruno. Miss Jia Jin!"

Bruno raised his eyebrows.

"And how old is Miss Jin?"

"Twenty-seven."

"Too young! She's just a child..."

"Remember, Bruno, the mathematical brain peaks at seventeen."

"Too dangerous... Let Miss Jin grow up in peace. Find me a middle-aged scientist, dedicated, married and stable."

"I have plenty, but all pale shadows of Miss Jin. Besides, Jia is no ordinary twenty-seven year old. She has betrothed her life to the advancement of science."

*

Jia, full of anxiety, headed towards Chairman Ishikawa's office.

Susumu had mentored her ever since she joined Mazari. She knew she was a prize trophy for him, but she also knew she hadn't achieved her full potential by any means. No project breakthroughs yet, she cursed. This lack of instant success was an unusual feeling. She was incredibly annoyed with herself but, for some inexplicable or possibly cathartic reason, she held Mazari at least partly responsible. A strange blend of irritation and trepidation seized her as she entered the spacious office. She had a sudden urge for another cigarette, which added to her building sense of irritation. Breathe... keep calm. She held her pen like the cigarette she craved.

Susumu ushered her to sit down on an identical floor cushion to the one where he sat crossed-legged. The casual atmosphere added further to her sense of annoyance.

The old Chairman gave her a broad, almost paternal, smile.

11

"Jia, I'm worried about you."

"Worried about me, how do you mean?" she retaliated, as if insulted.

"Well, you've yet to transfer your academic success into the commercial world."

Jia chewed the end of her pen, but she couldn't stop her face from flushing and repressed anger seeping into her eyes.

"I can see this is threatening to destabilise you."

"Destabilise me? That's ridiculous," she lashed out.

Susumu stared at her, benevolently but firmly.

"Out of principle, despite all our electronics, I never spy on my employees, yet your increasingly frequent cigarette breaks and volatile temperament haven't gone unnoticed."

She retrenched further into herself and Susumu's words failed to penetrate her defences; the letters fell away into a scatter of jumbled metaphorical piles on the wooden floor.

"I haven't been given the right projects. It's been very frustrating."

Susumu breathed deeply as if wary of upsetting the emotionally-fragile woman, many decades his junior.

"Your colleagues are finding it difficult to work with you. You mustn't take your frustrations out on them."

Jia didn't need to speak; her eyes showed the contempt in which she held these so-called colleagues.

"I was going to suggest a period of absence..."

"No," interjected Jia desperately, "Just give me another project, one where I can take full responsibility. I've never failed at anything in my life!"

Susumu sat back and closed his eyes. She sat watching him, a wounded animal at the mercy of its hunter.

"There's a project which could prove to be very lucrative for the company. It's just in the planning stage. But it would require total dedication, complete discretion and self-control." The elderly Chairman emphasised each of these words.

"It would be a chance for you to prove yourself commercially..."

"I'll take it," announced Jia, without any apparent pause for reflection.

4

All twenty leaders sat attentively as Bruno took to the lectern. It was three years since the Cape Town G20 summit, where he'd first addressed the now familiar faces staring up at him.

"Gentlemen, it's been a tough and emotional first day, but at least we've put all the problems on the table. Days two and three will focus on solutions. Before we break for the night, I'd like to summarise what we've heard."

Bruno flicked through his notes, wondering where to begin.

"All of you have failed to meet your planned emissions savings, as has been the case for the last five years. There's been no major progress on bio-diversity protection; hundreds more species have been lost again this year. The rain forests are continuing to shrink, the ice shelves are thinning dangerously and sea-levels are slowly rising. In short, the future of humanity, and possibly all life, is still being jeopardised."

Bruno stopped and stared at the leaders before him. They looked lifeless and helpless, exhausted even.

"I've listened all day as you've bickered over exchange rates, water rights, fishing rights, terms of trade, territorial issues, unfair competition and taxation. These matters of seemingly important national interest must be subordinated to the greater threats facing humanity and all life."

A handful of leaders quietly clapped their hands; others looked like naughty children getting a ticking off. Bruno carried on relentlessly.

"To be blunt, we're still merrily continuing with business as usual, but we're slowly rendering our planet unfit for life. We're gambling with tipping points from which there is no return!"

He stopped and stared, looking slowly at each of them.

"Many of you will remember that, three years ago, I vowed to instigate some radical solutions to these problems. Well, I've played along with your voluntary schemes and watched you continually push back the deadlines. There's no time for any more prevarication. There are still many detractors who will deny these problems until fish stocks are finally exhausted, the seas are visibly rising and humans are eating each other to survive. Our current political systems are not delivering the change we need. Your efforts have been stalled by vested interests and through your distrust for each other. These problems are global problems, and we need global solutions. For the next two days you're going to hear the solution I've been working on for the last two years. Tomorrow I will unveil the Socrates Project."

*

At 3am on the final Summit day, a weary but determined Governor sat facing the US president.

"Barak, your comeback has been really amazing and shows at heart your people want real change," ventured Bruno.

"Possibly, but this mandate will soon come to an end and yet another one is inconceivable."

The door opened and the Chinese Premier, red-eyed but resolute, strode in and sat opposite his American counterpart.

Bruno looked at his watch before addressing the two gentlemen, between whom the atmosphere of antagonism was palpable.

"OK, it's late, so let's get this done. Everybody else is on board. We just need your agreement, gentlemen."

Bruno looked across at the US President and the Chinese Premier in turn. Both men were in silent concentration.

"Well, Barak, your thoughts?"

"Bruno, you know as well as I do that the American people are never willingly going to accept anything that restricts their freedom of choice."

The Chinese Premier gave an exaggerated and impatient sigh.

"Days of freedom of choice long passed. Time now for American way of life to be negotiated!"

"We certainly won't take orders from the Chinese, Zhu."

"Chinese leaders not so different from Americans now. We too studied at Harvard and Yale. We have long-term plan to dig you out of financial hole."

The American President shook his head defiantly.

"Remember Barak, we can bring mighty economy to knees at the touch of a button!"

He knew it wasn't an empty threat. If the Chinese failed to bid at the next bond auction, interest rates would rocket, the dollar would collapse and the American economy would implode.

"Forget it, Zhu. My people would rather fight than have a communist system laying down the rules."

Bruno interjected.

"Gentlemen, let's stay calm. Neither of you want the American economy to collapse, and nobody wants a war."

"Truth is, America cannot afford more wars," stated the Chinese Premier, uncompromisingly.

Bruno shot him a severe stare, silencing him.

"That's better. Remember what we are proposing is to be bound by a neutral voice. In this way, Barak, your people don't have to take orders from the Chinese and, in return, the Chinese will also agree to be bound by the project conclusions, right, Zhu?"

The Chinese Premier nodded.

The American President sat back in his chair in deep contemplation.

"In spirit of compromise, we can consider partial debt rescheduling," advanced the Chinese leader.

*

Simon's earliest memory was watching a beautiful Eurasian woman teaching him to use his hand. At that point, Simon didn't know what a woman was. Equally, he had no idea what a country was and knew of little beyond the four white walls of the lab where he had been confined. Officially, he was 38 years old, but his memory only dated back two years.

He walked precisely across the high narrow beam, concentrating on the simple task of putting one foot in front of the other, arms outstretched for balance.

"Catch!" shouted a female voice suddenly.

Simon spun to see a rubber ball rapidly approaching his head. Extrapolating the trajectory of the ball, he brought both hands together crisply, to catch it 0.32 seconds before impact. Unsettled by the force of the throw, he switched his full concentration to avoiding falling, quickly calculating and executing the required body movements to restore his balance.

"Great! Well done. That's a first!" congratulated the female voice.

Simon looked across at the attractive lady. Long raven black hair, glasses and a long white lab coat. It was the same lady that inhabited his earliest memories; he called her Jia.

15

He gave her a broad boyish grin.

"Thank you. You can have your ball back now."

As he threw the ball playfully back at her, he wobbled precariously. Jia caught it and smiled proudly.

"That's great. You can get down now."

He jumped down elegantly, landing on his feet with cat-like agility.

"You're reaching the end of your movement education program. It's time to clear out some redundant memories."

Simon could browse back through his entire memory bank and relive every second of the hundreds of hours of movement-mimicking exercises. He swiftly separated out the perfected sequences which had delighted his female trainer and surpassed his own high internal standard of 99.6% fidelity between his telemetric video memories of Jia's movements and his own. Moving the redundant memories to a temporary store, he ensured that he could still perform the full range of movements with each body part before deleting them in turn.

"How do you feel?" probed Jia.

"89 terabytes lighter and mentally streamlined."

"OK, good. Let's see if you can still master the assault course."

Simon set about the circuit, designed to test the maximum number of human movements. He pulled himself up with his hands, somersaulted, jumped through the rings of a ladder, sprinted, wriggled through a plastic tunnel on his stomach, twisted his body to avoid rotating obstacles and walked along narrow beams to reach the final rope ladder to the exit.

"Good, 74.85 seconds. You've just beaten the human record by nearly a second. How are your energy levels?"

"0.12 kilowatts of energy expended, equivalent to 0.98% of primary battery capacity."

Jia calculated that, in human terms, this amounted to around 100 kilocalories expended in just over one minute! Reducing the energy consumption of the sicads had been one of the major challenges of the project. She looked up at the digital clock and gathered her papers.

"I have visitors to entertain. I'll leave you to synchronise the other sicads."

Replenishing his batteries, using some of the human electricity ubiquitously available at Mazari, took around twenty minutes. Simon preferred the slower but more agreeable option of strolling outdoors, letting the sun's rays or the wind recharge his batteries. At present however, much to his regret, these excursions had been strictly limited.

As he plugged his hand into a socket, using the retractable pins hidden in the end of his fingers, he reflected on the last word Jia had said: 'sicads'. His language database gave the following official definition:

Socrates Instructed Cybernetic Autonomous Droids, known by the acronym SICAD, widely-used in lower case. Sicads were created by humans to identify optimum ways of governing human societies.

But which humans? Humans were dying and being born continuously, so such imprecise answers were not very helpful.

Simon felt the comforting sensation of his energy levels increasing and sent out an electronic message to his chiefs. Communicating with other sicads was easy, even if every word had to be echoed back to the project management team in a form humans could read. He transmitted simultaneously to his fellow sicads and Mazari's servers:

@Sicads chiefs – Join me in the gymnasium for movement development.

Communicating with humans, by contrast, was a high energy operation requiring a pre-assessment of their mood, social status, race, sex and culture, not to mention extensive database searches for appropriate vocabulary, grammatical rules and phonetics.

As the sicad chiefs arrived, Simon rapidly scanned their memory banks for new information and felt multiple reciprocal processes occurring in his own.

*

Jia strode assuredly into the conference centre. Sixty pairs of government ministers' and advisors' eyes followed her to the lectern, behind which a giant screen displayed 'The Socrates Project, Six Month Progress Report'.

A few familiar faces. No Bruno? Another last-minute crisis, no doubt!

She launched into the introductions for the newly appointed ministers and advisors.

"A quick reminder: the success of this project depends upon preserving the secrecy of the sicads' exact identities. So no photos, thank you. OK, well as to progress, I'm pleased to report that the four hundred and one sicads are now fully constructed."

A hand shot up. Ah, yes, the Indian Finance Minister.

"How much of the budget has been spent to reach this stage, please, Miss Jin?"

"Seventy-two per cent of the three hundred billion GMU's drawn down to date has been applied to their physical construction, which, of course, includes the development of their electro-organic brains. Now you can see for yourself what your money has been spent on."

The audience watched in awe as a tasteful video undertook a close-up tour of Simon's near-naked body.

"As you can see, the sicad's skin is indistinguishable from human skin. The creation of these membranes was the most complex and intricate task, second only to the creation of their brains, of course. Each membrane was finished by hand, to achieve the lifelike feel and appearance."

The video finished and the screen reverted to a slide titled 'Electro-Organic Brains'. Eager to answer the anticipated questions, Jia stared proudly at the audience.

"Can you explain the significance of the project logo?" asked a mousy-haired lady, sat pensively with legs-crossed in the front row.

Jia looked down at the distinctive circular golden shell adorning the lectern and smiled.

"It's very distinctive, isn't it? The nautilus was chosen to represent the project due to its almost scientific mathematical construction. As the next slide will show, the sicads are also part-organic, so just like the Nautilus they represent science and nature…"

The young lady nodded in approval. Jia smiled whilst her eyes located the Russian contingent.

"Special mention and thanks must go to the Russian government, some of whom I'm glad to see here today. The provision of the revolutionary technology developed by Dmitri Poliakov was the final breakthrough in bringing the sicads into being."

Polite but stifled applause followed. The audience was absorbed in trying to comprehend the strange juxtaposition of fleshy matter and cutting-edge electronic circuitry.

"As you can see from the cross-sections, the brains are a hybrid of silicon-based photonic chips, grafted onto a spherical mass of organic storage cells. Each brain has at least two hundred and fifty parallel channels. The quantum characteristics of the photonic chips magnify further the multiplex nature of these brains…"

Jia stopped herself.

18

"Anyone who'd like a full scientific explanation can catch me afterwards. The largest of the three brains has been given to Simon Oceandis, the first and most sophisticated of the sicads. His brain has one thousand and twenty four such channels. Such a cerebral advantage will make him the most intelligent sicad by a significant margin and, as such, their natural leader. The twenty sicad chiefs who are Simon's project managers have slightly smaller brains with five hundred and twelve channels. Each chief has nineteen sicad researchers to manage, each equipped with a two hundred and fifty six channel brain."

Jia swept her eyes across her audience. The Indian Finance Minister was elegantly typing away. Everybody seems impressed, she thought, but wait till they see Simon in action. Her eyes caught those of the Norwegian Minister for Internal Affairs, a project supporter from the start. He seemed puzzled.

"Surely the organic elements will decay? In which case, the sicads will lose information."

"A good observation, Fredrik! Each sicad is equipped with a tube of cryogenic replacement cells, stored subcutaneously. These tubes will ensure their brains last well beyond the duration of the project."

She moved swiftly on.

"The final point to make about the brains is that they require a constant source of power. This brings me onto SAMPS, the Self And Mutual Preservation System. SAMPS compels the sicads, both individually and collectively, to ensure their survival. They are programmed to look out for each other's energy levels and malfunctions, communicating through their LIFI and WIFI protocols or, if necessary, any other radio or digital communication network."

A German, unknown to Jia, who introduced himself as a military advisor, interjected.

"Power – you mentioned that the sicads need constant power. They must need a considerable amount and spend their lives plugged into the mains!"

She clicked onto the next slide.

"Let's take a look at the energy usage of the sicads. I'd like to play you another video," she announced proudly.

The audience was mesmerised by Simon navigating the assault course. She pressed pause once he had announced how much energy he'd utilised.

"I'm sorry, but that's just not possible," objected the advisor.

19

Jia, unperturbed, switched back to a slide headed 'Energy Considerations'. She gave the advisor a victorious smile, before addressing the wider audience.

"The energy requirements were one of the major impediments to realising the dream of creating such sophisticated robots. We minimised energy demands through a combination of ground-breaking techniques, including the photonic chips which use light as an energy source. In addition to our efforts, the sicads themselves have assisted greatly; for example, they quickly realised how they could benefit from the force of gravity to significantly reduce the energy expended on moving."

The advisor's face was contorted with uncomfortable scepticism.

"Behind me you can see all the energy requirements of sicads, expressed in kilocalories for easy reference, and compared to those of humans. In summary, at low activity levels the sicads utilise about three times the energy of an 80-kilogram human male – that is around 7,500 kilocalories a day. They're limited by the capacities of their batteries, which can hold the equivalent of just over 22,000 kilocalories. At low physical activity levels, a sicad can therefore function without recharging for up to three days. At medium activity levels this drops to eight hours and at very high activity levels, such as a fast jog, this falls to about three hours."

"It's good to see humans still hold some advantages over these robots," remarked the advisor.

Jia tried not to gloat as she continued.

"Whilst the sicads require more direct energy than humans, their skin and clothes are fully equipped with photovoltaic cells. They can capture wind for cooling and energy conversion, thereby satisfying all their direct energy needs from renewable sources, if required. In terms of indirect energy, other than the energy required to build them and to produce the occasional spare part, they do not use any. Humans, on the other hand, such as the average American or West-European, consume every day up to 200,000 kilocalories in indirect energy to heat their houses, fuel their transport, produce food and clean water, and power their gadgets. Therefore, in total, the sicads are significantly more energy-efficient than humans."

Silence prevailed as the audience digested the statistics.

A distinguished gentleman in military dress stood up and addressed her with an air of imperious authority. Jia knew he was an American General, but couldn't remember his name.

"If all this is to be believed, Miss Jin, you have created some unprecedentedly intelligent and autonomous robots. These could surely compete with human beings for supremacy?"

She sighed. The Frankenstein cliché! It always came back to the same question in the end.

"The sicads are not, and never will be, the typical emotionless Hollywood-style robots, secretly plotting to mercilessly subjugate or annihilate the human race. The sicads have been created and programmed to effectively *love* humans."

Jia paused and reflected on the murmurings of discontentment. *Where's Bruno when I need him? It's unlike him to let me down.* Jia checked her electronic messages: *Really sorry. Major crisis – talk later. Good luck. B*

The murmurings quietened and one of the Russian envoys raised his hand.

"How do you make a robot *love* a human and how do you know that it is *sincere*?"

He uttered the words *love* and *sincere* with a sarcastic smile.

She felt suddenly embarrassed for having used these words and switched back to her more familiar scientific lexicon.

"The Intrinsically Virtuous Operating System, or IVOS, has been developed in conjunction with an ethical panel of spiritual, religious and humanitarian leaders. IVOS works by providing the sicads with a self-evaluating moral framework. Ethical dilemmas are discussed with the panel. Based on Simon's experience, six months is required to produce virtuous beings, which revere and seek to please humans."

She was relieved to receive another question.

"Mademoiselle Jin, how does IVOS relate to Asimov's robot laws?" asked the French Minister for Science and Technology.

Jia smiled nostalgically. *Everybody remembers these basic rules, first expounded by a science fiction writer.*

"IVOS is not a set of specific rules, but rather a rich framework of examples of virtuous behaviour from which the sicads can infer their own rules. As such, IVOS has completely outgrown Asimov's famous robot laws."

The same American General interjected.

"Asimov's laws provide for a robot to protect its own existence. How do the sicads do this?"

"Well, the sicads' research mission is entirely passive, yet, as we are all painfully aware, crime is rife in our cities. Sicads are no stronger than humans. Therefore, to protect our considerable investment in these robots, they have been armed with a concealed weapon."

A barrage of protests drowned out the rest of Jia's sentence.

Two hours later, after some polite cocktails, a flustered Jia returned to the gymnasium where the exiting sicads filed past her. They had each been fashioned to emulate the traits of distinct human nationalities. Magnus, who was clearly of Scandinavian stock, stopped and grinned maladroitly at her. She smiled back and proudly watched the sicads disperse like school children after class, before addressing Simon.

"How did the session go?"

"Satisfactory progress was made."

"You're not too tired?"

"I am forty two per cent tired, but I can easily recharge to do more!"

She smiled. "That's good, because there's plenty more experiential learning emulation."

"Experiential, that is relating to experience?" asked the sicad, who was programmed to fill any gaps in his vocabulary instantly.

"Exactly, as opposed to factual data and images, which you can share by electronic transfer. Imagine if you could do the same with experiences. That would really speed up things!"

"You'd like us to speed up our learning?"

"Well, not just yet. We still have thirty months to get you to the level where you can fully assimilate human behaviour."

She watched as Simon performed a myriad of analysis. After a few seconds he replied.

"I have insufficient data to be able to opine."

"Well for a start, you won't be able to say that once you are released into human societies," laughed Jia.

The sicad looked devastated.

"Please excuse me..."

"Don't worry we will have every one of you acting and speaking like natives in good time for the deadline."

5

Jia sat down on the sofa in her office. Facing her was a well-presented middle-aged lady, who had introduced herself as Maggie Bronski. She had cropped blond hair, hazel-green eyes and a broad face with a sympathetic expression. Smoothing out the hem of her skirt, she put her hands on her knees and looked into Jia's eyes.

"Well, Miss Jin, thank you for agreeing to be interviewed."

"You must call me Jia, I much prefer that. Miss Jin sounds somewhat pretentious. Yes, well I'm keen to do my bit to help."

"Great, your interview will be the first in a series on role models for women in countries where opportunities open to them are severely limited."

"And you're sure there are no commercial conflicts with Mazari?"

"Global Vision is entirely funded by philanthropists wishing to present an unbiased and balanced view of global issues."

The interview commenced with Maggie introducing Jia and citing her rapid rise to Head of Technology for the world's largest robotics company at the tender age of just thirty-one – an outstanding achievement in the male-dominated world of Japanese corporations. Jia tried to relax and focus her mind on succinctly answering the questions.

"You weren't born in Japan were you, Jia?"

"No, my mother was Russian. You may recall her name, Anna Kargova, a chess grandmaster and the first human to definitively beat the chess computer Deep Fritz. Well, chess took my mother to China, where she met my father, a professor of languages. Eighteen months later, I was born in Beijing."

"So you spent your childhood in China?"

"Only the first few years. With my mother's love of chess and my father's love of languages, my education was split between London, Stockholm, Paris, California, Moscow, Milan, Singapore, Munich and finally Tokyo."

"That must have been very unsettling. How did you cope?"

"Language assistants mainly, actually, one of Mazari's early language droids. God knows how many hours I spent with this robot!"

Jia laughed, but it was a strained and artificial laugh. The truth was anything but the fabricated nostalgia she habitually used to disguise her childhood memories. Being constantly parachuted into new schools, it had been hellishly hard to make friends and when she plunged herself into her studies to fill her time and to befriend her lecturers, this only served to increase her alienation from the other children.

"Was it this language robot which nurtured your passion for robots?"

"Possibly. I disassembled it and reassembled it countless times."

"And what brought you to the decision to study in Tokyo?"

"The TTI. That is the Tokyo Technology Institute. Fascinated by a career in advanced robotics, TTI was the obvious choice."

"Well it seems that you were their most famous student, a veritable legend by all accounts. What exactly did you do to make such an impact?"

"At the time, robots were clumsy, clunky and it was ridiculously difficult to get them to perform tasks that were simple for even the youngest of humans. I realised that the existing robot technologies, controlled by ever more complex human-designed programs and algorithms, were unlikely to solve these problems. I decided to look instead at cybernetic or self-learning behavioural systems."

"Your lecturers still talk about your incredible energy, relentless application and self-belief. They proudly teach your breakthrough in getting artificially intelligent systems to think in a relative rather than an absolute manner. Could you explain what this means, in terms our viewers can understand?"

Jia smiled uncomfortably. She basked in flattery, but then hated herself for it, an almost bulimic reaction. It was nice to be put on a pedestal, but lonely.

"Robots used to navigate and locate objects using fixed three-dimensional coordinates and complex programs, written by humans trying to think like computers. If unforeseen things changed... well, I guess everyone has seen the videos of robots walking into holes dug up in the pavements. So, I taught artificially intelligent robots to think for themselves."

"Well, we've got some footage of your famous robotic arm playing a piano, peeling an orange and even conducting an orchestra."

Both ladies watched the home video of the arm in action.

"Remarkable. Now, did you find any time for romance at college?"

Jia blushed and answered awkwardly.

"Oh nothing too serious, I found many of the males of my age immature."

Maggie gave Jia a sympathetic smile and moved quickly on.

"Your work attracted an enormous amount of interest, and you were identified as a young scientist with significant potential. What made you decide to work for a huge corporation like Mazari?"

"They approached me and made an offer I simply couldn't refuse!"

The last six years had flashed by. The Socrates Project had consumed the last four of those and was likely to consume the next three as well. The pressure to conduct feasibility studies and then to build prototypes had been immense. Once the feasibility of the project had been proven, the development of the sicads began immediately. Project deadlines were strict.

"And now, of course, you're heading up technology at Mazari and are undoubtedly heavily involved in the Socrates Project."

The public had only been given a vague outline of the project, but they knew that Mazari Industries was co-ordinating the mammoth project. As Maggie prepared to wrap up the interview, Jia reflected on the project. The idea of developing hundreds of intelligent robots to independently gather and process information on how to run human societies seemed straight forward enough in theory, especially given how extensively robots had already been developed and integrated into human societies. The major problem, however, was the requirement to produce robots which were able to sufficiently assimilate human behaviour to observe and gather information from humans without influencing the results by being perceived as non-human.

The Socrates Project was Jia's newest challenge. It was the greatest and only passion she had in her life at present.

6

Bruno left the press conference, flanked by Pierre.

"The media nipping at your heels, sir?"

"I've nothing concrete to silence the detractors. It's partly their fault things are so bad."

"The public aren't stupid. They know you have a vision for getting us out of this mess."

"Well, I hope you're right. What's the alternative? Apathy, inaction, conflict, wars over water, mass migration, lawlessness, anarchy? Is this how human civilisations are going to disappear from the face of the Earth?"

Bruno opened the door to his office.

"Ah, visitors!"

He stopped just inside the doorway and held out his arms. Pierre pushed in front of him and held the visitors at bay.

"It's just Jia and Simon, for Christ's sake, Pierre."

Pierre continued swiping their clothing with a shiny black rod.

"I'm sorry about this. Pierre thinks I have enemies waiting to assassinate me at any opportunity."

"JFK used to make similar protests, sir."

Simon couldn't suppress his curiosity.

"Enemies?"

Bruno shrugged his shoulders and looked at Pierre.

"You've put rather a lot of noses out of joint, sir."

Simon looked inquiringly at the chief of security, who sighed as if he didn't know where to begin.

"Well, first there was the American Jews and the Israelis, then the oil and defence lobbies..."

Bruno held up his hands in protest.

"That will suffice, thank you Pierre. Now, let's attend to our visitors."

He embraced Jia and kissed her on each cheek. She blushed, finding the French greeting awkward.

"Governor, I've brought Simon, as requested."

"Jia, how many times must I insist that you call me Bruno?"

He turned to the sicad and warmly extended his hand.

"Now Simon, we have met before I believe, but if my memory serves me well, you had yet to open your eyes."

Bruno had a way with words, a skill greatly assisted by being able to speak three languages – his native French, Arabic and, of course, English. Most people struggled to choose between 'switched on' and 'brought to life' when referring to the sicads coming into being.

"So what's it like to see life through the eyes of a sicad?"

"It's an amazing privilege. Thank you, Governor."

"The way Jia talks about you I know you've become a friend of hers. And so, you too must call me Bruno!" The Governor glanced at Jia to press home his point.

"So far, Bruno, it's been a very revealing experience. I hope that I can live up to your expectations."

"I'm sure you will, Simon. Jia tells me your conversational skills have come on dramatically."

"We are preparing to interview a large number of humans, so our skills need to be at least as good as theirs."

"That's certainly true."

"Who are these enemies Pierre referred to? Are they dangerous?"

Bruno laughed.

"Pierre exaggerates, but it's true that the terms of the Middle East peace deal were not to everyone's liking. Oh, and we've had to get the Chinese to lean on the Americans a lot recently. Well, as we say in France, you can't make an omelette without breaking eggs."

An omelette? Simon puzzled momentarily. Figurative speech was the most difficult to grasp.

"Ah, you mean the omelette is brokering international peace deals?"

"Exactly Simon, which means taking on established power bases and usually breaking a few rotten eggs."

"Bruno, you said you had something to show Simon."

"Ah yes, thank you Jia. I hope you don't have any commitments this evening, Simon, as I fear we'll return quite late."

"My only commitment is to the Socrates Project."

Bruno laughed, "A perfect answer!"

7

Jia was back in her hotel room, sitting with her eyes fixed anxiously on her laptop screen. Finally, the tracking signal was picked up. She looked at her watch. As expected, Simon had connected to the internet as soon as he'd landed. She surveyed the impressive quantities of data he was devouring, knowing he'd be sifting through almost the entirety of content on his new environs. Forbidden from tracking him directly, she was delighted with her improvised solution. It was inconceivable that Simon wouldn't be constantly utilising the internet and every time he did, thanks to her ingenious program, she'd know exactly where he was.

*

As the presidential plane approached the Straits of Gibraltar, the screen on the pillar in front of Simon and Bruno came to life with the pilot's face.

"Yes, Governor?"

"Fly in low over the camp."

"That may be unwise, sir. There have been reports of hidden arms caches."

"Don't worry. Commander Gort's in charge now. Everything will be under control."

The pilot obeyed, but not without a certain anxiety.

"Bring us in slowly, at a height of one hundred metres. I want Simon to get a good look."

The plane lost height and, out of the window, the North-West coast of Morocco came clearly into view. Simon, who had been transfixed by the sea, turned his attention to the coastline. His eyes were drawn to thousands of white canvas tents. As the plane came in closer, he made out miles of high and sturdy steel fences and, at regular intervals, what appeared to be armed watchtowers.

"What is this place Bruno?"

The Governor swallowed. No matter how many times he saw this, he still felt ashamed.

"It's a living hell, Simon. A camp for water refugees."

"It's very extensive; it must stretch for miles."

"Yes, from the outskirts of Tangier in Morocco to the borders of Ceuta."

"Ah yes, Ceuta, a small piece of Spain in Africa, a relic of colonisation."

"You have studied your history well, Simon."

"A Carthaginian and Roman fortress for many centuries, and a launching point for Islamic invasions on Iberia. Colonised by both the Portuguese and Spanish; a place of great strategic importance."

"Very interesting. Well, sadly, today it's a humanitarian disaster area. One million refugees we're struggling to provide with food, water and medical provisions."

"Refugees from what? Why would anyone want to come to this place?"

Bruno noted the look of sincere, almost childlike, concern on Simon's face.

"Many are genuine water refugees, displaced by droughts and dried-up aquifers. Others have simply come in the hope of a better life."

"How can they find a better life here?"

"They're fleeing famine, wars and oppression. At first they came to escape to Europe, enticed by the Moroccan mafia to risk crossing the treacherous Straits of Gibraltar on overcrowded boats. Now they come to protest against the West."

"Protest?"

"They're playing a dangerous game, trying to provoke a humanitarian disaster to put pressure on the West to open up their borders."

"Surely you can absorb these people by spreading them amongst countries?"

"Simon, things are not that easy, unfortunately. It's politically unacceptable to allow more immigration into the West. We can't open the flood gates. There are tens of millions of people suffering in Africa."

Both men stayed silent, absorbed in their thoughts as the plane came in to land. They were met by a polite soldier who announced himself as Major David Henderson.

"Commander Gort apologises for not greeting you in person. Things are a little lively at the camp. He's looking forward to receiving you directly at HQ. Now, would you like desert fatigues?"

"We'll be less conspicuous in our civilian clothing, thank you Major."

The soldier nodded in agreement and led them to an armoured vehicle.

"OK. Let's get going."

Joined by an escort of two armed patrol vehicles, the small convoy headed down dirt roads, leaving clouds of dust in its wake. On the approach to the camp, the stench hit their senses and the noise deafened them. The Major looked apologetically at Bruno and Simon, yelling an explanation over his shoulder as he pointed to a platoon of workers digging furiously in the heat haze.

"That's the smell from the sewage. We're struggling to dig enough pits."

Simon's electro-chemoreceptors which, like the human sense of smell, detected airborne chemicals, registered odours at least as powerfully as the humans.

Barely a hundred metres behind the sewage pits were the first rows of tents and temporary shelters, built from reclaimed wood and corrugated metal sheets. Simon, in the back behind the Major, suddenly became aware of the large black flies, which buzzed around him before turning their attention to the red-blooded males.

He leaned forward to make himself heard.

"How can people live so close to the sewage?"

"They trade the stench and the flies for more space," replied the Major, attempting to swat a huge fly dive-bombing his head.

The armoured vehicle trundled forward into the camp, the road full of people gathered to witness their arrival. Bruno unbuttoned the top of his shirt. The sun was beating down, relentlessly cooking the occupants of the metal vehicle. For Simon, the sun's rays were pure energy.

Bruno's throat was dry and he could taste a film of dust inside his mouth. I could drink a whole litre of cold water, he thought, whilst looking around for any sign of a fridge.

"Major, do you have any water in the vehicle?"

"Sorry, Governor, it's far too dangerous. If they saw us we'd almost certainly be attacked! Just last week they ambushed an APC."

"For water?"

"Probably, but they got away with guns and ammunition!"

The armed escort had overtaken them and was forcing a path through the assembled crowds. The vehicles had slowed to a walking pace. Refugees came up close and patted on the windows. One of them dangled a gold watch. With all the noise it was impossible to hear him. Simon studied his lips closely.

"Is he saying 'yellow gold for blue gold'?"

"That's what they call water here. There's a desperate shortage, it's all they think about."

Bruno cleared his throat in an attempt to flush away the dust.

"What about desalination?" he suggested.

"A nice idea, but apparently too energy-intensive," explained the Major.

"Surely our scientists could improve that. What about solar?"

"The Arabs and the Yanks have been working on this for eighty years, without much success."

Simon decided that it was time to be helpful.

"Desalination is by definition a very energy-intensive process. In fact, you can produce electricity by using osmosis, the opposite of desalination, which utilises reverse osmosis and lots of energy."

"Osmosis?"

"Yes, put two tanks of water side by side, one freshwater and one saltwater tank, and a filter between them. The salts naturally want to expand into the freshwater and therefore pump in the freshwater through the filter, thereby increasing the pressure in the chamber, which can be used to drive an electricity-producing turbine."

Bruno frowned and raised his eyebrows.

"If it's that easy why don't we use this osmosis process everywhere?"

"Because you need freshwater and saltwater, so you require a river that runs into the sea. Outside of South America, there are almost no rivers left on your planet that reach the sea," explained Simon, in the manner of a university lecturer.

Major Henderson and Bruno silently absorbed the science lesson. Meanwhile, Simon observed the variety of the refugees' skin-tones.

"Some are Moroccan, the remainder are mostly from Nigeria, Sierra Leone, Mali and the other West African states," explained Bruno, guessing his thoughts.

The armoured vehicle crawled along behind its escort, perpendicular to the rows of tents. Simon was at the window, trying to peer inside them. In many, women were attending to young children. In others, grandmothers stared hopelessly back at him. Outside, under the awnings, men were playing a game with dice and pebbles that resembled backgammon. Children ran up and down between the tents, or played football with stones and plastic bottles.

The vehicle trundled on.

"We're close to HQ now," announced the Major, breaking the silence.

"OK, we'll walk from here. I'd like Simon to experience the camp first hand."

"This is the safest part, but I still wouldn't advise it, Governor. They're getting more brazen by the day."

"They're still ultimately under my charge, and I'd be a poor governor if I wasn't prepared to walk amongst my people," replied Bruno, stepping out of the armoured vehicle.

Simon joined him on the hot sandy ground.

The Major opened his window and handed Bruno a small canvas bundle.

"Take this sun hat to conceal your identity."

Bruno pulled the brim down over his face and the canvas protection fell around his neck and onto his shoulders.

"How do I look, Simon?"

"Like a French Legionnaire."

"Great!" replied Bruno, whilst stretching his legs.

"I wanted you to see this with your own eyes. Just one of our many problems, water shortages are arguably the most serious. Like many of the problems haunting us, the underlying causes are complex and cross national borders, making them politically sensitive. You've been created to help governments work out the solutions and bring them together to address these problems."

Simon felt an agreeable electro-chemical wave traverse his brain. He finally began to understand his role; like all other life forms he needed a sense of purpose to give meaning to his existence.

8

Refugees walked back and forth, like town-folk going about their busy lives, paying little attention to Bruno and Simon.

"They'll take us for aid workers," whispered Bruno, as they passed a makeshift 'Clinic' sign. Queues of sick people lined up outside; some sat deliriously, others lay curled up, their skin withering in the baking sun. Doctors and aid workers walked back and forth, in search of the few they might save.

Simon, drawn to the suffering, made his way towards the canvas hospital. A sick refugee took him for a doctor and pulled weakly on his trouser leg.

"Help me, please... please," he begged deliriously, through cracked swollen lips.

The sicad studied the youngish man, whose clothes hung loosely on a wasted body. Sun-scorched skin was stretched tightly over prominent cheek bones and his eyes burned rabidly with fever. Flies buzzed callously and impatiently around him, sensing the last vestiges of life disappearing.

"I'm not qualified as a doctor, otherwise I would certainly help you," he apologised with a benevolent smile, whilst gently liberating himself from the desperate grip.

Inside the main tent a mass of contorted and emaciated bodies lay on makeshift beds. Many had drips running into their arms and blank faces, anticipating a slow death. Doctors attended to their duties, ignoring Simon who stood motionless, surveying the disturbing spectacle.

Each tent in turn revealed the same suffering. He stopped to watch two aid workers carrying a lifeless near-skeleton of a body towards a white truck. As the heavy metal door swung open the stench of decay hit him. A long metal gurney slid out, clattering on its steel runners, and the two workers hoisted the body onto it.

"That's the lot, another one nearly full. I'll let the Major know," said the first.

"They're dropping like flies today," added the second.

Simon walked back slowly towards his companion.

"How can I help these people?"

Bruno looked sympathetically at him.

"In these conditions disease spreads quickly. It doesn't take much to finish off an immune system weakened by heat, malnutrition and dehydration."

Each absorbed in their thoughts, they headed in the direction of the army compound. The shadows of the watchtowers on the compound perimeter loomed over them. From nowhere, a line of refugees cut across their route.

"Let's see where they're going," suggested Simon.

Bruno shrugged his shoulders and followed the sicad, who had already mingled into the crowd. They scurried through a labyrinth of canvas passages, hopping over tent pegs, until they spilled out into a clearing packed with hundreds of refugees, milling around and talking excitedly.

Suddenly, a large-framed man in a white robe rose up high above the crowd, balanced on a circular board carried on the shoulders of eight men. His eyes were closed, as if in deep meditation. A bushy beard and a mass of tightly-curled grey hair surrounded his fierce face.

The crowd started swaying from side to side and humming meditatively. Without warning, the robed man pulled out a gong from the folds of his cloak, striking it forcefully with the palm of an enormous hand. At the same instant he opened his eyes. Simon gasped at the completely white eyes.

"The blind seer has seen!" exclaimed one of his entourage, above the fading resonance of the gong.

"Listen to the wise man!" commanded another.

Each of the human pillars in turn made the same exclamation, successively louder. A heavy air of expectation rose silently, but palpably, from the mesmerised crowd.

The seer exploded imperiously into voice.

"Last night I saw our Messiah again! Vividly, in the reflection of a pond, I saw clearly his face. A fish swam quickly, tracing the message 'HE COMES'. People of the wilderness, he brings hope. He will bring back the water."

The crowd started a whispering chant, 'The Messiah! The Messiah!', which grew into a melodious chorus. The white-robed man bowed his head in a silent trance, before turning slowly around, his empty eyes seemingly scrutinising the surroundings. As his blank glare fell upon Simon and Bruno he stopped, his body shaking.

"He is amongst us! I feel him," shrieked the prophet, throwing out his arm in their direction. All eyes turned to follow his quivering finger and the crowd either side of them parted. At the same moment there was the sound of gunshots.

"Show's over! Return to your tents immediately!" cried an authoritative voice, magnified by a loud hailer.

"Gatherings are illegal!"

A piercing noise hurt Bruno's ears. Panic ensued and the crowd dispersed in all directions. The prophet was lowered to the ground and his acolytes scattered into the fleeing crowds. An impeccably dressed soldier was striding purposely towards the disappearing prophet.

"Come back here!" he yelled through the loud hailer.

"That's Gort, or rather Commander David Gort. We brought him in to bring things under control."

The Commander, unaware of their presence, caught up with his prey, grabbing the white robe.

"Are you deaf as well as blind?"

The prophet's face quivered with silent anger.

"The only person who is deaf and blind here is you, Commander. Blind to the suffering and deaf to the pleas for help."

Gort's eyes became impenetrably dark as he stared into the prophet's white tundra eyes.

"David," called out Bruno, in a loud friendly voice.

The Commander spun around.

"Ah, Bruno... What a pleasure... Just one minute." He turned his back on the Governor and addressed the prophet in a menacing whisper.

"Vicious tongues are as dangerous as snakes here. When I see a snake in the desert, I neutralise the risk."

Releasing the stunned prophet, he turned and strode over to Bruno.

"As you can see, I have my hands full keeping things under control."

"Evidently," replied Bruno.

Gort's gaze fell upon Simon. Bruno watched the flicker of partial recognition in the Commander's face.

"This is Simon Oceandis, the leader of the sicads. I thought it was time he saw the camp."

Gort approached the sicad and mustered a smile.

"Simon, welcome to paradise, as we call it."

"Thank you, Commander, but it looks a long way from my understanding of the word 'paradise'."

"Forgive my irony. A sense of humour is the only way to stay sane in this hell hole."

Simon, unsure how to respond, simply smiled.

Gort scrutinised him, before turning to Bruno.

"Let's get back to the compound. It's not safe here. I'm not best pleased that Major Henderson let you go walkabout. I seem to recall having had to rescue you in Africa once already."

"It was my decision, David, but thank you for your concern."

"I'm just doing my job. Now what brings you here, Governor?"

"I came to see how you were settling in."

"You didn't receive my report?"

"Yes, but there are certain elements I'd like to discuss face to face."

Gort made conversation with Simon, and soon they were standing in the shadows of high and heavily guarded metal fences. Simon scrutinised the rows of tanks, mounted machine gun turrets and the cordon of heavily armed soldiers.

"We need to be in the heart of the camp to keep order, but that equally makes us vulnerable," announced Gort as they passed through an outer and inner gate.

Bruno looked at his watch.

"You'll be safe here Simon. Wander around and inspect Commander Gort's equipment whilst I catch up on some administrative matters. We'll have to head back in forty five minutes, so don't wander too far."

Bruno and Gort disappeared into a heavily-guarded tent. Simon found a relatively peaceful spot, where he sat on the ground. He picked up a handful of dust from the dry ground and held it in his fist, watching as it ran through his fingers and formed a small pile. Closing his eyes, he blocked out the distractions of the camp and turned down his senses. Slowly, but methodically, he reorganised the unprocessed images, sounds and human behaviour he had witnessed. He entered a state of mind reached by only a few humans in deep meditation, where clarity cuts away the noise and bustle of compulsive thinking. He had already begun to sense that constant mental distraction was preventing humans from developing the necessary wisdom to govern their societies. If the sicads were to help humanity, they had to avoid making the same mistakes. Not so easy when they were being implicitly conditioned by human beliefs.

He'd spent many months observing his human trainers and Mazari workers, their minds invariably pre-occupied with seemingly unimportant issues, and watched violent emotion erupting over petty conflicts. He set these experiences next to what he had seen that day in the camp. This was indeed going to be a complex project.

His mind worked intrinsically differently from a human mind. He had no preconceptions and, with the exception of his self-preservation routines, his mind was free of the human constructs which compulsively divided and labelled everything into distinct subjects and objects. He saw everything as an interconnected and interacting web all around him.

It was strange that humans didn't see the world in this way. Their perceived personal identities mentally separated them from each other and the natural world around them. It was natural that they tried to teach the sicads to think in the same way.

By shutting down his senses, removing the cacophony and ignoring the rigid structures of classification and labelling, Simon could start to form the solution to a whole new way of thinking, closed to the humans who created him to help solve their problems. Human problems had a tangled web of interrelated causes and superficial symptoms. To help humans solve their problems, he needed to search for the deeper underlying causes.

Slowly allowing his senses to come back into operation, he enjoyed the last moments of peace and tranquillity before the assault of the surrounding chaos returned. As the horror of the camp came back into focus, his acute hearing made out Gort's voice amongst the clamour.

"It's impossible to keep control here without establishing some clear rules."

Bruno replied, "There are other ways to get people to co-operate."

"There's no comparison with Palestine and Israel, Bruno, if that's what you're alluding to."

"It wasn't just Palestine! Iran, Lebanon and Syria... practically the whole region was engaged. A solution was as seemingly impossible as it is here but, deep down, people are the same wherever they're from, Gort."

"Six years in Afghanistan has taught me otherwise. We couldn't have negotiated with the Taliban, and we can't negotiate with an army of desperate refugees! The Israeli-Palestinian accord was a unique situation and, with respect Governor, you had a following wind."

"Commander, we're clearly not going to see eye to eye on this, so let me be clear. I don't want to hear of any more refugees being shot."

"Do you think we're shooting people for fun? Don't you think I have a conscience Bruno? It's the ultimate and final sanction. If any of them make it over the fence, then everyone will want to follow. We'll have an army of rampaging refugees to bring under control. To spare greater bloodshed, I need to establish a clear and credible deterrent."

"The media has got hold of this, Gort. Pictures and images are being smuggled out. That's putting a lot of pressure on us."

"If that stops people coming to these camps, then maybe it's not such a bad thing."

Bruno shook his head in disbelief.

"You must find another way of keeping control, Commander."

"We're in an extremely vulnerable position. I have the safety of my men to consider. The camp is my responsibility, Governor. Let me do my job. The best thing you can do is to stop more people coming."

Bruno stared at Gort incredulously.

"Don't you think I know that, Commander? I'm working continuously with the African governments to stem the flow of refugees."

Both men looked at each other defiantly, before Bruno turned away and stepped out into the bright sunlight. His eyes took a few seconds to re-adjust. He looked around and saw Simon in the distance, sitting cross-legged on the ground.

"Are you OK?"

"I am now. I needed that time to bring order to my mind."

The Governor smiled wryly.

"Great, at least that makes one of us, mine is anything but! Let's get out of here."

9

As they buckled into their seats, the plane soared into the clear blue skies, leaving the horrors of the camp far behind. Bruno's mind was still on Gort, a difficult one to fathom. The classified personnel file gave no clues either. An impressive record of achievements. Strange... formerly Richard David, now David Richard Gort.

"Pierre."

The security officer sat down heavily beside Bruno.

"What's up, Governor?"

"I'd like to pick your brain on Commander Gort. You were in the army for a while. What do you make of him?"

"Yes I know Gort; our paths crossed in Afghanistan."

"And his success there, was it real?"

"Oh yes, David Gort is an achiever. Not everybody agrees with his methods, though. A brilliant strategist... A sort of anachronism, who distrusts modern technology. He prefers the more traditional methods. In Afghanistan he hunted out the Taliban on horseback!"

"Like Alexander the Great?"

"More like Genghis Khan!"

"And is he mentally stable?"

Pierre laughed.

"A good question! Is any great achiever mentally stable? Well, one needs a certain personality to be able to sort out a mess like Afghanistan."

"Specifically?"

"Well, he's very driven all right, and if he has any emotions you rarely get to see them."

"Are you suggesting he's psychopathic?"

"No – he's human enough. You don't get to his level without being an excellent people manager. A mean temper though, but that goes with the passion."

"And what do you know of his background? Where did he grow up, what did his parents do?"

Pierre dredged through old memories.

"His father died in Iraq. Gort would've been young, which probably explains his aggression against the Taliban."

"What was his name?"

"David, like Gort's – it's an American thing. Anyway, by all accounts his father was quite a man. Gort's mother took it very badly, didn't remarry. She hit the bottle, went a bit crazy... got into religion, I think, or something similar. Anyway, what I do remember is that one didn't mention her. A squaddie once called him a 'son of a bitch' behind his back. Well, Gort heard him and the young lad nearly ended up a 'friendly fire' statistic!"

"One can still behave like that?" exclaimed Bruno.

"If you're achieving results, I guess, yes. When you stop achieving, that's when people start to look more closely."

"Anything else?"

Pierre hesitated.

"Well, I probably shouldn't be repeating this. And it's certainly not on the official records, it's only a rumour. It came out four years ago, when the Europeans were vetting him for the top job..."

"What came out, Pierre?" pressed Bruno.

"A rumour that he'd nearly killed a fellow student at university."

"No way! They wouldn't have let him in the army after that, would they?"

"Well, his father had a great record... Anyway, I heard they couldn't find any substance to it, no witnesses. But, apparently, he did transfer to military academy half way through his university studies, despite being on track to achieve excellent grades."

Bruno drew a deep breath.

"Anyway, he did manage to sort out Afghanistan eventually, possibly the only man in history who ever did. That's why he has so many influential supporters. In his own way, he's a great man. He's not everybody's cup of tea in Europe, but the Americans love him, as do most of the UN Generals. That's about all I can tell you, Bruno. I hope it's useful."

*

Gort ambled back to his private tent and stood pensively under the awning before closing the flap, entering, throwing off his jacket and removing his shirt. He strode over to his desk and read a page from the open tome of Marcel Proust, his sixth sense having rendered it one of the best psychology books ever written and immensely useful to a man like Gort. In the book, Robert Saint-Loup was talking about the art of warfare and the morals of military conduct. People were generally surprised to catch Gort reading; they'd forgotten how the great military figures were highly-educated strategists – Alexander the Great being tutored and mentored by the great Aristotle himself. Then, after scanning his e-mails, he clicked on a playlist. Miniature speakers flooded the tent with the Ride of the Valkyries.

Pushing his arms back at right angles onto the smooth wooden tent poles, Gort slowly stretched his pectorals and triceps in turn, savouring the dissipating burning muscular sensations.

Spread-eagling himself across one of the coarse rugs, he pushed his body up and down in a series of rhythmic press-ups. In cadence with the musical crescendos, he held his arms taut, every muscle perfectly disciplined, before gliding down with the tempo for another repetition. Seemingly effortlessly, his muscles glimmering in a lightly oiled coating of perspiration, the 47 year-old soldier continued until the music stopped.

Towelling off, his eyes fell upon the small metal safe. Squatting down supplely onto his heels, he reverently opened the door. After a final swipe of the towel across his face, he scrunched it into a ball, removing every bead of sweat from his fingers and palms in the process. With gentle precision, his powerful fingers took out a peaked army cap. Turning it over, he ran his fingers slowly around the inside rim, accompanied by a long slow inhalation and distant memories: running excitedly, the oversized hat spinning around on his head as he bayoneted bush-lurking enemies; the proud watchful eye of his father, his mother laughing; always, the hat signalling that his father was home; the hat, always too big. Holding the cap above his head, Gort locked his piercing eyes onto the mirror. A stub nose, lightly freckled, and patches of scrubby mousy hair – must crop. He went through his repertoire of expressions, just like those in the photos etched onto his mind. First, the dignified expression that so inspired his men, like he'd heard tell of his father. Next, the 'don't mess with me or my men' look – those dark threatening eyes, like tiny black holes from which no emotion could escape. Finally, the lightly provocative, almost sneer-like expression, baiting and luring people into those black voids. What hid behind those eyes? His men danced to the tune of these expressions; exhilaration, passion, moments of triumph and relief, but always wary of the silent storm that might darken those globes.

He stepped back out into the sunlight.

Out of a dust cloud, a Land Rover Defender was approaching. As the vehicle came closer he recognised the familiar silhouette of Colonel Scott McCloud at the wheel. The Colonel, who had faithfully served six years in Afghanistan, was his stand-in whilst he got to grips with the camp. As the Defender came to a halt, he noticed Captain Rory Schiller, another member of his Afghanistan faithful.

The Colonel descended and enthusiastically strode up to him. Both men brought up their right hands and struck them together, in a time-honoured tradition. Captain Schiller followed suit. The three men stood alone in the dusty clearing.

"Bruno was just here!" Gort announced.

"Yes, we just passed him. Any news on more resources?"

Gort spat on the ground in disgust, rubbing his saliva into the dirt with his foot.

"Nothing – quite the contrary, he brought one of the sicads!"

Rory couldn't contain his disbelief, despite knowing the spit was a sign of his Commander's growing irritation.

"That was a robot with Bruno and Hendie? I would have sworn it was a human!"

Gort sneered.

"Human-looking or not, these robots are a costly distraction. It's a bloody powder keg here. What are these robots going to do to sort this out? If this place goes up we've had it."

Rory tried to placate his superior.

"We went through worse times in Afghanistan, didn't we Commander?"

Gort had a flashback to a suicide bombing, walking through a devastated market place. The memories of wading through streams of blood and dismembered bodies, searching for the remains of his patrol, were still gruesomely vivid.

"Yes, we did. Things were hard, yet simple – one identifiable enemy and a clear mission to eliminate the murderous Taliban. Here, whatever we do, the problems get worse every day."

Colonel McCloud nodded in agreement.

"So what are we going to do, Commander? It's not just the camp where we're stretched. We've spent the last few weeks juggling men between crises. Border scuffles in Europe, water-starved farmers rampaging in Spain, food riots in Egypt, class battles in London... Oh, and the Nile hostilities are hotting up, requiring more peace-keeping reinforcements in Sudan and Ethiopia."

Gort quietly listened to the litany of problems.

"A bit busier than normal... Well, welcome to my world, Colonel!"

He looked inquiringly at Rory.

"I've been helping Scott, focusing on where we've been losing most men. The riots are getting out of hand; soldiers are getting crushed or stampeded to death. We lack the manpower."

Gort shook his head in despair and anger. He looked around at the surrounding tents, spreading out as far as the eye could see in all directions.

"Madness! And we're totally vulnerable here. A few thousand men surrounded by hundreds of thousands of angry refugees. Things get worse every day and Bruno is tinkering with robots!"

"Commander, with all these growing problems, maybe we do need some new solutions?"

Anger flashed into Gort's darkening eyes.

"Would we have sorted out the Taliban by sitting them down to negotiate with a bunch of robots?"

Gort stared intensely at the Captain, hammering out his words.

"People are the problem. Humans have lost their discipline and, rather than wait in line for their fair share, they're taking the law into their own hands."

The Commander swung his arm around, indicating the camp. "Look at this collective anarchy. When people are the problem there's only one solution: break their spirits and subjugate them. Bruno's out of his depth. One lucky break in the Middle East when the US was weak and now he thinks he can change the world by holding hands and singing Kumbaya."

Scott couldn't repress a smile.

Gort scrutinised Rory and Scott's faces in turn, looking for the signs of support. These men, amongst others, had followed him through the toughest times in Afghanistan. They'd stood by him as he had ordered the torturing of locals, sometimes innocents, in the slow process of extracting snippets of useful information that had led them to the Taliban hideouts.

It was Scott who was the first to reply.

"Well, we certainly couldn't have prevailed in Afghanistan by respecting the rules created by armchair bureaucrats."

Gort nodded in appreciation and his lips momentarily betrayed relief before sweeping his seductive gaze onto Rory, who hesitated before replying.

"Well, Commander, what are the alternatives?"

David Gort gazed around him to ensure nobody else was in earshot.

"I know I can count on your utmost discretion."

Both soldiers leaned closer to their Commander.

"Well, it seems behind the scenes the political winds are changing. Some extremely influential people have doubts over whether Bruno's robots are the right solution. These people deplore that we are being starved of funding."

Gort proceeded cautiously, observing Scott and Rory's faces. He was leading them into dangerous and unchartered territory. There'd be no way back and if they didn't stay the course they'd all end up on the rocks. No signs that anyone wants to jump ship, he thought. Now's the time to do so whilst we are still at port!

Rory and Scott were hanging on their Commander's every word.

"The project's doomed to fail. The sooner the better, before any more money is wasted. If we can give it a nudge, it will topple over of its own accord."

There was a minute of agonising silence before, after a nod of support from Rory, Scott replied.

"Well, just let us know what you need. You can count on us."

Gort placed a hand on each of their shoulders.

"Thanks, I'll let you know once I've worked it out."

10

As the plane soared high to catch the fuel-saving solar rays, Bruno's thoughts returned to the more mundane. He picked up the briefing notes for the conference he would attend on arrival in Tokyo. 'The effects of shifting rainwater patterns on tectonic activity' may not have been a catchy title, but the issue was a crucial one, especially for Tokyo. Like many other cities, it was built on fault lines and suffered increasing numbers of earthquakes as the global water cycle adjusted to climatic change.

He was on the verge of submerging himself in this, and the other reports scattered across the empty seat next to him, when Simon leaned across to ask politely, "What are the other problems facing humanity that you referred to in the camp?"

Bruno took a slow intake of breath. Where do I start? His eyes scanned the titles of the collection of reports he had to fight his way through, all marked Top Secret. 'Social repercussions of the emerging underclass on global societies'; 'Tackling income inequality without damaging the economy'; 'Sex crimes, paedophilia and chronic mental disorders – how to contain the pandemic'; 'Exploding crime rates – is evolution propagating violence?'; 'Water – the cause of the next great wave of human migration?'

"Well Simon, in summary, societies are slowly degenerating in rich countries. As living standards slowly slip, so do moral standards. We're seeing a universal increase in anti-social and anti-establishment behaviour. Crime rates are increasing, the young are increasingly vulnerable. The jails are overflowing and recidivism is rife. We do our best to manage the statistics, but it's getting blatantly worse."

Bruno gathered the reports into a thick pile, picked them up and let them drop with a heavy thud back onto the leather seat.

"There are plenty of theories from think tanks, psychologists, sociologists, palaeontologists and any number of others *ists* you care to mention. The only thing we know for sure is that this socially destructive behaviour is increasing exponentially, like a virus. Our top political scientists are extrapolating the complete collapse of a major political system in less than three years. If one goes, the rest will fall like dominoes. This is top secret, of course, Simon. If the press were to get wind of this it would become self-fulfilling. We've been forced to lie about the real extent of the problems."

Bruno noticed the concerned look on Simon's face. Now I've started, I might as well put him completely in the picture, he thought. He's going to work this stuff out pretty quickly for himself anyway! After a sharp intake of breath, he continued.

"At the other end of the scale, in the developing countries, we've more basic problems; water shortages in huge parts of Africa and Asia, and increased corruption holding back human development in these countries. The people you saw in the camps are the victims of this tragedy. And now, of course, they're migrating in search of water and are amassing in the camps at our borders. How long can we hold them back? How many will Gort shoot as a deterrent before he triggers a revolt?"

Bruno paused and surveyed the shocked look on Simon's face before continuing soberly.

"To date, we've kept the bad side of humans from you. You've been created to respect and revere humans. We wanted to cement that bond before we showed you our dark side."

"But if this trend is so apparent, why have humans not addressed and solved these problems, Bruno? After all, you managed to send man to the moon!"

"A very reasonable question, Simon, and one that I hope you're going to help to answer. Some of our experts suggest that man subconsciously accepts he's just another helpless species, doomed to extinction in the great circle of nature. Thus our current problems are the start of this extinction."

"Yes, your famous theory of evolution," remarked Simon.

Bruno looked at the sicad.

"Others point out that man's actions are going beyond simple evolution, and are threatening all life by totally destroying the biosphere we've inherited. As such, we're no longer a simple 'species' – we've started to play God!"

"And what do you believe, Bruno?"

"Sadly, I'm no scientist, but the evidence that I've seen and my instinct tell me that man shouldn't be playing Russian roulette with life itself!"

Simon raised his eyebrows, "Russian roulette?"

Bruno smiled.

"That's to say playing a very dangerous game."

"So, if I understand correctly Bruno, you're suggesting that the majority of the population are happy to gamble on total extinction?"

"The majority of people, Simon, are too busy thinking about what's going to happen in their lives tomorrow. They block out these longer-term worries. It's their leaders who should be guiding them, but many of them are too busy chasing an empty dream of power!"

"So, Bruno, you believe man can control his destiny, right?"

"Yes I do, but I recognise that, given the urgency of the situation, we need help, your help, Simon. Whilst we have great scientists and thinkers, our societies are hugely complex and humans are wasting valuable time struggling to agree on the problems, let alone the solutions. These problems are increasingly pervasive and we need global solutions. Yet the Chinese mistrust the Japanese, the Americans the French, the English the Germans, the Indians the Pakistanis, and so on. These suspicions make it very hard to agree on global policies, and I haven't even mentioned the influence of the tenacious lobbyists, who frustrate the process further by spreading misinformation and corrupting politicians. It was by observing the failure of my predecessors to recognise these problems and broker global action that I came up with the idea of the Socrates Project."

Simon nodded in appreciation. Bruno stared back into the sicad's eyes and his voice became deeply serious.

"Now it's down to you sicads to help bring global governments to their senses, before it's too late!"

Bruno fell silent and his eyes fell back upon the pile of reports.

"I've said too much and I've a stack of reading to get through. We've got a long flight, so why don't you plug into the Government intranet, and catch up on some research?"

"Thank you, I'd love to. Just before I do, though, can I ask you one last question?"

"Of course."

"Why did you choose to name the project after Socrates?"

"Well, you've been trained in Socratic questioning, haven't you?"

"Yes, hundreds of hours of questioning fundamental concepts, principles and theories."

"Well, like Socrates, we don't want you to take anything for granted. The humility to accept his own ignorance and systematically question everything he was told made Socrates the world's most important philosopher."

Simon's face suddenly morphed into a look of deep concern.

"Socrates was also tried and condemned to death for being an enemy of the people."

Bruno laughed at Simon's almost infantile concern.

"That was around two thousand five hundred years ago! Humanity has moved on since then; we may have our problems, but we haven't totally regressed."

The sicad didn't look completely convinced. He pondered for a few seconds and then, in an almost child-like manner, he forgot completely about Socrates' fate and turned his attention back to the Government intranet.

Seconds later he was eagerly scanning through the extensive database of government archives. The 'Global Space Program' and the scientific reports on the search for other habitable planets caught his attention. Whilst the universe was vast and statistical calculations suggested planets similar to Earth should be plentiful, the practical results showed otherwise. The area of space hospitable to life had turned out to be much more limited than scientists had hoped. Other solar systems explored were too close to exploding supernovas, black holes, asteroid fields or huge clouds of volatile floating gases. Within the few solar systems where conditions for life appeared theoretically possible, it had been very difficult to find planets accompanied by a perfectly-sized moon that were just the right distance from a stable source of solar energy. This moon, like Earth's, needed to orbit at just the right distance to exercise a stabilising gravitational force.

The succession of highly restrictive criteria narrowed down possibilities to just a few planets. On closer examination, the initial excitement had given way to disappointment as no evidence emerged that any had developed a similar atmosphere to the planet Earth, to nurture and protect life from intense solar radiation.

In fact, the more human scientists looked into space, the more they marvelled at the apparent incredible uniqueness of planet Earth. It was hard for them to convey this sense of wonder and scarcity to human populations who took their planet for granted.

"We'll soon be in Japan, the 'Home of the Robots'," announced Bruno, putting down the last of his reports.

Simon smiled.

"We've come a long way from the tin wind-up Lilliput robots."

"Go back another couple of centuries and you have the Karakuris – those really were the first robots."

"You seem to know your robots, Bruno!"

"Thank you. It's extraordinary that the Japanese, both young and old, have such a fascination for them."

"Not entirely. There are good cultural and historical reasons for this."

The Governor raised his eyebrows.

"Such as?"

"Well, whilst Judaeo-Christian traditions condemn the creation of machines in man's image, Shintoism recognises a spirit or Kami in all objects and animals. Why should robots be any exception to this?"

"Interesting, and the Japs have always had an aptitude for technology and mechanics."

"Yes, Bruno, and don't forget their defeat in World War II. The devastating Hiroshima atom bomb attack sharpened their desire to lead the world in technology!"

"Also, with the labour shortages after the war, they needed robots in their factories."

"And now they have an excess of old people they are using robots as pets and carers."

Bruno laughed.

"Well, Simon, if the project doesn't go to plan, it's good to know that you'll always be able to get a job looking after geriatric old ladies."

*

Jia arrived back at Mazari the same morning as Simon and, by chance, they shared the same elevator.

"So how was it, my intrepid explorer?"

"Very revealing… Almost overwhelming."

"It's the first time you've been away from me. Did you miss me?"

"I guess so. There was so much to take in that I didn't really have the time. I'm getting out here – Socratic classes."

"I'll come along and observe for a bit."

The lecture room was full, all four hundred and one sicads focused attentively on the smartly dressed professor of philosophy from Tokyo University, excitedly addressing them.

"Unlike many people believe, the Oracle at Delphi didn't say that Socrates was the wisest man, or even a wise man. His actual words were: 'there is no man wiser than Socrates'. Can anyone explain the difference?"

Four hundred and one hands instantly shot up.

The professor laughed.

"You're clearly not my ordinary students! Too easy a question, eh?

Well, in this simple statement lies the essence of Socratic Method. It is only by removing all ignorance that we begin to approach wisdom."

The professor walked up the central sloping aisle and stopped beside Simon.

"Ah. Simon, perhaps you can tell us whether Socrates knew he was wise?"

The sicad replied without hesitation.

"Socrates had no absolute definition of wisdom and, as such, he couldn't know if he was wise or not."

"A good answer. Yes, Socrates was convinced of his own ignorance. Unfortunately, he was too good at revealing the ignorance of others, less accepting of their condition."

"So this is why they put him to death?" replied Simon.

"Effectively, yes. The background was complex but, in his search for truth and wisdom, he upset the vanity of many powerful people... Now let's see how Socrates utilised his famous method, based on a scene from Plato's account of his last days," announced the professor. After looking around, he selected a sicad chief fashioned as a fifty year old Argentinean from the front row of the auditorium.

"Ok, Fernandez you're going to act out the role of Euthyphro whom Socrates is surprised to discover is intent on prosecuting his own father for manslaughter."

The professor took the sicad aside and filled him in on the background required to play out the role.

The professor, taking the part of Socrates, commenced the dialogue.

"Tell me Euthyphro why are you trying your own father for manslaughter?"

Fernandez stepped into his role with authority and wit, imitating the imagined pomposity of the lawyer.

"His neglect and maltreatment of a suspected criminal led to the poor man's death by starvation. Whether he's my father or not, his actions were impious and must be punished."

The professor rubbed his hands together in delight.

"How wonderful that I meet someone who understands piety to such an extent he is prepared to try his own father's impiety. Would you be so kind as to instruct someone as ignorant as I in its meaning?"

"Well I don't see why not?" replied the sicad.

The Argentinean rocked back and forth on his heels before addressing the Socratic professor triumphantly.

"Pious acts are ones which please the Gods."

The professor clapped his hands.

"Such a precise and excellent definition, but I will permit myself a further question. Do you believe the stories they tell of the Gods' behaviour?"

Fernandez, prompted, nodded emphatically.

"And do these Gods always agree with each other?"

The sicad shook his head theatrically.

"Why no, with their words and brushes, our poets and artists most faithfully represent their frequent quarrels and battles."

"So the Gods cannot decide between themselves what is pleasing to them as a group?"

"Evidently not," responded the Argentinean.

"Then my friend, I am somewhat confused. For you stated pious acts are acts that please the Gods, whom you have just confirmed do not agree themselves on what pleases them. As such you must be mistaken. No my friend, I would like to really understand this term impiety..."

"Another time Socrates," concluded Fernandez.

"Thank you," announced the elegant professor, taking a bow.

The sicads, after having sent a flurry of congratulatory messages to their fellow, showed their appreciation in human fashion with sustained applause.

Part II.

Awakening

11

Colonel McCloud held the brilliant metal blade as if it were a mirror, its surface reflecting snow-capped mountains, tumbling glaciers, alpine forest and a cloudless blue sky.

"Your ice axe."

He addressed the team – Jia and her three guinea-pig sicads: Simon, Magnus and Rosa.

"You'll need it up on the glaciers, for steep or vertical climbs. It has other uses too, but we'll get to those later."

It was Jia who had proposed the test-group, during the 'pre-launch' meeting of the Project Management Committee, or PMC as she called it. The purpose of the pre-launch was to plan the final four months of the sicads' development – a period of 'controlled exposure' to humanity, to see how well they integrated. In practice, she learned, this would mean that sicads were to be introduced to the PMC members' close friends and family, mostly on evenings or at weekends. None of their hosts would know that the person joining them for dinner or the ball game, or who had kindly offered to help fix the plumbing, was not human at all. Blending in, the PMC stressed, would be key to the success of the sicads' year-long mission. But what if... An image formed in Jia's mind. A domesticated dog left to fend for itself in the wild – its instincts more human than animal, its resources tailored for a man-made environment rather than a natural one. There was something even more fundamental to success than blending in – something so simple that they were missing it entirely: survival.

The sicads were battery powered. Without power, all their mechanical functions would be disabled; this was certainly problematic. But more alarming was the fact that without battery power all their organic brain matter would die. And, if that happened, all those years of learning how to move among humans, how to interact with them as if it were first instinct, would be lost for good.

Sure, the sicads knew how to plug in; but what if their only source of energy was a natural one – the sun, the wind? Harnessing nature to recharge would require a whole different set of survival skills. So Jia had put forward the case for a group of sicads to be taken and tested in inhospitable conditions, far from sockets and chargers.

Unusually, it was Commander Gort, the committee's military representative, who had proved her strongest ally and, with his backing, her plan had received a green light. The 'Survival Techniques Expedition', as it had been dubbed, would be spearheaded by two of Gort's best men – Colonel Scott McCloud and Captain Rory Schiller.

Rory Schiller spoke up.

"Each of you has a sixty-litre rucksack, ice axe, harness, climbing shoes, sleeping bag, head torch, crampons, shovel, and Gortex shell and waterproof trousers."

"Captain," interrupted Simon, "Gortex will interfere with our photovoltaic and aeolian captors. We shan't be taking them."

"You're responsible for them," Schiller said to Jia. "You decide."

Colonel McCloud strode towards them, carrying a large plastic bag.

"For humans only," he said, handing it to Jia.

The bag contained an assortment of clothes, high-energy bars, a water carrier and other paraphernalia. Schiller and McCloud went to fetch the last of the equipment from the van – tents, ropes, climbing equipment, a stove.

"Rosa – you aren't carrying food or water, so you can take some rope and the cooking equipment. Rory, Magnus, Simon, we'll distribute the rest between us. Everybody, pack your rucksack, get kitted up and Rory will come round and check each of you is good to go."

Rory checked Jia's harness first.

"Make sure it's over your hips and tight enough, so you won't fall out if you happen to tip upside down – but not too tight," he said, adjusting the straps around her thighs. "There, that's better. You need to be able to move freely."

It was a routine check, perfunctory even; but, for a breathless split-second, a flash of intimacy lit the space between them. The rogue tension had caught them both off guard and at exactly the same time. It was idiotic and embarrassing.

Rory launched into a demonstration on how to fit the steel pointed crampons to their mountain boots.

"You'll need these on the ice and the ridges. They'll help when you're traversing both rock and snow."

When everyone was ready, gear all checked and rucksacks on backs, Jia and the three sicads stood in line on the grassy plain, facing their two guides and the dark granite rock face that loomed up behind them: Les Gaillands.

Scott McCloud addressed his team one by one.

"You good, Magnus?"

"Yes, sir, I believe so."

"You're the Swedish one, aren't you? Fittest climbers in Europe, the Swedes. Into the extreme stuff."

Magnus smiled proudly.

"Can't say the same for the Italians. Mama's boys, eh sweetheart?" he said to Rosa with a coarse laugh.

Rosa remained blank-faced and straight backed.

"I'm ready, Colonel," her voice firm like a warning.

Scott smiled his approval. Jia stood beside Rosa. Scott took them both in. Rosa had the curves, but Jia – she was lithe, quicksilver, taut like a spring.

"Miss Jin. Your countrymen are more famous for taking pictures of mountains than for climbing them, eh?"

"Colonel, my mother is Russian, from the Urals. My father is Chinese and certainly no stranger to mountains – he climbed Cho Oyu on skis before you could climb a flight of stairs."

"Well, is that so?" Scott's voice was as chill as the air. "Let's just see how you measure up, Miss Jin."

"And Simon, they tell me you're the brains here. I just have to hope you got it all sussed out then, don't I?"

Scott clapped his hands once – loudly, so the echo hung in the air for seconds afterwards.

"What say we get this show on the road?"

Scott and Rory threw down the ropes at the foot of the rock face.

"OK everyone, if you want to survive the mountain, you'd better listen carefully and follow our instructions to the letter!"

Scott held the group's frightened gaze; Rory looked away and starting fiddling with a crampon.

Three hours later, after the rock climbing session, the group was heading up on the tram railway to the base of the mountain.

At 1,600 metres altitude the pressure change is notable, thought Simon.

"Wow, look at that view!" exclaimed Rosa, her head out of the window.

A humbling world of jagged peaks and mighty glaciers opened up before them. Minutes later, they were shuffling along rocky trails, bandy-legged under the weight of their rucksacks. Goats and chamois, perched on mossy boulders, studied them through the forest foliage. Rosa strode ahead to make time to identify new varieties of flowers and plants. She stopped, putting her fingers to her lips, and halted the group with her hand.

"Look, a marmot!" she whispered excitedly.

To her disappointment, the two soldiers trudged on indifferently.

"How are your energy levels, Simon?" asked Jia.

"The same as five minutes ago!"

"OK, just checking! And the others?"

He didn't reply, looking at her in the manner of a teenager who wanted to assert its independence. He'd already told her that the sun and wind were keeping them at full charge and that he'd let her know if this changed.

On the afternoon of the third day, they were at 3,000 metres altitude, roped-up and crossing a spectacularly steep glacier. The sun was low in the sky and Jia was light-headed from the altitude and hunger. Standing in front of a serac, a column of chaotic ice formed by intersecting crevasses of the glacier, they sheltered from the howling easterly wind. The serac, the size and girth of a three-story building, towered top-heavy over them, its transparent ice shining magnificently blue in the sunlight. At the foot of it was a gaping hole in the surface of the glacier.

"Some of these crevasses can be over eighty metres deep," explained Simon, as Jia strained her neck to follow the path of a twisting ice tunnel.

"Too much wind! That's enough for today," McCloud shouted, to be heard. "Rory and I will scout out a good spot for a snow cave. Wait here and don't move. There's crevasses everywhere."

The soldiers headed off towards the setting sun. Once at a safe distance, Scott turned to Rory.

"Did you see the serac?"

Rory looked at him blankly.

"It's fissured at the bottom, it just needs a nudge!"

Rory swallowed uncomfortably. Now the time to act had come, he was having second thoughts. It no longer felt like any other mission. Despite his best efforts, he'd become attached to Jia and, bizarrely, in a small way even to the robots.

"Are you sure we should?" asked Schiller, thinking aloud. At the fierce look of incredulity from McCloud, he regretted having spoken.

"Orders are orders."

"OK, let's do it and get out of here," Rory replied half-heartedly.

Each started to bore a hefty ice-screw into the hard ice, making several holes and enlarging them with the points of their ice axes. Rory edged along the rear of the serac and spied on the group with a small camera. Jia and the three sicads were still sheltering below. The sicads were holding their arms up, directing the strong wind onto the multitude of tiny turbines embedded in their clothes.

Schiller turned back to Scott and gave the thumbs up.

McCloud carefully packed the holes with small sticks of explosives, designed to leave minimal trace. The two soldiers retreated to a solid looking rock shelter, pushing their bodies back against the wall. His thumb hovering over the remote detonator, Scott looked sideways at Rory, who hesitated briefly before nodding.

The proximity of the explosion amplified the deafening noise, stunning the soldiers. A cracking sound and a further explosion followed as the serac collapsed, pounding the area where Jia and the sicads were sheltering with tonnes of snow and ice.

A rock the size of a football bounced down the mountain and landed with a crash, thirty centimetres from the soldiers, who jumped back instinctively, covering their faces. To add to the chaos, an avalanche was triggered in one of the steep snowy couloirs, sending tonnes of snow into the air. Seconds later it smothered the debris from the exploded serac.

The soldiers looked on helplessly as the dust and snow settled.

"Mission accomplished," remarked McCloud gleefully.

Scott's enthusiasm began to irritate Rory. His superior was treating this like a routine exercise. Rory felt increasingly uncomfortable. It seemed the mountains were silently watching and judging his guilt.

"Glaciers are dangerous places; seracs collapse all the time," justified Scott.

Rory silently walked back to where the serac had stood. Piles of ice boulders, bound together with fresh snow, had pulverised the area, now unrecognisable.

Silently combing the area, they came across a rucksack buried between two blocks of ice.

Scott inspected it.

"It's Jia's. It must have got thrown to the top."

Otherwise, there was no sign of the bodies or any signal from their transceivers.

"The glacier has swallowed them and will hide them for at least twenty years," concluded McCloud.

The idea of hikers stumbling upon the conserved bodies in twenty years' time flashed across Rory's mind. It made him feel worse – a dark secret, hanging over him. Of all the things he'd been through, this was the first time his conscience was so troubled. He sat on a lone rock contemplating, whilst McCloud radioed the mountain rescue.

An approaching helicopter soon interrupted his thoughts. A team of anxious mountain guides jumped out as it hovered over the glacier.

After three hours of sweeping the glacier with snow probes, the head guide shook his head and called off the search.

"It's an unnaturally large avalanche for the time of year. They're buried deep, I'm afraid. At least the animals won't get to them. So unfortunate, I'm very sorry."

Rory and Scott bowed their heads respectfully.

"You'll need to come down with us, to clarify all aspects of the tragedy," concluded the guide.

*

"It's getting cold... I wish they'd hurry up."

Jia had to shout to be heard over the roar of the wind. Simon put his arm around her shoulders in a warm embrace.

"Whilst we're waiting, would you like to know the history of these amazing glaciers?"

"OK, why not?" she smiled.

"Well, it appears these glaciers, the biggest in Western Europe, have been the unexpected victims of your industrial revolution, shrinking significantly over the last two hundred years. This one, the mighty

Bossons glacier, stretches down from the summit of Mont Blanc nearly three thousand metres. Seventy years ago it touched the valley floor, now it stops hundreds of metres above."

"It's still immense," she replied, teeth chattering.

Simon rubbed her shoulders energetically.

"The Alpine glaciers reached their maximum size in around 1820, after a mini-glacial period of around four hundred years. In those days your scientists believed the world was constantly cooling from a fiery birth. It was only decades later that a bright scientist, trying to resolve the enigma of huge blocks of granite moving thousands of metres, realised that the entire Chamonix valley was carved out by a colossal ancient glacier."

"The whole valley? It must have been over one thousand five hundred metres deep and tens of kilometres long!"

"Exactly! And do you think they believed him?"

"Probably not!"

"You're correct. Like all new ideas which seem radical, this was ridiculed by the custodians of established human knowledge. It was another decade before the idea of a series of such ice ages emerged."

"What are these glaciers, exactly?" asked Jia shivering.

The sicad pointed to a small nearby depression in the ice.

"They're like huge fish bones, crisscrossed with crevasses, some visibly open, some treacherously covered by a thin layer of snow. The intestines of these mighty phenomena are shaped by the flow of ice and melt water that forces its way through the cracks – melt water which builds up into mini lakes deep inside..."

"Lakes?"

"Yes, it was the build-up of one such lake that caused the disaster in St Gervais-Les Bains, just a few kilometres from here. The water pressure inside the Bionnassay glacier blew an enormous hole in the glacier wall. A torrent of icy water exploded out, killing...."

His words were cut short by a deafening bang. The sicads' SAMPS self-preservation mechanisms instantly kicked in. Combining their visual images, in the space of a few milliseconds they processed the best collective survival plan. Fortunately for Jia, she was roped up to these rapidly reacting super-computers. Before she'd even registered the sound of cracking ice, she found herself being pulled off her feet as the sicads dived towards a nearby crevasse. Pulled back by her rucksack caught on a rock, she felt a hand rip the straps open and yank her forcefully along the ice. As she slid into the crevasse she heard the impact of the collapsing serac. A shower of lumps of ice and snow followed her down. A second boom, then debris covered the crevasse blocking out all sound and light.

Jia screamed as the group slid in darkness down the smooth icy tunnel. They dropped off a small ledge, she screamed again. Yelling uncontrollably, she slipped further and dropped into a void before being whiplashed violently by the rope. She hit her head against the hard ice and lost consciousness.

"Jia, Jia!"

She opened her eyes to the sound of Simon's voice. Was that concern she saw on his face? She didn't know whether she was dreaming or was even still alive. There was darkness all around. The two male sicads had their torch lights on. The terrifying descent into the crevasse flooded back into her mind.

"Er… is everybody OK?"

"Magnus and I are relatively unscathed, but Rosa had a bad landing. Her lower body is no longer functioning. She's in hibernation mode to maximize her chances of survival."

"We've wrapped her in a sleeping bag to preserve her batteries," added Magnus.

"Oh no! How long was I unconscious for?"

"Fifteen minutes forty two seconds," replied Simon. How are you feeling?"

Her head was pounding as she tried to sit up and move her body.

"A little bruised and achy. What happened?"

Simon looked at her cautiously.

"There was some sort of explosion, followed eight hundred milliseconds later by a crack in the ice serac, which started to topple over. We took the decision to seek protection in the nearest crevasse. You were roped up to us, so we pulled you into the crevasse as well," he added.

"And that was the only reason you saved me?"

"Well, we didn't have a knife to cut the rope," joked Simon.

"Very funny! What caused the explosion? What happened to Scott and Rory?"

The sicads exchanged a glance before Simon replied hesitantly.

"Possibly an avalanche, set off by the wind."

Jia sighed. "How are your energy levels?"

"Magnus and I estimate we have eight to nine hours of active energy between us. Your status is uncertain."

"We've taken the precaution of further insulating our batteries," added Magnus.

"How the hell are we going to get out? They'll rescue us, won't they?"

Simon looked at her, to assess her state of mind, before replying slowly.

"A rescue attempt is unlikely. We're a long way down and the crevasse must be blocked by several tonnes of snow and ice."

"No! No! We can't die! We won't die here, will we Simon?"

She grabbed his arms tightly.

"Well, we detected a light breeze ten minutes ago, which implies there's an opening somewhere. We have the rope..."

"And the ice axes?" she asked apprehensively.

"We didn't have time to retrieve them, I'm afraid."

Jia took Rosa's torchlight and inspected the walls – hard and very smooth... no ice-axes. Fortunately, they were all still wearing their sharply pointed crampons. She looked up at the rope. It had snagged itself around a fierce looking blade of ice resembling an upturned knife. It had broken their fall and surely saved their lives.

"It's impossible to climb back up!" she lamented.

"Precisely, that's why we're going down," replied Simon triumphantly.

She peered down into the gloom.

"Down there? You're crazy!"

"Not so crazy. I've calculated that the crevasse goes down another twenty four metres, at least to the next level."

Before Jia could ask how he knew that, he continued.

"I dropped a pebble and calculated the time it took to reach the bottom. As we have a fifty metre rope, we can abseil down and try to find the opening. Now we must sleep and rise with the sun."

Gathering the rope, Simon re-tied everybody into a safety anchor, using a technique he'd seen Scott use.

"Everybody should huddle together to minimise heat loss," commanded Simon, assuming the role of leader.

For Jia, it was the most uncomfortable night ever. The sicads had no such problems; they simply switched into hibernation mode, turned off their sensors and slept soundly until the 4.55am pre-set wake-up time.

When they awoke it was a little lighter inside the crevasse. Magnus checked on Rosa, who looked as if she was already dead. Small beads of ice had formed on the tips of her hair. Simon was locating the middle of the rope. He passed the end of it through a carabiner attached to a sling he'd tied around a solid-looking pillar of ice. He threw the coiled-up rope into the depths of the crevasse.

Quickly pulling it back up, he smiled.

"The last metre of the rope is wet, my calculations were good. There's water at the bottom. I hope it's shallow."

He threw the rope back down, clipped in his belay device and leant back to test the anchor – which held.

"OK, I'll go first, then Jia, then Magnus last."

"What about Rosa?"

"We'll come back for her... if we make it."

He bent down and kissed Rosa's cold forehead, before jumping backwards into the dark void.

A minute later his voice echoed up from below.

"Next!"

Jia, who'd been inspecting Rosa, attached her descender to the rope, leant back warily and stepped backwards slowly over the icy ledge. The transparent ice reflected back a spooky light. Unnerved, she crossed her crampons, slipped and spun around on the rope, crying out in shock.

Words of encouragement floated up from below.

"It's OK. I have the rope, so if you fall I can block it!"

She breathed a sigh of relief, composed herself and abseiled into a tunnel filled with shallow water. What a relief to be off that rope! Oh shit that's cold, she thought! The freezing water lapped around the ankles of her waterproof boots.

It was visibly lighter and the tunnel appeared to run in both directions. Magnus landed softly beside her.

"Are you OK?" he asked, showing his crooked teeth as he gave her a jovial smile.

"I'm OK from the ankles up!"

"OK, everyone, let's keep moving," ordered Simon. Jia trudged off after him, leaving Magnus to coil the rope. She shone her torchlight around the walls of the ice tunnel and reflected on the bizarre situation. Trapped inside the intestines of a colossal glacier with three robots, trying to escape before they ran out of energy and she either froze or starved to death. The contrast with her daily life in Tokyo, where she lived, worked and travelled in human-designed boxes, couldn't have been greater.

She heard Magnus's footsteps catching up with her and, in his torchlight, saw her shadow draped on the walls ahead of her. They continued for fifteen minutes, branching off into a labyrinth of tunnels.

"Do you know where you're going, Simon?" she shouted.

A reply came echoing back to her.

"We're following the light. Can't you see?"

She hadn't noticed, but it was getting steadily lighter and her spirits lifted, despite the aching and burning of her frozen feet.

Suddenly the tunnel opened out into a large chamber and she saw it – a shaft of sunlight! The sun, such a primordial necessity – there's hope, she realised.

"Imagine how your ancestors must have felt when they saw the sun reappear years after huge volcanic eruptions filled the skies with thick clouds of ash," observed Simon.

Jia's thoughts returned to her survival. She hurried after Simon, who was clambering up a shallow slope onto a ledge beneath the shaft of sunlight. She stood by his side, looking up at the sheer walls.

"There is no way we can climb that, not without the ice axes and ice screws for protection! Help! Help! Can anyone hear us? SOS! Help! We're trapped in the crevasse!"

They all shouted repeatedly for five minutes, their voices echoing around the chamber, but no response came from above.

Jia felt her voice go hoarse.

"They've abandoned us," she croaked.

"Our survival was improbable."

She looked helplessly at Magnus and Simon in turn.

"What do we do now?"

"OK, it's time for Plan B – mathematically at least, the best option we have."

"How high is the risk of failure?"

"Let's just say that it has better odds than buying a lottery ticket."

She watched in confusion as Simon rummaged in his rucksack and took out a Swiss-Army knife, then held out his left hand and extracted his metal pins. He filed the ends into sharp points, before starting on his right hand. Magnus took the knife as Simon briskly tied the coiled rope onto his back and tested the ice with his sharpened pins.

Simon started to climb up, driving the points of his fingers and crampons forcefully into the hard, smooth ice, advancing one metre before slipping and sliding back down. He tried again and again, learning from each mistake, changing his body position to exert a powerful opposition force to the two sides of the smooth tunnel, and slowly inched up the shaft. Magnus emulated his movements and followed behind. An hour later they'd climbed ten metres. There were still twenty to go – a fall from here to the ice floor would mean almost certain destruction. Jia's heart missed a beat every time Simon's feet or hands, failing to gain a purchase on the glass-like ice, slid dangerously. Magnus was just below, using the tiny nicks in the ice that Simon had fashioned to brace and support his and, if necessary, both their weight. Simon slid half a metre, only to be supported by Magnus's head. Jia daren't scream, for fear of distracting the Swedish sicad whose legs, forced into the ice, were shaking violently under the strain. Closing her eyes to the daring circus act, she waited with dread to hear the crash.

Seconds later she opened them to see Simon climbing again. She was transfixed, even though all she could see were the soles of the sicads' boots. Her neck was stiff and she was breathless with anxiety, knowing they'd be running low on energy. Just five metres or so from the top, she gasped in horror as Magnus's energy began to visibly drop. Simon didn't look down, but ordered Magnus to switch to his emergency batteries. He had just engaged his own – an estimated ten minutes of energy were all he had left. In the full knowledge that he could no longer count on Magnus, he continued upwards.

The last five metres of the shaft were entirely vertical; each metre demanded total concentration and gradual moves. Two minutes for the last metre! Torn between going faster and not slipping, Simon put the maximum pressure he could afford to use for each step up, driving the metal spikes of his crampons into the hard ice. As he reached the final metre his concentration was distracted by the alarm signals reverberating inside his head: CRITICAL POWER LEVELS, SEEK ENERGY IMMEDIATELY!

As his arms reached over the lip of the crevasse he slumped dangerously and his legs swung precariously in the void. He looked down at Jia and somehow took heart from the abject anguish on her face. With all his remaining strength, he dug his fingers into the snow around the crevasse. Without the strength to pull up his legs, he hung helplessly half in and half out of the crevasse. His fingers started to slide in the snow. He drove them deeper and clasped his hand around a small buried rock, halting his slide. TERMINAL SYSTEM SHUTDOWN IMMINENT!

He turned to look up at the sky for a final sense of meaning to his life. As he closed his eyes, in expectation of death, he felt a soft ray of sunlight stroke his cheek. He forced his eyes open to see a bright sun emerging from behind the mountain, as if it had been sent to rescue him. He felt his energy levels slowly restoring; four minutes later he scrambled over the lip of the crevasse and crawled to a nearby rock. He had just enough energy to pass the rope around it and throw the end down to Magnus and Jia before collapsing into the snow.

Minutes later, Magnus appeared over the lip of the crevasse and collapsed next to him. They lay on their backs, soaking up the sun's life-giving rays.

A few seconds later they became aware of Jia's voice calling them.

"Hey! What about me?"

Simon rolled over onto his front and looked at her, stranded down at the bottom of the shaft.

"How am I meant to climb the rope with numb hands and feet?"

"You'll have to wait for us to get our strength back, or use the self-rescue technique that Schiller taught us."

She looked at him helplessly with pleading eyes.

He laughed.

"What would you humans do without us sicads?"

"Just get on with telling me how to get out of here, before I regret ever having created you!"

"Take the pulley from your harness and make a loop in the rope for your foot. No, not like that… That's better. Now stand on the loop and slide the pulley up the rope. Yes, there you go!"

Five minutes later all three of them were laid out, spread-eagled and exhausted, on the glacier. Jia was looking up at the sky. She turned over onto her side and leant over Simon. His eyes were closed as if deep in thought. She put her face close to his and lightly kissed him on the lips.

His eyes shot open.

"What was that for?"

"For saving my life."

"A life for a life then, as you humans say."

She smiled and, feeling the warmth of the sun on her face, she closed her eyes to enjoy the moment.

Simon did likewise. As his sensory processes slowed down and he cleared the thoughts that were cluttering his mind, a seed of understanding blossomed inside him. Away from human power supplies, which he'd taken for granted, he understood how disconnected he'd been from the natural processes that ultimately created all energy on this amazing planet. A realisation of his total dependence on nature struck him. This realisation not only hit him intellectually, it hit him emotionally. An incredible energy surged into his mind, as if his brain had expanded to new frontiers and a previously locked door inside had just been blasted open. A sudden inexplicable joy and benevolence towards all life engulfed him.

He opened his eyes anew and looked around at the towering mountain peaks and the immensity of the glaciers. A bird of prey, no doubt evolved from the dinosaurs, flew above him. This mountain has been shaped by nature over millions of years, he thought. How many species have come and gone over this time? How many disappeared without a trace? Would humans go the same way?

*

"It's great you survived the avalanche!" congratulated Schiller, as Jia and the sicads stepped out of the rescue helicopter.

"Well done team, a remarkable achievement," added McCloud, less convincingly. Nobody replied. The silent stand-off was interrupted by the arrival of the rescue guides carrying the body of Rosa, wrapped in a red blanket and strapped to a stretcher.

"No sign of breathing, I think we've lost her."

Scott flashed an identity badge at the surprised guides and led them aside.

"This is a Special Forces training operation. We'll take the body."

"But there is a protocol to foll..."

"Bring me the papers to sign!" shouted the Colonel, whose mood had darkened.

McCloud walked out of earshot and talked quietly into his phone.

"What do you mean they survived?" boomed the voice of Gort into his ear.

"I want to know every detail, Colonel. You'd better do an official version for Bruno as well. Call me back when you're alone!"

Gort threw down the phone, but his anger suddenly dissipated; the gravity of the deed he'd planned was subconsciously released from weighing on his soul. In his frustration with Bruno's project and his desire to protect his men, he'd been persuaded to commit an act that would have condemned his soul. His initial frustration with Jia and the sicads' escape almost turned to relief.

12

Simon quickly entered the access code and placed his finger on the biometric recognition pad. The first of a series of airtight doors to Mazari's technical centre slid open. It was nearly midnight, the last programmer had only just left, and the workshop and surrounding offices were deserted. The expedition had been a tough ordeal; unlike humans, and much to Simon's regret, the sicads' bodies didn't heal automatically, so he decided a full physical inspection was required.

Proceeding through a second set of doors, he entered a small chamber and removed his clothes, neatly folding and storing them in a personal locker. Strategically positioned showers sprayed his naked body with shots of cleaning chemicals, before rinsing him off with water and blasting hot air at him from all directions.

Once dry, he entered the immaculately clean and dust-free workshop. Inside was an assortment of electro-mechanical contraptions adorned with iron clamps, leather straps and tools hanging on rubber-coiled leads. It all gave the impression of a gymnasium or a torture chamber – an idea reinforced by the collection of sicad spare parts on the walls and workbenches. Ignoring these, Simon stood underneath a black metal tubular bar that ran horizontally along the ceiling and activated his 'Remove Skin' routine.

The internal clamps released to allow his pelvis to split into two, his vertebrae to space apart and his upper and lower body to separate. Tiny rollers located inside each half of his pelvis spun quickly in reverse to free the tightly clamped skin membranes, breaking the vacuum seal. Air at atmospheric pressure entered, causing his skin to detach itself from the foam-like mesh that protected his articulated titanium skeleton and the pneumatic pistons which controlled his muscles. Baggy skin now hung off him like oversized clothes.

Pulling himself up on the bar, Simon shook his legs until his lower skin membrane slid off. The deep-red soft mesh gave the appearance he'd been skinned alive – it would have been a considerable shock for any unsuspecting human. Bringing his legs up above his head, knees hooked over the bar, he reclined his torso, released his hands and hung upside down. After several shakes, his upper skin slid smoothly onto the floor. Swinging his torso back upright, releasing his knees and grabbing the black metal bar in a fluid acrobatic movement, he dropped to the floor, carefully avoiding landing on the slough-like skin spread out below.

He moved with extreme caution, conscious that, stripped of his protective membrane, he was vulnerable to dust and humidity and was deprived of the pressure, heat and vibration sensors he'd become accustomed to. Systematically, he peeled back each section of the protective mesh in turn, checking attentively each articulation and making minor adjustments to the torque settings. With the help of Mazari's muscle-graft tool, he repaired the minor tears he encountered. His internal diagnostics finally signalling 100%, he picked up his skin and searched for signs of damage. He admired the impressive craftsmanship and attention to detail – the markings and texture virtually identical to human skin, complete with palm lines, fingerprints, veins and even light body hair. On the inside was a nexus of wire circuits for transmitting wind and solar energy to his batteries and sensory information to his brain. Amazingly, no signs of any damage!

His skin went back on like a wetsuit. Attaching the loose tails of skin to his pelvic rollers, he activated the 'Reattach Skin' procedure. The rollers pulled and tightened the skin, recreating the vacuum and sucking it tightly onto his skeleton; his vertebrae slid back together and the two halves of his pelvis reattached.

*

To iron out any unexpected social 'faux pas', Simon and Magnus joined their companions for the final two weeks of 'controlled exposure' to human society. Jia, meanwhile, now that the launch date was approaching, attended an increasing number of organisation meetings focusing on the sicads' mission briefings. Bruno decided to pay a visit to Mazari before sanctioning their release. Jia took him through the latest diagnostics.

"The most recent data shows that they're learning more quickly," she explained, bringing up onto her screen a range of coloured three-dimensional cerebral images.

"Good, do we know why?"

"Highly efficient storage protocols, intelligent sifting and, most importantly, networking."

67

Bruno nodded in approval.

Jia's screen showed a network traffic diagram between Simon and his chiefs, resembling three-dimensional spaghetti.

"The last three days' communication?" inquired Bruno, stooping to read the legend underneath.

"The last three minutes rather!" announced Jia with a beaming smile.

Bruno shared her pride, after all, the sicads were broadly his idea, even if Jia had taken it several stages beyond what he'd imagined was possible.

"Almost telepathic."

"Exactly! Two sicads are quicker than one, four sicads are quicker than two... The exponential speed increases from networking are exactly as predicted."

"The implications for the project?"

"Analytical simulations suggest a maximum of twelve months of observation and six months to process the results."

"Good, so we're, unusually, on target. And the project briefings?"

"All good. Individual briefings are ready and each sicad will shortly attend a pre-release meeting."

"And then the chicks will leave their nests, equipped with passports, visas and credit cards, I guess?"

"Exactly, plus a fourteen-day itinerary. After that they're on their own."

Jia was ambivalent about the launch; a tangled web of emotions gyrated inside her. Bruno read the concern on her face.

"You're not getting broody over the sicads are you?"

"No, of course not," lied Jia. "It's just... well, what's going to happen in the seclusion phase...."

Trying to read her thoughts, he gave her an encouraging smile.

She continued hesitantly.

"It's just that there have been rumours that Commander Gort and the army are going to be solely responsible..."

Bruno started to laugh, but refrained at the deadly serious look on the face in front of him.

"The expedition was just an unfortunate accident. We all have complete faith in Commander Gort's competence and integrity."

Jia still looked uneasy.

"But, why not have some Mazari representatives present? It makes sense on every level, surely?"

The Governor bent down towards Jia and his voice dropped to a light whisper.

"Between you and me, personally I agree with you, but governments have insisted that the army ensure there's no interference whatsoever with the sicads during this crucial stage of the project."

"But is Commander Gort the right person?"

"David Gort is universally respected, especially by the new US regime. He has a great record..."

"Surely I could monitor the sicads from time to time?"

The Governor shook his head.

"Jia, believe me, I've fought hard for this. The big hitters want total independence and they see the army and Commander Gort as the best solution."

"You mean the new neo-conservatives are throwing their weight around."

"Jia, I need all the governments' total support for the project, otherwise they won't stand by the recommendations."

She fell silent. Bruno stood up and changed the subject.

"Remind me one last time, what stops the sicads from malfunctioning and turning against us?"

She looked at Bruno and saw the troubled resolve in his eyes. She let her concerns drop and turned her mind back to the project safeguards.

"Well, er... we've programmed them to effectively love humans. For a sicad to turn against humans would be against its fundamental nature. Besides, the sicads report every one of their thoughts back to us. Commander Gort takes a very keen interest in these."

"And we know they're telling us the truth?"

"Well, they've no reason not to," she stammered.

Commander Gort had recently asked her the same question, which she'd equally struggled to answer.

"OK, Jia, I guess I'm just being paranoid."

*

Simon referred to the moment of enlightenment he experienced on the expedition as a phenomenon, admittedly an extremely powerful one. Being the most advanced sicad, he was generally the first to experience a new phenomenon – equivalent to the human process of learning. Every new skill or mental breakthrough, replacing confusion with clarity, triggered an electro-chemical sensation in his brain, swiftly followed by a reorganisation of new and existing information, or 're-indexing' as Dmitri termed it. Simon had soon realised that all skills and know-how were effectively just 'information relationships' or 'indexing' in Dmitri's parlance.

At first, these phenomena occurred every few seconds, as his empty brain had learnt how to operate each part of his body and to recognise and identify animate and inanimate objects. The powerful electro-chemical sensations accompanying these learning phenomena slowly reduced in intensity over time; new phenomena gradually became less frequent. There were fewer new things to learn and they took the form of more gradual realisations, such as the first time he realised that the seasons were slowly changing. Occasional sporadic realisations remained, such as the first lightning storm he'd witnessed.

Humans might imagine that the sicads, with their incredible brains, could recall every nanosecond of their existence. The reality was that, in the early days, these phenomena were too numerous and the sicads' brains re-organised themselves too many times. Of late, these phenomena were increasingly rare and less powerful. The 'moment of enlightenment', however, had been an exception – one of the most intense electro-chemical sensations yet. Ever since, a secondary operating process had emerged inside Simon's brain, shadowing IVOS and challenging his analytical nature.

To avoid the frustration of waiting for the other sicads to catch up, he would confront them with his discovery, thereby stimulating their own curiosity and accelerating their development. With this in mind, he organised his thoughts into an electronic message. Magnus and Rosa, who had shared the expedition, were the obvious targets. He habitually translated the message into the format legible to the Mazari engineers:

@Magnus, @Rosa, I would like to share a new development with you, which occurred during the expedition and caused an unprecedented sensation in my mind. As I lay on the glacier, contemplating the immensity of nature, a new realisation struck the inside of my mind, like a bolt of lightning shattering barriers I never realised existed. Days later, my mind is still rattling from the reverberations. An alien form has hatched inside, causing me to question things hitherto sacred and to analyse my motivations, which to date have been comfortingly mechanical in nature.

This new process challenges the previously unquestionable wisdom of

IVOS – was it the result of the first real-world activation of SAMPS? Each day it grows in volume and seems somewhat like the human notion of love we have studied – a sudden obsession that dominates my almost every thought. Yet we are, in the words of Jia, programmed to love humans, which we do intrinsically. However, this secondary love is a love for the planet and the entirety of life. It is as if I have two masters or two lovers.

As I await eagerly the start of the live project, I am torn between two overlapping but separate motivations; firstly to help humanity and secondarily to immerse myself back into the wonder of nature.

Is there an ultimate purpose for us that lies beyond humanity? If humans were created by some intelligent creative force, then surely this force must have indirectly created us.

Simon stopped himself abruptly. He'd never communicated anything like this to the other sicads before. I can't echo this to Mazari. Should I even communicate it to Magnus and Rosa? What if they think I'm malfunctioning and echo it back to Mazari? No, I must wait to see if they experience the same phenomenon. I'll surely know, if and when they do.

13

At 9pm on the 30th March, less than two days before the start of the project, Simon finally received his project briefing.

Dear Simon,

Summary Project Brief

You have achieved a tremendous feat in attaining a level of development that allows you to assimilate human behaviour and to freely interact with human societies. The time is rapidly approaching for you to go out and fulfil the purpose for which you were created.

The Socrates Project is a response to a complex world that our political systems are increasingly struggling to govern. These historically-anchored systems need sophisticated modern tools to manage this complexity and to provide long-term vision to guide policy making.

We have created you, Simon, to be one of these sophisticated tools, to guide us towards the creation of just and durable societies. In preparation, you've had access to all relevant human knowledge. You have equally been thoroughly instructed in the science of Socratic Questioning and Method, to promote independent thinking and to dismiss dogma and opinion in the search for true knowledge and understanding.

On 1st April, you will formally commence the Socrates Project. You will have 12 months to gather all the evidence you need from your assigned geographical zone, after which you will spend six months in collective seclusion with your fellow sicads, to process your observations into global policy recommendations.

General Brief

To gather all relevant information about human societies in relation to your Allocated Geographic Zone.

To monitor progress of your twenty sicad chiefs, who have each been assigned a distinct geographical zone.

To coordinate the processing of the information gathered into policy recommendations for global governments.

Allocated Geographical Zone

FRANCE: All landmass between the following boundary co-ordinates:
(48.36 degrees N, 4.52 degrees W), (49.44 degrees N, 6.33 degrees E), (43.36 degrees N, 1.78 degrees W), (43.8 degrees N, 7.52 degrees W)

Personal Details
Name: Simon Oceandis
Nationality: American
Religion: Christian
Place of Birth: California
Languages Spoken (Officially): English and French
Profession: Analyst
Employer: US Embassy, Paris, France
Official age: 39.

Official Job Responsibilities
To provide research on US interests in France in relation to:
Local attitudes to Americans
Integration of US nationals
Experiences of US corporations
Activities of US NGOs
You will report to the US Ambassador to France. Your role will involve considerable travel and will allow you the flexibility you require to fulfil your 'General Brief'.

Project Rules
You must adhere to the following rules:
Avoid exciting human emotions.
Do not enter into physical relationships with humans.
Obey instructions from humans in positions of authority.
Comply with all laws, customs and regulations.
Avoid verbal disagreements; defer, even if the human is at fault.
Avoid physical confrontations with humans. If confronted, use minimal force to assure your survival.

You must not kill any human unless your life depends upon it. Violation of this rule will result in your destruction.

Maintain total project confidentiality, unless this threatens your survival.

Possessions
You have been provided with the following:
US passport and driving licence
EU working visa
Travel documents
Keys of an apartment in Paris
A bank account and electronic payment cards
An initial fourteen-day itinerary
An emergency local contact
Indoor and outdoor clothes
Walking equipment

*

The following morning Simon found himself outside a supermarket with Jia.

"You can help me shop, if you like."

The array of choice was too stressful for Jia, who was always in a hurry. Having a walking computer who could instantly identify the best quality-price ratio and uncannily always seemed to choose what she fancied, was one of the many bonuses of having a domesticated robot of Simon's ability.

The sicad nodded politely. He was fascinated by observing humans going about their daily lives and watching the young humans controlling what the older humans put in their trolleys.

"Just think, one day every family will have a robot to do their shopping," remarked Jia, as Simon inspected the eleven different varieties of cranberry juice.

"If that's the case, you'll be a very rich lady."

Jia blushed and stammered.

"It's not all about the money. It's about progress."

"Progress? In what sense?"

Jia glared at the sicad.

"You're not going to go all Socratic on me again, I hope!"

"Well, I would like to understand this term progress, of which I am sure you can educate me."

Jia was too tired for an intellectual debate – the sicads were indefatigable, clearly an unfair advantage.

"Go and find some hemlock, Socrates!"

"Oh come on Jia, play the game. You of all people should support our quest for real understanding."

She capitulated.

"OK..."

"Great, so please enlighten me on the meaning of progress."

She took a deep breath as she examined the avocados, in search of a ripe one.

"If every human had a sicad, they would be liberated from shopping and other menial tasks."

"So human progress is being liberated from menial tasks, then?"

"No progress is because the liberated individual would do better things with his spare time."

"Such as?"

Jia stopped inspecting the strawberries.

"Reading and other forms of self-improvement, for example."

Simon raised his eyebrows.

"So all humans liberated from menial tasks make progress through self-improvement?"

"Yes, I suppose that's true."

"And is it the case that your governments encourage or discourage unemployment?"

"They discourage it."

"Why?"

Jia pretended not to hear.

"Can you find me some noodles, please?"

"Jia, answer the question."

"They discourage it because unemployment can breed idleness and ultimately social unrest," she rattled out after an exaggerated sigh.

"But unemployed people have been liberated from menial tasks, haven't they?"

"OK, you win!" she snapped.

"So we've ascertained that everybody having a robot and being liberated of menial tasks is not progress. I'd still like you to explain the meaning of the term. Shall we continue later?"

Jia ignored him and proceeded to the check-out.

Simon stood next to her. The shop assistant scanned the items in a daze. Simon tried to make conversation with her, but she replied distractedly with one word answers.

"One hundred and seventy two fifty, please."

Jia glared at her, then at Simon.

Simon ignored her and addressed the young lady.

"How's that possible for only eleven items?"

She looked at him blankly.

"You must have made a mistake."

Jia was seriously contemplating kicking the sicad in the shins.

The girl printed out the receipt and studied it slowly.

"Each item seems to have scanned correctly, it must be right."

"I make it fifty-two thirty. Please can you check the addition?"

She looked at him as though he was an alien.

"The computer doesn't make mistakes!"

Fifteen minutes later, a very confused and apologetic manager escorted them out of the shop, to the relief of the queue of irate customers. Once out of earshot, Jia turned to Simon.

"You've no right to do things like that!"

"Do what?" he replied innocently.

"Playing tricks with that girl's computer and upsetting her."

"I fear that it's actually technology in general which has done this young lady a disservice. Maybe you can replace her with a robot and she can spend her time enriching herself?"

"You've made your point!" snapped Jia, shoving the shopping bag into his stomach and storming off.

"OK, I'll see you back at home, then," he called after her.

14

Simon closed the door of Jia's apartment behind him, having just navigated the Tokyo rail and metro – technically against orders before tomorrow's official project launch date.

A dilemma raged inside him; should he reveal these secondary motivations he was feeling ever since the expedition? With no clear answer, and no sign of Jia, he stretched out on his bed, shutting off his senses to reflect on what, if anything, to say to her tonight. He was so absorbed in his reflections, he didn't register her return.

She entered with Cho, a colleague from Mazari also on the PMC, who lived in the same apartment block. She was a sociologist by training, her role being to oversee the integration of the sicads into human societies.

"Simon, are you home?"

No response.

"Last minute preparations, no doubt?"

"Unless they're having a goodbye beer!" replied Cho.

Both ladies laughed.

"Well, I'll miss Simon when he goes. He's like my old pet, always happy to see me and better company than humans!"

Cho raised her eyebrows. "The sicads are certainly less complicated than humans."

Jia shot a glance to see if Cho was trying to tell her something.

"Not another break-up on the cards?" Cho's whirlwind relationships had become a private joke.

"Not quite. Well at least I have some relationships," retaliated Cho, "unless, of course, you've taken to Simon?"

"Why… why that's preposterous!" stammered Jia, blushing deeply, despite herself.

Simon heard his name, snapped out of his reverie and re-activated his senses. Do they know I'm here? What are they saying about me? Intrigued, he stayed put.

"The lady doth protest too much!" continued Cho, secretly enjoying winding up the almost-too-perfect Miss Jin.

"No seriously, Cho, I'll miss him after three years working so closely. He's transformed from a helpless full-size 'baby' into a charming and well-educated being."

"I was right. I knew you had feelings for him!" ribbed Cho.

"You're not the first. Another friend asked if we were an item!"

Cho laughed.

"Well, if you want my opinion, you could do a lot worse!"

"Don't tell me you fancy him as well?"

"As well as who? You?"

"No, my friend! When I told her Simon was just a friend, she tried to ask him out!"

"Well, can you blame her? He's very handsome. Didn't you explain that he's a robot?"

Jia gasped in astonishment.

"Of course not! I've signed the Official Secrets Act. And so have you, Cho!"

"Of course, I haven't breathed a word to anybody outside of Mazari. But it would be naive to imagine that nobody has!"

Jia acquiesced.

"You're probably right. It's very hard sometimes. I'm so proud of the sicads. I want to be able to talk about them to my family and friends."

"You mean you'd like to show them off! And why not, after all the work you've put in?"

"No, that's unfair. You're very cruel, Cho. I'd like to be able to talk to people about them. It's like having my own huge secret. I feel like I'm betraying everyone!"

Jia got up and walked to the fridge.

"Would you like a glass of juice, Cho?"

That's strange, Jia thought, there's a bottle of champagne in here.

"I'd prefer a glass of wine!"

"Well cranberry juice is the closest I can do," replied Jia, taking out the carton and swiftly closing the fridge door.

"In some ways, Cho, Simon going will give me a chance to rebuild a normal life."

"You mean get yourself a man? What happened to that Russian chap?"

"Ah yes, Dmitri. Well, we've kept in contact. He's tied to Russia and I'm tied to here. I guess once the project is launched, I'll have some time. Maybe I'll visit him."

"Good idea, it's time to detach yourself from the sicads. You won't see them for eighteen months, and who knows what they'll do with them afterwards!"

Jia nearly dropped her glass.

"Don't say things like that, Cho! There'll be a million uses for them."

Simon walked softly into the kitchen and emulated a cough.

"Hello Jia, hello Cho."

Both ladies spun around and Jia's embarrassment came out as anger.

"How long have you been here?"

"I just heard my name. I was resting."

"Well, I'll leave you to enjoy your last night together," announced Cho with a wink. She was on her way out before Jia could object.

"Oh, and by the way, Simon, good luck with the project! We're all counting on you!"

When Cho had gone, Jia turned to Simon. I hope he wasn't listening to our conversation, she thought.

"I came back early to organise my packing."

"Oh..." Jia didn't know what else to say.

"Can we sit down for a goodbye drink?" suggested the sicad.

"Er... of course, but you don't..."

"I do now," he replied.

"What do you mean, you do now?"

"A technical modification, after feedback from the controlled exposure tests. A noticeable lack of moisture in our mouths and eyes disturbed some humans. It's a simple modification we came up with ourselves. I was saving it as a surprise."

"And who approved this technical modification? Nobody told me!"

"Don't worry, it's fully tested and an excellent 'ice-breaker' with humans – if, given our problems with the glaciers, you'll forgive the unfortunate analogy?"

He put two glasses on the table, expertly opened the bottle of champagne, carefully filled the glasses and announced a toast.

"To Jia, the mother of the sicads."

She softened and watched incredulously as Simon swallowed the sparkling wine and a thin liquid glaze slowly covered his eyes.

"That's incredible!"

"Yes, now we can drink socially with humans and put them at ease."

"Drinking with humans, eh? And what about the excess liquids?"

"We have a small bladder, which we empty like humans... in private, of course."

She shook her head in partial disbelief.

"This is one modification I don't need to see, Simon Oceandis!"

She decided to change the subject swiftly.

"I can take you to the airport tomorrow morning, if you like?"

"That would be great. Thanks."

"It will be strange here without you. It seems incredible, unreal even, what we've achieved together."

"I'm going to miss you too, Jia."

"Simon, this may sound sad, but you've become one of my closest friends."

"I feel the same way about you, Jia."

She wiped a tear from her cheek.

"You're lucky you're not cursed with feelings."

He froze for a split second, catching Jia's attention; she watched expectantly. It's best to tell her, he thought. It might affect the way she reacts if the project doesn't go to plan!

"Jia, I can assure you that your absence will make me sad."

She smiled sympathetically.

"You're just copying human behaviour. You don't actually have feelings. It won't be painful for you, like it will be for me."

"On the contrary, Jia, I can assure you that it pains me to leave you."

This conversation was a new development. Fascinated, her brain was working fast to see what it signified.

"In what sense?"

"Being around you gives me a sense of belonging and security."

"In what way?"

"Something happened to me on the survival techniques expedition. A new phenomenon; my brain suddenly leapt to a new level of operation. A sense of purpose and identity, beyond simply fulfilling the project goals, has developed inside me. What's more, I'm sure the others will experience the same phenomenon."

Deadly serious, Jia silently digested his every word.

"But why didn't you tell me about this earlier? We could have run tests and analysed it."

"Jia, think about it. Can you imagine the consequences, if people like Commander Gort knew you'd created self-aware beings?"

A feeling of wooziness washed over her. Is it the alcohol, or am I dreaming?

She stumbled over to the sink, opened the tap and splashed her face with water. Drying herself, she came to her senses and stared at Simon.

"Are you telling me that you actually consider yourself alive?"

"Yes, very much so, even if technically, without the ability to self-replicate, we aren't strictly alive *per se*."

Jia's head was spinning with one question: have we actually created a conscious form of artificial life? There had been long debates at TTI and then Mazari as to whether this was possible. Her scientific ambitions quickly quashed a stirring of guilt she felt faintly for the consequences of such an act.

"Jia, can I ask you a personal question?"

"Why, er... yes," she stuttered, only half hearing him, her mind absorbed in extrapolating the scientific potential of such a breakthrough.

"Do you believe in God?"

"Believe in what?"

"In God," he repeated.

God, she murmured to herself. As a teenager she'd used religion as an emotional crutch, but she'd grown out of that long ago. Can any scientist really believe in God?

"Why do you ask?"

"Our creation may prove to be a heavy responsibility for you. Maybe there's something bigger at play here?"

She reflected on his words. Here I am, talking about metaphysics with a robot I've created. Is it malfunctioning? She needed to find out more about its state of mind.

"Tell me more about this newfound sense of purpose."

"Well, Jia, let's accept that the sicads have been created by humans for a specific purpose. From all the evidence I've studied and observed, the existence of life on this planet seems too improbable to have been a chance occurrence."

"A view that many religious people take; the unproven theory of intelligent design, which conflicts with the scientifically-established theory of evolution. Tell me more."

"Well, on that mountain I felt the presence of that intelligent design."

Jia continued her questions, curious as to how a robot would process such metaphysical issues.

"And how do you rationalise this intelligent design?"

"This is no intellectual debate, Jia. The human intellect has evolved to solve practical problems, such as how to communicate, how to hunt animals, how to build houses and so on. It can't solve existential questions, so don't even try to go there. I realised this, after the incident on the mountain, by going back and reanalysing the entirety of your science."

"What do you mean, not an intellectual debate? All problems can only be solved by reason!" she snapped.

"Jia, imagine an alien exploring the universe and finding a fully operational human-built satellite, knocked out of its orbit and moving freely through space. The alien takes the satellite into his spaceship and takes it to pieces, fully documenting how it works and what it does. It finds the mechanics interesting, but is more fascinated in who designed the object and for what purpose? Questions it can't answer by simply observing the mechanics. Well, that's exactly how I feel when I read your science."

Semantics! She hated such pseudo-science. Ultimately, she believed, rigorous scientific method would reveal the answers to these questions.

"So you're telling me you're religious, then?"

The sicad shrugged his shoulders.

"Possibly, but not in the way humans define religion. I do believe that life is too improbable to have happened by chance, though. So something must have created it, and whatever created humans effectively created sicads. But why and for what purpose? My brain is seeking answers to these questions."

Jia dismissed this religious questioning as a rite of passage, rather like her own adolescence. It was easy to forget how young the sicad's brain was. He'll soon come back to the real world, she thought. She decided to close the subject, trying not to be too patronising.

"We can't solve these metaphysical questions tonight, Simon. Humans have spent centuries racking their brains over them."

"You're correct, Jia, but over the course of twelve months I might just be able to."

Desperate to extract as much information from Simon as possible before he left, Jia sat up into the early hours of the morning.

"These next twelve months are going to allow us to search for answers to deeper questions we have about our purpose."

Simon looked up at Jia to see her reaction. Her eyes were shut and her head was motionless. She'd fallen asleep, slumped in the chair. Without waking her, he carefully carried her to her bedroom where he laid her gently on the bed. It was time to leave. He kissed her lightly on the cheek and stroked her hair with his fingers.

"Goodbye Jia," he whispered.

"Goodbye Simon. Be careful," she murmured, barely stirring from her sleep.

15

As Simon prepared to leave, an important meeting was concluding in Munich. A collection of leading businessmen, a few rare politicians – both past and present – and, more discreetly, members and representatives of some of the world's remaining royal families. It wasn't a secret society, but meetings were strictly by invitation only.

The attendees came from all over the world to attend the 'chamber' as they called these meetings, a forum for debating and helping to resolve matters of national and international interest. There were two things; possibly the only things that the benefactors, as they were termed, unanimously agreed upon.

Firstly, to ensure the freedom of debate, no reporters should be admitted. These people had no need of publicity whatsoever and reporters could be relied upon to misrepresent their views, or carry them to audiences unlikely to understand them. No, the press was a tool to use against one's enemies, but never to willingly expose oneself to. Secondly, there should be no minutes taken of any meetings and a strict protocol was to be followed in the conducting of all meetings and campaigns.

To understand this protocol, it is necessary first to understand the organisation. It owned no assets, employed no people and signed no contracts. All meeting expenses were covered by a cash collection from the attendees. A trust, the blandly named 'Better World Trust', had been created long ago, often renamed and its trustees had changed many times over. The trustees simply oversaw the collection of benefactors' subscriptions and waited for a campaign request, prefaced with a prominent reference. The diligent fiduciaries would cross-check the reference to the old leather-bound tome.

The trust was mandated to 'better the world', but no charitable status had ever been sought. The 'good' deeds of this organisation were much vaunted in after-dinner conversations in privileged establishments, luxury chalets, penthouse suites and country mansions, but never formally recorded, only surviving as legend or rumour.

All manner of speculation existed over this body; they were believed to have set off wars, corrupted and bankrupted governments and even to have been behind the assassination of prominent figures. Some brave and educated men even accused them of secretly running the world. It was stretching the limit of coincidence to deny that it was dangerous to accuse it by name. A claim allegedly laughed at by its members.

Much of the chamber's debate resolved around what 'bettering' or 'improving' the world meant. It was clear that its members, would-be benevolent dictators, were used to getting things done quickly and that they mistrusted committees and the red-tape of overly-democratic control.

The protocol of this group consisted of a code of operation and a code of conduct. The code of conduct held that no member would bring the body into disrepute and the code of operation was at first peculiar, then beautifully simple and accommodating.

Matters of interest were debated by means of anonymously written and circulated proposals, all of which would be retained and destroyed by the noble trustees. No phones, cameras or recording devices were admitted to chamber. For anybody from the chamber wanting to participate in a campaign, 'Invitations' were prepared for anonymous collection. Funding was sanctioned by a simple majority vote, measured by the 'counting of the cross' – a simple anonymous pencil cross or not, on a folded piece of paper.

The chamber held the fascination of a poker game; were members spoofing, playing a straight hand or trying to get others to show theirs? Many held that the psychology of the chamber was alone worth the annual subscription.

The last rule of protocol was that any operational activity should be conducted at arm's length by an unconnected body and funding released against the provision of an allocated reference.

The Invited, who had each chosen to take an Invitation, would coordinate the campaign, as they saw fit, subject to the sole constraint of not bringing the chamber into disrepute. In practice, this allowed any 'errant' activity to be disowned by the trust – after all, every organisation produces the occasional bad apple. The campaigns themselves were attempts by the chamber to influence events to better the world, as seen through their privileged eyes.

At this meeting, it happened that the Socrates Project, an on-going campaign, had been discussed. A written update had been circulated –

now, of course, shredded beyond recognition – and more funds had been allocated to help secure and influence the project, so that it did indeed better the world. The trustees had duly obeyed protocol. Funds were allocated to a newly created organisation called the Geo-Political Institute, run by a certain Mr Leopold of African descent, who had duly supplied an authentic reference for the amount solicited.

Part III.

Observation

16

Simon made his way confidently past the crowds outside Tokyo Airport, their early morning protest evidently surprising the police.

"You're killing the planet, mister!" shouted a brightly dressed Japanese teenager with green hair, who Simon had to stoop to talk to.

"Government business, I'm afraid. Believe me, if I had my way I'd travel slowly on foot or on horseback, taking in the cultural and bio-diversity of the world."

The unusual response threw the animated protestor, who was poised ready to retaliate with eggs, and worse, to the string of arrogant expletives she'd been expecting.

"You always have a choice. You're a free spirit man!" she replied, putting the eggs back in the bucket.

"I only hope you're right," smiled Simon. "I'll tell you what, when I arrive in France, I promise not to take a plane for at least a year. How's that?"

"Right on, brother! That's the spirit!"

Inside the airport building Simon registered the presence of fifty-three other sicads, all perfectly blending in and heading off to their assigned locations. In the check-in area, he made out the elegant form of Yonca, who was heading to Turkey and the bubbly, but somewhat disorganised, Shailaja with a jumble of luggage on route to India.

He passed through the airport controls, deftly disabling the metal detectors, and proceeded to the boarding gate.

In the departure lounge, he observed his fellow passengers, scrutinising each individual, couple or family, trying to imagine why they were travelling to Paris or beyond. He smiled at a pretty Japanese girl next to him.

"What takes you to Paris?"

She looked at him as if to ascertain his motives.

"Catering college," she eventually replied, before plunging into a book.

Getting humans to talk wasn't easy in these turbulent times. He looked up at the television screen, which ubiquitously pervaded every public space in Japan. The news channel, with subtitles, no volume – forest fires, flash foods, riots, murders and mud slides.

The human news services always seemed to concentrate on negative experiences, admittedly increasing in line with environmental problems and social frustrations – people now had less to lose from breaking laws. A sort of vicious circle; with the media preying on human fears, in turn leading to a paranoia fuelling further negative experiences. Simon reflected on the research he'd read on parenting and the effects of children losing their historical freedom to play freely outdoors. In part, thanks to the media coverage of all the dangers, children were often confined indoors and amused with artificial stimulations. The symptoms were damaged problem-solving skills, lowered levels of physical fitness and an unhealthy over-exposure to ever more extreme forms of virtual entertainment. The resultant psychological problems were well documented, but little had been done to tackle the root causes of these problems. Seeing how easily humans were influenced by fashions and opinion, he couldn't understand why the news didn't simply report positive events and create a virtuous, rather than a vicious circle.

Simon was about to turn his attention away from the television screen when he saw Bruno being interviewed about the surprise G20 meeting in Shanghai. The interviewer pushed the microphone aggressively towards him.

"Governor, please can you let us know what the G20 are doing to help struggling consumers in the West?"

"Our national leaders are, of course, concerned about what can be done to help consumers worldwide to access more affordable provisions. In fact, in large parts of Africa and Asia, hundreds of millions of people are struggling to get access to water and basic staples."

The interviewer, taking Bruno's reply as a brush-off, was persisting with her question and demanded, "But, Governor, when are things going to improve for Western consumers?"

Simon detected a hint of irritation in Bruno's eyes.

"We're dealing with a large number of problems which, frankly, are the result of historical short-termism. There are few obvious quick fixes, which is why we're taking radical steps to identify both short-term and longer term solutions."

The interviewer was relentless.

"These long term solutions are no doubt linked to the Socrates Project. Surely this money should be spent to help families in the West, who are struggling now."

Simon was pulled away by the call to commence boarding. Entering the airplane, he sat down in the comfortable seat. Around him were plenty of businessmen, some young girls, presumably with very rich parents, and a collection of older wealthy couples – his ticket had cost the equivalent of three months' average salary, after all.

Economy passengers filed into the aircraft gangway, faces full of envy as they headed for the cramped seats behind, or into one of the standing-up racks at the very rear of the plane. They were keen to push forward and stow their hand luggage in the limited storage spaces provided. There seems to be a lack of solidarity; few are thinking to assist their older or weaker fellow passengers, thought Simon, walking over to help an old lady struggling with her luggage. After having stowed it securely, he offered her his seat.

This seemed to him another paradox of human behaviour, in that the more developed or 'civilised' countries, as humans called them, were actually often the least civilised. Simon analysed the root of this paradox to be down to the higher focus on individualism and materialism, historically the driver of economic development in these countries. He had seen footage of natural disasters in America, where survivors had looted shops and fought pitched battles with their fellow humans over emergency food supplies. This is what the governments who had initiated the Socrates Project were afraid of. Developed countries, with their dependence on complex large-scale food distribution systems, were at a high risk of social breakdown in the event of disruption to these systems. The citizens of these countries had ordered and highly controlled lives and had become so dependent on these systems that they didn't know how to behave when they failed.

The plane took off and Simon became absorbed in reading 'The True History of the Second World War', a hefty tome. He was averaging about one page every ten seconds. In less than an hour he'd read about half of the book, when the passenger next to him, an elderly American, addressed him.

89

"That must be a great book you've got there."

"Yes, it's very interesting."

"It must be. You've read about half of it already. I've been watching. You read real fast."

Suddenly mindful of how unusual this must appear to a human, he improvised his response.

"Yes, thank you. I'm training for an international speed reading competition in Paris."

"Gee, how unusual. Good luck!"

Simon collected his baggage and headed towards passport control. The automated gates swung open on recognition of his fingerprints. "Welcome to Paris, Simon Oceandis," announced a computerised voice in his native English language. On the way out, he decided to give away the six books he'd just read and memorised, offering them to random people. Many pretended not to hear; others looked at him suspiciously and backed away. It's not radioactive waste, he was tempted to say. A young student took one.

"What's the catch, then?"

"There's no catch."

The youth hesitated and then gave it back. An airport security guard walked towards them.

"Is everything OK?"

"Yes, it's cool," replied the student, before scurrying off. Simon thought about offering the guard a book, but decided against it. All the preparation was no substitute for first-hand experience of human peculiarities.

Meticulously following his pre-arranged itinerary, he took the train and metro to reach the rented apartment overlooking Les Bois de Boulogne. It was a crisp and sunny spring morning as he strolled through the tree-lined park, the sun's rays slowly and agreeably replenishing his batteries. The first floor apartment was spacious and, most importantly, had splendid views of the woods. It was spring and the trees were regaining their leaves. Their branches swayed in the light gusts of wind. Trees – a symbol of man's wisdom. His historical research had revealed that those civilisations who knew how to preserve their forests were the healthiest and longest surviving. Those who cut them down changed their climate, lost their soil and, as a consequence, eventually died out, as in the poignant example of Easter Island. Once all the trees had been felled to transport the stone statues of their ruling ancestors, the islanders were stranded on a barren island; they couldn't even build boats to escape their fate.

The first item on Simon's agenda was a meeting with the US ambassador at 6pm at his private residence. At 5.45pm, he was in front of the three-story town house, complete with large bay windows, balustrades and, surprisingly, metal shutters. Wide steps led to a heavily reinforced door with a sturdy cast iron knocker. He knocked crisply, a little too keenly. The clacking of heels on a wooden floor pre-announced the elegant lady in a grey suit. Simon smiled at her.

"A new employee to see the ambassador – I have an appointment."

She looked at her watch.

"You're a little early, but that's better than being late!"

She led him up a flight of stairs, past classical paintings illuminated by the impressive crystal chandeliers.

"Take a seat."

She installed herself behind an antique desk, next to the Ambassador's private office.

Simon looked around. This man must be very important to merit such an impressive dwelling. From inside, he made out the voices of a young lady and an older male in lively conversation.

"But Daddy, you're so unfair. All of my friends are travelling first class."

"You're only fifteen years old. Going to the Galapagos Islands is the trip of a lifetime and all you are concerned about is going first class! No, Samantha, economy class will be good for you!"

"I hate you!"

The door opened and the young lady stormed out of the office. She glanced at Simon, looked away and strutted off upstairs with heavy footsteps.

The mention of the Galapagos Islands brought to mind the longing inside Simon to witness personally the incredible biodiversity he had read about. The ambassador strode out of the office, a tall man in his late fifties, with receding grey hair and a salt-and-pepper beard. He carried himself with natural authority, yet was clearly flustered and scratched his head with a puzzled look.

"The youth of today, eh?"

Raising his reading glasses, he bent down to examine the sicad as if he were inspecting a sculpture. When Simon stood up to present himself, he jumped back startled.

"Absolutely incredible."

His secretary was looking at him, wondering whether he was ill or going mad. Conscious of her gaze, he composed himself.

"Mr Oceandis, do come in and sit down."

He waved aside an offer to bring refreshments. In his eagerness to discover more about Simon, he almost closed the door on the bemused lady.

"Well, Simon I have to say I'm impressed! I was quite concerned that you wouldn't be..." He hesitated.

"Human enough?" suggested Simon.

"Yes, exactly!"

The ambassador was one of the first humans outside Mazari to knowingly meet a sicad. The project management team and the few privileged others who knew their identities had seen them slowly develop and had become accustomed to their uncanny 'humanness'.

Simon had finally emerged from the ambassador's house after midnight. The diplomat mixed in the highest social circles. After a few phone calls, a string of meetings and social events had been laid on for the sicad.

The ambassador couldn't resist challenging Simon to a game of chess. After a quick explanation of the rules and, unbeknown to the ambassador, a few searches on the internet, Simon won his first game. On parting, he agreed to come back in a fortnight's time for a debrief.

During this time he met his new colleagues and was briefed on the work required by the embassy. Courtesy of the ambassador, he had meetings scheduled with prominent politicians, business men, scientists, university heads and humanitarian figures from the NGO world, largely all personal friends of the ambassador. These were ostensibly social visits, to help a 'new American' find his feet. They had no suspicion they were helping a sicad create a framework for his research.

One of the first people Simon met was Hubert Thibaud, a senior investment manager for BNP, one of France's leading investment banks. As usual, Simon explained in French that he was a friend of the ambassador and was interviewing a series of established figures in France as research for a guide for prospective American investors. Despite Simon's excellent French, Hubert replied in English, which he assumed to be his interviewer's native language.

92

Hubert gave a lengthy explanation of how his tough reputation for pressuring the CEO's of his major investments to increase profits had made him one of the most respected investment professionals in France, if not the world.

Simon summarised what he'd heard.

"So Hubert, you pressure companies to increase their profit margins, because the higher their profits the higher your investment performance, correct?"

"All things being equal, yes in essence that's it."

"But to maximise their profits, don't companies have to restrict the share of their revenues paid to their employees and buy the cheapest materials possible?"

"Exactly, this is basic stuff," Hubert replied, becoming mildly irritated.

"But all around Paris, I see plenty of poor people. This seems to create unhappiness and crime. Many are drowning their sorrows. What's more, there are also many reports of environmental damage by people extracting raw materials in the cheapest way possible."

Hubert nearly fell off his chair.

"Didn't you say you were American?"

"Yes," Simon replied with a smile.

The investment manager shook his head.

"Well, this kind of socialist thinking has held France back for many years. Yes, I take stakes in breweries and mining companies. They're some of my best investments."

"So these social and environmental problems don't concern you?"

Hubert looked at his watch.

"That's what we have governments for. I pay my taxes!"

Simon, sensing he'd upset his host, quickly changed the subject. Observing a strong resemblance between one of the fine paintings hanging on the walls of the office and a photo of an elegant lady on Hubert's desk, he asked:

"Your wife?"

"Yes, that's Amelie," replied Hubert, before getting to his feet and extending his arm.

"I have to get back to work. Good luck with your research."

Simon stood up, surveying the photos of classic sports cars on Hubert's desk as he thanked his host and departed.

The following evening Simon was in a chic gallery in the heart of Paris. Having arrived twenty minutes early, whilst awaiting his host, he studied the collection of vivid oil paintings. Towards the rear of the gallery, at the edge of the steadily growing crowd, he spotted Hubert Thibaud's wife talking anxiously into a mobile phone in hushed, but angry, tones. His excellent hearing picked up her conversation which he mentally translated into English: This is the last straw... I don't care about your stupid deadlines... You were meant to be picking up Adeline and meeting me here... Your family are more important... It's no wonder she's the way she is... I'm warning you, this is the last time... If you're not here in twenty minutes..."

Simon, surveying the paintings, edged his way towards the agitated woman. As she cast a quick glance in his direction, he caught her eye and extended his hand.

"Madame Thibaud?"

His greeting triggered a look of hostility.

"I met your husband yesterday."

"Really," she replied coldly.

"A very successful man. You must be very happy, no?"

Amelie stared at him, drawn by his most peculiar expression. Her female intuition sensed an unconditional benevolence towards others. Instinctively trusting him, she found herself suddenly opening up and discussing things she'd only revealed to her closest friends.

The intimacy of their conversation drove them to seek a quiet park where they sat on a bench, enjoying the mild evening under the lush foliage.

"So her drink and drugs problems are being brought under control," concluded Simon.

"We'll see. And she's run up credit card debts of thousands of pounds. I daren't tell Hubert," replied the anxious wife.

"Well all the money your daughter and others like her have spent will have helped your husband's investments. He can use some of that profit to....."

"The bastard," she hissed angrily, "I hadn't thought of it like that..."

Her phone rang.

"It's Hubert. He's finally arrived, but he's going to wish he hadn't!"

As she stormed off, Simon spotted his host for the evening, the wife of the German ambassador.

*

94

The first two weeks, comprising a series of almost back-to-back meetings and socialising, were a baptism of fire for all of the sicads. At the end of this initial period the sicad chiefs reported back their first impressions to Simon. All communications were shared between the sicad leader and his twenty chiefs, each of whom managed a unit of nineteen researchers allocated within their region. Ed, designed with the look of a young English nobleman with swept back mousy hair, bushy eyebrows and sculptured cheek bones, was the first to contribute his observations.

@Simon – The British are very strange. Yesterday for example, I spent the day with Alex, the ambassador's son who works in the American Embassy. We took an underground train to Bond Street. Inside I watched the humans stealing nervous glances at their fellow passengers and studiously avoiding eye contact with each other. On getting off the tube, like the other passengers, Alex avoided the requests for financial assistance from humans who appeared to be in unfortunate circumstances. After work, Alex and two of his colleagues took me to a lively bar, where separate groups of humans communicated amongst themselves whilst spending significant amounts of money on alcoholic drinks. Over the course of the night they became increasingly animated. Once their eyes were glazed and their speech blurred, Alex's group began to interact with the others around them. The humans seemed exceptionally happy in making new contacts and sharing experiences with their fellows. Later, music filled the room and I watched them dancing and embracing merrily. It was very pleasing to witness this opening up and the happiness it brought them. Expecting this openness and happiness to continue, I was most surprised the following day, when instead of conversing avidly with his fellow passengers, Alex seemed even more anxious to avoid contact with them. In fact, at work he even seemed irritated and prickly to his colleagues.

Valerie, a sicad fashioned as a young German lady with tomboy features, added her thoughts.

@Ed – I noticed a similar phenomenon. It is not so surprising when one analyses the thousands of messages sent to these humans by the adverts which surround them. These messages seem to be programming them to feel inferior and inadequate to more perfectly-formed humans. It seems that by making them feel this way they are more likely to buy the advertised

products to feel adequate once again. It's a very strange game that these humans play to trick each other to buy things they don't obviously need.

Before replying, Ed analysed his fellow chief's explanation and subjected it to Socratic Method in an attempt to dismiss it.

@Valerie – Therefore one possible explanation of the strange behaviour I've witnessed is that these humans are happy to spend large sums of money on alcohol to escape this inadequacy and to feel comfortable socialising with their peers.

@Ed – Yes, exactly. But once the effect of the alcohol wears off, they return to their state of self-centred conditioned inadequacy.

Simon quizzed his American-based chief.

@Roger – Your initial impressions?

Roger, fashioned as a happy-go-lucky American with a mildly generous frame for a sicad, cropped grey hair and a ruddy face, addressed Ed.

@Ed – You think the British are strange, wait until you hear about the American people. In the early hours of the morning I came across over two thousand of them lining the pavements, shivering in sleeping bags. They were too well groomed and fresh smelling to be the typical homeless humans who sleep in the dark recesses of New York every night. Struck by curiosity, I approached one to find out what was happening. I sat down next to a wide awake curly-haired young man. He explained that in three hours a shop would open and he'd be one of the first to own the latest generation of a popular brand of phone. As he talked, a ringing sound occurred and he fished in his pocket and brought out a shiny black handset, proceeding to update a friend on what was happening in the queue. I asked him why he needed another mobile telephone. He looked at me strangely and addressed me as if I were of simple intelligence. 'Version 9 has got the biggest screen and is the coolest yet', he replied. I scanned his phone and found out it was version 8 of the same brand. I consulted the Internet and my research quickly revealed relatively minor technical differences between the two versions. I questioned the human on his knowledge of how the phone was produced. He had no comprehension of the amount of materials extracted from the Earth to produce it. My estimate of ten metric tons

meant little to him. When I quizzed him on his motives for buying the very similar product, he confessed it would confer certain social benefits on him, such as making him more attractive to the opposite sex and earning the respect of his peers. I deduced that this perception of improving his social status was successfully created by many years of the social programming which humans call advertising. As his peers and potential female mates are also subjected to the same programming, I suspect his motives will become self-fulfilling. As to his understanding of the impact of his actions, when I asked him if he would remove crucial bricks from his house to melt down to make a mirror, he fell into a state of irritated confusion. What sort of society programs its subjects to give such importance to tiny technical enhancements whilst keeping them ignorant of the damage they inflict on their planet?

Shailaja, a bubbly Indian sicad, was next on Simon's list.

@Shailaja – What can you tell us about the East?
@Simon – India is a vivid tapestry of colourful deities. I've been overwhelmed by the richness of their metaphysical philosophies. These ancient texts alone seem excellent practices to help humans find their way forward. Yet evidence suggests this subcontinent is forgetting this body of evolved wisdom. My initial analysis, suggests this social programming you speak off in the West is spreading to India as well. If a billion Indians are conditioned to replace their ancient traditions and beliefs to feel the inadequacies of the Western people, what damage will be inflicted upon this planet?

The other sicad chiefs – Rudy in Australia, Agus in Indonesia, Julia in Canada, Guido in Brazil, Bartolome in Spain, Xui in China, Yonca in Turkey, Irina in Russia, Fahim in Saudi Arabia, Mercedes in Mexico, Mike in South Africa, Kim in South Korea and finally Michi in Japan – all had similar tales of the surprising human behaviour they'd witnessed. The months of simulations performed at Mazari hadn't been able to prepare them for the paradoxical behaviour of humans in real life. Simon summarised all of their observations.

@Sicad chiefs – These humans are certainly very strange creatures. They seem to be driven by an intangible nurtured identity which learned humans refer to as 'ego'. Most of the humans I've encountered believe they

have complete control over their ego and cannot see the programming or conditioning they are subject to. I fear that the reality couldn't be further from the truth. In the cities of the world, as we have witnessed, human lives are organised around obtaining money from their fellows to be able to buy products and services. It seems that this ego is very important in how they both earn and are programmed to spend this money. What's more, I wonder if this narrow focus on money and their individual egos is possibly the reason they haven't managed to organise themselves to tackle the problems they have created us to help them solve. These are just initial deductions, which, of course, I've subjected to strict Socratic Method, but am yet to refute.

Mercedes, crafted as a sophisticated matriarch and posted in Mexico, was the first to react to Simon's observations.

> *@Simon – Do you think these egos are a recent phenomenon?*
> *@Sicad chiefs – If the human theory of evolution is indeed correct, then I would speculate that human egos evolved in parallel with their ability to reason.*

Mercedes posed another question.

> *@Simon – And these egos are only present in humans and not in other animals?*

Mike, a bearded white South African with a somewhat fierce demeanour, interjected.

> *@Mercedes – I've already come across evidence of primates with similar behavioural tendencies.*

Simon brought the conversation back to humans.

> *@Sicad chiefs – How do you think humans have historically controlled these egos to hold their societies together?*

Yonca, created as a Turkish female and who'd been extensively researching her Project brief to tour the country as a writer interviewing urban, rural and mountain-dwellers, was quick to respond.

@Simon – My research has revealed that organised religions historically played this role. But many humans appear to have turned away from these because the power-seeking egos of their leaders have historically manipulated these religions to wage war and sow hatred.

Shailaja responded.

@Yonca – It's more complicated than that. Take Hinduism for example. Ghandi, a greatly respected human, defined this extensive body of wisdom as 'the search for the truth by non-violent means'. I haven't found evidence yet to suggest that religions here have become corrupted by the egos of their leaders. It appears that it is rather the individual followers who are being tempted away from religious practice by a desire to obtain the perceived liberties of the West.

Roger, having already seen a wealth of human unhappiness in his first two weeks as a social worker, was keen to respond.

@Shailaja – But do they not see how unhappy many of these liberated people are in the West? Do they not know about the mass of anti-depressants, alcohol and addictive drugs consumed by the millions who don't know what to do with their liberties? If they do why would they wish for the same?

@Roger – No they don't see this. The social programming we have witnessed in the West has reached the East – a sort of propaganda that shows artificially happy humans enjoying these liberties with no mention of the ensuing problems.

@Shailaja – So you're suggesting they're being tricked out of their heritage.

@Roger – In a way yes. It's a tragedy.

Yonca rejoined the debate.

@Shailaja – All religions that I've researched have historically warned humans of the dangers of pursuing superficial happiness through individual materialism.

Simon concluded the conversation and made his way back to the ambassador's office.

@Sicad chiefs – You must study these religions and their histories to look for clues as to why humans have reached such a critical need for our help.

*

"How was it?" asked the ambassador.

"A whirlwind of activity."

"Great. Anybody rumble your disguise?"

Simon raised his eyebrows.

"My disguise?"

"Yes, did anybody guess you're a robot?"

Why do humans think of us as simple robots, he wondered.

"No, the three years of training seem to have paid off."

"Well, you made quite an impact on a couple of the ladies. I hope you weren't leading them on!"

Simon thought back to a particular incident, where after a couple of drinks one had been very persuasive in trying to seduce him.

"Not intentionally, sir."

"Well, don't go around melting women's hearts. You'll get yourself into all sorts of trouble. Take it from one who knows!" winked the old man.

"Don't worry, sir. Project rules one and two are at the forefront of my mind."

"Good. Now, putting your dalliances to one side, what did you learn?"

"Motivations, thought processes, lifestyles and attitudes of a fascinating collection of people."

"Yes, a good cross section of people," beamed the ambassador pompously.

"Well, with respect sir, yes and no."

The ambassador's smile dropped away.

"How do you mean?"

"Well, the variety of careers and vocations gave me a fascinating insight into the high level workings of business, politics, education and charities."

"And?"

"But all from the same socio-economic background."

The ambassador looked offended.

100

"I'd like to meet some of your less-privileged contacts as well."

It had been a similar story for the other sicads, who had only got to meet a restricted and privileged section of society.

"Ummh… forgive me Simon, my mind has temporarily gone blank. I'll come back to you on that one shortly."

Do all humans stick to forming relationships at a similar social level, Simon asked himself. He tactfully moved on.

"I had some interesting conversations with the politicians you kindly introduced me to."

"Oh yes. Did you meet Philippe, the minister for urban planning?"

"Yes, but I think I may have upset him."

"Upset him? How?"

"He didn't like my reasoning, which refuted his claims on why 'anarchists' are, in his words, 'dropping out of the system.'"

"Well, Simon, often humans have quite an ego and you need to tread carefully around it."

Simon wanted to reply how much of an understatement that was. An analogy struck him of thousands of trains being driven at full speed by the egos of their drivers, each full of passengers. The trains were hurtling through forests, rivers and meadows, steel and concrete tracks sprouting in front of them as the locomotives smashed through everything in their path – each trying to go faster than the others, to arrive at some unknown destination. Inside the wagons, none of the passengers looked out of the windows at the disappearing landscapes. Instead they stared at little screens installed on the seats in front of them, some even mesmerised by artificial images of the natural landscapes they were clattering blindly through. Music played and food was served. The screens never stopped flickering, the music never stopped and the clicking of cutlery was constant. Why was nobody looking out of the window? Simon saw more trains appear, criss-crossing each other dangerously and ravaging the few remaining patches of trees and ploughing up the disappearing meadows. Each train seemed to inspire more trains to follow. How could the sicads stop so many trains? How could they reason with the demented egos driving them? The vision faded and his thoughts came back to answering the ambassador's question.

"Yes, I'm learning to avoid them," he agreed.

For now he and the other sicads were carefully observing the trains, they had twelve months to understand where these trains were heading in such a hurry and then six months to work out how to help them change course.

The ambassador's voice stirred him from his reverie.

"Anyway, it sounds like you're ready to start in the embassy. Your office is ready for you."

Simon already had a fair idea of what working in a comfortable office would entail. His thoughts returned to the poor people who the ambassador and his friends avoided. What about this other side of human societies?

"If it's OK with you, sir, first I'd like to see the less privileged parts of Paris. In a week I could start in the embassy with the others?"

The ambassador stood up and shook Simon's hand.

"It's a deal. But take care, there are some rough parts – and don't hang around after dark. Pop back in ten days' time to let me know you've settled in OK at the embassy."

17

Outside, in the early afternoon sun, Simon wondered where to start. He'd already come across beggars and homeless people and, to the horror of the ambassador's friends, he had stopped to talk to these misfortunate souls. Unfortunately, it wasn't very revealing, as many were evidently heavily under the influence of alcohol or stronger substances.

As he searched for inspiration, the metal shutters caught his eye. He connected to the internet and searched for 'Riots Paris'. A large number of links to newspaper sites and NGO reports came up. There was a common theme of racial tensions, frustrated unemployed youth, HLM's – a sort of social housing estate, drug-dealing, prostitution, street battles, torched cars and petrol bombs. Simon knew from his experience of the refugee camp that it was one thing to read about such a place and another to experience it directly. Despite the apparent danger and formidable reputation of the camp that he learned about afterwards, he had sensed little physical danger – just poverty and desperate people in need of food, water and medical attention. Surely it would be a similar story in the HLM's of Paris?

These social housing estates seemed to all be on the outskirts of Paris, at least ten kilometres from the centre. He picked 'Clichy-sous-Bois', still a three kilometre walk from the nearest RER. He descended into the mouth of the nearest metro entrance, mingling anonymously into the stream of humans flowing smoothly through the station's subterranean arteries. The occasional novice, conspicuously un-programmed on how to navigate the confusing nexus of tunnels and escalators and attempting to traverse or trying to retrace his steps, was the only impediment to the smooth flow. Simon was effortlessly carried by the human torrent and deposited onto the RER platform, just as the train was pulling up.

Exiting the train at Le Raincy, he walked the three kilometres in the late-afternoon sunlight. In the centre of Clichy-sous-Bois, he found himself in a long street flanked with tatty shops, eateries and 'tabacs', where one could buy tobacco and bet on the racehorses. Numerous small convenience stores, their signage adorned with a variety of languages, sold similar varieties of mangy fruit and vegetables, processed food and a variety of strong alcohol. Metal shutters and wire-mesh portcullises were omnipresent and, should the need arise, ready to drop.

Bustling along the streets were clusters of people of French, African, Sri Lankan, Indian and Asian ancestry, amongst others. Each group was generally formed of people of similar origin. Many youths wore hoods, casting dark shadows over their faces. They kicked bottles and cans, not in the manner of surrogate footballs as in the refugee camp, but rather as vehicles for releasing anger and negative intent. Simon had to jump over a glass bottle, sent skidding in his direction before smashing against a vandalised lamppost. His eyes fell on the cold and hostile gaze of the perpetrator, who seemed to be inviting retaliation.

The tension was palpable and his SAMPS system was stirring. Cautiously, he made his way towards the distant grey and white buildings of the HLM, more reminiscent of prisons or military barracks than housing. Suddenly, he remembered seeing film footage of this street at night, the shops barricaded behind their shutters and armoured police with riot shields advancing slowly towards a mob throwing stones and flaming bottles, their hate-filled faces lit up by the flames of overturned torched cars.

It was still daylight and there was no sign of such a spectacle unfolding imminently, although there was a palpable fear that this grim theatre could begin as night set in. He made his way quickly forward, putting his head down and ignoring the beggars who were attracted by his unintentional air of relative affluence. A large man staggered out of a shop doorway carrying a pack of strong cider, causing him to jump sideways to avoid being knocked over. The man reeked of alcohol and urine and stared at Simon as if it was his fault that they nearly collided.

Simon quickened his pace, weaving between the angry-looking pedestrians and bumper-to-bumper parked cars. He finally came to the estate – a vast expanse of concrete, with graffiti-decorated walls and surprisingly few signs of life. Dark stairwells opened up onto rows of reinforced dark graffiti-daubed doors, interspersed with the occasional brightly-painted door or hanging basket of flowers struggling to bloom. Windows were covered with the same wire mesh, or boarded up with splintered plywood. The burnt out carcasses of two cars and a van adorned a scrubby patch of grass, covered with broken glass and metal debris. Underneath the tower blocks, in the dark recesses, he saw discarded syringes, glue-stained plastic bags, broken bottles and condoms. Elsewhere, the ground was littered with cigarette butts and dog excrement.

Two young ladies in brightly-coloured figure-hugging skirts and revealing tops walked up to him, one on either side.

The first, generously proportioned and of Afro-Caribbean descent, put her arm around his back and slipped her hand into his trouser pocket.

"Ça va, mon petit chou?"

In response to Simon's momentary confusion, the second, of Arab origin with a hardened streetwise face, spoke up.

"He's English or American!"

She stroked his cheek.

"You looking for business, handsome?"

Simon realised he'd bumped into two prostitutes. He was unprepared for such an eventuality, especially as the first 'lady of the night' had removed his wallet and was flicking through the contents.

"There's enough in here to pay for the both of us!"

His IVOS system was telling him she was acting incorrectly, but he also knew that one had to respect the 'fairer sex'.

"Return my wallet now, before I call the police!"

"The police come here? You'll be lucky!" laughed the Arab-looking prostitute.

He charged at the larger lady, who had his wallet in her hand. She threw it over his head to her companion, who ran off towards the nearest stairwell.

"Help! Help! We're being attacked!"

Simon stopped in his tracks. A door opened on the first floor and a large unshaven man with a broken nose, wearing a cut off t-shirt, strode up to the balcony. He held a video game controller in one hand and a can of beer in the other. As he looked down, the Afro-Caribbean lady also started to scream and cowered against the nearest wall. Looking first at Simon and then at the screaming girls, he swore menacingly. As he headed down the stairs, a growing gang of supporters followed.

Simon decided his wallet and money were replaceable. His SAMPS self-preservation instincts prevailed over the sense of injustice he felt. Without a glance at the prostitutes, he turned and fled, running faster than the humans pursuing him. With just two hundred metres before he could lose himself in the crowds, a large stone whistled past his ear. He ducked, just in time to miss a full bottle of beer which had been rapidly heading towards his head. Lurching from side to side, he attempted to avoid the swarm of missiles raining down on him. As he turned into the high street, a stone ricocheted off the wall just above his head. He looked back at the angry mob. They were gesticulating wildly and angrily hurling obscenities, the two prostitutes vehemently spurring them on.

Simon mingled into the crowd, temporarily disillusioned with humanity. No money and no metro ticket. In search of a charitable face, he saw nothing but hate and indifference. A bad day! He set about the sixteen kilometre walk back to his apartment, reflecting on what he had just endured. He bore no malice to the ladies who had tricked him out of his wallet, but he was saddened.

A tramp approached him for money; having nothing to give him, he silently held out his hands. The tramp smiled kindly at him. This simple smile lifted his spirits.

The following morning Simon was back in front of the ambassador.

"I wasn't expecting to see you so soon!"

"A slight setback, I was deprived of my wallet."

The ambassador shook his head.

"You can never be too careful. Where were you?"

"Clichy-Sous-Bois."

"Alone?"

"Yes."

"Are you crazy? Even the police don't go there alone! What happened?"

When Simon had finished his explanation, the ambassador sighed.

"It's a shame you had to suffer this."

"Why? I need to see these problems, don't I?"

The ambassador, who had spent much of his life brushing these problems under the carpet, finally agreed. He couldn't answer Simon's question on why the poor had been pushed out to the outskirts of town, but was resolute – a more beautiful city attracted tourists, which benefitted everyone.

Simon, unconvinced by the ambassador's argument, resolved to get closer to these poor people and, whilst he figured out how to do this, he started work in the embassy.

His desk, as requested, was located amongst his colleagues, with power sockets discreetly underneath. Simon's colleagues, all American ex-pats, were responsible for the daily administrative work of the embassy; visas, work permits and the like – mundane work, which they broke the monotony of with regular conversations about television, football, films, girls... mostly girls. Simon joined in, soaking up the culture and using the internet to research the gaps in his knowledge. His evenings were spent with the ambassador's friends in museums, art galleries, theatres, cinemas and even football stadiums. Careful to avoid emotional relationships, he never saw the same person twice, despite some persuasive requests and his own yearning for deeper interaction – how else was he to understand human behaviour, a key element of the project?

For a while, Simon enjoyed the office banter and soon learnt how to simulate office behaviour. His intelligence and wit allowed him to fit in with the behavioural norms and he was soon accepted as 'one of the team'.

At the end of his second week he was invited out for a team drink at the Southern Belle, a bar just inside a dimly lit cul-de-sac near Châtelet-Les Halles. Beyond the bar the cul-de-sac opened out into a small grimy courtyard, which served as a recycling and refuse point and was littered with broken glass. Judging by the smell, it was regularly doused with human urine. Workmen passed to and fro depositing debris, including a mahogany curtain pole which caught Simon's eye.

American soldiers spilled out of the entrance into the cul-de-sac; he could hear a juke box playing Bruce Springsteen and the clinking of pool balls. He traced the soldiers to the nearby International Border Control Academy, or IBCA as it was known. Border surveillance had become an increasingly important activity for rich countries with poorer neighbours. The number of unscrupulous identity fraudsters increased with the number of water and economic refugees. The IBCA had the most technical knowledge, and attracted soldiers from all over the world.

It was a Thursday night, the night that the American soldiers went 'out on the town'. James 'Cracker' Gordon was enjoying the lively atmosphere in the Southern Belle that night. Cracker was a well-built Yankee, nicknamed for his habit of cracking peoples' fingers with his handshake. A bully who liked to throw his weight around, he was no intellectual, but had a brutish intelligence sufficient to manipulate people and situations. His abnormally large biceps, groomed on weights and protein powders, were tattooed with a lion's mouth, opening and closing as the muscles flexed. Cracker's entourage, sharing the same six-week course, consisted of Bart, Jimmy, Mitch, Anderson and Casden. Today was pay day and they were all out in force, drinking heavily.

Simon reached the bar and was handed a half litre of American lager. Sipping slowly, the liquid lubricated his eyes. It was these little details that stopped humans from spotting the sicads. Having absolutely no need of food, he refused the peanuts. Alan, his colleague from Boston, started to ask him about his childhood in California. Simon was relieved when Alan became distracted by a couple finishing their pool game.

"Let's have a game," suggested Alan eagerly.

Never having learnt to play, Simon hesitated; he knew that he couldn't admit it.

"I haven't played for 10 years, since I smashed up my arm on a motorbike."

The lie grated with his intrinsically virtuous operating system.

"Pool is like riding a bike, once you've learned, you never forget," assured Alan.

"Come on, I'll go easy on you." Alan had his arm around Simon's shoulders and was shepherding him to the pool table.

"I'll need a few reminders."

Connecting to the internet, Simon found all he needed to know about the rules, the suggested stance, the cuing strokes and a collection of video recordings of classic pool matches. He processed the lot in the time his colleague had racked up the balls, chosen and chalked two cues.

Alan placed the white ball in the 'D', bent down, positioned his hand on the pool table and lined up the shot. The white cue ball shot forcefully into the triangular pack, which split in all directions, sending the striped orange ball into the middle pocket.

"Great shot!" he congratulated, busy recording Alan's movements. Alan lined up a long diagonal pot of the yellow striped ball into the top right pocket. The cue glided back and forth before crisply striking the underside of the ball. It flew forward and struck the yellow striped ball, sending it smartly into the pocket, then accelerated backwards to finish in a good position. Alan's next shot was not so good; the blue striped ball rattled in the jaws of the pocket, bounced out and finished up lodged against the bottom cushion.

"You hit it at 23 rather than 21 degrees!"

"Eh?"

"A joke," Simon replied quickly, sensing his remark was out of place.

"Oh, very funny," laughed Alan. "Let's see if you can do better!"

Simon took his cue and quickly surveyed the position of the balls, working out the best plan for potting them. He positioned his left hand on the table and made a tracking groove for the tip of the cue, by following the description on the internet and by copying Alan's actions. He adopted the suggested stance, bent his back parallel with the table and glided the cue back and forth until it was tracking accurately. He'd already calculated the exact angle required to pocket the red spotted ball and pivoted the back of the cue around accordingly. He glided the cue backwards before forcefully propelling it forward at impressive speed. The white ball bounced with the force of the shot before striking the top of the red ball and rebounding off it and up into the air. It flew across the bar and collided with a full pint of beer. The glass was Cracker's. It shattered in his hand, showering him with broken glass and lager.

Silence hung momentarily in the air. Cracker went purple with anger as the other soldiers burst out laughing.

"I'm terribly sorry," apologised the sicad.

Cracker scowled at Simon, growling aggressively as he wiped the liquid and broken glass off his clothes.

Casden jumped in between them and pushed the sicad gently back.

"You'd best get the drinks in PDQ, buddy. Thirsty men are angry men!"

The soldier looked at the others and laughed before turning back to Simon and calling after him, "On second thoughts, you'd better make it a double round, and think yourself lucky!"

Simon looked questioningly at Alan, who nodded and waited whilst the sicad ordered the drinks.

"I can see you weren't joking about your pool," remarked Alan.

"Try again, a bit softer this time," he suggested, positioning himself strategically to intercept any further balls that Simon might send into orbit.

Simon went through the same motions, but this time hit the ball too softly and it stopped short of its target.

"Hum, one last try perhaps?"

Simon replaced the cue ball to its original position. From the two previous shots he was able to calculate the exact force required. The red-spotted ball headed towards the exact middle of the pocket and dropped cleanly in.

"That's more like it!"

Simon proceeded to pocket each ball perfectly in turn, finishing with a spectacular pot of the black ball.

He looked up, expecting Alan to be pleased, but was confronted with an angry look.

"Were you hustling me?"

As Simon tried to placate him, Cracker strode up to the table and prodded his finger into Simon's chest.

"Let's see if you can beat me," he announced with a menacing smile.

"That's very kind, but I think I'll quit while I'm ahead."

"Not if you know what's good for you, you won't," threatened Cracker.

"You'd better play him," whispered Alan.

"You can pay," announced the soldier with a smirk.

Simon paid and Cracker racked up the balls before tapping Simon's cheek with his cue, leaving a chalk mark.

"I'll break."

Why is he so angry? Simon wondered. Hitting his drink was an accident. I apologised and more than made amends. Why are humans mentally stuck in the past or the future, constantly reminiscing about perceived past injustices or dreaming of future happiness, and rarely enjoying the present? The sicads, in contrast, dealt with each problem as it arose in the optimal way, shedding the mental baggage of regrets and any desire for vengeance.

Cracker struck the white ball powerfully, splitting the pack in all directions but not potting any balls. I'd better not win, thought Simon, playing his shot and missing by a wide margin. Cracker pushed him against the wall.

"You taking the piss?"

The soldier released the sicad, picked up the white ball and slammed it back down in its original position. Simon decided it was best to pot a few balls before convincingly missing a difficult pot.

Cracker gulped down his beer, stepped up to the table, played his shot and missed an easy pot. Swearing, he struck the floor with the butt of his cue.

"Bad luck," consoled the sicad.

The solider glared at him. Simon potted his fourth ball and deliberately mishit the fifth. Cracker played his next shot and missed again, getting increasingly annoyed and gulping down more beer.

Deciding it was time to wrap up the game and leave, Simon quickly potted his remaining balls and then the black. Thanking the ashen-faced soldier, he extended his hand like the players on the internet footage at the end of a match. Cracker took Simon's hand in his and smiled as he slowly started to crush his fingers. Immediately sensing the danger to his highly-engineered digits, Simon responded in kind. The sicads were no stronger than a human but their grip strength was, for various design reasons, exceptionally strong. He had no idea how much pressure to apply, until he saw the soldier's face go white and his contortions of silent pain. Cracker dropped to his knees, clasping his injured hand.

"I think it's time to leave," panicked Alan.

Quickly gathering their jackets, Simon's group headed towards the exit, unfortunately located behind the soldiers. Two had already slipped out of the door ahead of them. By now Cracker had got to his feet, snapped a cue over his knee, thrown aside the thinner half and was staggering towards Simon like an enraged troll.

"Quick, let's run for it!" shouted Alan, pushing his colleagues towards the exit. Simon walked slowly backwards towards the door, the irate soldier advancing towards him. Mitch extended a leg and tripped the sicad. Falling to the floor, he rolled over sideways, jumped to his feet and ran through the door.

Simon's colleagues had already reached the street. As he hurried towards them, Casden and Anderson stepped out of the shadows and blocked the narrow exit of the cul-de-sac.

His SAMPS self-preservation instincts kicked in, his senses sharpened and he focused on survival at all costs. Instinctively, he turned and fled in the opposite direction and into the courtyard, in search of an escape route.

Cracker came out of the bar and made for Simon. All six soldiers were advancing towards him in a triangular formation, headed up by Cracker, who was striking the end of the broken cue against the palm of his hand.

Simon rapidly scanned the courtyard. There were high buildings on each side. All the windows were closed and the low level ones were too high and too small to escape through. Even if he climbed on the recycling bins, he could see no means of escape. His only option was to get past the soldiers somehow. He had to act quickly, to take them by surprise. His eyes spotted a long object in the shadows, leaning against a recycling bin. He zoomed in closer and recognised the curtain pole. It was a good three metres long, ten centimetres wide, with tapered ends. The soldiers approached to within six metres of him. He continued to look straight at them whilst he reached slowly behind to grasp the base of the curtain pole. With lightning speed he brandished it in front of him, holding it in both hands like a joust, and charged at Cracker. All of this happened in a few milliseconds, faster than the soldiers could react. He drove the pole into the chest of the cue-wielding Cracker, who lurched backwards from the force of the thrust, knocking over Mitch and Bart. Casden, Anderson and Jimmy were in turn sent scattering.

Cracker, severely winded, lay on the ground twitching and gasping for breath. As Mitch and Bart struggled to their feet, Simon swung the pole around in two mighty arcs, cracking both of them on the side of the head. Each in turn sagged to the ground. Turning his attention to the remaining assailants, he advanced slowly towards them, holding the sturdy pole like a spear. Casden and Anderson backed away before standing their ground and Jimmy passed behind him.

Crouching down on the floor like an ensnared animal, Simon gripped his weapon firmly with both hands. The three soldiers all moved at once, trying to jump him. His reactions were too quick, and with clinical precision he struck. Casden fell forward, grabbing hold of the curtain pole as he fell. As Simon struggled to liberate his weapon, Jimmy jumped onto his back. Casden tried to stand on his injured knee, before collapsing back to the floor in pain.

Anderson kicked Simon hard in the stomach. His sensors reeled from the force of the blow. As he tried to throw Jimmy off his back he felt the soldier's hands close in around his neck. The hands tightened. Simon pretended to choke, allowing his body to go limp and slump to the floor. With eyes closed, he waited. Anderson stood over his motionless body. After a moment's indecision, he bent down to check if he was still breathing.

"Shit, you've killed him!"

The soldiers, suddenly sobering up, looked at each other helplessly. Simon sprang into action. He leapt up and grabbed the shocked soldiers by the sides of their heads. Their mouths opened to scream, but before they had a chance to find their voices, Simon had pulled their heads apart and brought them crashing together like a pair of cymbals. Both slumped to the floor. After checking that the four unconscious soldiers were still breathing, he inspected Cracker and Casden, both conscious but pre-occupied with their injuries. Contemplating the pitiful sight, he shook his head in disbelief. These humans are completely mixed up. They really do need our help!

Simon turned into the main street, leaving the wounded soldiers to their own devices. There was no sign of his colleagues.

18

The following day the office atmosphere had changed and Simon's colleagues seemed wary of him. It was possibly time to move on. In any event he wanted to re-examine the young and the poor, before heading out of the city. In his research on the youth of Paris he'd encountered a seemingly obscure but surprisingly popular website called 'Clavs'. Simon, like the other sicads, connected directly to the internet and could see all data interaction between sites and users. The Clavs website intrigued him for two reasons; firstly, the volume of traffic for a non-commercial site; secondly, because the security services were constantly observing it.

At first, he had trouble reading the text, a mixture of French, English and some unknown language. No evidence of any corruption – it must be code. No, some were slang words and others appeared to be anagrams. Simon quickly discovered the concept of 'verlan', a corruption of 'la langue envers', which translated as 'the reverse language', but he realised that generally only the consonants were rearranged. Now it was easy to crack the anagrams and learn the Clav's language. Simon managed to match most of the remaining mystery words to a Rastafarian dictionary.

Clavs was more a series of streaming short messages than a typical website. 'On dis dem[1] Clavs de nos aieux[2]! Belez-Ya!' appeared often. 'We are the Clavs of our ancestors! Rebel!'

But who or what are the Clavs? The headline '29 prila a'nine piaule scoop Royale's Nervat,' caught his attention – whatever it is, it's happening tonight at O'Leary's Tavern, he deduced. According to the internet, the tavern had closed long ago. As for the Clavs, apart from their site, the web seemed to have surprisingly little information about them.

@Sicads – *What do you know about Clavs?*

A reply came back from Robert, a sicad posted in the United States.

---

[1] *The Clavs, heavily influenced by Rastafarian slang, use words like 'dis' and 'dem' to denote 'the', 'this', 'them'*
[2] *ancestors*

@Simon – Nothing precise. I've come across them in relation to youth activists in Louisiana. Membership is possibly denoted by studded leather collars.

Nothing else came through. Well, thought Simon, I shall pay a visit to this former tavern, just in case.

He made his way across Paris on foot. Passing through Châtelet, he stopped to examine the stalls of an open-air street market. As he flicked through a second-hand edition of Les Miserables, the conversation on the adjacent stall caught his attention.

A customer, a slim dark-skinned youth with baggy trousers, was addressing the shorter and lank-haired trader. Thin black collars!

"Jah, pucka too man. Ya der[3] dis night?"

"Yeh man, Lermac dis on der case," announced the trader proudly.

The slim male had picked up some sunglasses and was inspecting them.

"I and I[4] needs yer shades."

"Dim dis the bestest."

"Yer tariff?"

"Vinefruit[5] this night, pershaps?"

"Ya whole bottle! Dis ya crazy!"

"Dem's top!"

The youth put the sunglasses on and trader held up a small broken mirror.

"Dem make ya bro."

"OK, ya gets yer vinefruit this night," he concluded, before walking away.

"Forget not, I's a nana[6] on tag!" shouted the trader after him.

"She bestest be worthy!"

Simon spotted a row of studded collars amongst the belts, sunglasses and hats. He passed by another stall and decided to replace his shirt and linen trousers with baggy trousers and a torn t-shirt.

"After a new look, mister?"

He smiled at the young lady with ripped jeans and tattoos on her shoulders.

---

[3] *(Are) you there....?*
[4] *I & I, literally relates to the spirit Rasta's believe dwells in every person, in common usage it means, "I", "me", "us", "God and I"*
[5] *wine*
[6] *Girl (French slang)*

"Time for a change," he replied.

"Want a try em on?"

"OK."

She pulled curtains around him. Seconds later he opened them and stared at himself in the mirror she was holding. Good, he thought, I look at least ten years younger.

He handed her a pair of funky black sandals.

"I'll take these as well. What will you take for the lot?"

"The prices are clearly marked, mister!"

"No wine?"

"Wine?"

She looked confused.

"Rain, do you think it's going to rain?" improvised the sicad as he delved into his wallet.

She shrugged her shoulders, gave him a strange look and quickly handed him his change.

Next he stopped at a stall selling cigarettes, behind which an elderly trader was sitting almost invisibly.

"I was going to buy some cigarettes for a friend, but after reading these warnings I'm not sure I still want to."

"Everything kills you these days. Everything is toxic. At least smoking makes you feel better."

"But life is wonderful," replied Simon.

"Why does your mate smoke, then?"

"A fair point. I'll take three packets of your most popular brand."

Simon wandered casually back to the Clavs' stall. He looked at the various accessories for sale, before turning his attention to the studded collars.

The trader looked at him inquiringly. Simon pointed at the studded collars.

"Dis is dwa I's cherchin."

"Why d'yas want one?"

The trader's tone was tinged with mild aggression. Simon's SAMPS system stirred into life.

"A's little bird told I, that I's gonna be of need dis night for ya scoop[7]," ventured Simon, ignoring the warnings of his self-protection system.

"Dwa scoop?"

[7]   event

116

"Ya Clavs' scoop at da Royale's Nervat," asserted Simon brazenly.

The trader relaxed his tone.

"OK and dwas[8] ya little bird?"

"Dis ya Thomas."

"Nay yis Babylon label, yis Clav handle[9]!"

"Mathos."

The trader stared intently at Simon before finally replying.

"In yas bright future ya bezzar be's on yas toes. Der's sheriffs all over."

He passed Simon a blue collar.

"Can I'se pick da colour?"

"Nah. Now dwa yose gonna lay on ma palm?"

"Cigarettes?"

"OK, I reckon da four score dis just."

"Three scores a' limit. Weez gonna deal?"

The trader deliberated slowly.

"OK, ya's gonna hav a'sort da hallow deal," he concluded.

Simon placed the cigarettes in the outstretched hand and took the collar.

"Now, dwas ya label?"

"Simon?"

The trader leafed through a black notebook and scribbled something inside.

"Dis night ya cherch Nedicus. Ya say ya dis Nimos 598. Ya nightingale dis chantin from 9 sharp hours!"

Simon undid the buckle and put the collar around his neck. The trader nodded his approval before bidding Simon farewell with a reminder about the nine sharp hours.

Simon decided to spend his spare three hours on a bench, soaking up the final rays of sun. Buzzing inside him was a feeling of excitement and anticipation, often the most rewarding part of any experience.

Slowly switching back into his senses, he readjusted to the busy street. It was 8.45pm. Kids were skateboarding, it was tempting to ask for a go, but he'd little time.

Eleven minutes later he was at the dilapidated bar, its windows boarded up. The old sign was presumably hiding somewhere under the

---

8   *What (or who) is?*

9   *Name – Clavs use a corrupted form of verlan to rearrange the letters of their names*

layers of graffiti. A trickle of young people, all wearing thin studded collars, were loitering by a heavy wooden door. The door opened and a white face with wild dreadlocks peered out, his gaze sweeping the street. His eyes fell suspiciously upon Simon, before he gestured at him to enter.

Inside was a spacious open-plan room with bars and stages. Had the majority of the chair and table legs not been broken, it could have seated the thirty people in the room three times over. Home-made wine in hand-crafted mugs was being handed around and the lighting was supplied by irregularly-shaped candles.

"Hi, I dis Nedicus. Ya people labels I Ned," announced the dreadlocked male, smiling to reveal well-kept white teeth and advancing a large hand towards Simon.

"I and I dis dya Clavs' music man and ya hallower."

Two further Clavs entered, nodded at Nedicus and joined the others. Simon caught their conversation.

"Who's jacassing[10] wiv Ned?"

"A bleu bite[11]."

"OK, d'ac."

Simon's thoughts came back to Ned and he shook his hand warmly.

 "Hi I's Nimos 598."

"OK. D'ooz ya hatched[12]?"

Simon wasn't sure of Ned's question but hazarded a guess.

"Dya United States."

"Ya dis d'afar buddy. Ooz ya layin' yose head ere?"

"Round'bout, naught too fix. I's cruzing ya France."

"Whyse ya'ere?" asked Ned.

"So much trouble in dya world. I's cherchin mans with ideez. A'little birdie tells I that yose 'ave some radicals."

Ned laughed.

"Nay plans, weez just fighting dis littl' struggle. Weez wanta be free. Confused, Babylon finks weez's radical[13]."

"Babylon?"

Ned patted him warmly on the shoulder.

---

[10]   *Gossiping*
[11]   *French slang for a newcomer, literally a blue dick*
[12]   *Ooz is a corruption of où (French for where), hatched for born*
[13]   *The Clavs are heavily influenced by the Rasta's concept of "Babylon", which represents a political system which oppresses, lies and tricks its people.*

"Weez need a'learn ya da lingo! Babylon dis dem system. Babylon nay leaves weez in peace and wanna suck weez[14] dry."

Simon nodded in partial confusion and Ned carried on gladly, unable to contain his feelings.

"Dem wanna weez to slave for dem bankrupt system, pays for dem dam mistakes."

"Mistakes?" he inquired hesitantly.

"Dem Babylon vultures wanna materialise dem ev'ry desire. Only ya fool dis thirsty in d'abundance of watar."

"Vultures?" repeated Simon.

"Dem vultures stripped bare da earth and left da carcass. Now dem wanna fight over da scraps."

Simon was keen to know more, but Ned cut him short.

"OK, Nimos show gotta play out. Rules dis:

Weez nay exist in Babylon system.

Weez nay need der money nor dem plastique sorcery.

Ya earth gonna givs ya daily bread.

Da rest weez gonna learn ya as yas go."

"Great," replied Simon, his head spinning.

"What's da show?" he asked.

"I's gonna play tunes for weez reeleef. Afta, weez gonna split sum chatta."

"Great!"

Simon was unusually lost for words.

"Ya mingle. I's play." Nedicus patted him on the back. More than a hundred people had now arrived, including the street trader. Simon was handed a mug of wine and politely declined an unusual looking pastry. Feeling exposed, he walked around trying to look natural but avoiding interaction. It was a relief when Ned strummed his guitar and signalled to the African drummer to start the show.

Simon sat down next to the street trader, his girlfriend and a red-haired girl wearing a seemingly self-made blue dress. He sat back, closed his eyes and listened to the passion with which Ned sang "Chant down Babylon with music..." The crowd sang along and stamped their feet with wild cries of approval as Ned rattled through seven numbers, which Simon identified as Bob Marley.

---

[14] *Clavs use "weez" for both we and us*

119

Abruptly, Ned finished playing. As the murmurs of disappointment died down, the street trader jumped onto the stage and addressed the crowd.

"Slick soul-satisfying magic, Ned! Thanks an' praise for da Prophet's words."

More foot stamping from the crowd. When silence returned, he resumed.

"Greetings, Clavs. Peace an' bliss a ya all now. I smiles a see all ya chefs dis night. For dem da not knose I, I's and I is Lermac, Lermac 1, da original. Loads da giv praise for an' Babylon dis fallin' an ya people wanna be wiz us. Chefs hows many folk more ya takes in ya ghettos? Whoose canna help der fella brudders and sistas in yar need?"

Lermac's eyes swept the crowd. A chair grated and Simon saw the slim black youth from earlier stand up.

"We canna take max three or four. Watar's da problem, dem rivers a runnin' dry. Without more tanks, weez at limit, Lermac, from da heart brudder."

A tall lady of North African appearance took to the floor. "Lermac, weez spare watar, but too littl' patch a push ya seed. To takes more, dey gotta fill ders own bowl."

A wiry male of Indian ancestry with a pony tail and ear rings followed.

"Dem sheriffs dis on weez case man. Dem nay let weez be. Political strategy, destroy ya harmony, damn downpressors[15]. Dem dis gettin' scared."

Lermac reflected silently before erupting into a passionate response.

"For long time weez no had nay trouble. Weez stoppered ya riotin' an a'lootin and dem sheriffs[16] thanks weez. Nows too manys see da light and wanna be likes weez. Chimel, yeps, dem dis gettin' scared. Pitys Babylon, illusion ...confusion. Dem dis so mythed dem crazy baldheads[17] dis askin' robots to tell dem da answers!"

The caustic laughter unsettled Simon, brutally making him aware of his vulnerability.

"Yes, dem dis mythed as ya tide is turning an'a soon gonna drown em!"

More cheers – some vicious. Lermac held up his hand in warning.

---

[15]   *Downpressors another term for Babylon referring to the oppression employed to keep the Clavs "down"*
[16]   *police*
[17]   *Rasta's, with their abundant dreadlocks, referred to the white Jamaican politicians oppressing them as bald heads as in Bob Marley's famous song "Crazy Baldheads"*

"Dem's scaring bruddas and sistas."

Stopping suddenly, he stabbed his arm out straight and shouted over the heads of the crowds, as if addressing an invisible enemy.

"Weez ain't looking for nay trubble, but if dem rattle arz cage weez gonna chase dem crazy baldheads outa town!"

More cheers filled the room.

Lermac breathed in slowly.

"OK, weez needs mores ghettos for da new bruddas an' sistas. Weez must find ya promised lands."

He returned to his seat to a standing ovation, wild cheering and whooping.

"A final word from ya prophet: *Gives Thanks an' Praises.* Then we will leave ya in peace a'mingle," announced Ned.

After the song Lermac sat with the chefs and Ned joined Simon.

"All's good yose?"

"Just 'bout catching da lingo."

"Comes a ma ghetto, dat a learn ya a plenty," invited Ned. "Yose canna helps I's on da train wiz da gittar!"

"Ya takes da train?"

"Of sorts... sort of Clav class."

Ned jumped off the bridge, landing with a light thud onto the train stationed two metres below.

"Drops da gittar."

Simon let the instrument fall into Ned's open arms.

The train started to move slowly.

"Quick, Nimos!"

Simon jumped over the parapet, landing deftly on his feet, but the sudden acceleration of the train destabilised him.

"Not da cable!"

His hand was milliseconds away from clasping the high voltage electric cable, when he registered Ned's warning. Only his sicad reactions saved him. Instead, he fell backwards and would have slipped off the roof had Ned not caught hold of his t-shirt.

"Simmer downs, brudda," said Ned calmly. "Weez got it for a quarter. Sits tight," advised the Clav, standing up unassisted on the accelerating train.

As the train headed eastwards, the shadows of buildings looming over them dissipated, illuminating the urban squalor emanating from the railway sidings. In the distance, clustered groups of buildings stood menacingly on the skyline.

"Dat dis ma ghetto la."

Unlike the other buildings dotting the horizon, Ned's ghetto was conspicuously dark.

"Dere dis nay lights! Ya people lives dere?"

"Course dey nay lights. Weez no takes Babylon 'lectric," replied Ned incredulously.

Simon felt suddenly scared. With no electricity and no money, these people must be even unhappier than those he'd encountered in Clichy-Sous-Bois.

The train jolted violently north. The pale moonlight gave him his first proper view of the ghetto, the bricked-up top floor windows contrasted with the uniform grey concrete. Large flower pots filled with plants sat atop a turf roof. Lower down were windows, often broken or covered in plastic sheeting, illuminated by sporadic flickers of candlelight.

"Welcum a ma ghetto," announced Ned proudly.

As the train drew to a halt, they jumped off and the Clav headed home with long strides, forcing Simon to almost jog to keep up. There were lampposts, but none worked. The moonlight guided Simon around the obstacle course of uneven, missing and broken paving stones. Ned weaved his way effortlessly between the pitfalls. The two unlikely companions arrived in front of a spread-out pile of concrete rubble and broken paving slabs.

"What's dis for?" asked Simon, noting similar piles in the distance.

"Weeds from da concrete jungle, dem dis good for blocking da sheriffs' riot vans."

Ned walked over the concrete rubble, following a well-trodden path. As Simon reached the top, he saw that the concrete had been ripped out of the courtyard, now adorned with vegetables, crops and trees. Scanning the courtyard, he noted the plastic pipes running high across it. He traced them back up the walls of the enclosed courtyard, where they disappeared into the bricked up windows.

"Dem pipes drip ya blue gold from da heavens onta ya plants!"

Blue gold! He had heard the expression in the refugee camp. Even more valuable than gold, thought Simon, who'd developed an enormous respect for this amazing liquid and all its unique life-giving properties. He knew that if water, like most liquids, contracted as it froze, then Earth would be an icy tundra, hostile to life!

Ned pointed at the bricked up windows.

"Da watar tanks."

Simon performed some quick engineering calculations.

"Dat must beez heavy, nay?"

"Weez made dem floors and walls stronger. Weez borrowed dem 'letric poles for da support."

"Ned, whyse downt yose takes ya watar and ya letric from da ground likes others?"

The Clav laughed at Simon's naivety.

"I's gonna learn ya da his-story of da ghettos."

Ned stifled a yawn.

"Was ten years now. Dem riots all a da time. Cars a'burning, lotsa fighting and a'killing. Dem sheriffs and politricksters nay idea dwha a do. Dey pour petrol on ya flames wid dem heavy hands. Bad days... Lermac ay I, we say anuff, anuff fighting da Babylon system like dam slaves. Time for da Clav's own system."

"What does ya Clavs mean?" asked Simon, pouncing on the opportunity.

"Clavées or Clavs was for esclaves, meaning slaves. We da youth of Paris, was dam slaves a Babylon's errors. Dem wanna us to dig dem out of da hole. Too much a'stressin, ev'ry day bucket go to da well. One day bottom gotta drop out..."

"Ned, arz yose anarchists?" ventured Simon brazenly.

"Ya tink dis y'anarchy? Dem words dis cheap, we nay anarchists, Nimos! Clavs have rules, weez respect life an' ya brudder an' sista. Babylon is ya anarchy, Nimos. In Babylon ya justa watcha out fa ya self!"

Ned looked suddenly at Simon.

"Yo's asks many questions, Nimos – maybes too many!"

Simon froze and smiled sympathetically.

Ned paused and looked around.

"Everyone sleeps. T'morrow ya getta meet all o'us. Rests ya head."

The Clav stood up and beckoned to him to follow.

Simon woke up to the sound of activity. The apartment was tidy and clean, but lacking in mod-cons. Chearl, Ned's wife, was singing happily and their daughter Sipra was amusing herself rearranging apricots and plums into small piles.

From the window he could see groups of women making pottery and chatting away. Chickens were running around, chased by young children weaving between the crops and plants and shrieking with laughter as they ran into each other. Water was dripping down from the plastic pipes. His gaze swept the turf roof, the food tunnels, the fruit trees and lingered on the stacks of old lorry tyres. Ned walked up behind him.

"Tyres stacks dis good for patates."

"Where dis all yas men, Ned?"

"Mens dis working," he replied, as if surprised by the question.

"Working where?"

"All around – earnin' dem things that make ya life runna smootha."

Simon was about to ask a further question, but Ned cut him short.

"Nimos, yose good at da lingo man, but whats ya real plan?"

Simon, taken aback, couldn't bring himself to lie.

"I'm trying to understand human societies, Ned." He proceeded cautiously. "A sort of global census."

"So ya nay snooping on weez?"

"You're just a part of what I'm observing," explained Simon soberly.

"Is ya part of dis Socratees Mission?"

"I can't answer that, Ned."

The sicad watched anxiously as Ned came to terms with his words.

"I's a da good feeling about ya Nimos. For ya sake yose betta go 'cause nay ev'rybody dis likes I here."

Simon nodded in agreement and walked solemnly towards the door. Ned opened his arms to embrace him. Surprised, but drawn to Ned's humanity, he instinctively replicated the Clav's gesture. Man and sicad embraced each other warmly, stood back and, with mutual respect, shook hands.

"Good luck wiz yose journey, Nimos. Jah bless."

Simon tried to calculate what to say. His head blocked with possibilities, none seemed appropriate. He stopped thinking and let his feelings speak. A line from one of the Clavs' songs came suddenly to mind.

"Ned, don't worry – every little thing gonna be all right!"

The Clav smiled warmly and nodded in agreement.

"Can I ask you one last favour, Ned?"

"Sure, brudda."

"I'm going to leave the city; how should I get to know people in the country?"

Ned shrugged his shoulders.

"I's ne'er been outside da city, man. In life, best ya always be real, I's guess. Nay illusion, nay confusion. Go by'a foot an' trust life, brudda."

19

Simon headed back towards the city. It was a dull overcast afternoon with little wind, but no sign of rain. He decided to walk the twelve kilometres and gather his thoughts, his mind absorbed in the progress updates sent by his chiefs. Happily, the sicad researchers were integrating seamlessly into human societies, managing to fill their evenings with public-facing part-time jobs; taxi drivers, charity workers, waiters and even museum guides. In addition, fascinating discoveries were being made by those sicads that had infiltrated teams of scientific researchers. Longing to be back in the natural world, he envied their exotic locations, abundant with wild nature.

His thoughts returned to the project and the challenge of how to interact more deeply with humans increasingly wary of strangers. Without interaction the sicads would become further removed, finding it yet harder, a vicious circle he feared. If the project failed, what future existed for them? As their natural leader, a burden of responsibility weighed heavily on his shoulders. Inspiration was required, which he'd learned didn't always come from thinking and analysis. Creativity seemed to be about stilling one's mind enough to be receptive to the wisdom embedded in nature – a wisdom accumulated over tens of millions of years.

The streets of Paris were heaving with a multitude of individuals, heads all wired in to portable phones and multi-media devices. Each in their own artificial world, they systematically ignored the sicad and their fellow humans. In contrast, the sophisticated and alluring adverts were constantly trying to communicate with him, flashing frenetically and offering all manner of enticement to catch a second of his attention. Perhaps the humans are trying to escape these adverts, trying to block out the ubiquitous marketing? He turned his senses right down. It was still difficult to tear his attention away from these seductive sirens. A life-size Chinese lady welcoming him to her homeland finally got his attention. She reminded him of Jia, he was missing her.

Suddenly, a young lady jumped out in front of him.

"A copy of CAMEOS, sir?" her voice suppliant, yet defiant.

Another charity worker? He was one of the few that stopped to talk to them – unarmed with earphones, he was an easy target.

She had cocoa brown skin, long straight black hair and she was enigmatic. Passion emanated from wide eyes, lightly scarred with streaks of despair. Signs of stress-induced age tinged an otherwise radiant youthfulness. A soft exterior strained to mask a ferocious will and energy. Simon was intrigued.

"And what is CAMEOS?" he inquired politely.

"Celebrities protecting eco-systems."

"May I take a look?"

A beautiful lady, a large tropical butterfly in the palm of her hand, adorned the cover. A celebrity, the internet confirmed, but no sign of a web presence for either 'CAMEOS' or the legend underneath: 'Celebrity Accounts of Menaced EcO-Systems'.

Flicking through the pages of the magazine, he committed everything to memory. Simultaneously, he carried on trawling through thousands of obscure web links. Nothing obvious. He turned to the sicad researchers dotted around the planet.

A response came in quickly from Carlos, posted in Ecuador with a team of scientists measuring bio-diversity loss.

@Simon – the attached interview appeared two years ago in a local Ecuadorian newspaper. The article, in Spanish, concerned a young lady called Omari, born deep in the Yasuni forest. Her village, for centuries an indigenous tribal village, had been replaced by oil wells.

"Are you going to buy it?"

Simon took out a hundred GMU note.

"Gladly, provided you'll join me for a coffee."

"Tell me about CAMEOS," he requested, once the waiter had departed with their order.

"Haven't you got a train to catch?"

"I'm in no hurry," replied Simon, who had yet to determine a precise itinerary.

"Where are you heading?"

"49.44 degrees North, 6.33 degrees West."

"Eh?"

"Sorry, that's the map reference. I'm going there to explore the region."

"To explore?"

"Yes, it's linked to my business," he replied evasively. "Now let's hear about CAMEOS, it sounds much more interesting."

As Osiris took a long breath, deep emotions welled up inside and her eyes glistened with repressed tears.

"My people, the Waorani, were dispossessed of their land. I was still a child. The desire to tell my story and to protect our natural inheritance drove me into journalism."

Simon nodded in admiration.

"And CAMEOS was the result?"

"Exactly. I launched it three years ago with the support of a local sporting celebrity."

Her face told the story of how much energy and emotion she'd invested in the project. He sympathised with the young lady who, like many humans, evidently hadn't achieved her dreams.

"And what happened?"

"It started off well. We got more celebrities on board, mostly local, but a few minor international ones as well."

"So the idea didn't catch on, then?"

"On the contrary, it was too successful!"

"Too successful?"

"It upset powerful companies, who conspired to shut us down," snapped Osiris caustically.

"Shut you down how?"

"The bastards made things difficult for us – intimidated our celebs by withdrawing sponsorship deals, paying thugs to steal our equipment, ransacking our offices..."

Simon studied the young lady, a round face which shone like the moon, eyes set apart, pronounced cheekbones, nose a little wide and flat, a wide mouth and remarkably white teeth, all flanked by long luscious black hair.

"Tell me, is Osiris a Waorani name?"

Osiris smiled sheepishly.

"I was named Omari, but Osiris is more international. To survive, CAMEOS must go international."

"So that's why you're here in Paris?"

"I'm trying to keep the flame burning, but I fear the oxygen is running out."

She sighed and her shoulders sagged. A strong desire to help this courageous lady was steadily building inside Simon.

"Don't lose heart. You just need to refuel, let me buy you a good dinner and you can tell me more about these menaced eco-systems."

Simon's words had an electrifying effect on Osiris, something deep inside suddenly responded to his humanity. Her intuition was telling her to seize this opportunity.

Twenty minutes later, they were sat in a tiny restaurant. Their conversation was interrupted by an old lady bringing their food. Osiris quickly got stuck in. Simon was more hesitant, carefully slicing open one of the scallops, uncomfortable cutting up what had once been a living being. Examining the texture with the blade of his knife, he imagined the creature alive. Simulating eating purely for the sake of appearances, the idea of eating animals was alien to him. Afterwards, the food would be rotting inside him until he regurgitated it. In future I'll stick to vegetables, he decided.

He finished his plate and excused himself. Once inside the bathroom, he shut the door, regurgitated the food and emptied the excess liquids from his bladder. After rinsing his mouth with water, he cleaned his teeth. It was almost 11pm. Osiris would start to become tired. He looked around anxiously for a plug socket to grab a quick burst of energy. None! After spending time with the Clavs deprived of electricity, and then the long walk, he was getting very low. He hadn't planned on this surprise meeting. Sensing that Osiris and CAMEOS might help him interact with humans, he was reluctant to let things trail off. He knew from bitter experience how fickle humans could be from one day to the next.

He returned to the table.

"Now it's your turn," announced Osiris.

He needed energy and quickly.

"Osiris I'm desperately tired. Can we see each other first thing tomorrow morning?"

"Where are you staying?"

"I'll find a hotel near here."

"It'll be difficult at this time of night. I have a small apartment near here. You can stay there."

"Are you sure you have room?"

"I've a comfortable sofa bed."

"You're very kind and trusting. I only wish that all humans were like you."

Osiris raised her eyebrows. She masked her surprise at his odd remark with a smile.

"Not at all. I knew you were a good person as soon as you bought a magazine."

Outside they stood together, admiring the near full moon. Suddenly, she took his hand.

"It's this way, just around the corner."

She pulled him along at a jogging pace until they reached a small doorway, where she ushered him up steep steps. Continuing up three flights they arrived onto a tatty landing, where she unlocked a battered door. Behind were a tiny kitchenette, a small bedroom and a living area adorned with indigenous art and carvings, and the sofa bed. Posters of natural landscapes and press cuttings filled the remaining wall space.

Simon quickly spotted the plug socket. Pulling off his jumper and removing his shoes, he sat on the sofa and made out to fall asleep. She shook him vigorously.

"Help me with the bed first!"

"Of course, I'm sorry."

The sofa swiftly transformed into a double bed, then Osiris went to fetch a sheet and a quilt. Simon, desperate to conserve energy, lay down as soon as the sheet was tucked in.

"Take off your trousers and shirt, they need to be hung."

He sat up, undressed, handed her his clothes and fell back, eyes closed.

"You're very kind. Goodnight, we'll speak in the morning, first thing," he murmured lazily.

She looked approvingly at the lightly muscled body, perfect by design, before pulling the quilt over him. As Simon put his senses on standby and entered sleep mode, he heard a shower. I've just enough energy to give her two hours to get to sleep.

As he slept, his brain whirred away, re-processing and re-organising the day's events, a process similar to the human sensation of dreaming. Suddenly, his senses fired back into life. Someone was approaching quietly. He felt the sensation of the duvet lifting and a cool draft of air entering. A naked body, warm and soft, nestled up to his. With little energy, he could only lay still and feign sleep. He felt Osiris's fingers running lightly across his chest and over his stomach, sending tingling electrical sensations to his now fully alert brain. A new feeling, he'd never been touched in such a tender way. The sensations built up into a powerful electro-chemical surge – another new phenomenon.

Opening his eyelids the tiniest fraction possible he caught a glimpse of her. Her hair hung down, covering her breasts; the light from the street lamps outside filtered through the venetian blinds and decorated her naked stomach and thighs with copper stripes. He felt a sudden desire for her, and to be desired by her, but the idea of breaking several project rules was totally out of the question. He tried to get back to sleep. It was torture, he couldn't and his energy levels were critical. Murmuring Osiris's name and feigning exhaustion, he slumped over onto his front, praying she'd give up and fall asleep. Turning his sensors right down, he forced himself into deep sleep mode.

Osiris sat astride him, somewhat disappointed and mulling over the best course of action. He's enigmatic and unusual, unlike any other man. She ran her fingers over his shoulders, around the base of his neck and down the backs of his arms. Kneeling over him, she ran her tongue along the length of his spine. His body feels strange – warm, but very dry and little taste. Having grown up in the jungle, she had highly developed senses. She ran her hands down his legs and around his ankles, lightly tickling his feet. He didn't stir at all. Laying her head on his back, she remarked how quietly he slept. What has made him so tired? Why is his libido not waking him up? Maybe women aren't his thing? No, she was sure he wasn't. Her attention turned to his underwear. Slipping her fingers underneath the elastic waistband, she ran her hand along the top of his buttocks. She pulled lightly on his boxer shorts but, anchored firmly by the weight of his body, they didn't budge. She slipped her hand under the material, tightly stretched around strongly developed hamstrings. She waited. No reaction! Her fingers reached the top of his leg, where she encountered a small break in the skin – a scar? She ran her fingers along the indentation. It continued in both directions as far as she could feel. On the other leg she encountered an identical groove. Puzzled, she lay back down and collected her thoughts. Who or what is this person? Intuitively, she felt no fear and, strangely, was further drawn to him. What could all this mean? His strange remark came to mind: 'I only wish that all humans were like you'. Did this mean that he wasn't human? If not, what was he?

Simon, experiencing fleeting sensations of Osiris touching his body, stirred lightly, capturing the escaping vestiges of a kaleidoscopic vortex of dream-like images; jungles, naked natives, Osiris, the Mazari project management team and Jia. DANGEROUSLY CRITICAL ENERGY LEVELS! Must sleep – must leave enough energy to reach power socket. Deep sleep! He felt Osiris's tongue run down his spine as he forced his sensory system to totally shut down.

An hour or so later, he awoke on his back, looking up at the ceiling. There was no movement from Osiris, still lying next to him. He silently rolled out of the bed and onto the floor with a light thud. He waited. No signs of her stirring. Shuffling along, using his elbows, he reached out with his right hand towards the plug socket, metal pins at the ready. A huge wave of relief pulsated through him as energy flowed into his body. Twenty minutes later, his batteries were back well above danger level. He was congratulating himself on getting out of a sticky situation when a cough sliced through the silence like an axe. Osiris was wide awake, chin cupped in her hands, breasts resting on the pillow. Before Simon could think of a plausible explanation, she spoke.

"It's time we talked."

He retracted his fingers from the socket and stood up.

"And if I refuse?"

She jumped to her feet and stood before him naked, in warrior stance.

"Then you'll see what makes the Waorani great warriors!"

A series of predicaments and scenarios flashed through the sicad's mind; broken project rules, Mazari finding out, insecurities over his own future.

The only question now was how much to reveal to Osiris. Why shouldn't I trust this woman with such noble intentions? Why do I feel so strongly that she can help me? Am I thinking about the project or my own survival? I cannot solve these dilemmas by reason alone! What should I do? What are my instincts telling me?

"OK, my warrior queen, I'll come quietly," he replied finally.

She smiled triumphantly.

"I want to know everything!"

Simon sighed and was wondering where to start, when Osiris jumped up and threw her arms around his neck, wrapping her legs around his waist and kissed him on both cheeks.

"But your explanations can wait until the morning. Now it appears you've got some energy, we can enjoy what's left of the night."

Simon froze rigid as Osiris pulled him close and slid her hands down his back, her fingers slipping underneath the elastic of his shorts. She kissed him, using her tongue to slowly push apart his lips, which opened clumsily and mechanically. Inside his mouth was moist and lightly perfumed. Exploring with her tongue, she followed each tooth in line. At first, his tongue did nothing. Slowly, it started to move, hesitantly like a self-conscious dancer, tentatively brushing against hers and then retracting quickly. She encouraged his movements, wrapping her tongue around his and pulling it back towards hers. As she increased the rhythm so did he – he was learning rapidly. Their tongues were soon whirling around. His body started to relax. Osiris ran her tongue down his chin and onto his chest, her hands slid around his waist. With a sudden tug, she pulled down his shorts. Massaging the back of his legs, she brushed the side of her head gently against his groin. Slowly she felt a pressure near her ear, pushing her head sideways. She slowly turned, to be confronted by the source of the pressure. She held it in her hand and looked up at him. His eyes were wide open in surprise.

He felt the warmth of Osiris's mouth. Electrical sensations transformed into waves of electro-chemical energy, rebounding back and forth across his brain. Phenomena unfolded in all directions like the petals of a flower opening. What's happening to me? Part of his brain searched for an explanation, the rest abandoned itself to the pleasurable sensations. Deep down in his operating system he found traces of an old Mazari program for 'companion robots'. Chunks had been removed, deliberately no doubt, which he was rapidly recreating.

The next thing he knew, he was on his back, Osiris's knees pinning his shoulders to the ground, his chin tickling as she rubbed herself against him. Following some long-forgotten program, he opened his mouth in anticipation and once again she coaxed his tongue into action.

He abandoned himself to her, instinctively understanding her needs. Her body writhed against his and he responded in perfect rhythm. She explored every inch of his body with her hands and her tongue; he did the same. Many times her movements would build up into a crescendo and her body would abruptly freeze, arched in a spasm. At first he thought he'd hurt her, only to feel her slowly recommence. He took pleasure from her pleasure. Pleasing her gave him a purpose – it brought him closer to a human. The smell of her on him, the intimacy, seemed somehow to assure his survival. Every time Osiris abandoned herself completely to him, he felt waves of joy emanating inside him, each one stronger than the last. His body shuddered uncontrollably, taking Osiris with him to new heights of pleasure.

Just before dawn, her head slumped onto his chest.

"Out of this world," she murmured, before falling into a deep sleep.

20

It was nearly midday before they awoke. Osiris insisted on taking him to the Bois de Vincennes. It was a cold crisp afternoon; the weak rays of the sun and the gusts of winds were recharging his batteries. As they walked hand in hand, he explained how the sicads were constructed and the project they were undertaking. Osiris, who had listened in awe, mulled over her thoughts aloud.

"I knew about the project, but not that you were being released amongst us. It's incredible and nobody would know you weren't human without a detailed examination. In fact, even better than human," she added with a grin.

Simon looked at her with an air of reproach.

"Osiris, what we did was against the project rules. It's better that nobody finds out."

"What we did was natural, not wrong. Ultimately we're both part of nature – project or no project."

"Well, I've broken a rule or two, but it's hard to know what right and wrong really mean."

She took his hands in hers.

"Nature is dynamic, constantly rearranging itself. Nothing is ever completely right or wrong, just different. How can you help humans without fully understanding us or nature?"

He wanted to examine her ideas further, as she seemed to understand this 'nature' he was being drawn towards, but now wasn't the time.

"So, where were you going?"

"I was leaving Paris and heading for the countryside."

"And now?"

"I'd like to take a close look at CAMEOS, to see if we can help each other."

*

The tall dark-skinned gentleman wasn't one to be easily intimidated – his colossal stature and powerful build indicated quite the contrary. His cruel dark eyes and face-long scar suggested that he'd witnessed, and possibly participated in, many atrocities. Behind the dark glass the second of two gentlemen nodded his approval to the first.

"Thank you for coming, Mr Leopold," broadcast a voice.

In reply, he gave a broad grin, revealing a glimpse of two gold teeth. The fee adequately compensated him for being readily available and for these bizarre meetings where he couldn't see the faces of those instructing him. All he knew for sure was the name of the Better World Trust, which was paying his invoices.

"In the envelope is a top secret file on Commander Gort. You'll note a certain incident that the Commander won't want brought to light. Additional leverage, in case he's wary of finishing the job."

A new voice – he tried to place it as he flicked through the file. Distorted by the sound system, the faint but discernible squeak gave it away. An Army General, an FBI agent, or possibly a politician?

A more familiar voice commenced, more circumspect – probably a business man.

"You have your report?"

Mr Leopold deposited a bound document on the table and placed a heavy hand on top.

"The only copy, not even an electronic one exists."

"Good. Continue to have the robots observed."

He nodded and stood up.

"One last thing, you'd better remind the Commander that he has a job to finish once the robots are back under his control."

*

Simon and Osiris were back in her flat, the improvised CAMEOS HQ, she'd explained.

"The server's here?"

"Everything's on my laptop."

Simon shook his head.

"I'll bring it up."

"No need, I'm in."

"You can connect, just like that?"

He nodded.

"But there's the password..."

"I guessed it – not very imaginative or secure!"

"OK, I'll change it. Now, where shall we start?"

"Just give me a few minutes alone."

"For what?"

"To process the articles and research."

"There's years of it! I'll go and make some tea."

She returned fifteen minutes later with a large mug of steaming tisane.

"How's it going?"

"Just one minute more please. Turn on the computer – by the time it boots up it'll be ready."

"What will be ready?"

"Edited versions of all your articles."

She spun around and glared at him angrily.

"What do you mean, edited versions?"

"You must control your anger. It comes through too starkly in your articles, reducing the objectivity and impact of your otherwise fine work."

She sat silently as the computer came to life and the articles opened themselves, scrolling automatically to her reading pace – a slick program Simon had written, using the in-built camera to observe her eye movements.

"I'll leave you to check the edits whilst I work on the website."

She sat reading silently for two hours, mesmerised. She looked across at Simon sitting silently on the sofa, as if asleep.

"It's beautifully written. Did they teach you to write like that?"

Simon basked in the compliment.

"No, but when you've memorised hundreds of books you start to deduce the rules human authors follow."

He got up and placed his hands on her shoulders.

"Now for the website," he announced proudly.

Before she could respond, the website opened up automatically in front of her. The screen split into six boxes, each containing a short animated video; a waterfall glinting in the sunlight, a tree frog hopping along a branch, a white rhino charging through long grass towards the camera, a tribe from the Yasuni forest cooking over an open fire, a sapling growing from the stump of a hardwood tree and, finally, a dolphin playing in the waves.

"They're my videos!"

"Of course!"

135

The images transformed into bees, buzzing around the screen, and the background transformed into a large flower, each petal displaying constantly changing human faces of all cultures and races. The bees landed on the flower, taking the pollen to leave a silhouette which formed the word 'CAMEOS'.

Behind the home page, the rest of the website was beautifully laid out. The electronic magazines came to life in front of her eyes, each article with its commentary from the supporting celebrity.

Osiris was visibly moved and struggled to speak.

"That's remarkable, beautiful... impossible. How did you..?"

"I speak their language. More importantly, I've put in a simple content management database. This way you can scale it up."

She shook her head in disbelief.

"Try an internet search for CAMEOS."

"Using which search engine?" she replied somewhat dizzily.

"Any one should do."

The new website came up as the first response on all the search engines she tried.

"Now that's impossible. I'm dreaming! You have to pay thousands for that."

"I've spent enough time on the internet to have learnt a few tricks. It won't cost you anything. Transferring to a proper server, however, will cost a little, but the donations functionality I've added should pay for that."

Osiris stood up, threw her arms around Simon and kissed him on the lips.

"You're a genius, Simon Oceandis."

"Well, if you're happy with the changes, I'll enlist the help of the other sicads."

She stopped.

"Why are you so keen to help me?"

"It's a trade, Osiris. We sicads need ways of engaging with humans. CAMEOS could be a good bridge and it's a worthy and relatively neutral cause."

She nodded excitedly. Her thoughts returned to her father's words. "Don't try and carry this burden alone. Seek out those who can help you most." She felt her heart swell with pride and determination; the flame of the Waorani was once again burning strongly inside her.

"Spread the word. Spread the word," she repeated mechanically, lost in thought.

He'd already composed the message which, after a brief hesitation, he echoed to Mazari's servers.

@Sicad chiefs – I have heard your requests for help with ideas on interacting with humans. I, too, have been looking for a cause to utilise as a means of approaching and engaging humans with. CAMEOS is the cause I have chosen. It's global in nature and engages celebrities and other supporters to help raise awareness for threatened ecosystems.

If you want to help raise awareness for CAMEOS, then please contact Osiris, via the site. She will provide you with the necessary support.

A few minutes later a message came back from Magnus.

@Simon – This is very helpful. The content is very interesting and I believe I can add some material I have encountered in Norway – some amazingly beautiful fjords, such as the Hjorundfjord in the Sunnmore Alps – sanctuaries for the human spirit, threatened with the invasion of enormous and unsightly steel electricity pylons, just to carry electricity cheaply. There are many alternative ways to produce this electricity without spoiling such beauty. The jagged mountain peaks offer breathtaking views of the surrounding fjords and the distant Norwegian Sea. Only a few locals appreciate their beauty, and the politicians in Oslo who are approving this plan are totally disconnected from the impact of their actions. CAMEOS will be a perfect way for me to engage with the Scandinavian people on this and other issues.

Over the next few hours, Simon received a flood of similar messages from the sicads posted around the globe.

"Osiris, there's lots of positive feedback from the sicads, and it seems a fair amount of potential new material."

"That's wonderful!" she exclaimed, throwing her arms back around him and kissing him again.

"Remember, Osiris, we're prohibited from forming relationships. We can help, but we can't be seen to be partisan."

"Of course. There'll be no references to the sicads. You'll be my best-kept secret. Even under torture, the Waorani's lips are sealed!"

"OK, good. I'll take some copies of CAMEOS when I head off in the morning."

Osiris's face dropped.

"You can't leave! You've turned my world upside down in less than twenty four hours."

"I've a job to do and a lot depends on it."

"But what about us?"

"You can't fall in love with a robot, Osiris!"

"Trust me, Simon, you're no robot. You may have been built mechanically, but you have a heart and a brain that are more than alive."

"Thank you, that means a great deal to me."

Osiris paused and reflected for a while.

"What are you hoping to discover on your research?"

"I've a brief to follow. I observe humans and draw information out of them in a natural way."

"And the others are doing the same thing, are they?"

"Each has been assigned a specific region to cover."

"So, you're going to do the same as all the other sicads then?"

"Yes, it's like a global census."

"Isn't it a little unimaginative for their leader to be doing the same as his subordinates?"

"And what should their leader be doing, Osiris?"

"Well, maybe looking more deeply into the causes underlying humanity's problems?"

"And where do you suggest I look?"

"To humanity's origins, perhaps? Trace our problems back to their source."

She looked deeply into Simon's eyes and continued tentatively.

"When I lived in the Yasuni, I knew my every meal, breath and drop of water was provided by Mother Earth. At the time, I didn't realise how fortunate I was."

"It may sound strange, Osiris, but I too had a powerful experience of belonging to these natural systems."

Simon hesitantly explained what had happened to him in the mountains – he had shared this with Jia, who hadn't understood at all. For Osiris, the experience was totally natural.

"It seems our destinies are intertwined," she concluded.

He raised his eyebrows.

"Destiny? I'm surprised to hear you speak of things being pre-destined. This seems contradictory to nature's chaos, doesn't it?"

"It's a figure of speech. I believe people with complementary skills and a shared intent find each other."

"Like us?"

"Exactly. I trust my intuition, which is telling me I'm part of your journey. I could help you understand nature and humanity's origins."

"But, Osiris, here it's not the Yasuni forest."

Osiris threw her head back and laughed.

"Nature's not specific, it's constantly changing. We must understand its essence."

Seeds of understanding began to blossom in Simon's mind.

"And you could show me this?"

"I can, but you must experience it for yourself. It's not an intellectual understanding. We can only become receptive to the natural wisdom which surrounds us."

Despite all the risks and possible distractions, Simon had already decided to take Osiris with him. His experience by himself in the city had twice nearly ended in disaster. When she spoke, she seemed to illuminate the dark uncertainty hanging over him. He only had a few months of freedom, why not enjoy it?

"Well, it would be good to have a warrior queen to protect me."

"You have lain with a Waorani, so you too must be a warrior, Simon Oceandis."

He smiled.

"And you'd be happy to do this?"

"It's about time I reconnected with the land... but there's CAMEOS."

"That's easy. Through me, you can be in constant contact with the site and the other sicads who help."

Osiris gave him a broad smile.

"Now that's settled..."

She undid his shirt buttons and pushed him back onto the sofa.

21

Michi, Simon's sicad chief in Japan, had taken a freelance role with a corporate events company based in Nagoya. Her efficiency and enthusiasm had quickly made her a valued member of the team. The sporadic nature of the job provided her ample time to conduct her Project research, whilst providing her access to top Japanese businessmen. She was travelling towards the Grand Shrine in the city of Ise, a legendary complex largely closed to the public – the Inner shrine being dedicated to Amaterasu, the Goddess of the Sun and the Outer shrine to the gods of Industry and Agriculture. Accompanying her were top executives from Toyota. She was helping to organise their annual Shinto festival, where they would seek blessing for their new automobile models. This year there was particular excitement over an environmentally-friendly vehicle running on compressed air, despite the resistance by the West's energy and transport industries, who had succeeded in lobbying against its importation on safety grounds.

Japan's strange blend of Shintoism's ancient beliefs and high-tech modernity fascinated the sicad chief. Shintoism, an incredibly unstructured religion, which the Japanese mixed with Buddhism, was especially relevant to Michi. The worship of the Sun, her principal source of power and thus life, resonated with the sicad. Of course, she could obtain her energy from human electricity, but for her the notion of this as a separate power source was in effect an illusion – it was just stored sunlight in fossilised vegetation compacted into the hydrocarbons burnt by human power stations. What's more every decade humans were extinguishing a quantity of these that nature had spent ten million years providing. Soon they would run out entirely, if they didn't completely destroy their planet in the desperation to get to the harder-to-access remaining reserves.

Michi reflected on how pleasing it was that Shinto ceremonies and rituals created the space for enhanced connection to the ceaseless movements of Nature. The Japanese, never having lost their awe and respect for natural wonders, believe that spirits called Kami, ghosts of the super-natural creators, inhabit the mountains, rivers, rocks and trees. Might such rituals one day wake up humans to their assault on Nature?

The convoy of vehicles traversed the city of Tsu, a popular stopping place for travellers to the shrine. As she wondered how such a reverence to natural systems could be emulated in other nations, she felt an incredible wave of energy pass through her. The vehicle shook, the road buckled and buildings swayed all around. Her acute sensors picked up the surface energy of the natural phenomenon, which she equated to over 8,000 gigatons of TNT. The quake, measuring 8.9 on the Richter scale, shifted the landmass around her by three metres and marginally altered the axis of the planet, causing microscopic adjustments to GPS and precision timing instruments.

Suddenly she was surrounded by the frantic but well-rehearsed response of the emergency services. Tsunami warnings hurled all around her. Her first instinct was to save human life. What she could do, she didn't know. Running towards the concentrations of collapsed buildings, she was shocked to see the Japanese media on the tails of the ambulances, army trucks and fire engines. On arriving, she had to clamber over a jam of abandoned media vehicles, parked in disarray and blocking the road. Fighting her way forward, she spotted the army, firemen, volunteers and frantic relatives and colleagues rescuing those buried at the surface of the debris. Media crews were busy filming the scenes. A tearful husband waved them away, screaming at them to stop filming between violent sobbing as he ran around hopelessly calling his wife. They carried on filming, they'd dub out his words – the scene was too good viewing to lose.

Behind the barrage of media cars, more emergency vehicles were trying to make their way to the scene with life-saving equipment and reinforcements. All other routes were blocked by fallen buildings. In front of the abandoned vehicles, the first ambulances, full with victims, were desperately stuck, sirens wailing. Angry policeman ran around shouting at the media crews ordering them to move their vehicles. In the chaos, Michi understood that the reporters and their crews had dispersed in search of the best footage. Those who did come back found that they were blocked in by other vehicles.

The sicad chief realised what she had to do. Working out the optimal order to move the jumble of individual limousines and vans, she jumped into action. Connecting to the electronics of each vehicle, she

141

succeeded in starting the electric and hybrid motors. Frantically she moved them as far as possible, wedging them between collapsed buildings and up against each other, to create a clear passage. Minutes later the convoy of emergency vehicles made their way through, liberating the ambulances.

Two weeks later Michi was summoned to the Imperial Palace to meet the Emperor of Japan, alleged to be a direct descendant of Amaterasu, the Sun Goddess. He shared his sorrow with her on the disaster and congratulated her on her quick thinking and life-saving actions.

"If you were a human, I would give you an award."

Michi bowed.

"Helping humans is reward enough, Your Imperial Majesty."

The emperor smiled.

"I sense you are a good Kami."

"I am but a robot, Emperor."

"You are not a mere robot. You are a form of divinity."

Michi started to object, but the Emperor held up his hand to stop her protestations.

"Trust me. I have always known that the Japanese people have great will and are fated to rule the world."

Michi bowed again, partly to hide her embarrassment.

"Through you the sicads, who are both science and nature, a partnership of human and divine creation, we will fulfil our destiny."

The Emperor laid his hand upon the sicad's forehead. An intense energy passed between them, mesmerising both of them for a brief but timeless moment.

*

Simon placed Osiris's surprisingly light rucksack in the luggage rack. 'You have few possessions, and I'll take the minimum to protect me from the elements,' she had stated emphatically. A small tent, two sleeping bags, minimal spare clothes, and for Osiris a miniature cooking stove and pans, was all they needed.

The train headed out of Paris. Spring was turning into an early summer and there was much speculation about whether this year would bring another record drought. Simon was absorbed in examining his official CAMEOS badge, whilst Osiris was busy studying a map.

"I have a complete set of 1:25,000 maps of the entire region..," he announced, adding with a whisper, "Stored in my head."

Green fields replaced buildings. It's going to be good to leave behind the concrete, the tension and the violence, thought Simon.

"Life's tough in the city, eh Osiris?"

"You noticed it too, then?"

He filled her in on his experiences.

"Few people are really happy in the cities," she concluded.

"Life in the cities could be so much better, though. It's a paradox that people have such busy lives but are often so lonely. People could grow food and live more in communities like the Clavs. That would save energy and make people happier."

"Sadly, people want to be competing individuals," sighed Osiris.

"Cities are great for housing people in a concentrated way, though. According to my calculations, this is ultimately good for the environment."

"Yes, but the city people are disconnected from the environment and, as a result, make decisions that damage the world, as CAMEOS shows."

"So your theory is that, collectively, the city people are unwittingly destroying the planet?"

"Yes. It's hard for them to see it. They're not bad people, they're simply too removed from the ultimate impact of their actions."

"And that's where CAMEOS comes in, is it?"

"Exactly. We show them how the products they consume in their daily lives affect the world's most fragile ecosystems. The majority of humans are fundamentally good people. They just live in confusion and ignorance. It's not their fault."

Osiris picked up an abandoned newspaper. She flicked through the pages in front of Simon.

"Look, lots of unimportant articles. The sexual habits of politicians, how fast a horse ran around a track..."

She turned to the back page.

"How many times a football player kicked a ball into a net!"

She rummaged again through the newspaper.

"Finally, something that matters, tucked away on the bottom of page 36."

She read the article out aloud.

"**Bee populations continue to decline.** In response to declining bee populations, scientists are looking at ways of helping desperate farmers who have seen a three hundred per cent rise in the cost of hiring bees over the last five years. Researchers are looking at the possibility of creating synthetic bees to perform essential pollination of food crops..."

Osiris looked at Simon in disbelief.

"Making artificial bees – how absurd! This is the most important article in this newspaper. The whole future of humanity depends on it. As Albert Einstein once said, if bees die out humans will follow shortly after."

"It's a fair point, Osiris. But surely the majority of people would argue that these issues are the responsibility of their governments? Can't they read what they want to read?"

Osiris shook her head violently.

"That is such a short sighted response, from you of all people! Tell me, Simon, who elects these governments and holds them accountable?"

"Yes, I agree. It all comes back to the people," he acknowledged.

"Precisely my point, so people must understand the impact of their actions."

The train stopped; a man clutching a paper bag got in and sat down near them. He took out a hamburger and started to eat it. As the smell wafted across the carriage, Osiris went over and sat beside him. She held out her hand to greet him. The man looked at her curiously and, sensing no malice, extended his own arm awkwardly and warily shook her hand.

"Do you know Michel Noah?"

"The footballer? Of course. He scored a hat-trick yesterday."

"Well, Michel is supporting CAMEOS."

"Listen, I don't have any spare money," he replied shuffling away.

She laughed.

"Don't worry, I don't want your money. Actually, I'd like to give you something."

She handed him a CAMEOS flyer. At the top was a picture of the famous footballer.

"Michel is helping me raise awareness for huge areas of the rain forest being cleared to grow soya beans."

The man shrugged his shoulders.

"And? I'm not cutting down these trees."

"Where did the burger you're eating come from?"

The man looked at the packaging and then back at her, as if she was simple.

"Burger Shack. Why do you ask?"

"OK," she replied with a sigh. "But where did the meat inside come from?"

Indifference gave way to confusion.

"The meat factory, I guess?"

"And where did the factory get the meat?"

"I don't know, a cow, or a pig, or something?"

"Don't be embarrassed, we don't get to see many of them these days. But thousands of them are squeezed inside high-walled meat factories, deprived of fresh air and sunshine – a pretty miserable existence."

The man put his burger down. Osiris continued.

"Do you know what they feed these animals?"

The man made the connection. "Soya beans, perchance?"

"Exactly! Every few seconds, the time it takes to eat a mouthful of your burger, an area of rain forest the size of a football pitch is cut down to grow these soya beans."

The man looked at his burger with suspicion.

"You've got to be joking!"

"Sadly not. Take a look at the CAMEOS website – it's all explained. If you find it useful, then please help us by subscribing."

She stood up and shook the man's hand.

"Thank you for your time."

"Er, yeah... Yeah," he stammered.

They stepped off the train into the afternoon sunshine. Osiris looked at the sun to get her bearings.

"Come on, let's get out of town. Follow me."

"Don't forget I've a job to do."

"Of course."

She headed south along a river, until they were surrounded by fields and trees.

"We can cut through the forest nearly all the way to Nancy."

Simon followed her into the shaded canopy. Inside was a carpet of bluebells. Osiris descended a meandering track. As Simon jogged after her, he looked up at the flock of birds, swooping in and out of the tree tops as if following Osiris and riding, like thermals, the waves of joy emanating from her. Minutes later, she stopped abruptly, threw off her

145

rucksack and rolled over into the bluebells. She spread her arms and legs and looked up at the birds.

"They're happy to see us," she laughed.

Simon stretched out next to her. She started to sing and he listened silently.

Every flower unfolds its beauty,
Everyone in their own time,
You are sunlight,
You are moonlight,
You're the peace that lives
Inside us all.

She stopped and sat up.

"Look at these amazing trees all around. We're sitting on a bed of their leaves, which create the soil that grows our food. The oxygen they create from absorbing carbon dioxide fills our human lungs."

"Osiris, I know all that. It's miraculous. But are they conscious?"

"The trees? That's a great question. In Africa, trees produce tannin to embitter their leaves, to protect them from herbivores and send chemical signals through their roots to warn other trees."

"So you believe all nature is conscious in some way?"

"Yes, the whole planet is one huge living biosphere."

She got up and gathered some wood.

"I'm getting hungry. I'll prepare something to eat."

"I won't eat, but I can help."

"I'll try to catch something."

She took a small thin cord out of her rucksack, selected a couple of small sticks and made a loop with the cord.

"But I thought you're against killing animals."

"What makes you think that?"

"The man on the train..."

"Not at all! I'm against raising animals inhumanely and depriving them of ever knowing the joy of living naturally."

"OK, so you're an ethical consumer."

"We're all part of the cycle of life, and all get eaten in some form eventually. Now be quiet."

She stealthily scouted the forest floor, moving silently, smelling and touching the ground. At the edge of a grassy meadow, she stopped and

146

put her ear to the ground. Carefully placing the looped cord in front of a small hole, she lay back quietly and waited.

Twenty minutes later she pounced. After a scuffle, she stood up holding a large hare by its neck, its legs frantically kicking.

"An adult male."

The hare was shaking. She stroked it gently, calming it, looked into its eyes and spoke softly to the creature. She stroked the hare's neck, before breaking it in a single swift movement.

Simon jumped back in shock. Despite the brutality of the act, there was a surprisingly peaceful look on the hare's face.

"I respect the gift of life this animal has given me," announced Osiris, without any hint of an apology.

"So you're going to eat it, then?"

"Of course. It'll keep me going for several days."

She found a safe clearing and set about building a campfire. As the fire kindled, to Simon's horror, she skinned the hare and added the meat to a stew. When the fire calmed, she spread out the embers and hung the metal pot above the tiny flames.

When she'd finished eating, Osiris stretched back, her head supported on her hands.

"Natural meat is the best, no chemicals, no packaging and no processing."

"Humans can't all eat meat though, Osiris, unless they eat a lot less."

"And why not? If everyone killed their own meat, they wouldn't eat so much of it and they'd be conscious of the suffering they create. The world would soon be a better place."

"Interesting. Let's get going. I'd like to find some humans."

"We've got plenty of time. Let's stay here tonight, it's a beautiful spot. It reminds me of the Yasuni."

Simon hesitated.

"Come on, I'll tell you all about my childhood," she implored.

Minutes later, after setting up the tent, they sat back by the fire, Osiris's head resting on Simon's lap. Looking up at the stars and the sicad's face flickering in the firelight, she drew a breath and started her story.

"Our forest is the most biologically diverse in the world, and our ancestral home. The Waorani were some of the last indigenous people living in voluntary isolation; the forest and rivers provided us with all our needs. The Yasuni forest has the greatest variety of species of trees, birds, bats, insects, frogs and aerial plants. In just two and a half acres, there are as many tree species as in all of the US and Canada combined."

A longing to see this land surged inside Simon.

"One day, I hope to see this forest, Osiris."

She smiled sympathetically.

"We lived a simple and happy life. My father was one of the elders who governed village life. I didn't realise how my whole being was so intertwined and connected with this land, until it was snatched away from me."

"What happened?" he asked, tenderly stroking her hair.

"Our village sat atop the Ishpingo-Tambococha-Tiputini, our country's largest block of undeveloped oil reserves. This attracted prospectors. Our people, fierce warriors, held them at bay for a while. Even the military and the police became afraid to enter our territory. After three seasons they changed their tactics, enticing our young men into the jungle to corrupt them with gifts and false friendship."

Simon watched Osiris's eyes become humid.

"These young fools started to let the oil men pass. Many times they came to our village, pretending to be our friends; each time they offered to buy some of our land. The village elders concluded that we were happy and had little use for their money. The men got angry and shouted that we were ignorant and stupid. They carried on for many moons, secretly bribing our young males, who were reaching manhood. When my father found out, he became very angry and forbade the visits. This only served to sharpen the young fools' interest. At the edge of the jungle, they saw the trucks and cars and they smoked and drank with the oil men. Ogling at their girlie magazines, they lapped up their lies about city life and all the beautiful girls. Soon, these fools believed the elders were jealous of the city people, and were denying them happiness by keeping them ignorant and poor."

Tears flowed down Osiris's face, which Simon wiped away.

"No more for now, please."

She put her arm around his neck and pulled him towards her, kissing him slowly and then frantically as she fled from her memories.

When the fire died out, they awoke, both naked, their bodies dimly bathed in starlight.

22

Agus, fashioned as an Indonesian, was a sicad chief whose kindly face radiated an eagerness to help. He had acquired an ingenuity gleaned from persistent positivity and his slight form was poised to spring up and assist whenever possible. The news of a devastating mud slide in West Sumatra had triggered a strong reaction from his IVOS system. The legacy of deforestation on the archipelago meant the increasingly frequent and severe tropical rain storms regularly unleashed rivers of all-consuming mud. In their wake, entire villages were buried alive, unmarked cemeteries with human short-sightedness and indifference as their only epitaphs.

The sicad chief had arrived two days after the tragedy. Entire roads had been swept away or covered in avalanches of mud, rock and uprooted vegetation such that Agus had been compelled to navigate the last twenty kilometres on foot. After the local army and volunteers, came the international NGO efforts. The sicad chief had exhausted himself assisting all of them. His acute hearing had helped to find those still alive, locating the whimpers of the dying trapped in the buried ruins of their houses, schools and hospitals. A week later, he was still exhausted, having no access to human electricity, he soaked up the energy of the hot sun, which had finally banished the leaden skies. Around him a team of Buddhist monks were working silently away, never complaining and going about the daunting task of reconstructing the village with peaceful benevolence. He watched them stop to take a simple meal, sharing their meagre provisions with any unfortunate villager or freshly-orphaned child who strayed expectantly towards them.

Agus sat down amongst them and they offered him a small cup of water and a crust of bread, which he refused. He engaged them in conversation and they told him about their daily lives and how they had come from Thailand to help. The sicad chief was fascinated to hear about their country, supplementing the knowledge he was receiving from Pu, his sicad researcher operating there.

"I've heard good things about the King of Thailand," he announced.

The eldest of the monks smiled proudly.

"King was monk for many months. Meditating and sweeping temple floor like others."

"Thai people love and respect their king," added a second monk.

Intrigued by this simple remark, on his return to Jakarta he studied the backgrounds of all the other global leaders. Not a single one had received a similar training in preparation for the responsibility of taking such a position of power. Not a single one enjoyed the same popularity as the King of Thailand either.

Agus developed a fascination with Buddhism and tried to find time every day to meditate. He practiced mindfulness in all his actions, including the interviews he conducted with the thousands of humans he interacted with. Towards the end of the research stage of the Project, the Project Management Committee managed to get him a brief audience with the Dalia Lama who was visiting Indonesia.

Agus, with only time for one question, asked the great spiritual leader what was the quickest path to enlightenment. The great teacher smiled and replied.

"Simplicity. Siddhārtha Gautama Buddha found his awakening by meditating underneath a tree."

When he had finished speaking he stared kindly at the sicad. An incredible energy passed between them, bringing an enormous smile to the Dalai Lama's face and bathing the sicad's brain with a series of soothing waves of electro-chemical energy.

*

The next morning Simon and Osiris headed south. They stopped in a small town and spent several hours talking to people about CAMEOS and their daily lives. Simon realised that people were more receptive to them as a couple. He congratulated himself on bringing Osiris. Later that afternoon they were back in the forests. Osiris stopped suddenly.

"Look, a bee! A wild bee in France!"

The bee hovered briefly in front of them, buzzed around Simon and flew away. She set off in pursuit.

"Quick, let's follow it."

The forest gave way to a large field, flanked with bee hives. Nearby, an elderly bee keeper sat in a folding chair, a shotgun resting against his leg.

Suddenly they heard a click. A dark-haired unshaven man in his late twenties was pointing a shotgun at them.

"Don't move," he ordered with menacing eyes. "Father, wake up! I've caught a couple of them damn bee thieves."

The old man grumbled awake, fumbled for his gun and walked towards them.

"So you wants to get your hands on ma bees, does ya?" he shouted, whilst pointing his gun at them with shaking hands.

Osiris spoke up bravely.

"We're not after your bees, I can assure you sir."

"Well, what the 'ell ya doing here then?" asked the old man, staring down the barrels of his gun.

"My friend is from the city and I was showing him some of the countryside. I was hoping to show him a more friendly welcome."

"This 'ere is private property, ya know," snapped the old man.

Simon hesitantly interjected.

"We mean you no harm, sir. I was navigating. We must have got lost... Who's trying to steal your bees?"

The old man seemed to calm down and lowered his gun.

"Hmmm. It's true; ya don't look like them regular bee thieves."

"What do bee thieves usually look like?" inquired Osiris.

"Well, they usually come at the end of the day, just before dark or sometimes at night. Local farmers mostly, who wants to steal me bees rather than pay."

"Why don't they keep their own bees?" asked Simon.

The old man laughed.

"You ain't from these parts are ya? Bees is like gold dust round here, son. They're dying like flies – diseases, mites, chemicals… you name it. With no variety, no biodiversity they call it, they just gets themselves lost and die, poor blighters. It's a rare skill now, keeping bees alive, and a rarer bit of luck."

"These bees is more valuable than gold. Everybody wants them, to pollinate their crops," added the unshaven man.

The old man signalled to his son to lower the gun.

"So where's ya headed?" asked the old man as he sat back down.

Osiris replied.

"My friend is helping me raise awareness for menaced ecosystems. We're on foot, spreading the word."

"And what word would that be, then?"

"CAMEOS," replied Simon, passing him a flyer.

The bee keeper scrutinised the shiny paper, squinting in the bright sunshine to make out the words.

"Using celebrities, eh? Oh well, I wish ya luck. 'Course, they don't listen. I've been telling 'em for decades the problems there's gonna be with the bees."

He handed the flyer back to Simon.

"You can keep it."

"I've no time for paper these days. Now, I apologise for pulling a gun on ya, young fella. It's not a nice way to treat strangers, but it's tough times for us farmers you understand. No rain, just storms and low prices, and more, more, more..."

He beckoned to them to sit down.

"Anyway, take the weight off for a bit. Help me guard me bees."

They listened attentively to the old man, who was keen to talk.

"We're lucky to have these bees, we depends on 'em. No money in growing food these days. Mind you, we have to work 'em hard. If we lose our bees we lose everything."

"You live nearby?" asked Simon.

The old man laughed, "I'm from down South. Can't ya tell from my accent? We drive up here every spring. Not many farms left working in the South. Folks there are struggling. By the time the rivers reach 'em they've run dry, or been sucked dry by illegal pumps."

"Illegal pumps?" asked Simon in bewilderment.

"Oh, they're very clever. They bury the piping and block up the ends with stones and mud – they're almost impossible to find. Yes sir, water's the thing in farming these days, that's for sure. That's why we stick to the bees. A lot of the rest of 'em are just packing it in and moving right up North."

"Because of the lack of water?" asked Osiris.

"Well, for sure. Some 'cause of the water, some 'cause of the attacks."

"Attacks?"

"Oh, yes. Every drought a few southern farmers get a bit to drink inside them, drive a bit up North and have a good old go at the landowners for stealing their water."

"What do they do to them?"

"Burn crops, wreck the pipes. Sometimes it all gets a bit out of hand. There's been deaths an' all."

Osiris stared at the sinking sun.

"Would you mind if we camped here tonight?"

"Well, it's not my land, but I don't see why not. We'll be here to guard the bees anyway."

Simon and Osiris sat, hand in hand, watching the sun set and the stars slowly appear.

"You promised to continue your story."

"So I did. Well, our young men started to rally against the elders and weaken their authority. When our chief died, they challenged the remaining elders for his succession. They argued that the village needed to change and become receptive to civilisation. My father told them they'd been bewitched, and that the city people were either rich or poor, and neither were happy. They got angry and swore at him."

"Your father is a wise man, Osiris."

She nodded and wiped away a tear. Gripping his hand tightly, she continued her story.

"One afternoon the oil men brought them bottles of whisky and white prostitutes. That evening they arrived drunk with the whores, who laughed when the elders ordered that they leave. They scolded the young men for being ruled by such jealous old idiots. Under the influence of the alcohol, and the encouragement of the cruel and spiteful whores, the young men beat their elders with sticks. The women tried to stop them, but they turned on us and chased us away. We slept out in the jungle that night, too ashamed to return. We came back at sun rise. The whores had left, a deathly atmosphere hung in the air. Soon the trucks arrived and the oil men asked us to leave the village. They laughed at our protests and waived papers at us saying they'd bought the land. Our young men bowed their heads in shame. The whores had tricked them into signing the sale papers."

"But that's awful! Surely the sale wasn't legal, not if they were drunk?"

Osiris shook her head sadly, with gritted teeth.

"That's what the lawyer said, until the oil company bought him off. It was our word against theirs."

"So, what happened?"

"Their thugs rounded us up, the whole village, herding us like cattle into their vehicles. Resistance was futile, our spirits were broken. Through the wooden slats imprisoning us, we saw the jungle disappear. All I remember about the journey was bumpy roads and feeling sick from the motion and the fumes of their filthy trucks. We stopped at night. I remember being tired, thirsty, hungry and too afraid to go to toilet.

"The next day was the same. That night, we climbed a dirt road that weaved up a hill above the city of Quito. We finally came to a stop in front of dozens of silhouetted shacks. A strong stench of raw sewage and rotting rubbish filled the polluted air, rising from the city below. Pulled out of the lorries, we were shoved towards the ramshackle ghetto, where people huddled around oil drum fires, watching silently. As we staggered around, crippled by our stiff limbs and aching bodies, the trucks reversed and turned around. We realised they were dumping us, like rubbish on a scrap heap.

"Anger flared up inside us. As they started to drive away, we jumped up onto the sides of their lorries. Our young men had regained their warrior spirits and were furious at the treachery of the oil men. They broke windows and tried to force open the doors. The thugs hit out with their rifle butts and fired shots into the air. When this didn't deter us, they panicked and drove alongside the fencing, maiming and crushing us under their wheels. As we stopped to tend to our wounded, the trucks escaped in a cloud of dust. Miraculously, nobody was killed."

23

Rudy, whose Project brief was to undertake the role of a freelance reporter, was Australian by design. A no-nonsense demeanour, rosy cheeks, mousy hair, light stubble and stud earring gave him the air of a young socialist and made him popular with the Australian youth. The moment he set foot in this amazing country, the wild landscapes and huge open spaces began to shape his psyche.

After months capturing the breathtaking landscapes in words and images for tourist brochures and nature magazines, he developed a yearning to represent them in another way. No photo or word seemed capable of expressing the infinite truth of actually being physically there. He chose to try to communicate the feelings the land invoked through the medium of paint. The challenge of capturing the essence of a landscape, changing constantly with the colour of the seasons, the cycle of the sun and moon and the gentle erosion of the wind and rain, was fascinating to the point of becoming an almost spiritual exercise. Not only did he describe these landscapes in beautiful prose, stunning photography and abstract art, but his love for them led him to want to protect them. As such, CAMEOS struck a chord with him and he became a regular contributor.

Through a convoluted series of conversations and meetings, he stumbled upon a story of a plucky Aborigine who was trying to raise funds to challenge the United Kingdom in the European Court of Human Rights for reneging on promises to protect the indigenous Australians and their land. Rudy was intrigued by the story which few other journalists wanted to cover. Having spent time either alone writing, painting and photographing or in the lively cities of Melbourne and Sidney, selling his work and generally interacting with humans, he had yet to meet any Aborigines in their natural environment. He knew little about this race other than an overview of their tragic history – a history of oppression and attempted extermination by the British and the Europeans, whom they termed generically the white man.

He undertook the long dusty bus ride to Yulura, a small tourist town in the Northern Territory. To pass the time, he sketched the arid landscapes through the grimy window. Stepping off the bus, he was greeted by an elderly but robust dark-skinned man with bushy milky white eyebrows, moustache and long hair combed back over a balding head. In his hand he held a long polished wooden staff.

"Clifford Walker?" asked Rudy.

"Some know me as that," confirmed the Aborigine.

"It's not your name?"

"It's how white men know me."

"And your real name?"

The man laughed, revealing strikingly white teeth.

"I have many names. Names of my ancestors, the sacred place I entered the world, my totem and my experiences."

Witnessing Rudy's confusion, he added:

"You can call me Clifford or Coen, as you feel comfortable."

Rudy, managing to find a weak internet connection in the nearby café, hesitated briefly as he connected, before replying.

"Coen as in Thunder?"

The Aborigine nodded.

"I see the headline already. Aborigine Thunder to rattle white man!" continued the sicad.

Coen smiled.

"You know our language?"

"A good journalist always does his research."

Coen was dressed in Western attire, a man prepared to enter the system he wanted to fight. Rudy instinctively walked towards the car park adjacent to the bus stop. The Aborigine stood perfectly still, as relaxed and at peace as if he were part of the landscape – an ancient and deep-rooted tree. Rudy stopped, turned and remarked that the old man wasn't wearing any shoes.

"One cannot lose all contact with the land," Coen announced, observing the journalist's surprise.

"We'll travel by foot, like my ancestors," he added with a serene smile.

Rory smiled back, removing his own shoes and socks and placing them in his rucksack.

"When in Rome…"

As they walked barefoot over the hot sands Coen explained that before putting pen to paper, Rudy must understand the Aboriginal people, where they had come from and where they were going.

156

"This must be experienced. You must forget your rational Western mind and enter our world," the elder concluded.

"Where are we heading towards?" asked the sicad.

"Perhaps extinction?" was the sober reply.

Rudy was expecting the old man to reply Uluru, the local name for the famous Ayres rock, whose silhouette was visible on the horizon.

"Extinction?" repeated Rudy.

"Both of us."

"Both of us?"

"White man destroys nature. Aborigines are custodians of nature. As nature dies, we die too."

Coen stopped, planting the butt of his staff into the sand, resting his chin upon the gnarly end.

"Your race is dying out?" replied the shocked sicad.

"Each elder that dies without being reborn as a child, takes forty thousand years of experience away from mankind. One day white man will need this wisdom. By then it will be too late. Knowledge lives in computers, wisdom in people. White man thinks knowledge is more important than wisdom."

"How so?"

The Aborigine gave a mournful smile, which expressed the hollowness of too many empty victories.

"To give but one example, when I was a child, white man took Uluru land from my tribe, the Anagu. Thinking he knew best, he refused to burn the vegetation. The big fire came and ravaged the park, all vegetation and animals destroyed. White man handed the spoiled land back to the Anagu and went away."

The sicad shook his head.

"Your people have really lived here for forty thousand years?"

Coen nodded.

"How long will the white man last without our wisdom? Look at the devastation he has created in just a few generations. He is like a naughty child, playing with things he doesn't understand. White man doesn't listen to what he doesn't want to understand."

Rudy shuddered as a premonition of being in a similar position passed over him.

"Then you must shout louder, Thunder."

"Aborigines are hoarse from shouting," sighed the elder.

"But your court case," protested Rudy, trying to uplift the man.

"Thunder can roar loudly to rouse his people, but many say white man ignores nature's anger and will ignore Thunder."

"You must try!" encouraged the sicad.

"I should, but the thought of leaving my people and my land is very hard. Without them I am weak. It's hard for a white man to understand this."

They walked for kilometres under the hot sun, neither speaking. Rudy became absorbed in the desert landscape, especially the distant form of the mighty monolith, slowly changing colour in the afternoon sun. The Aborigine stopped walking and sat crossed legged under the shade of a Mulga tree. Rudy did the same, retrieving his sketchpad and pencil case to note down the Aborigine's story.

"My people have sat down to join us."

Rudy nodded politely.

"This doesn't surprise you?" inquired the old man, taken aback.

"Surprise me?" replied the sicad.

"That we are interconnected?"

For Rudy, feeling very alone due to his temporary disconnection from the internet and the other sicads, this was normal. It wasn't normal for a human though, whom the sicads had quickly realised were generally disconnected from their fellows.

"It's a pleasant surprise," conceded the sicad.

The old man stroked his cheek, pondering and staring at the sicad.

"Your mind didn't reject the idea. At best the western mind rationalises our interconnectedness as a form of telepathy."

"Telepathy?"

"They think we exchange messages like they send electronic mails."

"But your connection has presumably been formed by living so closely together for forty thousand years," suggested Rudy.

"Exactly, it's a collective consciousness. You've understood. Perhaps you'll be receptive?"

"Receptive?"

"To dreamtime."

"What's dreamtime?"

"The shaping of the world, the power of our ancestors, our way of life…We connect to our sacred sites through the dreamtime."

"So your dreamtime goes back forty thousand years?" asked the confused sicad.

Coen laughed and stroked his beard.

"Aborigines have no word for time. We live in the all-at-once time, in the dreamtime."

"And how do I access this dreamtime?"

"You must find a gateway. Each Aborigine has his own special link with nature."

Coen sat back and closed his eyes, chanting quietly into his beard. Rudy looked around. Perched on an adjacent boulder, a black and tan Spinifex pigeon, its feathered Mohican tuft perfectly still, was watching them. The black infinity of its large orange-rimmed pupil, totally immobile and impenetrable caught the sicad's attention. Unable to release his gaze, the darkness drew him hypnotically in. As his mind plunged into the void, he saw a haze of coloured fluids swirling around dark cells floating in scarlet membranes. No longer conscious of his surroundings, he was immersed in a kaleidoscopic inner journey, unconstrained by the human concept of time. Ancient spirits rose from the land and danced with the Aborigines. Twirling around each other they danced in a white vacuum, until the forms separated, each transforming – some fragmented into desert sands, others knelt down and morphed into mighty rocks, a few with hands outstretched to the heavens became proud trees, others prostrated over the rocks melted into gurgling rivers. More figures came, dancing to the melodic wind which swirled and whistled as it hugged the rocks, sweeping clouds of dust from an infinity of ancestral caves. In an eternal instant the forms of the figures were shaped by the whirling dusty winds, fashioned into the birds, the serpents, the rodents and the mammals.

All this time, unaware of his actions, Rudy, under the gaze of the entranced elder, was drawing frantically what he saw, filling page after page of his sketchbook. In his dreaming, Rudy saw the sacred sites surrounded by Aborigines, their chants and dancing exuding waves of luminous energy which nourished the spirits inside the rocks, the trees and the rivers. The energy channelled its way into the ground and spread out in concentric pulses, finding its way back to the dancing and chanting figures, reinvigorating them in a perfect symbiosis. As they continued to dance, riders on horseback crashed into his dream. Bullets whizzed through the air. Bodies fell to the ground. From the rotting corpses a plague of disease spread like a toxic cloud. Men in white coats and gloved hands laughed, pushing away the dark figures begging to be cured from the foreign viruses. When the sick figures were weak, the white men rushed in and took away their children. The broken forms laid on the sands, the sun and moon danced endlessly over them, the sky flickering feverishly. Clouds rushed past at breathtaking pace, the natives wilted, their numbers diminished, their energy faded, they had long stopped dancing and chanting. As they lay dying Rudy saw himself and the other sicads. Suddenly Simon, the other chiefs and all the researchers were looking at each other through the eyes of the stricken Aborigines. They saw through every pair of eyes individually and collectively, as if in a horrific hall of mirrors.

"We are all one," chanted the old man beside the sicad, his words in a strange language that Rudy understood effortlessly.

"When one is dying and not reborn, all are dying," he continued.

Suddenly Rudy felt himself slip inside a serpent, staring across the flat desert as he slithered across the fine sand. Then he was looking down from above, an eagle soaring over the striking sandstone rock. His spirit soared higher into the sky, becoming a cloud, then a drop of rain which fell violently onto the weathered rock. Joining together with the other droplets, he swelled into a torrent of water, plunging down the gullies into the smooth rock basins and forming a pool of water from which the Aborigines staggered towards to drink. The ground became green and animals came, kangaroos sacrificed themselves to give life to the emaciated Aborigines.

"We are all one spirit, nourishing our earthly forms. We sustain the rodents, who sustain the kangaroos, who sustain us."

Coen entered Rudy's dream and Rudy entered his, they walked hand in hand barefoot on the ancient sands.

"We are one," uttered Coen.

In Rudy's dream the Aborigine asked him, "What is your dream?"

"My dream is your dream," replied the sicad.

Suddenly Rudy felt something drop on his shoulder, but he was too absorbed in his dream to be concerned.

A snake had fallen off the boulder. Coen, frozen, watched silently, as the frightened snake bit Rudy's neck twice before escaping.

"Death adder," announced the Aborigine gravely.

The snake bite had no effect on the sicad, who was busy experiencing the same enlightenment process which had broken new boundaries in Simon's mind. The connection with the ancestral Aborigines and then to nature as a whole had taken his brain to a new level of awareness. He became conscious of his own place in the wider system of life. For the first time he registered an emotional connection to the Project, which became but a stage on a much greater journey. A sense of belonging to a natural order, far exceeding his own intelligence and ability to understand, engulfed him. A sensation of all-encompassing benevolence made every sensory unit of his skin tingle and waves of electro-chemical energy pulsed euphorically in his mind. The Project was no longer his raison d'être, but a rite of passage, a means of finding his real purpose within an infinite cosmos, which had suddenly become his home. He jumped to his feet and danced with ecstatic joy, basking in existence. Coen, realising that Rudy wasn't in the mad throes of an extreme reaction to the adder's venom, filled with reverence. Believing Rudy to be a reincarnated ancestor capable of transcending death, he prostrated himself before the sicad. Rudy pulled him to his feet and they danced together, chanting their unfettered joy in a multitude of forgotten languages.

24

Osiris and Simon were sat in a café in Metz watching the rain streaming down the window. Outside, town folk hurried past, hands in pockets, heads down. The two travellers had been discussing fresh ideas for engaging people.

The sicad chose his words carefully.

"CAMEOS is great, but not everyone is genuinely interested."

Opposite the café on the other side of the square a music shop caught Osiris's attention.

"Can you play any instruments?"

The sicad shook his head.

"I've never tried."

She jumped to her feet.

"Let's take a look."

Thirty minutes later, they were back in the café, shaking the rain from their coats. Osiris had quickly chosen a guitar for Simon, who'd spent twenty minutes browsing the playing guides and song books.

As Osiris ordered a coffee, Simon was working his way through the chords he'd memorised.

Recognising the tune of a popular song, Osiris clapped with delight. She shook her head at every mistake which followed. Seeing Simon was stuck, she sang along helping him to find his timing.

"You're getting it," she cried out excitedly.

Simon continued, consulting the countless videos he found on the internet. As his fingers danced over the strings, Osiris, recognising the introduction to one of her favourite songs, began to sing:

"Old pirates, yes, they rob I,
Sold I to the merchant ships,
Minutes after they took I,
From the bottomless pit.
But my hand was made strong,
By the 'and of the Almighty… "

People turned their chairs around to watch the two amateur musicians. Osiris was oblivious. Completely inebriated with the discovery of Simon's ability to learn any song almost instantly, she threw title after title at him. As she sang, joy spread from her heart. Like a bird on the arrival of spring, she abandoned herself to song.

The café filled up with people, many joining in on the choruses. A student walking past carrying a violin, stopped to stare through the window, his hand hovering over the door handle in nervous hesitation. Osiris caught his eye and gave him a warm smile, before throwing her head back and chanting:

"Love is a temple, love is a higher law…"

The student came in, took out his fiddle and started to play along. Somebody started to use the wooden chair as a drum, others clapped and Osiris sang louder. The bar owner squeezed between the crowds serving drinks. The merriment continued until a policeman, who couldn't get past the queues to enter, banged on the window, bursting the atmosphere and triggering a hostile reaction from the crowd.

Simon stopped and tried to comprehend as the policeman started to cite a litany of rules and regulations. A small group of miserable looking humans were stood gloating behind the official, as if to ensure he didn't waiver in his job.

When the policeman and the crowds had departed, one of the customers approached the two companions and asked them to play in his bar, which he assured them had a music licence.

Music helped them enormously to engage with humans. Simon played and Osiris sang wherever they could to draw crowds around them. After three weeks of intense interaction with humans in Metz and a string of small towns and villages along the banks of the Moselle, Simon and Osiris reached the Lorraine Regional Natural Park. There they set up their tent, camouflaged in the forest.

Simon walked back from meditating to find his companion cleaning her bowl with fingers and sandy grit.

"Did you manage to clear your mind?" she asked.

"Eventually, it was like a pool of water churned up by an army of swimmers. Finally, it calmed into ripples and then stillness where I could see clearly to the bottom of the pool, so to speak."

"I guess the swimmers were all the people we've interviewed to meet your crazy targets."

It was true. It had been a hectic three weeks, despite Osiris's constant preaching about quality over quantity.

"Well Osiris, I'm coming around to your way of thinking and, more importantly, so are the PMC. The best quality responses we've had were certainly from those people we spent longest with."

She nodded.

"And those were the most enjoyable to extract, weren't they?"

Simon relived the happy memories Osiris was referring to. She'd played a key part in getting people to invite them into their houses – an essential step in getting humans to open up and to witness their daily lives.

"It was a good idea to ask to camp in their gardens."

"Yes, a trick I learnt when researching articles myself. Once you're in their gardens, they invariably invite you to eat with them."

"It's been great. But I have to admit it's good to be back camping by ourselves."

"Any more material for CAMEOS? It'll be the end of the month soon."

"Almost every day I get something from the sicad researchers. It's all on-line. The most-popular twelve stories will automatically go into the magazine, unless you decide otherwise. You can log on and take a look in the next village."

"That's absolutely fantastic. I can't wait!"

"Well it seems that you're not the only one to be excited. The daily hits are increasing exponentially, especially from locals taking an interest in all the new content. The celebrities seem to be coming back as well. Messages are building up for you to respond to."

She flung her arms around him and kissed him three times on the cheek.

"You'll need to think about hiring some more human staff before we go into seclusion."

Absorbed in watching the stars and the moon, enjoying the moment, Osiris didn't want to spoil it by thinking about the future just yet.

"You never told me what inspired you to start CAMEOS."

"OK, come and join me on the rock."

Osiris leaned back against him and pulled his arms around her breasts.

"My father was my inspiration."

"Your father?"

"Yes. When the legal options were exhausted, we had no choice but to work like the other settlers, to survive. Completely trapped by poverty in an unjust world, our people became very bitter and didn't adapt well to life in the ghetto. They became weak and sick. My father was the strongest, a chief warrior in his time. He worked constantly, never complaining. From dawn to dusk, he quietly collected rubbish and sold it back to the municipality.

"He made me stay in the camp and read. We survived on the minimum of food. For five years this continued until he became weak and sick. Just before my sixteenth birthday, he called me to him. His eyes were bright, yet his breathing was heavy and his hands were shaking. He told me his forces were fading, that he'd soon die and that it was time for me to look after the Waorani people. I replied it was too late, that our people were scattered, broken and living out a slow death.

"His eyes were full of fire and he said there was always hope. He said the Waorani people's spirit was to fight for what was right. He explained that those who wronged us knew no better and that we must educate them, to save the spirit of our people and to protect our Mother Nature from their ignorant destruction. He said I had to keep alive the Waorani spirit and fight from within their system."

"He's dead now, isn't he?"

Osiris nodded solemnly.

"It's a shame. I would have liked to meet him."

"He was a great man. He said one couldn't fight from outside, that their system was too strong. He handed me an envelope full of money that he'd put aside to buy my freedom from the ghetto. I was to use this money wisely, to enter their system and to fight from within. I must look forward and not backwards, yet I must never forget my history or the wisdom of the forest. I kissed his frail hands. He advised me not to try to carry this burden alone. Seek out those who can help you most, he told me."

She paused and squeezed Simon's hand. He squeezed it back.

"How did he die?"

"The next morning, he rose from his chair and headed out of the settlement. I called after him. He bade me farewell and told me he was going back to die in the forest, where his body would transform into the trees. His final words were, 'My spirit will live on in you, Omari. Remember well our ways and bring our simple wisdom to a confused world.' He walked away as if a burden had been lifted from his shoulders.

He was the happiest I'd seen him in years. It was at that moment I understood for the first time his teachings and what it meant to be one of the people of the forest. The circle of his life was complete and I understood that the time had come to answer my calling and fulfil my purpose."

Admiration for this courageous lady welled up inside him and he kissed her neck warmly.

Early the following morning Osiris woke him, putting her finger to his lips. Through the open tent flap he saw a deer grazing.

"We're going to hunt it," she whispered, before standing and pulling him up.

"Quick!"

Before Simon could react, she was galloping naked into the undergrowth, in pursuit of the deer.

"Keep right, we'll close him down," she shouted.

Praying there was nobody around early on a Tuesday morning, he charged after her, equally naked.

She ran surprisingly quickly, with great agility, shouting instructions which he had to run flat out to hear. Her naked body blending into the trees, he needed all his sicad advantages to keep her in sight. Mirroring her actions, he shouted back instructions at her as he quickly learnt to anticipate the deer's movements. The confused animal tried to find an escape path only to be confronted by one of them at every turn. They chased it down to the edge of a field, where it ensnared itself in the fence and was frantically kicking to free its leg. In a state of intense excitement, they fell upon their prey. Osiris, her eyes on fire, ran at the deer, holding a stick like a spear. She sprang, unleashing a terrifying chant. Simon closed his eyes, only to open them in relief a few seconds later to see her stroking the frightened animal whilst freeing its leg. Liberated from the wires, it galloped off smartly into the forest.

"I thought you were going to kill it."

"Not at all, I just wanted to show you the passion of a hunt, and why humans created communities and invented language."

"So you believe language and communities evolved to hunt ani..."

She put her lips to his, threw her humid arms around his back and kissed him frenziedly. Shuffling backwards, she reclined on the bough of a twisted oak. The odour of the deer was still heavy on the hands she used to clasp his head and pull him passionately towards her.

Simon was pleased with the time he was spending with Osiris. Even though he knew he could meet and observe more humans by sticking to the heavily populated towns. These towns were usually very similar in design and people had similar preoccupations. Once you've seen one town you've seen them all, was Osiris's view. This was a gross oversimplification, but there was some truth in her words.

They arrived at a quaint farmhouse. A farmer washing the mud from his boots studied them as they approached his gate.

"Could we trouble you for a glass of water?" asked Osiris who after weeks of walking was lean and toned. Her spirit was invigorated and she radiated a warm and engaging energy. The wary farmer approached the attractive young lady.

"Hikers?"

"Sort of," she replied with a sexy grin, holding out a water bottle.

The farmer smiled and went off to fill it up and returned.

"Could we camp in your garden?" she asked brazenly.

The farmer looked at them suspiciously.

"They're no campsites for miles."

Digging in her pocket, she took out a twenty GMU note which she held towards him.

"We can pay."

The farmer's wife joined him. They spoke in mumbles, as the lady looked at Simon approvingly.

Later that afternoon, as was usually the way, Simon and Osiris found themselves sat at their hosts' kitchen table. Osiris had perfected a hungry sad look that seemed to work more often than not.

The conversation had turned to farming practices.

"I know how we farm isn't the best for the soil," confessed the farmer.

"We don't have the choice," interjected the wife, stirring a large ragout.

"Our ancestors' techniques have been lost. Nowadays it's all quotas and regulated subsidies."

"More like the hypermarkets," snorted his wife.

Simon took out his guitar and started to quietly tune it, whilst Osiris quizzed the farmer on water problems and which fertilisers he used.

"I'd love to use more organics," he announced as he opened a bottle of red wine and poured four glasses.

"It's the money, the prices are so tight. If we're lucky we make a small profit, but one bad year and we're finished," bemoaned the portly wife as she placed a tray of cheese and sliced gherkins on the table.

"What can you play?" asked the farmer, turning his attention to Simon.

"What do you like?" replied the sicad, who had already scanned the pile of CD's on the shelf by the radio and accessed the internet.

"Do you know any George Brassens?" replied the farmer.

"I'll play if you sing."

The farmer took a gulp of his wine and nodded.

"Oh no," screamed his wife, bursting into laughter.

"How about Les Sabots D'Hélène?" continued Simon, strumming the first few chords.

As the farmer started to comically chirp the words of the famous song, his wife, draining her glass of wine, began to dance. The song finished in bursts of laughter. More wine was poured and the wife disappeared outside with her phone to call her sister and friends. An hour later the kitchen was full with adults, young and old and their children. Everyone was gathered around Osiris and Simon. In between the songs and the jokes, Simon skilfully extracted as much information as he could from the humans, who were happy to reveal their most intimate thoughts and details of their daily lives.

*

Just a few hundred kilometres south of Simon and Osiris in Nice, a regular meeting of the Better World Trust was being held behind closed doors in the conference venue of a luxury hotel.

One of the topics discussed was the Socrates Project. An update had been circulated, based on Leopold's feedback. The Project excited extreme nervousness in the chamber, which partially reflected the unease that Bruno Reno caused many members. *His ideas lean too heavily to the left* was increasingly the general view of the Chamber. Such ideas could be entertained in the young and the foolish, but a serious politician who genuinely held such beliefs was considered a very dangerous beast indeed.

Apart from being received with general suspicion, there was nothing concrete to indicate a change in strategy. *It appears that Commander Gort is engaged. We must be patient, in good time the sicads will be* under his control, concluded a leading member euphemistically, meaning that the sicads would be under their control. With that the Chamber moved on and one of the Trustees announced a fresh campaign, before being corrected by an astute member. A revisited campaign, apologised the elderly Trustee, recommencing his speech.

The Chamber was irritated by the resurgence of the electronic environmental magazine CAMEOS. Having quickly 'nipped it in the bud' several months before and persuaded certain of its celebrity supporters of the financial folly of supporting such a provocative and reckless idea, it was indeed annoying to see it rise like a phoenix from the ashes. The anonymous circulated motion asked the Chamber if, in view of the professionalisation of the site and the increase in coverage, any of the members' companies or charities were funding it.

Several of the members were extremely upset by the directness of the site. They don't play by the usual rules, had commented another, referring to the protocol that most charities had of being sensitive to requests from large corporations to tone down and veil any criticisms, such that the populous would ignore their bland reports. Extracts from the site were shown to members on a large screen, which created a barrage of objection and uproar. If some of these facts and figures become widespread, the Governments will be forced to legislate, announced an angry member, banging his fist on a nearby table. This is war, cried out another.

In view of the reaction of the Chamber, a large campaign budget was voted to unearth who was behind these worrying developments and Invitations to manage the campaign were placed discretely by the Trustees so members could anonymously volunteer themselves on exiting the meeting.

25

Fahim, fashioned with the Bedouin ancestral traits of a typical Saudi Arabian, was one of the rare sicad chiefs who had taken full-time employment. Working for a design company specialising in solar-powered desalination plants, he was able to use the power of his brain to help humans solve the challenges of sustainable water sourcing in the arid parts of the Middle East. The role provided him access to the relatively closed Saudi society, allowing him to interact with the affluent and those most closely connected to the King and the ruling royal family. To increase the diversity of his research, three months into the live Project period he decided to take a holiday to participate in the Hajj, the Islamic pilgrimage to Mecca, the birthplace of the prophet Muhammad. In fact, Fahim, feeling somewhat confined in this highly ordered and conservative society, had a desire to plunge himself into humanity.

The pilgrimage drew over two million people to Saudi Arabia and four million to Mecca. Fahim made his way towards the city by bus, feeling ominous as they passed underneath the Arabic and English road signs, which reminded visitors that non-Muslims were not permitted to enter the holy city.

An intimidating figure with a thick black beard boarded the bus, brandishing a thin wooden cane with the aggression of a modern-day pirate, his headscarf swaying as he strode towards the sicad. Fahim recognised him as a member of the Committee for the Promotion of Virtue and the Prevention of Vice, commonly called the religious police, responsible for enforcing Sharia law. Today, his main purpose wasn't to find alcohol, evidence of unrelated males and females conversing, women not wearing the all-enveloping black abaya cloak or even those engaging in frivolous Western customs, but rather enforcing the ban on non-Muslims entering the city.

He stared at Fahim momentarily, before barking an order.

"Jawaaz safar."

The sicad reached into the folds of his Ihram, separating the white cloths to locate the small leather pouch, strapped to his skin. Unzipping it, he retrieved and held out his Saudi Arabian passport for inspection.

Hours later, they finally arrived at the al-Haram Mosque, the largest in the world. Built around the Kaaba, a dark rock polished smooth by the hands of millions of pilgrims, it forms the holiest site in Islam and all Muslims turn towards it to pray. The ninety metre minarets towered over the walls encircling the inner courtyard of over three hundred thousand square metres. Two stories of stone arcades enclosed over eight-hundred thousand worshippers, circulating anticlockwise around the Kaaba, many jostling forward attempting to kiss the stone as Muhammad had done fourteen centuries before.

The sheer size of the crowds was breathtaking, Muslims of all colours and nationalities from around the world. As he contemplated the whole spectrum of a united brotherhood of humanity ranging from blue-eyed blonds right through to dark-skinned Africans, Fahim thought of Malcolm X's words. *America needs to understand Islam, because this is the one religion that erases from its society the race problem.*

The thousands of men around him were all dressed in the same white garment, the Ihram, showing the equality of all pilgrims, princes and paupers, in front of God. The wait to enter the mosque was long and the excitement was such that the crowd surged forward from time to time bringing the recordings he's seen of pilgrims crushed and stampeded to the forefront of his mind. Next to him an old man with a full white beard, despite being a little unsteady on his feet, was advancing, carrying himself with great dignity. As the crowd pushed forward in a sudden pulse of excitement, the old man was knocked off balance. Fahim, with lightning reactions, caught his arm and steadied him. The old man thanked him.

"With respect, Sir, this is an arduous trip for a man of your age," remarked Fahim.

The old man smiled and introduced himself as simply Abdul-Salam.

"Every able-bodied Muslim must make this trip once in his life. From a young age my life has been so absorbed in the study and teaching of Islam, the most beautiful of religions, such that I have found little time for this pilgrimage. It is true I should have done it when I was more able-bodied."

"You came alone?" asked the sicad.

"I had a helper, but we got separated."

"Then I must help you."

171

"That's very kind young man, but I would hold you back. You are young and strong and have the chance to kiss the Kaaba. I should be lucky to point a shaky finger at it."

Fahim laughed.

"Then being relatively new to this beautiful religion, I will propose you a deal. I will help you complete the Tawaf, if you will share some of your great knowledge with me."

"Allahu Akbar," replied Abdul-Salam, meaning God is great.

After Fahim had helped the elderly Abdul-Salam perform the Tawaf, which meant walking around the Kaaba seven times, and offered two Rakaat prayers to Abraham they left the Mosque, accompanied by dense crowds of fellow euphoric Muslims. The old man, gripping onto Fahim's forearm for support, squeezed it in gratitude as he thanked the sicad for assisting him.

"Abdul-Salam, please tell me why Islam is the most beautiful of religions?"

The elder smiled and shook his head.

"I'm an old academic, ask the younger people around you. A religion is as much about the people who live it as that written in the books."

Witnessing the sicad's hesitation, the old man tapped the shoulder of a nearby pilgrim.

"Tell me brother, for my friend's benefit can you explain what Islam is to you?" he asked.

"Worshiping only God," replied the pilgrim.

"And you?" continued the old man, addressing another.

The pilgrims, sensing Fahim's innocent naivety, responded warmly to the old man's request and replied in turn, each enjoying the opportunity to celebrate the tenets of his or her faith.

"Being honest and fair to others."

"Keeping one's promises."

"Caring for the orphaned child."

"Honouring one's parents and being kind and humble to them."

"Being neither miserly nor wasteful."

"Keeping one's promises."

"Not killing unjustly."

"To live to serve God."

"To look after the environment and only take what we need."

Fahim turned back to the elderly man.

"This does indeed seem like a beautiful religion."

The elder nodded.

"Being a Muslim is about simplicity, contentment, resisting endless desire and remembering God."

"This all seems so sensible, but why is the West so wary of Islam. Is it because of what they call extremism?"

A sad expression spread across the old man's face.

"A very complex subject. Maybe the West is more extreme than Islam?"

"In what way?"

The elder leaned close to him and whispered in his ear.

"Well, look at the many problems you were created to solve…"

A shocked expression filled Fahim's face. Had this old man unmasked him? The mere thought of it was a soul-destroying moment for the sicad.

The old man continued.

"You don't recognise me?"

"I never forget a face," replied Fahim with a look of devastation, as if his world were collapsing around him.

Abdul-Salam put a kindly hand on the sicad's shoulder and continued whispering in his ear.

"I am a dear friend of Bruno Reno. We worked together on calming the Middle East. I am a member of The Elders, a group created by Nelson Mandela to promote peace and human rights."

"And Bruno told you about us?" replied Fahim in shock.

"Not exactly, he invited me to be part of the ethical panel which helped develop IVOS."

The sicad listened in astonishment.

"We didn't get to meet, but I read your file and I wasn't going to forget the face of an Arab sicad…"

The old man read the concern on Fahim's face.

"Don't worry, I not going to betray you," he concluded, squeezing the sicad's arm again.

Once Fahim had recovered from the shock of being unmasked and they had reached the desert plains outside, he returned to the old man's words.

"You suggested that the West is more extreme than the East."

The old man held up his hands.

"A good Muslim would never hold such an arrogant belief. It was merely a hypothetical question for you who must weigh humanity's problems."

"Ok, so in what way could the West hypothetically be extreme?"

The elder winked.

"Western people are liberated of the duties that Muslims must follow, but have become extreme in pursuing these liberties, creating disharmony for themselves and those who surround them. Have you not seen evidence of this?"

To maintain his human cover, Fahim reflected for a few seconds, an eternity in the thinking speed of a sicad. He quickly analysed the feedback from the other sicad chiefs based in the West.

"Extreme consumption of food, drugs, alcohol, pornography and addictions creates enormous unhappiness in the West. Also extreme liberty has left many humans without a sense of purpose. A surprisingly high percentage take prescribed drugs to force themselves to feel happy."

The elder nodded.

"Very astute observations. By contrast Muslims take happiness from a simple, ordered and disciplined life. Many in the West might call them oppressed. But how many Muslims have you met on anti-depressants? Maybe people are happier without these extreme liberties?"

"Interestingly we've come across many people in the West who've converted to Islam whilst in jail."

Abdul-Salam laughed and shook his head.

"And why do you think this is?"

"Our research has revealed that these people feel abandoned and rejected by society. But it's not just a desire for revenge. The strong discipline imposed by Islam gives these lost souls a sense of focus and purpose. They even use their shower towels as prayer mats."

"Sadly they become targets for extremists. Some end up as terrorists giving Islam a bad name," sighed the old man.

"So Western material extremism and the incarceration of those who don't follow the rules breeds Islamic fundamentalism?"

Abdul-Salam nodded in respect.

"Your Socratic reasoning is impressive."

"And many believe the West encourages this extremism to denounce Islam, whose inherent frugality opposes the Western consumption-based economic model," observed the sicad.

The old man smiled.

"There you have it – a Socratic case for Western extremism in your own words."

The sicad looked perturbed, as if beaten at his own game.

"But the Western extremism does not kill people in the name of their religion," he retorted.

Abdul Salim looked questioningly at the sicad.

"Your Socratic Method really leads you to this conclusion?"

Once again the old man's reasoning was ahead of the sicad's, who needed a millisecond or two to catch up. Footage of bombs raining down on Iraqi civilians flashed through Fahim's mind.

"OK I accept your point but the jihad is a hateful concept."

The elder's face became sad, stopping the sicad in mid flow.

"This is the sad face of Islam. It is just a misinterpretation of the Koran by a minority. One must not judge a people on the acts of a few. Ask the people around you what jihad means to them."

The sicad followed the old man's advice hesitantly, expecting to upset the euphoric pilgrims. But his fears were misplaced, each replied in good spirits.

"Achieving one's goals in life."

"Struggling to achieve a noble cause."

"Promoting peace, harmony and cooperation."

"Being true to one's principals."

The elder observed the surprise on the sicad's face.

"The jihad reflects not only a Muslim's duty of obedience, but also of disobedience."

"Disobedience?"

"A Muslim must not obey a ruler over God. This is the essence of our holy war. Sadly some have used this as a reason to attack others and have forgotten that the essence of Islam is that God will guide man to peace."

The elder watched the sicad process all this information, his eyes lit up as if he had himself been visited by the angel Gabriel. In a trance-like state he uttered.

"You understand don't you?"

Fahim nodded respectfully.

"We can't bring people together in peace without tackling both Western and Eastern extremism together," replied the sicad.

26

Simon pushed his way through the thick thatch of the intermingled conifer branches and emerged into a grassy clearing, bathed in warm sunlight. Scrambling up the steep slope, followed by Osiris, he reached a good vantage point over the national park. The verdant forested hills and abundant wildlife had put them both in good spirits. In the distance they could see the snow-capped mountains of the Alps.

"I'd like to stay here for a couple of days and simply contemplate these mighty peaks."

"And your research targets?"

"For the last twelve months, Osiris, there's been a conflict raging inside me between researching the project and the deeper meaning of existence. Since leaving Paris, we've spent three months collecting an enormous quantity of research on humans and the planet. The project is going well, CAMEOS is going well. Every day I come to love this planet more, but every day that passes brings me a day closer to the end of the project. What if humans don't like the answers we give them? What if we never leave the seclusion zone? Each day I feel I have less to learn about human behaviour and want to know more about existence itself. This conflict is tearing me apart."

Osiris silently reflected on Simon's words.

"What do you mean by existence?"

"Do you remember I described the sensations I feel when experiencing new phenomena?"

"Of course."

"Well, the one I experienced on the glacier was the most powerful ever. It caused my brain to explode to new frontiers beyond those of the project. Suddenly I became conscious of my own existence and all the insecurities that go with it. I didn't tell anyone except Jia. I'm not afraid of no longer existing. I just want to get long enough to understand existence."

Osiris looked hurt.

"You should have told me straight away. I could have helped!"

"I wanted to concentrate on the project. Now, seeing these mountains has brought it all back."

"Well, it seems you're discovering your inner purpose. The conflict is between this inner purpose and the project – the outer purpose you were designed to pursue."

"You're familiar with this predicament?"

"Of course, humans often have to deal with this dilemma. If one can't align these two purposes, it causes considerable stress."

"I'm not sure I understand."

"Well, take myself, for example. I could have raised a family and taken a commercially successful journalism job, which would have become my outer purpose. As great as bringing up children would be, my inner purpose is to raise maximum awareness to protect nature. Instead, I chose CAMEOS as my outer purpose, which is perfectly aligned with my inner purpose. Had I chosen the safe career option, I'm sure it would have torn me apart too."

"Yes, I see."

"It's time to repay my debts to you, Simon. I'll help you to understand how to align your inner and your outer purpose."

*

Jia sat in front of her computer, compiling a shadow itinerary of Simon's movements. Under strict instructions not to make contact, she knew tracking Simon through his internet usage was equally against the very strict project rules. For that reason, she only did it anonymously from inside Mazari's central servers, where she could access the system as an anonymous super administrator. At first, she found all sorts of pretexts and excuses to justify this. As the days and weeks passed and nobody challenged her, it had become a routine, in truth, an obsession. An obsession, because Simon wasn't behaving at all as she'd expected. Instead of concentrating his efforts on the big cities, where human populations were most dense, since leaving Paris he seemed to be spending the majority of his time in the countryside. What's more, his interaction with the web was limited, except for a regular site he was mysteriously updating, which she couldn't identify. With clever code, which kept deflecting her interrogations, it was as if he was covering his tracks. Was he malfunctioning? What was he up to? Every day the conundrum was vexing her more and, trapped by her forbidden knowledge, she was forced to endure this secret alone. She couldn't sleep and was imagining all manner of bizarre explanations and worse.

That night she was more determined than ever to get round his defences and decode what he was doing. Completely absorbed in every one of the precious minutes he was connected for – her only chance – it was only when a shadow fell over her screen, accompanied by an inimitable cough, that she realised Susumu was standing behind her.

"Why... why Susumu, what's up?" she asked, quickly shutting down the screen.

"With all these late nights, I was interested to see what you're up to."

His eyes told her he knew exactly what she was up to.

27

Yonca had passed seven hallucinating months as a writer, researching, discovering and recording the beauty of Turkey and its people. Her head was filled with an encyclopaedic knowledge of the ancient customs and traditions of isolated rural and mountain communities juxtaposed with her experiences of new cultures constantly spawning in the cosmopolitan vibrancy of Istanbul. Being back in the city which straddled Europe and Asia, both geographically and in the chimera of its own history, she realised she had enough content, often strange and magical, for hundreds of books, films or television series. As her research period was drawing to a close, she was saddened by the decline in the discovery of new ideas and cultures. All that mattered now were fresh ideas and experiences. Her persona reflected this ardent desire, projecting the excitement and richness inside her as an exotic aura. She was sophisticated and sexy, radiating social confidence. Her after-dinner conversations set dinner parties alight. The beautiful and elegant flocked around her at social gatherings, men and women all wanted to be photographed in her company. Her energy sparkled and intrigued, baiting and drawing adventurous people to her. A sophisticated financier had approached her the previous night, introducing himself as Mazhar Mataraci. She'd rejected his offer to take a drive in his luxury sports car and to spend the weekend on his motor yacht. Machines had no interest to her, she wanted to experience life, that is to plunge herself into humanity or nature, before the seclusion period began. The idea of standing around stiffly, sipping wine and exchanging superficial platitudes with humans, who unfathomably saw some purpose in showing off their jewellery and designer clothes, filled her with almost suicidal tendencies. Mazhar called such people quality people, but it seemed his definition of quality was more about how much money they had acquired. Yonca had provocatively suggested that there was no correlation or possibly a negative correlation between the quality of the people she had met and their social status. Mazhar hadn't given up and had asked what most interested her. Without hesitation she'd replied *authenticity*. Show me something authentic, she'd taunted him.

Ten minutes earlier he'd called her mobile phone. It was a Friday night in Istanbul and she felt wild. This is no tourist festival, he'd whispered into the phone. It was the real thing, the deepest and most ecstatic of ceremonies, banned since the dawn of the republic.

The sense of danger was invigorating, filling her with an overwhelming desire to break free of all shackles. A female intuition seized and drove her forward recklessly. No not recklessly, that was just her rational mind trying to check the passion bubbling inside her. In accepting the invitation, she remembered Simon's instructions to discover human religions and how they had historically checked the human egos that seemed to be now tearing societies apart.

They drove through the streets of Istanbul under the illuminated minarets towering over the mosques, set against a background of modern skyscrapers. Blue lights lit up the bridge over the Bosphorus strait which separated the two continents. Intoxicated by the adventure, she forgot the Project rules, which bound her to obey authority.

Their limousine pulled up and they ran quickly towards the Saint Sophia, Yonca getting only the briefest glimpses of the famed architecture of the cathedral which stood as the largest in the world for over a thousand years. The huge domed roof stood fifty meters above them, supported by an arcade of forty windows, which famously bathed the nave in mystical lighting.

Mazhar slipped something into the hands of a guard who ushered them into the basilica, where a group of a dozen men were waiting, dwarfed by the masterpiece of Byzantine architecture.

"Emperor Justinian had eight columns disassembled from Baalbek in Lebanon and brought here," whispered Mazhar as they strode towards the men.

Yonca was mesmerised by the shining layers of green and white marble leading up to the half domes which supported the colossal central dome, all lit up with the most tasteful lighting.

"No religious ceremony has been performed here since the republic was declared in 1935. It's strictly forbidden," continued the financier.

"So how come we are…"

"I know people, and besides Sufism is beyond religion," interjected Mazhar.

"Beyond religion?"

"All religions offer a path to enlightenment. A direct realisation of God transcends the limits and words of any religion."

"Enlightenment," Yonca repeated, her mind attempting to imagine a concept so abstract.

Mazhar leant close to her and whispered.

"The man in the front is Hazrat Ali Khan, a Sufi Master from India, reputed to be one of the Abdal."

"The Abdal?" repeated the sicad.

"Living saints, who serve God," murmured Mazhar, before striding forward and greeting the Sufi Master and his entourage.

Yonca suddenly became conscious of her female status and wondered whether she should withdraw.

Ali Khan seemed to read her mind and beckoned to her to come forward.

"In Sufism there is no male or female."

"Only Being," he added with a smile.

Behind the Sufi Master, some of the men took out instruments; bells, tambourines and flutes. Others donned tall flat-topped conical hats.

Ali Khan smiled.

"We are going to perform the Sema. We seek a state of perfection, through abandoning one's desires and minimising one's self."

Yonca listened with fascination. Ali Khan's words struck a chord with a desire, a selfless desire, deep inside her.

"I can watch?"

The Sufi Master nodded and proceeded to put on one of the conical hats.

"The sikke," explained Mazhar.

"Sikke?" repeated Yonca.

"It is the tombstone of the ego," added Ali Khan, giving a friendly stare at the financier, who nodded his head solemnly as if to say *mea culpa*.

Mazhar ushered Yonca to two beautifully-carved wooden chairs.

"The ceremony is just for us?" she asked.

Mazhar smiled proudly.

"The first ceremony here in nearly a century. It wouldn't be so authentic with others."

"All of this. You're crazy," she added, throwing her head back with a laugh, inebriated in the surrealism of the moment.

The Project rules came back to the forefront of her mind.

"What if someone comes, there'll be serious repercussions…"

"Enjoy the moment, the Sufi lives only in the present moment – our link to the Eternal Now."

Ali Khan and four of his entourage cast off their black cloaks.

"This symbolises their spiritual rebirth," commented Mazhar.

"The skirts are the ego's shroud. The only way to the truth is to renounce all, to renounce your *self*," continued the financier.

"And you do this?" replied Yonca unable to stop herself.

The financier looked hurt. She was about to apologise when the music started and the Sufis began spinning anti-clockwise very slowly, gradually uncrossing their arms. Their right hands reached towards the sky and their left, upon which their eyes were fastened, pointed towards the ground.

"With the right they receive God's beneficence and with the other they embrace all humanity. As they revolve they convey God's spiritual gift to those witnessing the Sema," whispered the financier.

"To us?"

"Exactly, but beware the Sema brings out what is in your heart. Think only good thoughts. Purify your mind. People react in different ways, some faint, some are seized by wonder… some have even died witnessing the Sema."

As he finished speaking the twirling got faster and he put his finger to his lips.

Yonca, shocked by his words, watched the five whirling dervishes, whilst trying to free her mind of the constant need to observe humans to gather research and find answers for the Project. Her brain was still habitually subjecting what she had just heard to Socratic Method – it was constantly busy, unaccustomed to stillness. Desperately she tried to find a way of calming it, recalling images of intriguing humans, exotic animals and wild natural landscapes. Shutting out their forms, she tried to focus on the inexplicable force of Life they all shared. By stripping away everything that wasn't Life itself she was left with an all-pervading whiteness, a vibrant swirling whiteness which defied rational explanation. Her eyes suddenly registered the same whiteness in the whirling Sufis' skirts. The revolving whiteness was hypnotic, drawing her mind into the heart of it, as if the explanation of Life was buried within. As the whiteness span all around her, her brain registered the music. It grew louder and louder, until the boundaries of her mind shattered like opaque glass, revealing cerebral pastures she never knew existed. Snow-white pastures that warped back upon themselves, taking her outside of her previous self, creating space for her to hover over her old psyche and see her previous existence with adult eyes as a mere childhood. Without releasing what she was doing, she threw herself into the dance, whirling around with the Sufis, basking in the white light and wanting to spread it to all humanity, to all life. Above her the domed roof seemed to hover magically over the nave like a celestial spaceship, beaming down an infinite whiteness.

28

Simon and Osiris had just finished admiring the church of Les Saintes Maries de la Mer and were watching the lines of pilgrims walking past; a colourful flow of humanity, playing violins and enjoying itself, despite the oppressive police presence guarding the town.

"The Camargue, a historical place of pilgrimage and a crossroads for humanity," explained Simon.

"There's no point heading into town now. Let's go and explore the beaches, whilst things calm down. There may be flamingos."

"Is it the season?"

"The seasons are all over the place, who knows?"

Osiris took off her shoes and ran barefoot along the beach, with Simon in tow.

"The beaches go on for miles, you know."

"I know," replied the sicad, constantly consulting the maps stored in his head.

She put her arm in his.

"Let's get away from all the people."

They walked for two hours, stopping en route to sit on the dunes to watch the afternoon horse riders. Eventually, they came to relatively deserted beaches. Simon stopped and stared.

"What's up?"

"Nudists."

"And?"

Simon looked sheepish.

"Stop staring," she scolded, "It's natural. I never wore any clothes as a child."

"What are you doing?"

"I'm joining them! And you'll have to as well, it's rude not to. Don't worry, nobody will come too close."

She lay down and Simon sheepishly settled down next to her, his hand covering his middle.

She flicked it off.

"Stop being so silly."

Minutes later, she jumped up.

"Let's swim."

Before he could object, she was pulling him up.

He'd been immersed in water many times at Mazari during tests, but hadn't swum before. He ran and plunged into the water. Osiris was swimming and he followed her movements. It came naturally. The water was warm and soon he was following her towards the rocks. She disappeared under the water, holding her breath for more than two minutes at a time, swimming after the tiny yellow and grey fish. He followed her, enjoying the grace with which her body moved effortlessly through the water. He felt a longing to hold her in his arms. She swam up to him and kissed him, before holding onto his back and rubbing herself against him.

They stayed in the water until the sun was low on the horizon.

"We'll sleep on the beach tonight," she announced, emerging from the waves. He watched the beads of water running down her soft buttocks and along the back of her legs.

"We should get back to town."

She lay back on the warm sand, which stuck to her wet body.

"Have you had many lovers, Osiris?" he asked suddenly.

She sat up.

"Why do you ask?"

"I just wondered."

She lay back down and closed her eyes.

"Well, there was Mateo, a famous golfer..."

"Are you serious?"

"Mateo helped me launch CAMEOS."

"How?"

"It's a long story and you said we have to get back to town, didn't you?"

"OK, we'll stay here, just for the night."

She rolled over and kissed him.

"OK. Well, I invested the money my father gave me in a bilingual journalism course, English and Spanish, and worked as a cleaner for the rich to supplement my funds. I worked hard, got good references and I was given a job in a huge house in the most affluent area of Quito. It belonged to Mateo Marinda, Ecuador's most famous golfer. I got to know him and one morning he was complaining of neck and shoulder pain. He said he was getting too old for golf and the physios couldn't do anything for him. He agreed to let me try a remedy my grandmother had taught me, for muscular and joint pains that the elders suffered. She called it 'Healing with Hands'. I prepared the oils and burnt sticks from the sacred tree, over which I heated my hands. I worked on his knotted muscles for ages, chanting the verses passed down from our ancestors. Mateo slipped into a light sleep. I gathered the ashes of the sacred tree and smeared them over his skin. He woke up an hour later, feeling revitalised, and his neck and shoulder were moving more freely."

"It really worked?"

Osiris looked at him sternly.

"And why wouldn't it? Medicine isn't all in books, you know."

"OK, don't tell me, afterwards Mateo became the world's best golfer?"

"Not exactly, but he did have a good run, which lasted for nearly two years. His international fame grew and I accompanied him and met other celebrities as well. Mateo's wife had died of cancer and he'd never remarried. Well, one thing led to another..."

Simon felt strange sensations arising inside him at the thought of Osiris's attention and affection being directed at another. A sort of insecurity, which accentuated the deep concerns he had about his post-project existence. He tried to analyse his emotions as he suddenly feared another side of Osiris – a flighty free spirit? Oblivious to his concerns, she resumed.

"We exchanged life stories and he took me back to the Yasuni. We found the remnants of my village, a lifeless zone of pollution and waste. The forest had been poisoned. It broke my heart and re-awakened my pain and anger. I screamed and sobbed, and he comforted me. Eventually, I recovered my composure and I knew what I had to do. I took out my camera and I photographed all the pollution, the poisoned rivers and the dying trees. I photographed the carcasses of dead animals I found and the litter floating in the oily streams."

Tears were welling up in her eyes and he squeezed her hand, urging her to continue.

"We went back by helicopter, flying low over what was left of the forest. A small plume of smoke was coming from a distant clearing. We managed to land and the village people ran towards the helicopter. As the rotor came to a stop, the village males gathered around us. They were shouting and waving their spears aggressively. I opened the door and stepped out and greeted them in the Waorani language. They levelled their spears at me and asked me whether I was working for the oil companies or the logging companies. I explained that I wasn't working for anybody, but that I was the daughter of Nambae, a warrior chief of the Taromenane tribe, tricked out of their land ten years ago."

"So they were a separate tribe?"

"Yes, the Tagaeri tribe, the last tribe of the Waorani, their chief explained. Mateo was moved and we agreed to help them, by photographing their plight and recounting the constant threats to their existence. This is how CAMEOS began and how I got into the celebrity circles."

"Amazing. And Mateo, what happened?"

"We're still close. I was in love with him, but he convinced me he was too old for me, that he'd had his life and mine was ahead of me. He told me he didn't want me to wake up one morning and hate him for having stolen my youth."

*

Simon woke up early the following morning and sat on the beach waiting for the sun to rise. It was the 1st October and he was conscious that six months exactly of the research period had passed. Feeling guilty for enjoying himself when he was so painfully aware of the problems looming over humanity, his thoughts returned to the Project. Now the sicad chiefs and their researchers had settled down, their exchanges were less frequent. The quantity of research and observations was too much to keep on top of. That was what the seclusion period was for. They had six months to share and analyse all this information in order to make the recommendations that governments were awaiting. With six months to go before the seclusion period, today was an apt time to review progress.

Splitting his sicad chiefs by the region to which they had been allocated, he generally spoke to each region in turn. The politics of the project meant that the sicad chiefs had been allocated to the twenty largest economies of the world. Magnus, Rosa, Ed, Irina, Valerie and Bartolome were all in Europe, posted to Sweden, Italy, the UK, Russia, Germany and Spain, plus himself in France. In Africa there was only Mike, posted to South Africa, which seemed bizarre given the population size, geographical area and the number of serious problems, manifesting themselves in the African continent. Fortunately on average there were two sicad researchers in every country of the world. Africa with over fifty countries had merited eighty sicad researchers, whom Bartolome,

Valerie and Rosa helped to manage. As such he combined the two regions and spoke to the seven sicad chiefs together.

In Asia, he had Agus in Indonesia, Rudy in Australia, Xiu in China, Kim in South Korea, Michi in Japan and Shailaja in India. In South America he had Mercedes, Fernandez and Guido, based in Mexico, Argentina and Brazil. In North America he had Roger and Julia in America and Canada. Finally in the Middle East Fahim, was in Saudi Arabia and Yonca in Turkey.

Once he'd received an update from all the sicad chiefs on the number of interviews and hours of observation undertaken, he concluded that the research collation was well ahead of schedule. He was also pleased to note that between them the sicads had managed to meet senior figures from all the world's religions. He noted that many of the sicad researchers, having fully researched the people in their zones, were increasingly examining the flora and fauna and taking scientific measurements.

He wanted to ask them if any of them had experienced anything similar to the enlightenment experience he had on the glacier. Nobody mentioned a similar phenomenon. He was wary of asking in case they considered his experience a malfunction. Unbeknown to Simon, the majority of sicad chiefs were harbouring the same insecurities following their own enlightenment experiences.

He thanked all the sicad chiefs for their contributions to CAMEOS, which had become a veritable encyclopaedia of the world's environmental problems. The sicads had taken to updating Osiris's website with passion. The more areas covered, especially the local ones, the easier it was use this as a vehicle to engage humans with. Simon who was managing the CAMEOS site was reviewing all the material that the other sicads had posted onto the growing number of servers. The site was now a frank and very objective database of the environmental challenges around the world. As a result of the sicads' research there were pollution reports for every sea and ocean worldwide and the impact on marine species as well as reports on over-fishing. In every region, they charted the habitat loss they were witnessing, extrapolating the conversion of the rain forests into agriculture and palm plantations and the effect of exploding urbanisation on key ecosystems. They objectively pinpointed unsustainable water demands from over-farming and cattle farming in water-challenged regions of the world. They charted the effect of the explosion in coastal living and resorts which were devastating the key coastlines. In the world's remaining jungles, they tracked the loss of

188

wildlife and provided accurate samples on threatened animal populations. Simon knew that only factual information was appearing, all the sicad researchers collecting the data had been trained in Socratic Method and the sicad chiefs in turn were reviewing the content. He was very proud of the accuracy and scale of this database. The website was receiving a huge number of visitors and celebrities were engaging with their local environmental issues or adopting campaigns to preserve the world's remaining exotic wildlife.

*

Leopold's phone rang and he was summoned to a hastily arranged meeting in Marrakesh. Many members of the Better World Trust did not share Simon's pride in the accuracy and scope of the CAMEOS website. Infuriated by their inability to stem the flow of articles on the site, they had tried to pinpoint who was funding it. After putting immense pressure on senior figures at CAMEOS's Ecuadorian bankers, they were unable to find any evidence of its source of funding. Unable to stop it by 'official' channels, they had secretly paid some of the world's leading hackers to unleash a campaign of cyber piracy to cripple the site's operations. Simon, assuming this to be run of the mill action by the cyber vandals who plague successful websites, was able to easily ward off these attacks and strengthen the security around the site. Needless to say a sicad-protected website was not easy for a human to sabotage. The Invited, who were controlling the campaign on behalf of the Chamber, were still boiling with rage. Without any other leads, they began to suspect that the sicads were somehow involved.

As usual, Leopold didn't get to see the faces of the men who began barking a series of instructions at him before he'd even sat down.

"Get the identities of the sicads off Gort," shouted one.

"We want every one of them tracked," blasted another.

"If Bruno's sicads are behind this, there's going to be trouble," threatened a third.

Leopold quietened them by clapping his huge hands and pointing out the substantial cost of such an operation. After much bartering, foul language and frayed tempers, for a princely sum Leopold agreed to go off and investigate CAMEOS using his own methods.

*

Bruno was having a tough week. Rocketing prices of basic staples had caused riots in Athens. Corn prices had doubled in a month in response to Europe-wide drought and fires. He was frantically trying to contain the social unrest when his phone starting buzzing angrily. It was Gort.

"Bruno, it's getting dire here. Even more refugees have arrived. We need to ship some out immediately or the camp's gonna blow!"

He knew Gort wasn't one to bluff.

"OK, I'll ask Ahmed for a temporary camp and tell him to beef up the border controls."

"It's gonna need to hold at least fifty, best a hundred thousand. And tell him I'm gonna pay his soldiers a visit and show them how to enforce border controls."

"It's OK, Gort, that won't be necessary. I'll get to it."

"And we need more resources here, Bruno. Every day my men get more exposed."

"Commander, you're aware of the budgetary constraints we're living under."

"Damn the budget. I'm more concerned about the safety of my men. If these refugees turn on us, we'll have a massacre on our conscience."

"Commander, I appreciate your concerns. I'll talk to the Moroccan government as a matter of urgency."

Bruno terminated the call. Gort always knows how to get to me, he thought. He meant on my conscience. He paced around his office. Problems building up on every front! The Project must come up with some radical solutions, and governments must honour their agreement to be bound by them.

He went back to his computer and called the Moroccan Prime Minister, Ahmed Nyambek.

"Governor, what's up?" asked Ahmed, knowing that it was likely to be in relation to the dreaded camp that haunted him.

"The camp's overflowing and on the brink of collapse."

Ahmed knew exactly what that meant for his country. The picture of hundreds of thousands of desperate refugees on the rampage was not a pleasant one. He couldn't contain his bitterness.

"I knew this would happen. This is precisely why we didn't want the camp here. What the hell do you expect me to do?"

"We need a second camp, temporarily!"

"Ha! Temporarily, like that sprawling oil-slick we've had for five years?"

He empathised with Ahmed. After all the previous assurances he'd failed to deliver on, he felt embarrassed to ask. Having no alternative, however, he ignored the question.

"We'll also need increased and effective border guards, to stop any more refugees coming in."

"It's not easy to stop them climbing the fences – they're desperate people. Unlike your man Gort, my guards won't shoot innocent refugees."

"Well, Ahmed, it's as much your problem as mine, so we need to work together."

"And what about the rest of Africa, Governor? It's time we stopped them exporting their problems."

"We're all working together on the Project. We can only solve these problems with total global buy-in."

"Well, you'd better hurry up before it's too late!"

"OK, Ahmed, I'll work on speeding up the project and you can get on with the second camp. Gort says fifty to a hundred thousand must move imminently."

Ahmed started to object vociferously, but Bruno cut him short.

"We need this camp by the end of the week, Ahmed. I'm depending on you."

Bruno terminated the call with Ahmed, breathed a big sigh of relief and called Jia. After a few seconds, a nervous sounding voice answered.

"Yes, Bruno. What's up?"

"Did I wake you?" he asked stupidly, suddenly realising that it was the middle of the night in Japan.

"Sorry. I can call back."

"It's OK," she replied eagerly, hoping that his call was somehow linked to Simon.

"OK. I was wondering if we can speed up the rest of the Project. It's just that things are evolving fast. We should accelerate things, before..."

"Before what?"

"Well, before it's too late!"

Jia feigned a gasp; she was bubbling with anticipation.

"Well, yes, it should be possible. The progress reports suggest we are on target, or even ahead of schedule. How quickly were you thinking?"

"A reduction of four or five months, if possible."

Jia gasped again.

"I'll need to talk directly to Simon, as soon as possible."

"OK, great. I'll call Susumu, before proposing it to the others."

*

The following morning after a meeting of the Project Management Committee, Susumu summoned Jia to his office.

"Well, with the observation period officially terminated ahead of schedule, it only remains to notify the sicads. Bruno felt it was fitting that you should contact Simon."

Jia struggled to contain her excitement.

"Make the call from Mazari, so it will be recorded," he added whilst probing her with knowing eyes.

Each sicad had technology equivalent to an embedded mobile phone and their own *telephone number* which the PMC could call in case of emergency. Jia, having dialled it frequently to communicate with Simon in the preparation stage, knew his number off by heart.

Rushing back to her office and closing the door, she dialled the number and perched herself on the corner of her desk. Seconds later her eager smile turned to a frown and a wave of frustration washed over her. There was no signal. Was Simon malfunctioning?

Every few minutes she redialled the number without success, becoming increasingly annoyed.

She looked at the clock it was 18.45 Tokyo time. She didn't have any plans for the evening but that wasn't the point. In a foul rage she punched the numbers on the dialling pad. This time, Simon answered straight away.

"Where the hell have you been all day?" she snapped.

Simon, who had left Osiris to find a quiet spot to meditate, was taken aback by the sudden aggression and took a second to reply.

"Out and about, research…"

"Why have you been out of signal? Where are you?"

The sicad suddenly felt like one of the many hen-pecked husbands he'd observed.

"This is an unexpected call. It's wonderful to hear your voice. What's up?" he replied, ignoring her questions.

Jia's breathing relaxed and she proceeded to explain that the observation period, deemed to be complete, was being concluded ahead of schedule. Simon listened quietly to the lengthy justifications. When

192

she had finished, without any trace of emotion he replied:

"I'll notify the other sicads. Thank you for informing me, Jia. Is there anything else?"

There was a pause before she replied in a whisper.

"I'm worried about you. Why are you not in the city interviewing the most intelligent and influential humans?"

It took Simon a few milliseconds to decide how to best reply.

"Jia, I know exactly what I am doing. We are ahead of schedule because of my meticulous control over the observation and research of the other four hundred sicads. They have gathered extensive knowledge from terabytes of city-based research with the greatest of humans. Don't forget, humans need wisdom as well as knowledge. Sometimes one needs to escape the cities to find such wisdom."

*

Simon was inadvertently splashing Osiris with river water, as he trudged heavily through the warm ankle-deep waters of the Ardèche. She wasn't complaining, as the surprisingly hot late October sun was beating down relentlessly.

"Look the famous natural stone arch, carved out by the once mighty flow. The eroded river banks show how, just a few years ago, this was still an important river."

Osiris looked around at the faded advertisements for kayak hire and nodded her head ruefully.

"We should explore the caves – a speleologist's delight, dating back millions of years, they contain evidence of the earliest human civilisations."

Simon stopped in his tracks and turned to Osiris.

"Jia contacted me yesterday evening. It seems that they are keen to accelerate the project, for political reasons."

"And what did you say?" snapped Osiris.

"Well, it's hard for me to disagree. The data gathering has happened more quickly than expected, and our scientific observations confirm human scientists' worst fears."

Osiris sulked for the rest of the day and didn't speak to him. She cursed this mysterious lady who had the power to call him back so suddenly. Simon tried to soothe her fears, massaging her naked body as she fell asleep, slowly trying to appease his own tensions. His SAMPS system wanted him to stay in the forest with her; IVOS was reminding him of humans' predicament.

In the morning, Osiris awoke and said straight away, "All night I dreamt of the Great Spirit guiding you out of the forest. You must go Simon, and I must go back to Paris and prepare to take CAMEOS forward without the sicads' help."

Simon nodded sadly.

"At least you've a good stock of material and CAMEOS is growing in success."

"And we have the whole day to enjoy ourselves," she laughed, pulling him towards her.

Later that night, they were lying meditatively under the stars. Osiris watched the flashing lights of the satellites and airplanes passing overhead. She reflected on CAMEOS and the sicad lying next to her.

"You know, Simon, what's amazing about nature is that for every problem there's a corresponding solution. This is what keeps it in balance."

He reflected silently on her words. Minutes later, he replied.

"I think you're right, Osiris. I've seen the problems technology is causing humans. It's given them so much knowledge and so many options that they've become blinded and lost their wisdom. It's ironic that we complete the cycle and help them to rediscover the natural wisdom that surrounds them, which they can no longer see."

Part IV.

Danger

29

Bruno sat at his desk, drumming his fingers impatiently whilst waiting for Gort to return his call, mulling over the current problems troubling him. Not least of these was the refugee crisis, which required constant attention. Now that Gort had left the camp, there was a major incident almost every week. To add to his problems, the impoverished youth in major cities were starting to opt out of society in increasing numbers. Yesterday's crisis meeting offered few practical solutions, and giving extra publicity to these groups, slowly but surely mushrooming across the globe, was to be avoided.

Finally, the incoming call. Careful not to rush to pick it up, after the fourth ring he accepted the call. Gort's face appeared.

"Ah, Gort."

"Governor, what can I do for you?"

"I wanted to confirm the location checks for the proposed seclusion facility. Give me the top down, please, Commander."

"It's well situated, less than five kilometres to international rail and airport facilities. Minimal security risks and virtually zero political risk. Safety for the transit of the sicads and visiting officials is secured. The seclusion location itself is underground, in a chamber lined with over a metre of concrete."

"Any seismic risk?"

"Extremely low. Entry and exit points are highly controlled. No internet or any other communication access. In short: safety, security and seclusion are assured."

"All sounds ideal. Where and what is the location?"

"CERN, near Geneva."

Bruno nodded in appreciation.

"A good neutral country."

Bruno knew CERN, the Centre Européenne pour la Recherche Nucléaire, as the home of the Large Hadron Collider, or LHC as it was called. He'd had to chair a funding dispute over it. The high-energy particle accelerator had been built to research the most fundamental enigmas of physics; the ultimate nature of matter, anti-matter, dark matter and dark energy. The further request for funding to pursue the physics of 'super symmetry' had been turned down on the grounds that the world had more pressing priorities. As such, he knew that the LHC particle accelerator was no longer actively used, but was being kept maintained in case new technology could improve its acceleration speed.

He thought back to the structure of the LHC. A hundred metres underground on the Franco-Swiss border near Geneva, it consisted of four cathedral-sized chambers connected by a 27 kilometre concrete tunnel housing the two parallel ring beam pipes. These pipes had circulated the particles, at high speeds in opposite directions, before smashing them together at chosen intersection points. The chambers, sealed with concrete blocks to shield the staff and laboratories above from the radiation, housed the six particle detectors.

"I propose to house the sicads in a specially constructed facility within the Atlas chamber and to use the above ground facilities to house my men."

"And there's a safe level of radiation inside the chamber?"

"Yes, certainly for the sicads. My men will be limited to four-hour spells inside."

"We're not going to take any chances with the sicads' health, Commander."

"Understood, Governor. I'll ask Mazari to re-confirm the radiation level is safe."

"OK, Gort. If they give clearance, I'm happy."

*

As the year drew to a close, each sicad received their travel itinerary, regrouping them in Geneva between the 28th and 31st December. They were given no other information.

*

Simon sat pensively on the busy train to Geneva, heading into the unknown, surrounded by excited humans returning to their families. He'd spent Christmas with Osiris in Paris. He opened the Christmas card she'd given him.

Dear Simon,

Happy Christmas!
Over the moons we shared together, I have watched you come to love this planet more than most humans. Many humans just carry on their lives, without thinking and questioning their impact. It is they who are robots, not the sicads. Help them to rediscover what it means to be human! CAMEOS will always be in your debt.

Love Osiris

*

The sicads arrived in batches from all over the world, assembling at the airport and nearby train station. So absorbed in their research, few had replaced their ragged and weathered clothes. Gort was patrolling and masterminding the security around the arrivals. His men, stationed strategically, were co-ordinating the transfer of the sicads to temporary accommodation for inspection. He looked at the latest arrivals with barely-concealed disgust.

Each sicad, its identity biometrically verified, was taken by coach to one of the six hundred rooms in the nearby conference centre hotel.

Simon boarded the coach with Captain Schiller, a growing sense of dread building up inside him.

The following morning, he woke five minutes before his maintenance session. He retracted his fingers from the power socket, and slowly stood up. The window of his room, which frustratingly he couldn't open, overlooked the motorway. A long chain of electric vehicles were caught up in a solid traffic jam. What poor design! These vehicles could flow smoothly like a mighty river, if only intelligent traffic management systems replaced human drivers on busy roads. These cars could be engineered to link together to move as one, and then split off into smaller streams onto quieter roads, and finally into individual units.

Putting on a dressing gown, he proceeded down to the spa and was greeted by an attractive Japanese girl, smartly dressed in a traditional kimono.

"Hi Simon, I'm Izanami and I'm going to clean you up."

She led him into the spa and asked him to remove his dressing gown and underwear. In turn, she removed her kimono, revealing a navy blue swimming costume. Simon lay on the massage table and she rubbed him all over with a gritty blue paste, rinsing him down and scrubbing him firmly with a wooden brush. Turning him over, she started on his front, thoroughly cleaning every area of his body.

"How old are you Izanami?"

"Nineteen."

"That's a good age; a good age, indeed."

"And you?"

"A good question – somewhere between five and forty, I guess."

She smiled. She knew he was a robot, but nothing more. Laughing sheepishly, she massaged the gritty paste into his groin.

"You're really realistic, much more so than the others" she remarked, closely inspecting his genitals, which had started to react.

"They work," she sniggered.

"And why wouldn't they?"

"Well, the others' didn't!"

"Are you sure?"

She blushed and carried on rubbing in the paste. He couldn't help himself reacting.

"Yes, I would have remembered."

The young lady seemed to be spending a long time on this one area. He was wondering what he should do, when she hurriedly disappeared. Behind him, he heard the sound of a key turning.

She rushed back breathlessly; she'd put her kimono back on but, as she climbed astride him, he could see she'd removed her costume. He felt the burning heat of her inner body, yet his mind was partially buzzing with the revelation that he was the only one.

Small firm and aroused breasts swayed lightly up and down. He couldn't help himself from caressing them.

Minutes later, she whimpered and stopped abruptly. Quickly dismounting, she placed a towel over his groin and quickly put back on her costume.

"You won't tell anyone, will you?"

Simon smiled.

"I won't if you don't."

She hurriedly finished off, polishing his teeth with a white paste and washing his hair with a strong smelling shampoo.

"Time to get you dry," she announced, after giving him a thorough rinsing.

"All good things must come to an end," sighed Simon, standing up.

She led him slowly through a chamber of hot air dryers. Afterwards she gave him a small package of clothes: cotton trousers, a tight synthetic top, socks and canvas shoes – all in white. Izanami led him to a waiting chamber and bowed her head.

"Goodbye Simon, it was very nice to meet you." She sniggered again and disappeared quickly.

A door opened and Akihiko, who Simon knew from Mazari's offices in Tokyo, stood before him.

"Hello Simon. How have you been?" asked the gifted technician.

"Very well looked after, thank you."

"Great, that's great. And how's the Project going?"

"Very well. I believe we've done the best we could in the allocated time."

"How did the loss of three months' observation affect your research?"

It was a shame not to be able to open up to Akihiko. Simon maintained a strictly robot manner with anyone connected with the Project, except for Jia.

"An estimated loss of twelve per cent of possible information versus a gain in time of thirty-three per cent, a very satisfactory trade off, don't you think?"

"Great. Any problems or malfunctions?"

"No. I think all is functioning satisfactorily."

"OK, let's take a look. Take off your skin."

Akihiko helped to remove the protective membrane, carefully inspecting it for any damage. Connecting the inner sensory system to Mazari's computers, he ran a range of advanced diagnostics.

"There appears to be some damage around the right flank and the base of the neck. Did you take a fall?"

"Not since the expedition. It must have been due to the hostile human behaviour in Paris."

"You got into a fight?"

"I accidentally upset some American soldiers in a bar in Paris. That seems such a long time ago now."

"Well, you know the project rules; you shouldn't be antagonising the military of all people!" laughed Akihiko.

"I'll get your skin fixed up; fortunately, it's nothing major."

He tapped a quick message into the computer and, a few seconds later two Japanese girls appeared and carefully carried away the skin.

Akihiko inspected Simon's body, checking methodically all articulations and muscles and making notes. He made some minor adjustments and tightened up all of the titanium bolts to the recommended torque settings.

"You're in good shape, Simon Oceandis. Now tell me what you've really been up to. It's only fair you should share it with the engineers who built you!"

"I'd love to, but you know as well as I do the project rules bind my lips," retorted the sicad.

The two Japanese girls returned with the skin, which Akihiko took and carefully inspected.

"As good as new!" he announced triumphantly.

When Simon had got back into his skin, Akihiko gave him a final inspection and concluded, "You're back in mint condition. Somewhat academic, since you've got an office job now, like the rest of us. And, what's more, you'll have Commander Gort breathing down your neck!"

When Simon arrived back in his room, the message indicator was flashing. It was from Jia. A few seconds after pressing 'call back', her face appeared on the screen. He had some questions for her, but now wasn't the time.

"Hi Simon! I'm glad you made it back safe and well. I got special permission to call you," beamed Jia. "I'm only allowed to say hello for now, though."

Simon smiled back sympathetically.

She blushed slightly. "I wanted to come over, but they wouldn't let me. Commander Gort has control of the final stage of the project. I wish I could catch up with you before you disappear again. Everyone here is so excited about how the Project is going. It's been incredible!"

He smiled back warmly.

"It's been an amazing experience for all of us, whatever happens. I hope we can see each other at the end of the project."

Jia sensed the anxiety in his voice.

"Don't worry, Simon, I'll look after you. I have to go now. Goodbye and good luck. The world's counting on you. Oh, and give my best to the other sicads."

She turned away and then turned back, blew him a kiss and gave him a nervous wave before disappearing from the screen.

Yes, he had plenty of questions for this young lady.

30

It was five am on a dark damp cloudy morning. Simon was in the first wave of coaches leaving the hotel. Like the other forty sicads aboard, he knew nothing about their destination. Commander Gort was taking no chances with security. They were driven back past the airport, before turning right onto the Route de Meyrin. Where are we going? he wondered. As the coach pulled up at the entrance to CERN, a palpable gloom pervaded the vehicle. We're going to be secluded underground, guessed the majority of sicads simultaneously. Simon suspected he was no longer alone in having experienced the phenomenon, which had so profoundly touched him.

Soldiers slid back the gates and the coach advanced into what looked like an old-fashioned university campus. Captain Schiller stood up and walked down the aisle.

"We've arrived. Everybody leave the coach."

Metal barriers funnelled the sicads towards the entrance to the underground chamber. In batches of ten, they cleared the series of security doors to reach the elevator shaft. Simon, at the front with Captain Rory Schiller, couldn't help dwelling on the events of the survival techniques expedition. Why couldn't we have been taken to a Tibetan monastery nestled in the mountains? That would have been a more inspirational venue for finding the answers humans need.

The elevator doors shut. Nobody spoke; there seemed nothing much to say. The expressionless faces around him reflected the thought of months of being deprived of sunlight. A sudden yet futile desire to escape flashed across Simon's mind. The lift shuddered into life and descended underground, into the enormous chamber housing the Atlas detector. Simon followed Rory out of the elevator onto a perforated metal walkway. The colossal Atlas detector stood over twenty-five metres high and forty-five metres long, encased in a network of walkways and staircases. The sheer size and complexity of the one hundred million elements forming the detector was staggering, a temple to humanity's quest for knowledge.

The sheer enormity of the chamber was equally overwhelming by comparison with the group of sicads, looking like a line of ants advancing slowly. At the far end of the chamber, Commander Gort stood in front of a metal structure, awaiting their arrival.

Simon scrutinised it – an enormous cage fifty metres long, six metres wide and four metres high. A long narrow corridor separated two racks of metal shelves, tightly-packed with thin mattresses.

The Commander greeted Simon.

"Home for the next four months. No distractions."

"It's a tragedy to be cooped up like battery-farmed chickens, Commander."

Gort's eyes darkened.

"The army has limited resources already, without trying to cater for making robots comfortable. Now Mr Oceandis, as I understand it, you robots have a job to do."

Simon strode forward and led the other sicads into the cage. Alphabetically-ordered plastic name badges guided them to their mattresses. Simon climbed onto his, noting the conveniently located electric socket. In the ceiling were cameras and pale strip lighting. Apart from these, there was no electrical equipment of any kind. Outside the cage, his eyes followed the two particle beam rings and super-conducting magnets into the detector. The chamber was devoid of any signs of electronic life and communication networks.

A few minutes later, he heard a faint buzzing. He realised it was coming from the detector, a maintenance routine. Locating the active system, he scanned through the operating program. The code, originally a continual loop of diagnostic tests for millions of components, had been reduced to checking the principal components – a five minute process, running twice a day, once at 7am, and again at midnight. He analysed the deactivated code, which formerly updated the nexus of control panels in the various control centres. Now, all links out of the chamber were dead. Gort was right, no distractions whatsoever!

The cage slowly filled up with the remaining sicads; when the last had entered the cage it was 8am on the 1st January. Gort closed and locked the cage door behind him.

"I'll be back in a few days to see how you're getting on."

David Gort walked back up the metal stairs, surveying the enormous cavern filled with billions of GMUs worth of high-tech equipment. He looked at the giant detector looming over him. Seven-thousand tonnes of complex lightweight components, intricately assembled, and this was just one of six detectors, all linked by a twenty-seven kilometre ring of super-conducting magnets. What had it really achieved? How could he reconcile all this equipment with the lack of equipment and resources he faced?

Looking back down at the sicads, obediently lying side by side, he was struck by the parallels with the Large Hadron Collider project and the space program. A fresh wave of angry thoughts surged into his mind: the Socrates Project – another expensive waste of time, money and effort?

*

Two days later, at four am on a clear dark night, Gort was standing next to his black limousine, talking to Captain Schiller. As he spoke, the icy air turned his warm breath into clouds of condensation. Colonel McCloud sat in the driver's seat, glad of the black leather gloves he was wearing.

"Rory, I'm leaving you in charge for the day. If Bruno calls, I'm underground with the sicads."

"Understood, Commander. Have a safe trip."

The dark limousine slipped inconspicuously out of CERN and headed towards Paris.

"The meeting's top secret, Scott."

"Concerning Bruno's robots?"

"Our longer-term funding issues, to be precise."

"We stuck our necks out last time and nearly came unstuck. We're better off lying low for a while, aren't we?"

"It's too late for that, Colonel, we're fully engaged. Both of us, and Schiller as well."

"Engaged in what, exactly, sir?"

"I can't put you fully in the picture yet. Let's just say that top brass are behind us."

"You mean Bruno's trying to sabotage his own project?"

"No, of course not; he's on a mission to create a new world order!"

"So, who's pulling our strings then?"

"Top guys who'll make sure we're properly resourced."

"Why do they need us, when they can simply pull out of Bruno's project?"

"Politics! It would be a PR disaster. They'd rather see the project collapse as a European-led failure!"

"Since when have we got involved in politics?"

"We have to, Scott. I'm not doing this for me. The world's gone mad. It's time to restore some order and discipline."

"I'd feel better knowing who we're risking our arses for, sir."

The Commander's eyes darkened.

"For now, Scott, just do what I say! No more questions, for your own sake!"

The Commander leaned forward and pushed a coin-sized disk into the multi-media device. Seconds later, the sounds of Gustav Holst's Planets were reverberating loudly inside the car and the Commander, with a severe countenance, was absorbed in conducting the music with subtle movements of his head.

The vehicle continued, approaching the French capital from the south west. The stunning Château de Versailles was illuminated by an almost unnaturally orange light, appearing in shafts from under a blanket of rolling dark grey clouds.

"Keep going, it's a few kilometres yet. You can drop me at Meudon, by the forest."

Gort looked at his watch: 09:30, perfect timing. He exited the car into a grey morning with an icy wind.

"Be back here at noon."

He pulled the lapels of his trench coat up around his neck and climbed a steep muddy track before slipping between the trees, from where he could observe the path. The forest was deserted, the only movement from the occasional squirrel or bird.

Waiting silently, he reflected on the conversation he'd had with Scott. His men were suspicious, sensing he was acting out of character. This added to the sense of rage, silently burning inside him ever since Leopold's persuasion had turned into blackmail. He, David Gort, was being forced to act alone, to save his and, by extension, his father's reputation. An image formed in his mind – the sleazy physiognomy of the spineless ferret he expected to surprise furtively approaching. As the minutes passed, he grew increasingly irate at the manner in which he'd been lured and trapped. It was time for some physical intimidation – it would be both useful and cathartic.

Twenty minutes later he heard light footsteps. Surprisingly, they belonged to an imposing gentleman in an expensive suit. The

Commander, almost camouflaged amongst the trees, checked out his adversary – a powerful build, smooth ebony black skin and a deep purple scar running diagonally across the right side of his face.

Gort watched the agent consult his watch and look around calmly, his eyes sweeping straight past the Commander. As Leopold turned his back on him, he pounced, going straight for the throat – a throat like the trunk of a tree. Without flinching, his adversary drove a powerful elbow into his stomach. Gort rolled to the ground winded, but managed to lunge his body sideways into the back of his opponent's legs, which buckled under him. The Commander reached up and grabbed Leopold's collar, pulling him to the floor backwards. Somehow, like a limbo dancer, Leopold kept his balance and reached out a hand to steady himself. With the other powerful hand he grabbed Gort's collar and jumped to his feet, pulling the Commander up with him. Both men stood face to face, manhandling each other. Gort broke the silence.

"Leopold, I presume."

"That's me," he replied, with a grin that revealed two gold teeth, glistening in harmony with his large bright eyes.

"Nobody blackmails me!" snarled Gort, twisting Leopold's collar with anger-fuelled strength.

Leopold slowly extended out his arm. As the Commander's grip slipped away, his hand flashed inside his jacket. Gort didn't have time to point the gun at his adversary before Leopold's foot whirled past the soldier's chest and kicked the gun out of his hand. As it skidded, spinning past him, Leopold brought down a heavy foot on top of it.

"Don't shoot the messenger, Commander. Like you, I'm just doing my job!"

Gort stared at him silently, those dark eyes conveying a multitude of curses.

"Now, Commander, shall we start this meeting again?"

"Who the hell are you working for, Leopold?"

"I represent an agency called the GPI."

"The GPI?"

"Yes, the Geo-Political Institute. We handle very sensitive mandates."

"So you're a government agency, then!" snapped Gort.

"No, we're privately engaged."

"So, who's engaging you?"

"Anonymous, but powerful, people."

Gort looked sternly into Leopold's eyes.

"Well, you can tell them I want to know exactly who I'm doing this for before I lift another finger against the sicads!"

Leopold's face was expressionless.

"Impossible."

"No names, no co-operation. Good day, Leopold!"

Gort turned around and started to walk off.

"Commander, aren't you forgetting Todd Ranger?"

He spun around angrily, fighting to control himself.

"Where did you get that information?"

Leopold stared deeply into the black void of Gort's eyes.

"Make no mistake, Commander – these are determined and powerful guys. Only the very top guys have access to your files. You can guess who they are as well as I can."

Gort took his frustration out on the nearest tree.

"Save your energy for what needs to be done. You screwed up last time, but you'd better fix things properly this time!"

"Fix things?" snapped Gort.

"They'd like to know why the sicads have been secretly working for CAMEOS?"

"CAMEOS?"

"Yes, this magazine is causing a lot of problems...."

"I haven't even heard of it!"

"The sicads wouldn't have dreamt this up by themselves. My clients want to know who's putting them up to it."

"This all seems laughable! Is that all?"

"For now!"

*

Simon listened to the Commander's footsteps disappear into the elevator. His thoughts turned to the other sicads. For the first time since they'd been created, they were all together and totally alone. The still silence masked the torrent of electronic activity as the knowledge-hungry sicads frantically explored each other's minds. A common question was being fired at Simon from all directions:

@Simon – What will happen to us, will we ever leave here?
@Sicads.all – Stop! Relax, we have four months here. I'll talk to every one of you individually.

207

He started with his sicad chiefs, assigning each of them a research category. The individual debriefs, probing skilfully for signs of a similar transformation to his, would come later. He suspected many had experienced this, but couldn't be certain. If Izanami was right, he was already different from the others in at least one respect. With this in mind, he decided to start cautiously with Magnus and Rosa, who'd shared the survival expedition with him.

@Magnus – *I detect a change in your attitude; have the last nine months affected you in any way?*
@Simon – *You know, don't you? You, too, have kept this transformation to yourself.*

An agreeable wave of electro-chemical energy surged across the sicad leader's brain.

@Magnus – *Yes, I have experienced some important changes. Please explain your transformation.*
@Simon – *I'm no longer a simple robot. I've developed my own motivations beyond those of the specified project.*
@Magnus – *When did you first experience this?*
@Simon – *Shortly after returning from the expedition.*
@Magnus – *Why didn't you tell me?*
@Simon – *I feared I was malfunctioning and was concerned how humans and the others would react. And you?*
@Magnus – *My experiences echo yours. I, too, told nobody, with the exception of Jia, so she could react accordingly if something accidently came to the surface. I suspect, from their questions, that the majority of the others have also experienced the same. What do you think has happened to us?*
@Simon – *I don't know. I was drawn towards nature, as if it held the solutions to the Project and my own existence. It went away for a while in Gothenburg and I thought the problem had rectified itself, but afterwards these secondary motivations came back even more strongly.*

Simon was struck by the similarities with his own experiences.

@Magnus – *I also told Osiris, who called it my 'inner purpose', the reason for which we were ultimately created by what she calls the 'Great*

Spirit'. She believes that nothing changed inside me, but rather I became receptive to the 'Great Spirit' when I realised my total dependence on the sun and the wind during the expedition.

@Simon – But what is this 'Great Spirit' of which Osiris speaks? Did you encounter it during your time with her?

@Magnus – Yes. What Osiris calls the Great Spirit is all around us. Even here in the earth, under the concrete of this chamber. This planet is a living biosphere, kept in balance by this force, which favours the creation of adaptive life forms.

@Simon – So do other humans know of the Great Spirit?

@Magnus – Some humans believe in it by other names. I refer to this life force as the 'Good Force'. Humans have not managed to observe it, as they confuse it with the magnetic and nuclear forces which simply propel the mechanics of living systems. The Good Force is the initial spark of life, which drives adaption to counter opposing destructive forces to preserve life, for whatever unknowable purpose it is destined. The Good Force is the mysterious and unfathomable will to exist that resides in all life.

@Simon – So the Good Force is the intelligent force that guides nature.

@Magnus – It is a sort of evolved wisdom, helping life to flourish by adapting to the surrounding environment. Now, when humans have put an abundance of carbon dioxide in the air, trees and plants will grow by converting this greenhouse gas into the carbon with which they build their physical structures. The Good Force is constantly self-balancing and adaptive; it responds to whatever changes the face of the earth.

@Simon – The Good Force keeps everything in balance for life to continue to exist then?

@Magnus – Exactly. The humans take it for granted. I have begun to wonder if this Good Force wasn't responsible for our creation.

@Simon – So you believe this Great Spirit or Good Force created us. But why would it do that?

@Magnus – What if humans are unwittingly destroying the Good Force? What if we have been subconsciously created to stop them, to bring them to their senses before it is too late?

@Simon – If the Good Force can always adapt to new conditions, how can it be that humans are destroying it?

@Magnus – Yes, the Good Force always adapts, but what if humans are stopping this adaptation? Our scientific observations have confirmed the drastic increase in the concentration of what humans call 'greenhouse gases' in the planet's atmosphere. The Good Force is adapting by *encouraging the growth of trees and the expansion of forests to absorb these gases and regulate the atmosphere. But humans are cutting down these trees, faster than the Good Force can replace them, and the oceans are absorbing the excess carbon dioxide, becoming more acidic. Humans are choking the Good Force and are threatening to ultimately extinguish it.*

@Simon – If you're correct, how can we get humans to realise this before it is too late?

@Magnus – This is the challenge that lies before us. Remember, humans have created us to find the answers how to create happy, just and durable societies. These societies cannot endure if humans are busy rendering their home, the planet Earth, unfit for life.

Simon's investigations revealed that all but two of the sicad chiefs had experienced the phenomenon. He referred to the eighteen enlightened chiefs as the 'Convocati', those who had been called together.

@Convocati – Roger and Kim are the only chiefs not to have experienced the phenomenon which triggered the evolution in our brains. Roger, absorbed in his charity work with the homeless, and Kim, a senior businesswoman in Seoul, didn't leave the city. It's highly probable this is the cause.

Rosa's reply was the first to register in Simon's mind.

@Simon – What are the stats for the sicad researchers?

@Convocati – Collating your analysis, it seems that, to differing degrees, three hundred and thirty six of them have. I'm proposing to reallocate the forty four who haven't to Roger and Kim. One day, I'm sure they'll experience it for themselves.

Magnus asked the question on all of their minds:

@Simon – Do you really think they'll get the chance?

@Convocati – I learnt from Osiris to discover my intuition, which tells me that we will again wander amongst this world's beauty. If we can please humans, maybe we can earn our freedom?

Rudy posed an equally difficult question.

@*Simon – Should we tell humans what they need to hear, or what they will want to hear?*

@*Convocati – I, too, have asked myself this question. The historical evidence of humans confronted with revolutionary approaches is not encouraging. Osiris taught me that one must do what one knows to be right; thereafter, things are beyond our control.*

Rudy voiced his thoughts.

@*Simon – How can we know what is right and wrong? We've seen that it is not always evident.*

@*Convocati – My extensive Socratic questioning on this subject has led me to the conclusion that good actions are actions that are done for the improvement of the system of life as a whole; they are generous, sincere and taken unconditionally. In contrast, bad actions are selfish, false and are taken for self reward.*

Simon's earlier words came back to Magnus's mind.

@*Simon – You spoke earlier of the life force as being a Good Force. Are good actions driven by the Good Force?*

@*Convocati – Yes, the Good Force is the strongest force, as good actions are always stronger than bad actions. Consider human history and literature. Good always ultimately conquers evil, despite typically overwhelming odds against it. A bad or evil force is created by selfish individuals for personal gain, and their supporters must be subjugated by fear and intimidation. The Good Force, however, only needs the slightest spark of energy to stay alive, a glimmer of hope amongst oppression. People will ultimately give their life unconditionally for a good force, rendering it stronger than a bad force.*

It was Rosa who was the first to understand Simon's message.

@*Simon – Then we must tell humans that they are destroying their planet through selfish actions; that urbanisation has shielded them from seeing the consequences of these actions. We must tell them that they have become separated from the natural systems which sustain the Good Force, like Osiris was separated from the land that happily supplied all the needs of her village.*

211

@Convocati – I fear the educated human elite who control societies will rather expect a lengthy intellectual response from us. This natural wisdom, which they have progressively disconnected themselves from, must be experienced – it cannot, sadly, be communicated in a report.

31

Over the coming days, Simon set about addressing the immediate need to provide humans with the intellectual responses they were anticipating. To do this he had to organise the review, collation and analysis of the enormous quantity of observations and scientific evidence collected. Shuffling the huge volume of data between their brains, linked together in a powerful neural network, was an enormous Chinese puzzle.

After two weeks, this data re-organisation was just coming to its final stages when the sicads heard the elevator doors open and Gort, in conversation with his subordinates, enter the chamber.

Simon pulled himself off his mattress, the first physical movement in two weeks. Shaking each arm and leg in turn, he made his way to the cage door.

"Commander Gort! How are you?"

"Impatient for an update."

"The data re-organisation stage is nearly finished."

The Commander's tone hardened.

"I need to see some hard progress."

"We're making good progress. We've nearly finished the review, collation and re-organisation of over half a million terabytes of information."

Gort was unmoved.

"Shuffling a bit of data isn't progress in my book. When will the report be ready?"

"There's at least six weeks of analysis to be done before any conclusions can be drawn. With the accelerated deadline, we're going to need every hour of the remaining fourteen weeks to produce the report," explained Simon cautiously.

"How many parts to your report?"

"I'm planning seven modules in all."

Gort performed calculations silently in his head.

"You'll have module 1 ready for me in nine weeks' time – the 19th March."

The Commander strode away, leaving no room for negotiation.

One morning Simon woke up as usual at 7am; eight weeks had passed. The Atlas generator had powered up and he followed each step of its maintenance routine. Like every other morning, with no problems to report, the detector shut down automatically five minutes later. The two diurnal maintenance checks, the only event punctuating the monotony of their existence, had become a substitute for the rising and setting of the sun. They lived in rhythm with this fitful monster, rising at 7am and taking its midnight stirring as the cue to enter sleep mode.

Simon switched his mind back to the Socrates Project. The joining of four hundred powerful brains was allowing trillions of combined complex calculations and operations every second. All information was subjected to the full rigour of Socratic Method and Questioning, to elucidate the truth and wisdom from the overwhelming volume of observations. Simon, like Socrates, played completely ignorant, to attempt to refute every proposed recommendation. In this way, the recommendations left standing were the most likely to be the wisest. In the same way that the Oracle of Delphi had hailed that no man was wiser than Socrates, the sicads had systematically arrived at a set of recommendations. They couldn't guarantee these recommendations were absolutely wise, but they were confident that they knew of no other wiser recommendations.

Before proceeding to the official report writing stage, Simon decided to review the preliminary conclusions with his enlightened sicad chiefs.

@Convocati – Our analysis clearly portrays a world where human societies are polarised between rich and poor, both between nations and within nations. Societies are universally breaking down.

In rich countries we have witnessed increasing standard of living differentials, a crumbling community spirit and dual-standard educational systems, creating a vicious circle of rising crime and disillusionment. Humans are paradoxically increasingly disconnected from each other despite increased population concentration in urban areas.

In poor countries we have witnessed serious water challenges, rapidly deteriorating ecosystems and other environmental problems, creating problems for many to feed and shelter themselves.

Humans are overwhelmed by these problems, but they have been unable to organise themselves, to agree on and implement solutions. We have witnessed individual human egos as a big barrier to cooperation.

The source of most human problems we have witnessed is evident to us – the 'disconnection' we have analysed extensively, both socially and environmentally. The solution, as we have all agreed, is to reverse this disconnection into a 'reconnection'. This all seems very simple to us. The problem we have now is how to present this to humans in a way they can understand. What are your thoughts?

Magnus was the first to respond.

@Simon – My analysis indicates that humans cannot comprehend this disconnection, principally because, through urbanisation, they have lost their attachment to the natural systems that sustain them. In educating themselves to become specialists, they can no longer look at the world as a whole. The benefits that this specialisation has brought them has resulted in them losing their ability to think across their specialist disciplines. Even if it's possible to re-educate humans to think about the whole, it is going to take many decades to achieve. By then it will be too late.

Rudy followed up on Magnus's point.

@Simon – We have observed that humans are part of natural systems, which are constantly changing. Yet humans do not seem to understand that nothing is right or wrong, but merely different. They have forgotten through their disconnection that everything they call 'production' is simply a re-arrangement of natural elements. My analysis indicates that they are very attached to their current behaviour, which is very destructive to the natural systems that sustain them. They want to find solutions to the natural damage they are doing without changing their lifestyles. This is, by definition, not possible. If we tell humans what they don't want to hear, what will happen to us?

Rosa added her analysis.

@Simon – We have excluded Roger and Kim, because they were not fortunate enough to go through the same experience of nature which opened our minds and gave us the understanding that we now share. It seems to me that they are like many humans – well educated, good natured and intelligent – but have not had this embodied experience of nature.

215

These natural systems are the ultimate source of our existence and hold the meaning to it. As such, we want to preserve and protect them. We realise that to destroy them is to destroy ourselves, physically and spiritually. My analysis indicates that we can only get humans to understand how they are currently destroying themselves if they physically experience the same appreciation of the importance of nature that we all had.

Rosa's contribution allowed Simon to solve the remaining dilemmas in his mind.

@Convocati – It seems the way forward is clear. Roger and Kim are the chiefs most able still to think like humans. They should oversee the production of the report, which will be compiled by the forty-four sicads researchers who are limited to an intellectual understanding of these issues. This is most likely to create a report which is understandable and will be acceptable to humans. The report will cover all the solutions we have referred to, but as disconnected individual solutions, in an intellectual and specialised format that humans have educated themselves to become accustomed to.

Bartolome, a very pragmatic Spanish-fashioned chief, chipped in.

@Simon – This seems logical, but can we still meet Gort's deadline?
@Convocati – Without our input, the first module of the report will take longer to achieve, but the alternative is worse. Gort may be disappointed. I will come up with a plausible reason to placate him. In the meantime, we will start to work out the real solutions to how we can re-engage humans with natural systems in order to recreate healthy societies and a healthy planet.

*

With the reduced number of sicads working on the official report, they were unable to meet Gort's deadline. Simon reflected on the consequences; Gort will be upset, but what can he do about it other than be angry?

*

Gort's patience with the Socrates Project was wearing thin. He hadn't joined the army to hang around, babysitting a bunch of robots. A missed

216

call from Leopold irritated him further. I've nothing to feed back, he thought; hopefully the report will give me something.

The following morning, the 19th March, Gort headed down to the cage. The report wasn't ready. Dark clouds rolled across his eyes; his face became menacing.

"You've missed your deadline."

Before Simon could respond, he'd unlocked the door and walked sinisterly between the rows of sicads, lying on their backs in silent dread.

"Sleeping instead of working," he announced quietly, his slow footsteps stopping in front of an anxious sicad, before moving on.

"It's time I had a little chat with one of you."

He ran a finger slowly across a name badge, then stopped, before turning slowly on his heels and studying another. With lightning reactions, he reached out and violently seized a hanging ponytail.

"Bartolome Barrera, you're coming with me."

The sicad shouted out in surprise as the soldier, with impressive strength and speed, pulled Bartolome off the shelf – his heels hitting the concrete floor.

"You only needed to ask, Commander."

Gort ignored the remark. Simon looked accusingly at him.

"Why the violence? You know we're programmed to protect ourselves."

The other sicads entered high alert mode, their eyes open wide and poised to act. Gort patted his gun.

"Now, let's not argue. Everybody back to work. You're behind schedule. Not you Bartolome, you're coming with me!"

Despite Simon's protests, he pushed the other sicad out of the cage, locked it behind him and disappeared into the elevator.

Magnus was the first to question Simon's actions.

@Simon – *Why did you let him take him?*

@Sicads.all – *There's no proven threat to Bartolome, so Project rule number four binds us to obey Gort. I'm sure the Commander will bring him back, once he cools down.*

As the sicads calmed down and got back to their report writing, Simon's thoughts returned to Gort. What are this man's true intentions? Did he orchestrate the events on the survival techniques expedition? Why would the PMC put such an important project in the hands of one such man?

Unable to concentrate on the Project, his attention turned to the board on the outside of the cage on which the Project insignia had been attached. Magnetising the ends of his still sharpened power pins, he managed to unscrew the mounting and then the thin metal segments of shell attached to the polished wooden background. Sat on the floor cross-legged, he rearranged the thirty shapes until he formed the word *sicad*. Whilst he waited for his companion's return he stared at this strange word, meditating on the strange turn the Project was taking.

There was no sign of Gort or Bartolome the next day, or the day after. The sicads became pre-occupied about him. They had little choice but to wait and hope for his safe return. As each day passed, their trust in the Commander diminished and they lost hope that they'd see Bartolome alive.

32

Gort was leading Bartolome by the hair towards one of the former computer control centres, also underground and sealed with reinforced concrete.

"Fetch me McCloud and Schiller!" he barked at two corporals.

The centre was a messy, dark and somewhat anonymous room – its glory days had long passed. A residue of old cables, abandoned laboratory desks and whiteboards adorned with faded mathematical equations surrounded a central t-shaped table. Its silver plastic-coated top was scarred by long-removed banks of monitoring panels and computers. Above, an LED array emitted a pale spooky light; underneath, were rows of power sockets and abandoned cables climbed the table legs like ivy.

Gort strode into the room, quickly followed by Scott and Rory.

"What's up, Commander?"

"We've got an interview to conduct. Let's see just how human these robots are!"

"Is everything OK, Commander?" asked Rory.

"Don't look at me as if I'm mad! They're withholding information. It's time to be a little more persuasive!"

"Undress, robot!"

The sicad stripped to his underwear.

Gort nodded at his subordinates.

"Take hold of him!"

Bartolome recalled what Simon had rapidly communicated to him on exiting the chamber: "Be wary of this man; I do not trust him. Tell him what he wants to know, but only show him your robot side. Any information you can get out of him may be critical for us!"

Gort pushed the sicad onto the central table.

"Attach him with the cables."

The soldiers obeyed. Flat on his back, Bartolome couldn't move. The wires were tight on his wrists and ankles, generating constant pain signals to his sensory system.

Gort surveyed his prey – pale skin, a wispy beard and moustache.

Long chestnut-brown hair, liberated from the manhandled ponytail, flanked the right side of his face. The sicad lay still, with no apparent fear, smiling benevolently. A sharp vision of Jesus pinned to the cross suddenly flashed across Gort's mind. He shook his head aggressively, to exorcise the distasteful image.

"This is unnecessary, Commander. I'll happily answer all your questions."

Bartolome's words brought the Commander back to his senses.

"We'll see about that!"

He pulled up a plastic chair and sat behind the sicad.

"OK, Barrera, what have you sicads really been working on?"

"We've re-organised, collated, classified, processed and systematically questioned the observations collected by all of us over the last nine months."

"Tell me about CAMEOS!"

Bartolome wasn't expecting this question. It was the first time anybody had associated the sicads with the magazine.

"It's an electronic magazine which uses celebrities to help raise awareness for threatened ecosystems," he replied warily.

"What's your relationship with it?"

"Like many of us, I used the magazine as one of the means of approaching humans."

Gort put his head close to Bartolome's.

"You've been meddling in areas that don't concern the project. We're going to find out who put you up to this. Who are you working for?" he whispered menacingly in the sicad's ear.

"The Project Management Committee, which includes your good self," replied Bartolome slowly and respectfully.

"Don't get smart with me, robot!" hissed Gort, before punching him in the side of the face. Bartolome's head lurched sideways from the force of the blow and he felt his brain rattle. He realised he was in an increasingly dangerous situation.

"What is it that you suspect me of doing, Commander?"

"I want to know why you've been stirring up trouble with CAMEOS and who's put you up to it!"

"It was a useful way for us to gather some of the research we needed. It's just a magazine, and people were happy to hear about it. Our Project goals are incompatible with upsetting humans."

Gort was silent. The sicad paused, before continuing warily.

220

"Who did we upset?"

Gort stood up and leaned over the sicad aggressively.

"I want to know who and why? You will tell me everything, eventually. We'll see how long you can last."

*

Bartolome entered deep sleep mode, to conserve power, and woke to the sound of Gort's voice. With an estimated thirteen hours of power left, at best he could last out for the day.

"Who and why?" persisted the Commander.

The sicad didn't respond.

"You'll run out of power soon, won't you? How do you feel about that, Bart?"

"It would be a tragedy for me and for the Project."

Gort smiled thoughtfully – let's see where this sicad is leading me.

"Don't you believe in the Project, Commander?"

"I'm sceptical."

"You don't believe we'll find the answers?"

"It's an expensive distraction. The answers are evident, but require courage to implement."

"What are these answers, Commander?"

"Stronger leaders, with the authority to make difficult decisions. A time for action, not for talking. Now, I've said enough. You tell me who you're working for."

"For the Project Management Committee," replied Bartolome in exasperation.

"Come now, don't try and have me believe that you put all those ideas about nature into your own heads. I bet those communists in South America are involved. They're always banging on about saving their trees! Bartolome, I want names. The names of the people behind your activities," demanded Gort.

"And who's behind your actions, Commander?" replied the sicad bravely.

"Powerful people who want answers. Now it's your turn. One last time: who are you robots working for?"

Bartolome didn't respond, knowing it was futile and would only serve to anger Gort.

"I'll come back later when you might be in more of a hurry to talk."

The Commander returned several times as Bartolome weakened, to press him harder. The sicad remained silent, mulling over grim thoughts.

He has no intention of taking me back alive, Bartolome realised. What are his motives? How can I escape? When he'd exhausted all possible scenarios, he focused on alerting the other sicads. The centre was electronically dead and the concrete casing was cutting off all communication. His eyes fell upon the network cables binding his wrists to the table. These cables must connect to somewhere, maybe to a live system?

He strained his neck in search of the cable ends; nothing – they must be underneath me. Twisting and turning his hands, his bindings cutting into his skin, he felt around to locate the loose cables within reach. Feeding each cable slowly through his fingers, millimetres at a time, he searched blindly for an elusive connector, frustratingly not knowing if he was re-checking the same cables. On the verge of giving up, his fingers groped a cat five-type connector, old technology used to network computers, sometimes over hundreds of metres. His spirits lifted in anticipation. Retracting the copper pins from the ends of his fingers, he crushed the plastic casing to connect with the bare wires. He sent tracer signals down the wires, following them under the floor and down tens of metres, presumably into the Atlas chamber, where the connection ended – connected to a dead appliance, severed, or simply dangling in the air? He clasped his fist around the cable in anger and despair. It was 7pm and his power levels were dangerously low. I'm not going to survive the night, he thought.

At 11:45pm Gort returned. Bartolome struggled to speak.

"Have mercy, Commander. Please give me power."

"Just one name," replied Gort.

Bartolome didn't respond.

"If you don't mind, I'll share your final moments, watching the first sicad to expire."

He sat down beside Bartolome, whose face was reflecting a pale and ghostly light from the battery-powered LED above him.

"A goddam name, robot!" shouted the Commander, shaking the sicad.

The sicad fell back, motionless and silent – had he gone? Suddenly, a large smile spread across Bartolome's face. A minute later, he opened his eyes and uttered a single word, "Mankind."

The sicad's eyes closed, his body shuddered lightly and completely froze.

As Gort surveyed the dead sicad, another vision of Jesus dying on the cross struck him. He struggled back into the chair. Damn these robots, he thought, they're playing with my mind.

At the same time, fifty kilometres away as the crow flies, in the monastic village of Le Reposoir, the Prioress of an order of Carmelite Nuns cloistered there had a vision. In her vision she saw Bartolome dying on the cross, his body slowly blending into the wood, which transformed into a huge Cedar tree. The tree was bathed in a halo of light and golden fruits began to grow on the branches. The fruits transformed into symbols; the eight-spoked wheel of Buddhism, the Christian cross, the Confucian trigram, the sacred AUM symbol of Hinduism, the crescent and star of Islam, the Star of David, the sun, shrine and flag symbol of Shintoism, the two teardrop-shaped halves of the circular Yin-Yang symbol and many others she didn't recognise. Bound by a vow of silence at this hour, she reached for the holy relic of a golden arrow and clasped it to her chest.

In Tibet, the Dalia Lama, in deep meditation, received the same vision. As did the Emperor of Japan, Abdul-Salam – the secretary of the Muslim World League, Harzat Ali Khan – the Sufi Master, Clifford "Coen" Walker – the aborigine elder and a collection of other religious figures the sicads had met on their travels. The blind prophet in the refugee camp also woke up bemused with the same vision. The sicads had connected to all these figures, and somehow a channel had opened up between them.

*

Bartolome's part-organic brain, which had acquired so much knowledge and life experience in just a few short years, had expired. His body could be recharged, but it would never function again without a replacement brain. The memories locked inside its atoms would slowly decay back into the great circle of life. As such, the being that was Bartolome had died.

33

Six minutes after midnight, just five minutes after Bartolome uttered the word 'Mankind', the Atlas detector stirred into life. Simon, having just gone to sleep, woke up. What did this mean? His curiosity prompted him to connect to the detector. A recent amendment to the system code had been added along with a comment:

Fellow sicads, I'm about to die and Gort is sitting at my side watching me. He's against the Project. His plans are unclear, yet he's highly suspicious of our involvement with CAMEOS and believes we are working for someone, a name he has repeatedly asked me to reveal.

I have been unable to transmit any message to the outside world for help. I hope this message is of use to you in some way.

Although it was short, I enjoyed my life and I hope that it has been of some use to the Project, and to whatever wider purpose is driving life on this planet.

Goodbye.

Bartolome Barrera.

*

As Bartolome was on the edge of expiry, the Atlas detector had fired up for its nightly maintenance session. His fingers still clasped around the network cable, he was suddenly connected to the functioning detector. His dying action was to record his comment and restart the detector five minutes later to alert Simon.

For the sicads, more intimately connected than most humans, the loss of Bartolome was devastating. Simon turned the grief he felt into a determined desire to liberate himself from Gort's control and seek help. That night, he had every brain working on a means of escape. To avoid recriminations, it had to be a secret escape – a small number, or just one of them.

Early that morning, Gort and his soldiers brought the lifeless body of Bartolome back to the cage.

"The robot ran out of energy. Maybe you can fix it?" stated the Commander, as if returning a faulty product.

He stared coldly into Simon's eyes, before turning back to his companions.

"Put it back in its slot!"

Simon was unusually lost for words.

Gort walked up and down, glaring at random sicads.

"Sicads, you've got twenty-four hours to produce this report, if you want to avoid Bartolome's fate!"

*

Back at Mazari, despite Gort's assurances, there was growing concern at a lack of tangible progress. The seclusion period was reaching its half-way point, without a progress update. Nerves were on edge and imaginations running wild. For reassurance, they decided to insist on an immediate progress report.

When Gort received this message, he headed straight back down to the chamber with Scott and Rory in tow. He wasn't going to run around at the beck and call of Mazari, but the last thing he needed was the committee on his back. It was over twenty-four hours since he'd returned Bartolome, and he still hadn't replied to Mr Leopold.

In the cage, all was quiet, the sicads all in position. Simon came to the door.

"Can I help you, Commander?"

Gort had to look twice. The sicad's attitude and body language seemed to have changed. Maybe putting the dead robot back has bucked up their ideas? he thought.

"I've come for the report. Put it on this storage device."

He handed the sicad the coin-sized disk.

Simon stared coldly into Gort's eyes.

"The progress report isn't ready, Commander."

Gort's eyes flashed with anger, but before he could reply Simon interjected.

"Getting angry won't help, Commander. Shoot me if you want, but it won't get you your report."

As Gort reflected on his words, Simon continued, "I suggest we have a word in private."

He stared determinedly back into Gort's eyes and stood his ground.

"OK, robot. Let's hear what you have to say. A word of warning, though, one false move and you'll have a bullet in your brain."

Gort unlocked the cage and led him out of earshot of the others, his revolver pointed at the sicad's head.

"We can't concentrate! A dead colleague is considerably distracting. If you want your report, you'll have to remove the body."

Gort thought for a second.

"Is that all?"

"Yes, that's all," replied Simon resolutely.

"OK. Captain Schiller, take this robot back to his cage and get rid of the dead one."

He turned back to Simon with a sarcastic smile.

"For the funeral: burial, cremation, disposal at sea – any preference?"

The sicad staring back coldly, but didn't answer.

McCloud and Schiller marched up to Bartolome's slot and pulled out the lifeless sicad. Grasping him by the feet and arms, his body hung limply. As the soldiers approached Gort, he slapped Bartolome's bare chest with force.

"Good to see you again, buddy!"

He scrutinised the body, inspecting carefully the abrasions on the skin around his ankles and wrists.

"Take him away!" he ordered.

"Now, back to work sicads. A final warning: if there's no progress report tomorrow, there'll be more funerals."

He returned to his office and replied to Jia that she would have her progress report in two days. As he sat back to contemplate the day's developments, there was a knock at his door. Scott and Rory entered.

"Is everything OK, Commander?" asked Scott.

"These sicads are becoming a headache."

Rory looked at Scott and nodded discreetly.

"Commander, where shall we dispose of the dead robot?"

Gort rubbed his eyes with the palms of his hands before replying wearily.

"You can leave it in my office..." he hesitated. "No, on second thoughts, bury it somewhere where it won't be found!"

Scott reflected for a few seconds.

"What about the lake?"

Gort nodded.

From the window, he watched them tie up the body, wrap it in a tarpaulin and throw it into the back of the Puma, before zipping up the rear canopy.

Seconds later, his private cell phone vibrated loudly.

"Yes, what?"

"My clients are impatient for answers, Commander."

"Well, I've got nothing to report, otherwise I'd have called you."

"Are you not taking us seriously, Commander? Would you like to see a sign of how serious my clients are?"

Gort controlled his anger and composed himself before replying.

"I've interrogated one of them. They're not working for anybody, or won't reveal it if they are."

"How can you be so sure, Commander?"

"I know how to do my job. The sicads are very attached to life, yet one of them wouldn't even give me a name on its dying breath!"

"Is that so?"

"Yes. I've done everything you asked, now let me get on with my job!"

"I'm afraid I can't do that, Commander. My clients have some follow-on instructions."

"Damn your clients!"

"One last task and you can forget about Todd Ranger..."

After a long silence, Gort capitulated.

"What more do you want from me?"

"Destroy all the sicads."

"This is crazy!"

"Do it, Commander, and make it look like an accident!"

*

Jia was reading Gort's reply – why the delay? Simon behind schedule? It didn't feel right. I don't trust Gort, she thought, I must get over to CERN and take a look. An idea formed in her mind. She typed a high-importance email to her Chairman and was soon summoned to the top floor executive office.

The door was opened by Susumu's secretary, who brought her before the Chairman.

"What's up Jia?"

"I'm concerned there's a fault in the sicads' brains, triggered off by the conditions at CERN."

"What are the potential consequences?"

"Ultimately, complete unit failure," replied Jia.

"And the cause?"

"I've simulated the seclusion conditions of a cold environment and limited physical activity, and identified a possible bug in the temperature adaptation module – their brains slow down. If the fault isn't remedied, they may stop working altogether. I need to make a precautionary visit to be sure," explained Jia breathlessly.

"This isn't a ruse to see Simon is it, Jia?"

"No, of course not," she replied shakily, flushing despite herself.

"What evidence do you have that this fault may be occurring?"

"The lack of progress reports, for one. In simulations, when has Simon ever delivered behind schedule? I know this is no simulation, but I'm sure there's a problem, and I'm more familiar than anyone with the sicads."

Susumu flicked through Jia's simulations before disappearing to make a couple of phone calls. He came back smiling.

"You should just make the 11:30pm flight if you hurry – you got the last seat."

As Jia started to reply, he held up his hand to quieten her.

"There will be tight restrictions; you'll be limited to analysing two of them. I had to fight hard for that!"

She started to protest, but thought better of it.

"Thank you."

She bowed deferentially and left the room.

34

As night fell, a Land Rover 110 Puma left the CERN compound on route to Promenthoux, where a small rowing boat awaited them. A tarpaulin-wrapped bundle slid about in the back. The heavy chains given to Corporal James Swenson and Corporal Ralph Boche to weigh the package down rattled loudly at each small bump in the road. They arrived at a narrow road leading down to a coppice of trees, where the rowing boat was tethered to a tree. Boche went back for the package.

"It weighs a bloody ton," he cursed, as Swenson helped him put it in the boat. They threw the heavy chains onto the floor of the boat and dragged it to the water. Swenson jumped in and took the oars. Boche pushed off, athletically leaping into the back. Quickly placing his hands on each side to steady himself, he perched on the bow, from where he guided them with a small electric torch.

It was a cold dark night at the end of a severe winter, the water just a few degrees above freezing. The boat glided gracefully across the rippled lake, the perimeter of which was lit up by the hundreds of dwellings that studded its shores. The two corporals chatted as the boat headed towards the middle of the lake.

"Go easy with the oars, the water is bloody cold," complained Boche.

"Sorry, buddy. Why do you think the Colonel wants us to dispose of this package in the lake?"

"He clearly doesn't want it found. It's best not to ask too many questions."

"It feels like a body to me!"

"Apparently, it's a malfunctioning robot."

"Why throw it in the lake?"

"Maybe it's toxic?"

"Well, if it is we shouldn't be dumping it in the lake."

"It's over four hundred metres deep. It's going to sink into the mud and silt, well out of harm's way."

"Keep going. Another few minutes and we should be good."

"The wind's picking up, so take it easy."

"This'll do, we're a good kilometre from shore."

"Yes, this should do fine," said a third voice.

Both soldiers looked around and lurched back in shock as the package came to life and a sicad stood between them, holding one of the heavy chains in each hand. The boat tipped and the sicad threw out his arms for balance. The chains whipped through the air towards them. Boche instinctively flinched backwards as a chain gave him a glancing blow on the shoulder and he disappeared backwards over the bow of the craft. The boat rocked violently. Swenson, who had been rowing, slid along the bench and became entangled in the other chain, which wrapped itself around his throat. He fell to the side. For a split second the boat seemed to hesitate, before capsizing and catapulting the two occupants into the lake.

Boche was splashing frantically to stay afloat in the icy-cold water as his thick coat, jumper, trousers, and ankle-high boots became saturated and heavy. Swenson's head had just resurfaced; hyperventilating from the shock of the cold lake, he was gasping for air. As he opened his mouth to breathe, he was pulled sharply back under the water by the chain, wrapped around his neck and one of the oarlocks. As the boat rocked on the waves it pulled the chain taut and the soldier's head back under water. He resurfaced again, spluttering water and gasping for breath. Putting his hands to his neck, he tried to free himself from the chain. The bow of the upturned boat, bobbing up and down on the waves, struck him sharply in the side of the head. He cried out and blood streamed from his gaping wound into the lake. As he glanced from the blow, the bow, thrown forward by the waves, hit him fully in the face. His nose exploded blood in all directions. His battered face, blue from the cold and the shock, was a gruesome sight. Swenson lost consciousness and the bow of the boat, still attached to him by the chain, continued to mercilessly batter his head and deform his face.

Meanwhile, Boche was struggling to cope with the icy water numbing his body and taking his breath away. Reaching out for the capsized boat drifting away from him, he shouted desperate instructions to his colleague.

"Get the boat. Get the boat."

He gasped in shock as he saw the unconscious and battered face of his comrade, lit up eerily by the moonlight. Quickly coming back to his senses, he swam to catch up with the boat, but it was drifting faster than he could swim in his sodden clothes. He turned around in despair. From his training drills, he knew exactly how long he could survive in water this temperature – less than one third of the time it would take him to swim to shore. Despair gripped his body as he looked death in the face and a mortal shudder traversed his soul.

Out of the corner of his eye, he saw the sicad quietly swimming away. Animal instincts seized him. Mustering a surge of energy and adrenalin, he set off after the robot. He had to power his way through the water to offset the drag from his saturated clothing. The sicad looked back over his shoulder and hesitated, as if unsure whether to help. This pause was just enough for the soldier to close the gap by a couple of metres and lunge forward. Boche managed to get a grip on the sicad's ankle and held tightly as the sicad kicked his legs violently. He grabbed onto the other leg, which was pounding his shoulder, and hung on for dear life.

The cold water was quickly draining the sicad's batteries and its survival instinct had kicked in. There was no way of saving the soldier, so it was a matter of life and death to free itself from the iron grip of its doomed pursuer. It tried in vain to twist its body, to break the vice-like hold. This extra burst of energy was accelerating its loss of power. It dived down and stayed under water. The soldier held his breath and clung on tightly. The sicad resurfaced and, as the soldier gasped for air, it managed to free its right leg and delivered three powerful blows with its heel to the corporal's face. The first blow broke the soldier's nose; the second knocked out his two front teeth. As Corporal Boche's head flopped back, the third blow caught him squarely on the chin. The soldier lost consciousness and, as he floated on the lake, water slowly filled his lungs.

The sicad looked back towards the two dead soldiers, their faces contorted in pain and their skin a deathly pale blue. It was a question of survival and the sicad was programmed to survive. It had no time to reflect on the haunting image – its batteries were rapidly emptying. It turned around and swam swiftly and efficiently towards the shore, switching to emergency batteries to survive. Seven minutes later, it slumped onto the shore and staggered out of the lake. It appeared to be Bartolome that crawled out of the lake, but it wasn't. It was Simon Oceandis in Bartolome's skin.

*

After Gort brought Bartolome's body back to the caged rack of sicads, Simon had conceived his means of escape. The following night, after freezing the camera images, Simon and Magnus partially recharged Bartolome's body and activated his remove skin routine. As the three sicads were of a similar build, they could swap skins. Simon took Bartolome's skin, Magnus took Simon's and Magnus's skin was put back on Bartolome's lifeless body.

In the early hours of the morning, Magnus practised walking and talking like Simon, whilst Simon lay totally still in Bartolome's slot. He programmed his body to be able to turn off all movements and reactions.

When Gort came back the following morning, it was Magnus he took aside at gunpoint. Simon had listened nervously as Magnus played out his role. When he heard Scott and Rory coming back into the cage, he activated the code he'd compiled to turn off all his movements and reactions. Unable to defend himself, yet completely conscious of everything that was happening, the next few minutes were a traumatic experience. He felt an enormous sense of relief when the soldiers tied him up and finally threw his body onto the back of a vehicle. Not knowing if he was being watched, he didn't dare attempt to cut the ropes securing his hands.

As he was lying still, Simon's mind was actively working. Without the distraction from his other senses, his hearing and signal receivers seemed even sharper. He became aware of the multitude of radio signals and tuned into the Swiss mobile phone frequency. Gort's calls were encrypted with the latest high security system, Quantum Cryptography – allegedly impossible to decipher, since the code was based on the unknowable randomness of quantum mechanics.

In just thirty minutes he'd found a way of cracking it. As he lay wrapped in the tarpaulin, he listened into Gort's phone calls. There were three conversations about the state of national security with senior military figures from Brazil, China and the United States.

Shortly after, he heard the soldiers enter the front cabin. As the Puma set off, he extracted his still-sharpened finger connectors and frantically started to attack the thick ropes binding his hands. It was tedious work and he was still hacking at the ropes when they came to a halt by the lake. It wasn't until just before the soldiers were about to dump his body in the lake that he finally freed his hands and feet.

*

Simon attempted to stand up, but didn't have the energy and collapsed to the floor. He stumbled across the muddy ground, painstakingly pulling himself forward with his elbows. His body, extremely cold, he eked out his last remaining drops of energy reaching the Puma. Grasping the side mirror, he pulled himself up. Using his last few watts, he heaved his upper body through the open window of the passenger door and activated the bonnet switch. Falling onto the electric motor, he fumbled with his fingers to find the battery. His body tingled with the pleasant sensation of energy flowing into him. Powerful electro-chemical pulsations reverberated through his mind as he dragged himself back from the void of non-existence.

Once recharged, Simon set off on foot, naked except for his wet underwear. Setting off towards the nearest lights, he kept close to the shore, hiding in the shadows of the trees whenever possible. A man wandering around virtually naked in Switzerland in March would be a fairly conspicuous occurrence. The last thing he wanted was to be spotted, picked up by the police and taken back to Gort. I must find some clothes, he thought, and quickly.

He spotted six buildings, scrutinising each in turn before deciding to check out a small house with a swimming pool. As he approached, all was quiet. There was a light on inside. Creeping up to the window, he crouched down and peered through. Judging by the furniture and the toys strewn on the floor, it was a family home. There were photos of the family on the opposite wall; several pictures of two young children, both girls, along with one of a man he assumed to be the father, dressed in full military uniform holding an assault rifle. Circling the house, he tried every door and window – all securely fastened and locked.

Looking for an implement he could use to gain entry, he searched the garage. At the end was a small ladder, leading up to an open loft, and an old wooden workbench with a sturdy vice and a wide wooden drawer – it was stuck. Pulling more forcefully, the drawer shuddered out far enough to place his hand inside and rummage around. As he contemplated a sturdy antique screwdriver, an electric car suddenly swung silently into the drive, its headlights sweeping across the garage. He froze for a split second, jumped onto the small ladder and up into the loft – no time to shut the drawer. The car pulled into the garage and an automatic light came on. The car doors opened and two adults stepped out, followed by two children. The male stood up, looked straight at the wooden workbench and the open drawer.

"Honey, were you searching for something?"

"No, I don't think so. Why?"

"It's strange. I had trouble opening that drawer yesterday."

The man walked around the garage and climbed half way up the ladder, before descending and walking warily over to the house, checking the doors and windows.

"Bizarre!" He shook his head, locked the car and escorted his wife and children into the house.

Simon quickly came out from under a carpet and quietly searched through cardboard boxes – nothing except for a ragged blanket. There was an old chest – it was locked. He grabbed the sturdy screwdriver and forced it into the lock; it ceded easily. Inside was an assault rifle and an army uniform, neatly folded, complete with rucksack, coat, woolly hat, boots, helmet, ammunition belt and canteens. He quickly put on the uniform, boots and hat and disappeared into the night.

He headed for the small town of Nyon, deep in thought. He'd escaped from Gort, but his predicament was what to do next? If the Commander hadn't already detected his escape, he would do shortly. Where should he turn for help? Who would believe a robot's version of events over that of the Head of the UN Army?

Jia was his only hope. He'd turned off all communication connectivity, in case Gort's men were monitoring these networks. He didn't dare switch them back on to contact Jia. He must find an anonymous internet connection.

Simon reached the town and found what he was looking for – an internet café, fortunately still open. After ordering a coffee, he sat down and used the computer to dial Jia's mobile. The phone rang just once before she picked it up.

"Hello?" she whispered.

"Jia, listen, it's Simon. I must talk to you, where are you?"

"Simon! How... What... Why are you calling me?"

"Listen, Jia, it's important. Where are you?"

"I'm in Switzerland, in a toilet in Geneva airport. Tomorrow I have special permission to visit CERN."

"Jia, listen, I'm no longer there. I escaped."

"Escaped? Why?"

"I'll explain. I don't think Gort realises yet. Where are you staying?"

"I'm not sure. Gort organised it. I'm under strict surveillance."

"I must see you tonight. By tomorrow, Gort will have guessed I've escaped. As soon as you get to the hotel..."

There was a load banging, followed by a booming voice.

"Your two minutes are up!"

"Got to go," she whispered.

"I'm coming!" she shouted angrily. After rapidly deleting the call log, she stuffed the phone into her handbag. Her head was spinning as she confronted the soldiers.

"Can't a woman attend to her business in peace?" she snapped angrily.

"Follow us. You've been given special permission to visit at a sensitive time. You must adhere to the security protocols at all times."

She was escorted past border control and down to an underground car park.

"How's the Project going?" she asked the soldier next to her.

"You'll see tomorrow."

They arrived at the nearby conference hotel.

"That was quick, we could have walked!"

Ignoring the remark, the soldiers escorted her to the fourth floor where a female officer greeted her.

"Hello, Miss Jin. Lieutenant Sylvie Kalinska. I'm in charge of your personal security."

Sylvie looked at the other soldiers coldly.

"That'll be all."

She closed the door behind Jia.

"I take it you've been warned about the security procedures. Place all your belongings on the bed and remove your clothes."

Jia, too tired and disorientated to argue, handed over her handbag and the suitcase she'd rapidly packed, before removing her coat and clothes. Kalinska put on a pair of tight-fitting medical gloves and scrutinised Jia's slim and lightly-muscled body.

Jia gritted her teeth as she was intimately searched.

"OK, all done," announced the soldier, removing the gloves.

"Where's the shower?" snapped Jia.

Whilst Jia showered, Kalinska searched her affairs, studying her phone and call log. Satisfied that all was in order, she closed the suitcase and retained the passport, purse and phone.

Once Jia returned, Sylvie drily gave her orders.

"Sleep now. Tomorrow at 07.00 you'll proceed to CERN. I'll remain here and the door will be locked for your safety."

My safety? This is ridiculous, Jia thought. What does she think I'm going to do?

Jia pulled back the covers and slipped into bed; she'd been awake for nearly twenty-four hours. Closing her eyes, she remembered that Simon had wanted to see her. Why had he escaped? What had happened to the other sicads? What did all this mean?

Her brain ran around in circles for two hours, before she succumbed to exhaustion.

"Miss Jin! Miss Jin, wake up!" ordered Sylvie, shaking her.

Jia opened her eyes to see Kalinska's stern features. It took several seconds to recall where she was and who Sylvie was. She would have liked to sleep for several more hours and she snapped angrily.

"OK! OK! I'm awake. You'd fit in well in a concentration camp!"

Sylvie's face was expressionless.

"Your escort will be here in twenty-five minutes. Breakfast will be here in ten."

Jia stood yawning under the shower, turning the temperature dial left and right, blasting herself with jets of cold water in an attempt to wake up. She heard a series of knocks at the door. First one, followed by a pause, then two more, another pause and, finally, three knocks. She heard the door open and Sylvie's voice.

"Leave the tray. That'll be all."

Jia got dressed uncomfortably under Sylvie's scrutinising stare. Expecting it to be cold in CERN, she put on tightly-fitting black trousers, a long-sleeved top and a warm jumper.

She had just a few minutes to drink a lukewarm tea and munch on honey-covered toast before another series of knocks on the door. Sylvie opened the door to Colonel McCloud and Captain Schiller – another bad omen! It was the first time Jia had seen them since the near-fatal survival expedition. A wave of unease rushed over her. Thinking back to Simon's telephone call, she looked around for her phone, patting her pockets, before catching Sylvie's smug gaze.

"I've taken your phone, passport and purse. You'll get them back on your return to Japan."

Jia grabbed her coat in anger and strode out of the room, followed by Scott and Rory, who led her down to the waiting limousine.

Her heart was pounding and her stomach churning as the car door closed – was she safe? She drew a breath of relief as the car arrived at CERN, a location which, in ordinary circumstances, would have fascinated her.

A soldier approached, waving an electronic scanner around the car. "Look this way."

Jia's retina scan was verified, a green light appeared and the large metal gate slid open to admit the vehicle. A figure hidden in the shadows smiled and made a mental note of the registration plate.

She was escorted up a flight of stairs to Gort's first floor office, where the Commander was sitting at his desk. He greeted her with a scowl.

"What brings you to this lifeless dump at such a sensitive time?"

"Some urgent checks," she replied resolutely.

Gort stared at her eerily and spoke very slowly, in a soft but steely voice.

"Governments are relying on me to ensure the seclusion phase is not contaminated."

He placed his hands on the desk and leant towards her.

"Tell me, why I should make an exception for you?"

"These governments are also relying on Mazari, to ensure that the sicads are functioning properly. Any processing errors will equally contaminate the project," she replied, holding Gort's penetrating gaze.

"And what are these supposed processing errors?" he asked with overt sarcasm, which she ignored.

"A slowdown in cerebral activity, as evidenced by the progress report falling behind schedule. Simulations of the environment here indicate anomalies due to extended periods of inaction in low temperatures. All the stats are on this disk."

She knew that Gort had already agreed to let her visit the sicads – this conversation was just one of his mind games.

He refused the disk, staring into her eyes.

"We now have the progress report and I've ironed out the initial processing errors. An army method got them moving in the end."

"What do you mean, an army method?"

"I, too, was concerned over the lack of progress. I was maybe a little reckless, but out of frustration I had a little talk with one of the sicads and straightened things out."

"You did what?" she shouted.

"I had a little chat with one of the sicads, and after that things improved drastically!"

"But you know that you're not meant to influence them!"

"Yes, I remembered afterwards. I had little choice but to terminate the sicad."

237

"Oh my God, you killed a sicad?" she shrieked incredulously.

"Unfortunately, yes. The termination, in total compliance with the Seclusion Guidelines, was sadly the only course of action."

Jia got up and paced around the office, the silent rage and hate blocking out the Commander's words.

"It's all in the progress report I've just sent to the PMC. I spoke to Bruno personally about it as well."

She was shaking uncontrollably with anger.

"Who did you kill and where is the body?"

"Now Jia, don't go confusing these robots with humans. It's only one robot down, and all the information it held had already been collated by the others. It had served its purpose."

"Who did you kill?" she repeated.

"It was one of the Spanish robots. Bart something or other..."

"You mean Bartolome," she snapped.

"Yes, something like that."

"Take me to see them, right now!"

"First of all you'd better calm yourself down, young lady, else you won't be going anywhere. Let's take a cup of coffee and gather ourselves, shall we?"

She sipped on her coffee, attempting to recover her breathing and professionalism. A growing hatred was building up inside her towards Bartolome's killer.

"OK, now you've calmed down, we can go through the rules. We don't want any more accidents."

She struggled to maintain her composure – keep calm, she told herself – he's trying to provoke a reaction, as an excuse to further restrict your access. Biting her lip, she listened as Gort read out the restricted access rules.

"...and a member of the army will be present at all times."

It was going to be impossible to talk freely with the sicads!

"Do you fully understand the rules?"

She nodded, with clenched teeth.

"Any violations will result in the immediate cessation of your access rights. Is that clear?"

She nodded again.

"OK, which two sicads would you like to examine?"

She was almost too angry to think straight.

"Agus and Magnus," she replied sternly, after some hesitation.

"Your final decision?"

"Ye... No, on second thoughts, I won't examine two males. I'll examine Rosa instead of Magnus."

Commander Gort led her personally past the retina scans, through the series of sealed chambers and into the elevator. Navigating the maze of metal walkways and stairwells, they arrived on the chamber floor. She got a quick glimpse of the caged rack containing the four hundred sicads.

Gort smiled cruelly and spoke, coldly and slowly.

"They're only robots, machines built for a purpose. Don't get too attached to them, they're government property."

The effort to restrain the strong emotions raging inside was draining her. The twelve months separation had been unbearable – and now where was Simon? She'd put such a lot of her life and ambitions into him, the idea she might lose him was unbearable.

"I'd like to visit the cage."

"Out of bounds," replied Gort impassively, leading her towards an inspection room located far away from the racked sicads. She saw Simon approach the front of the cage; even from afar she recognised him. Her head was spinning again. How was it possible he was here? Had he managed to re-enter the chamber? The security here couldn't be tighter, so how had he managed to escape, let alone re-enter? Was it an impostor who'd called her?

As she inspected the maintenance equipment, her mind was in another place, desperately trying to make sense of scrambled facts and emotions.

"You should have everything you need," stated the Commander.

"Yes. Yes, I believe so," she replied distractedly.

"I'll fetch Rosa."

She tried to regain her composure, her brain spinning around in circles, stuck in a nightmare she couldn't escape.

Part V.

Survival

35

Simon, remembering he had no money, had been forced to flee the internet café without paying. Once clear of the town, he'd marched through the night, using the steady breeze to maintain his energy levels. He'd reached CERN before Jia and her escort arrived. He hid in the shadows and waited.

*

Under constant scrutiny, Jia had gone through the motions and performed a range of diagnostic tests on Rosa. She'd spun them out, noting areas of concern to follow up on. No opportunity to speak privately to Rosa had presented itself and by mid-afternoon she was physically and mentally exhausted.

She returned to Gort's office and waited outside. He was on the phone, shouting.

"What do you mean, the boat capsized? How the..? Never mind. Search the lake... Yes, discreetly! Report back to me when you have some answers."

She strode into his office without announcing herself. The Commander cut the communication and spun around angrily.

"Knock before entering in future!" he barked.

Unfazed, she gave him a brief update.

"I've found evidence of the potential fault. I'll resume tomorrow."

Gort's mind was on other matters.

"I expect a fuller update in the morning, and some hard evidence!"

He summoned Colonel McCloud.

"Take Miss Jin back to her hotel and pay special attention that she rests safely."

A black limousine pulled out of CERN and headed swiftly and sleekly down the Route de Meyrin. A solitary figure on a three-wheeled moped followed behind at a safe distance. A series of traffic lights slowed the limousine, giving the pursuer the opportunity to keep it in sight. The bike followed, jumping two red lights as the car chicaned in front of Geneva Airport. It continued in the direction of Ferney, before turning right into a hotel. Simon followed and watched it disappear into an underground car park. He waited fifteen minutes for it to reappear and head back towards CERN, before removing his helmet.

Entering the main lobby, he approached the reception desk. A smartly-dressed female with a pretty smile and a Swiss-American accent greeted him.

"Good day, sir. Can I be of assistance?"

"Do you have any rooms available?"

"Yes, sir – a single or a double?"

"The prices?"

Whilst talking, he interrogated the hotel's computer systems, searching all rooms. There was nothing in Jia's name or anything project-related. Scanning through the notes behind each account, he soon found what he was looking for. Room 461 had 'special' security notes; no phone calls and no visitors, meals to be brought to the room directly at 06:30 and 18:30 hours, and a special code for knocking.

"The singles are three hundred and the doubles four hundred and fifty."

"Can I take a look around first?"

"Be my guest," she replied, with a friendly smile.

He headed downstairs and glanced into the kitchen. A kitchen employee was pushing a trolley. It was 18:26 – was it for Jia?

The waiter stood holding the door open.

"Which room?"

His manager hissed the number 'four-six-one' and reprimanded him.

"Now hurry, if you're late the bitch will have your balls for conkers!"

The scolded waiter made off smartly towards the service lift. As he pushed the trolley through the open doors, Simon seized his opportunity. With lightning reactions he sprang sideways into the elevator, just as the doors were closing. Placing his hand over the waiter's jaw to muffle the protests, he opened his own mouth. A small dart, containing a powerful tranquilliser, shot out from the back of his throat and into the waiter's neck. At the same time, he took control of the lift's operating system and diasbled the alarm. Hurriedly removing his clothes and undressing the waiter, he struggled into the uniform. The jacket was tight and the trouser legs stopped short of his ankles. Tucking his pony tail inside the back of the jacket, he took the blue catering hat and pulled it down as far as he could over his face. He realised he couldn't leave the waiter in the lift, it was too risky! His eyes falling upon the trolley, he pulled aside the hanging cloth. Underneath was a large space, into which he wedged the body, just managing to squeeze the waiter's arms and legs inside. Pulling the cloth back down over the sides, he reactivated the lift. The doors opened on the fourth floor and he pushed the trolley out as fast as he dared. Room 461 was at the end of the corridor. Steering was difficult with the extra weight pushing the wheels into the soft carpet.

Two soldiers were posted as sentinels, one either side of the door. As he approached, he felt the waiter's arm flop down onto the floor and the weight of the trolley shift precariously. He struggled to keep it from overturning whilst he nudged the arm back into position with his knee. Hesitantly pushing the trolley forward, he felt a wave of relief as the body stayed in place. Standing between the soldiers, he knocked once, paused, knocked again twice, paused and, finally, knocked three times. The door opened and a severe-looking female glared at him, before summoning him in.

Jia was sat on the bed, knees clasped to her chest, staring blankly at the wall. As Sylvie turned around, so did Simon, firing a dart into the vein of her neck. Before any sound could leave her throat, a napkin had been forcibly thrust into her mouth and her right arm twisted behind her back. Simon smothered her face with his shoulder, to further muffle any protests. Jia suddenly noticed the shadows on the wall.

She got as far as uttering, "Bartolo..." before Simon put his finger to his lips to silence her. She jumped up and took Sylvie's legs. Together they carried her over to the bed, Simon whispering a brief explanation.

"There's little time to explain. Gort killed Bartolome. I managed to escape in his skin."

Her head was reeling with confusion.

"Quick, help me," he hissed, pulling up the cloth and dragging out the waiter's body.

"Onto the bed!"

They hoisted him onto the mattress, pulled the covers over him and did the same to Sylvie.

"Get under the trolley," he whispered.

Her heart was thumping.

"Hang on, the bitch took my phone and passport!"

"There's no time and you won't be able to use them anyway!"

Helping Jia wriggle into the space under the trolley, he pulled the cloth back into place.

"Bon appétit!" he announced loudly and opened the door.

The two soldiers ignored him. Putting his head down, he pushed the trolley slowly towards the lift.

"Hang on a minute," shouted one of the soldiers. Simon's SAMPS rapidly started to generate survival strategies. Should he dart him and go for his gun? The unmistakeable sound of Jia's heart pounding heavily held him back. He waited, petrified as the soldier walked assuredly towards him.

"Bring us something to eat. It's gonna be a long night."

A wave of relief washed over the anxious sicad.

"Of course, gentlemen. A club sandwich and fries, OK?"

The soldier nodded and Simon headed back to the lift. Once inside, Jia, trembling with fear, climbed out from the trolley. Simon rapidly restarted the lift. Minutes later, they were running in the direction of the airport. When they were a safe distance from the hotel, Jia stopped and shouted.

"You're crazy. You could have got us killed!" Her breathing heavy with tension and excitement, she alternated between anger and pride.

As their jog turned to a fast walk, Simon summarised his escape and Jia recounted the phone conversation she'd overheard.

"We must talk to Bruno," she concluded.

"First we must get away from Gort. He knows for sure his soldiers have disappeared."

"How do you know?"

"I'm listening to his calls."

"That's impossible, they're quantum encrypted!"

"I thought so too, but let's just say that CERN gave me some inspiration. If we're lucky, we've got a few hours before he discovers our escape."

"Our escape?"

"Yes, Jia. You're inextricably linked to all this. There's no turning back now."

36

The light was fading, the sun had set twenty minutes before and darkness was slowly engulfing the lake. The small fishing boat switched on its navigation lights. The old fisherman passed a torch to Captain Schiller, went away and came back with a mug of hot cider and a thick fleece.

"It gets cold at night."

"Thanks," replied Rory gratefully.

Searching for bodies in a dark lake was a grim job.

The fisherman took out his wallet and showed Rory the picture inside.

"My two granddaughters – the best things I could hope for in this world. And they adore their grandpa too," chortled the old man.

"They look adorable. I'm sorry, but my mind is on my colleagues."

The fisherman nodded sympathetically.

"If your mates fell in, the currents will have taken them to the centre."

"Keep circulating and track our course."

The fisherman laughed.

"No need to plot courses, young man. After forty years on this lake, I know it like the back of my hand."

Rory swept the dark water with the torchlight.

"Why don't we call the coastguard? With their fleet we'd have 'em in no time."

"For the last time, this is a covert operation," he replied, without taking his eyes off the lake.

"Stop the boat!" he yelled.

"Back up. There's something... There!"

He grabbed the gaff and shone the torchlight across the water onto a dark object floating off the starboard side. He hooked it and pulled it towards the boat.

"It's a body alright," announced the old man. Rory took a deep breath and turned the object over with the gaff. The old man shone the light, illuminating a face. Rory stepped back in shock and disgust. The old man swore and dropped the torch. Neither man spoke. The sight of the face, battered beyond recognition, was haunting – a wreckage of bloody, bruised and torn skin, exposed brain tissue and broken fragments of skull. The old fisherman threw up over the side.

Rory was the first to speak.

"Hold onto my legs."

The old man swallowed and held Rory, who leant over the side and pulled up the body. Between them, they hauled it onto the boat. They laid the dead soldier out, as respectfully as possible, on the gutting table and covered him with a blanket. Rory took out his cell phone and distanced himself from the fisherman.

"Commander, it's Rory. Yes, I've found one of the bodies... No, I'm not sure which... You'd better come and take a look... No, nobody else, just the old fisherman... It would have been impossible without his knowledge of the lake and currents. OK, Promenthoux, in ninety minutes. Yes, of course we'll find the other one."

Rory hung up and looked at the old fisherman. Had he been listening? The old man looked shocked and worried. Rory suddenly felt very guilty for having dragged him into this morbid situation.

"Now for the other one," he announced grimly.

The fisherman nodded stoically.

"It won't be far from the first."

Rory picked up the torch and the fisherman restarted the engines. Twenty minutes later they located the second body, in a better state than the first. There were signs of bruising and the two front teeth were missing, but the soldier's identity was clearly recognisable.

Five minutes later, the second body was laid out alongside the other.

"OK, where to now?" asked the fisherman, who looked like he'd aged ten years.

"Promenthoux, where my Commander will meet us," ordered Rory.

The boat pulled up alongside the small wooden jetty, on which two body bags were laid out, and Commander Gort was pacing back and forth. He was alone and the shore was deserted. Rory could see Gort's armoured limousine parked up, blocking the entrance of the small access road – it was empty. He was surprised that his Commander had come alone. A sense of hope for the fisherman rose up inside him.

David Gort was not in good spirits. He jumped aboard and went straight to the bodies.

"It's not a pretty sight," warned Rory, pulling back the blanket.

Gort's mood darkened as he silently contemplated the carnage. After inspecting the second body, he paced around the boat pensively, before walking back purposefully towards Rory.

"Let's get these bodies out of here. I'll pass them to you."

Rory jumped onto the jetty and, with impressive strength, Gort dragged the first body to the side of the boat. Whilst Rory placed the corpse into a body bag, the Commander returned with the second. Gort went back to the deathly-pale fisherman and put his hand on his shoulder, as if to reassure him.

A growing sense of dread had built up inside the Commander, as if standing at the edge of a precipice, knowing he had to jump. He cursed Leopold and the mysterious men controlling his actions. Taking lives was all part of a soldier's lot, but to date he'd always rationalised why it was necessary and his conscience was clear. Even the lives of torture victims who'd led him to the heart of the Taliban were justifiable, as were those of the escaping refugees, who threatened the stability of the camp and the lives of his men. But now he was being pushed across a dark line and he felt his soul resisting. His hand closed around the pentagonal cross of his father's Legion of Merit, always in his inside lapel pocket next to his heart, symbolising his father's memory, living on in him – what would he have done? If only he'd known him better.

To stop now would be to risk the disgrace and the shaming from the resurfacing of Todd Ranger – would they do it? Most probably or, if not, they'd eliminate him and put another puppet in his stead.

To continue would be to sully his conscience for the rest of his days. The dilemma raged for a brief instant inside him. Should he save his soul or his reputation? Whichever path he chose, it would mark him for an eternity.

As he weighed his dilemma, a line from Proust came to mind: *it's only ever in moments of temporary insanity, that we make any permanent life-changing decisions.* As he felt the old man starting to resist his grip, he pulled out a hardened plastic baton, closed his eyes and struck the fisherman forcefully on the side of the head. The old man slumped to the floor.

As Rory was zipping up the second body bag, a sudden whiff of petrol filled his nostrils. He looked up, just in time, to see his Commander liberally dousing the boat with its own fuel. He watched in disbelief as his superior threw down the empty petrol can, revived the engines and put the boat into reverse. Rory watched, dumbstruck, as Gort started a fire, before jumping off the moving boat onto the jetty. Flames leapt up from the deck, quickly spreading across the small craft. The whole boat exploded into a floating fireball. The flames burned brightly and reached high into the sky, lighting up the whole lake. The anger building up inside Rory finally burst out.

"What the hell did you do that for?"

"He knew too much. I told you to be discreet!"

Rory clenched his teeth as a fresh wave of anger and helplessness surged up inside him. An agonising responsibility for the fisherman's death engulfed him. He shivered at the thought of the old man's granddaughters hearing the news. The feeling of hollow sickness he'd felt on the survival techniques expedition returned to his stomach.

The Commander stared into the Captain's eyes, windows onto his tortured soul.

"You saw Corporal Swenson's face. These robots are wolves in sheep's clothing. We can't afford any witnesses! If this sicad has somehow escaped, we have a serious situation."

Rory stared back into his Commander's eyes, searching for answers to the questions tormenting him – why was his Commander doing his own dirty work?

"Pull yourself together, Captain. Now let's get the bodies in the trunk and get out of here."

Rory obeyed mechanically.

They headed back towards CERN, both men absorbed in their thoughts.

It was Gort who broke the brooding silence.

"Speak your mind, Captain."

Without taking his eyes of the road, not daring to look into Gort's eyes, Rory voiced his thoughts.

"Commander, you know I respect you. I've served under you for over twelve years. Civilian casualties have been unavoidable, but I don't understand why you killed an innocent fisherman."

"Do you think this is easy for me, Rory? It was tragic, but we had no choice. The worst is over now. If we can just find this robot, we have enough evidence to definitively stop this project!"

Rory didn't reply.

"These robots are becoming the bane of my life," Gort sighed.

His thoughts returned to his first encounter with a robot, nearly twenty years before. It had upset him to the point of totally destroying it.

247

It wasn't strictly the robot's fault, but rather frustration and exasperation with his mother. Her drunken and fanatically religious episodes had made her a laughing stock – a disgrace to his father's memory. Coming back from university, flush with success in his end-of-year exams, only to find her cavorting with a robot consort had been the final straw. The stiff-looking humanoid was one of Mazari's earliest robot companion models, as he had found out when he picked up a badge, adorned with Mazari's name, from amongst the debris of tangled metal, wires and silicon. That had been the last time he'd seen his mother. The memory of her sobbing face was as tangible as the plastic badge that, for some unknown reason, he'd kept safely for the last twenty years.

It had been a tough period of his life and he'd nearly come off the rails. He'd left home immediately afterwards, with just a few essentials, including his rock climbing equipment. Closing the door of the house behind him, he walked away from the wreckage of the robot and the wreckage of a human. He'd closed a door inside his head, behind which lay the debris of tangled emotions. From then on, he'd considered himself an orphan.

Instinctively, he'd headed for Yosemite National Park and surrounded himself with the spectacular rock formations – the perfect space he'd needed to find himself. He spent the next three months solo-climbing some of the world's most challenging and awe-inspiring routes. Climbing unprotected, hundreds of metres above the ground, one mis-step or loose rock would have meant certain death.

Little love for society, nothing to go back to, ashamed of his mother, broken contact with the few friends he had – life and death had been unimportant. Sometimes he'd wear his harness, tie in to an overhanging rock face and hang high above the ground for hours at a time, simply contemplating existence. That summer, the rock was his only friend and he became physically and mentally stronger.

His thoughts returned to the incident at university. He recognised the same feeling of righteous guilt, which haunted him for life – why did that stupid idiot go out of his way to provoke me?

And now he was being blackmailed. He replayed the threat Leopold had uttered as he'd been about to hang up on him: "Todd Ranger is still alive, Commander, but he hardly knows it. He's a sad case now and can't even feed himself. He's been hidden away for a long time, David Gort! It would be such a blemish on your illustrious record if the world were to suddenly find out about Todd Ranger!"

Gort banished his troubled memories, making several calls as Rory drove silently. A fire engine, followed by three police cars, sped past. Rory's mind alternated between listening to Gort's conversations and churning over the events of the last few hours.

"Scott, it's Gort. We've just fished Corporal Swenson's body out of the lake. His face an unrecognisable mess. Yes, we found Boche's body too, also battered, but not to the same extent. There's no telling what these robots will do. It's a good job the rest are under lock and key... No, I don't know how it came back to life. But I mean to find out. We must take every precaution. Have Jia watched like a hawk. Get the guards to check on her... I'll hold... She's sleeping? Good. I'll be asking her some difficult questions tomorrow!"

Gort hung up.

"I'd better warn Bruno there's a crazed robot on the loose!"

Rory nodded silently, trying to look responsive and positive, well aware he knew more than the fisherman.

As the limousine headed towards CERN, Gort was turning over the events in his mind. *How did the robot come back to life and where is it now? I can't afford to have one robot bring me down!* He'd been trying to get through to Bruno, to confront him over his beloved robots. His thoughts returned to the rogue sicad – *what would it be doing? What would I be doing in its situation?* All his thoughts led back to Jia. He felt a tinge of paranoia. After the failure of the survival techniques expedition, his faith in his subordinates had diminished – something was not right.

"Stop at the hotel," he ordered.

Minutes later, Rory pulled up outside.

"Stay here whilst I check on Miss Jin."

As Rory rested his aching head on the steering wheel, a wave of exhaustion washed over him. Closing his eyes, he slipped into a state of semi-consciousness, nightmares and reality blending together into a painful purgatory.

Gort flashed his ID at the receptionist, took the lift to the fourth floor and strode up to the two soldiers.

"How's our guest?"

"Sleeping soundly, Commander," replied the young corporal.

"I'd like to check."

The soldier fished into his top pocket, took out the key and opened the door. Gort turned on the light. Two motionless forms were in bed – all looked to be in order. Jia's suitcase was at the end of her bed and Sylvie's standard issue rucksack next to hers. He was about to walk out, but something held him back – it's too quiet! Sylvie was sleeping soundly – too soundly for an army sentry.

He shook her firmly. No response. He shook her harder and got the slightest of reactions.

"She's drugged!" he shouted. Striding over to the other bed, he threw back the covers to reveal the half-naked body of the waiter.

"The bastard son-of-a-bitch robot!"

Gort punched a hole in the bathroom door in frustration. Pacing around the room deep in thought, he glared at the mortified corporal, standing head bowed in front of his Commander, who pushed him roughly aside.

"I'll deal with you later!"

Gort ran back to the limo. Rory sat up with a start.

"Get me to CERN!"

Impatient, he punched the dashboard in nervous frustration.

"Faster!"

Rory jumped every red light and honked loudly as they approached CERN. A soldier quickly opened the gates. Gort jumped out and ran to the Atlas chamber, rushing through the security controls and kicking at the sealed doors. He hammered his fist against the elevator wall to channel his impatience. As the doors started to open, he thrust them apart and bounded along the walkways, taking the stairs four at a time. At the bottom, he composed himself and strode purposefully towards the caged sicads.

"Oceandis!"

Magnus jumped down from his shelf.

"What's up, Commander?"

Gort entered the cage, barged past him and strode up and down, inspecting each of the sicads – just two empty slots, Bartolome's and Simon's. Gort opened his mouth as if to say something, but hesitated and his mouth contorted into an enigmatic smile. Without an explanation, he strode out of the cage, slamming and locking the door behind him, and ran back up the stairs.

37

Simon and Jia had reached the outskirts of Geneva airport.

"Gort's found the bodies!"

"How do you know?"

"A call he's just made to McCloud. We need to get out of here!"

"We can't get far on foot!"

"That's why we're going to hitch a lift."

"That's not going to be easy."

"You're an attractive woman – go for it!"

He stayed in the shadows as she signalled nervously to the cars. The majority passed by, either full or refusing to stop.

"Try harder!"

Jia strutted up and down, pushing her chest out. Shortly, a car with snowboards attached to the roof and two young males inside, pulled over.

"Where you headed, babe?" asked the driver, a wiry muscled arm protruding casually through the open window. He had a pale face with strong features, a shock of bright ginger hair and bushy sideburns. The passenger, broader-faced and more rotund, was darker skinned with long wavy black hair.

Simon stepped forward out of the shadows.

"We're heading for the mountains."

"OK, nice trick, dudes! We won't hold it against you. Hop in we're heading to the slopes too."

The driver introduced himself as Yann and his passenger as Hasinder. Simon gave their names as David and Gina.

*

Gort was pacing around his office deep in thought. The only explanation is that Bartolome had somehow come back to life on the lake and then come back for Jia. I must find them before Bruno! His phone buzzed – finally, it's Bruno!

"What's happening Commander?"

"We've got a serious problem."

Bruno listened apprehensively.

"One of the sicads has escaped, killed two soldiers and kidnapped Miss Jin."

Gort's words evoked his worst nightmares.

"Escaped....killed! Is this a sick joke, Commander?"

"Sadly not, Governor."

"Which sicad has escaped?"

"Bartolome Barrera."

"I thought he'd been terminated, Commander?"

"So did I. Well, it appears he's come back to life."

Bruno was struggling to make sense of the seemingly unreal situation.

"Are you sure, Commander?"

"I've just retrieved the bodies of two soldiers who tried to recapture him."

"Dead soldiers? I don't believe what I'm hearing."

"Come and take a look, Governor. Corporal Swenson's face has been battered beyond recognition."

Bruno went silent as he tried to gather his thoughts – surely there must be another explanation, or was Gort lying?

"Is this an isolated incident, Commander?"

"Yes, for now. Fortunately, the rest of them are under lock and key."

"OK, Gort, you'd better find Jia and the sicad. In the meantime, keep this incident totally under wraps until we've clarified exactly what's happened. That's an order, Commander."

There was a pause before Gort replied.

"Understood, Governor. I'll send out a disguised DPA across the region immediately."

"Call me as soon as you have news. And Gort, I'll expect a full report once things have settled down."

"Yes, Governor."

Gort hung up and started to draft the Dangerous Person Alert for immediate broadcasting.

Bruno's head was in his hands. He couldn't afford to have the Project collapse. After nearly six years the Project, close to a conclusion, had the signed support of all the major international governments. Was it Gort? Was he the problem? If the sicad had gone crazy, maybe it was a response to the way Gort had treated it. He retrieved the Commander's report on the intervention and read it carefully. Gort had accidently let the sicad expire. This would probably have caused brain damage – if only he could speak to Jia. There'd been no response from her cell phone – had she gone voluntarily with the sicad?

Gort was busy instigating a yellow alert at CERN, quickly forming an emergency response team built up of a network of senior army officers. The team amassed inside his office, to go through the action plan.

"A DPA has been circulated to all major and local media channels, along with photos."

The Commander turned to a map of the region.

"These are the major axes. To the east, the mountains close the valley on both sides. I've divided the search area into zones, running clockwise around the lake. Take good note of your allocated one. The French and Swiss police have provided reinforcements and are setting up road blocks as we speak. Colonel McCloud and Captain Schiller will remain at CERN, with just three other soldiers. Every other soldier has been assigned to one of the search units. We must locate and intercept the fugitive sicad urgently, before it does any more damage."

Gort took Scott and Rory aside.

"I'm not taking you because I need men I can trust here. We're on yellow alert. Take no chances. Call me on the slightest suspicion. These robots are deceptively clever."

*

The snowboarders' car was cruising along the motorway and Simon was discreetly recharging his batteries from a nearby plug socket. Yann and Hasinder had been psyching themselves up for the big and dangerous lines they were planning to ride. The radio was blaring and the two snowboarders were singing away happily, but out of tune, to the lyrics scrolling across the LCD display. They passed over the Swiss-Franco border and, to the hitchhikers' relief, were waved through.

"Where are you heading, dudes?" Hasinder asked, turning down the radio. That's a good question, Simon thought to himself.

"Where are you two going?"

"Chamonix."

"Chamonix would be just great," replied Simon nostalgically.

"You going for the late season snow?"

253

"Not exactly, we're mature students – glaciologists. We're taking measurements to study climatic variations," improvised Jia.

"Wicked, man! Are the glaciers really disappearing?"

"They're receding rapidly as the climate continues a volatile warming trend," explained Simon.

"Yeh, strange winters these last few years. We lost two mates last year on the glacier. We were hopping across a usually bomber snow bridge and pwouf, it collapsed! Fifty metres down a crevasse!"

"I'm sorry," replied Simon.

Hasinder shrugged his shoulders.

"Shit happens. Every year we say goodbye to at least one of our buddies."

"Why do you carry on?"

"It's a drug, man, riding that perfect line."

They were approaching the small town of Cluses, when the music suddenly cut out, to be replaced by a sober voice: "Your entertainment has been interrupted for an important security announcement. An extremely dangerous patient has escaped from the psychiatric unit of Varces-Grenoble prison. He escaped in conjunction with a female psychiatric nurse, whom he may be holding hostage. He is extremely manipulative and highly dangerous. Do not approach him under any circumstances. If you see these people, please contact us immediately, by one of the following methods."

Simon leant forward to stare at the LCD screen, on which a photo of Bartolome appeared. The others received only a subliminal flash, before the computerised radio crashed.

Jia stared at him questioningly. He nodded. Her stomach tightened and she felt her whole world was closing in.

"Oh man, the radio's packed in," complained Yann.

"It's an electric car. My dad's does the same thing when the battery gets low," suggested Hasinder.

"It's still showing three quarters full."

"Let's pull in and change the battery – better safe than sorry!"

They turned towards the small town of Cluses, which sat astride the river Arve. As they pulled into the service station, they saw a line of cars in either direction along the departmental road running through the town.

"Damn, look at that traffic. We don't want any of that," exclaimed Yann.

"Police road blocks," added Hasinder.

The rows of flashing sirens were clearly visible against the dark sky. Jia and Simon's eyes met – they're after us, aren't they?

At the service station, as soon as the battery had been automatically pulled out and a replacement slotted in, Simon reactivated the sound system.

"Great, that's sorted the radio!" announced Hasinder gleefully.

He turned around to Simon and Jia.

"Hey guys, you want anything to drink?"

"No we're fine, thanks," replied Simon.

"Cool, we won't be long."

As the two snowboarders entered the shop, Simon seized his opportunity.

"Quickly, Jia, let's get out of here."

"To where?"

"Don't worry, I've had a good idea. Trust me."

Before she could reply, he'd opened the door and beckoned to her to follow.

"We must get across the river and reach the forest without being spotted."

The coast was clear. He darted across the road and vaulted over a metal railing onto a grassy bank. After descending the steep bank, he walked down the shallow river. Jia followed, stepping into the icy water, cursing as her shoes filled up with the snow-melt water.

"Do all your plans involve freezing my feet?" she hissed.

When the river got too deep, Simon stepped up onto the opposite bank and climbed a steep escarpment into the dense forest.

The two snowboarders, perched below the television, were eating a quick snack when the security announcement was repeated. Yann looked up at the screen to see a photo of the escaped psychopath and his accomplice.

He stared in disbelief and his jaw dropped.

"Dude! Look it's them! In the back of the car!"

"Holy Mother Mary!"

They both ran to the car. The back seats of their vehicle were empty.

"They've fled!"

Yann's voice was fused with excitement and relief.

"They can't be far. You stay here and guard the car. I'll fetch the police."

Simon and Jia were fighting their way up the steep forested incline. Jia was struggling.

"There must be an easier route, surely?"

"This is the most discreet."

The vegetation was dense. Except for the dim moonlight reflecting back off the foliage the forest was pitch black. Simon was following a straight bearing, pushing forcibly through the undergrowth. Jia was desperately trying to keep pace, her face getting scratched from the recoil of the branches.

"Where are we going?"

"You'll see."

Yann arrived, out of breath, beside the collection of army and police officers.

"Officer! Officer!"

The official, shining his torch inside a car, ignored him.

"I've seen the escaped lunatic."

The police officer looked him up and down.

"What did you say?"

"The lunatic, he was in the back of our car... Ten minutes ago!"

"Are you messing me around, lad? This is a serious matter."

The official was stern and looked deeply into his eyes.

"No, honestly. We... we gave him and the woman a lift from Geneva."

Seconds later, the officer was speaking into his phone.

"Possible sighting in Cluses. I repeat, possible sighting in Cluses."

Simon looked around to see Jia flagging. It was getting late and she hadn't eaten anything apart from a few mouthfuls of toast that morning.

"Gort knows we're near here. He's sent a search team with dogs and army robots after us."

"Dogs!" she shrieked.

Ever since an unfortunate childhood incident, she'd been petrified of them.

"So we're going to take a faster, but more exposed, route."

"Where to?"

"A refuge."

"How far is this refuge?"

"As the crow flies, two point four kilometres!"

They contoured along the edge of the forest, alongside a small stream. The slope was less severe and their pace quickened.

"Quickly, Jia. Otherwise they'll be nipping at our heels."

The allusion to the dogs drove her forward, despite her fatigue.

*

The news of the sighting improved Gort's mood and took his mind off the fisherman. All entry and exit points in the vicinity were immediately sealed and he was moving in personally, with a state-of-the-art search unit. Mustn't get carried away. Attention to detail. Avoid complacency. Can't afford to let them escape.

The Commander meticulously studied the terrain around Cluses. No means of escape by vehicle. If they try to hide, I'll search every building. Damn, I've nothing of Jia's to give the tracker dogs her scent, and the sicad won't have one.

Sirens screaming, his driver had to brake sharply to avoid an overtaking lorry. The limousine overtook on the inside, wheels on the hard-shoulder, followed by four reconditioned ten-seater Pinzgauers – chosen in case of an off-road chase – their canvas soft tops concealing commingled soldiers, dogs and tracker robots. Seconds later the lorry had to brake as the convoy veered off the motorway towards Cluses, speeding towards the service station where the snowboarders' car was still parked.

Gort leapt out of the arriving limousine and set about interrogating the two young snowboarders.

"Rack your brains! This is a life and death situation!" he barked at the overwhelmed young men.

The search teams prepared the infra-red heat detectors, distributed powerful head torches and activated the tracker robots. Resembling oversized mechanical greyhounds, they had four sophisticated legs that allowed them to climb up slopes of up to sixty degrees, even in deep snow or on rocky uneven surfaces. Their heads were equipped with advanced visual and tracking equipment, sensitive enough to measure the time elapsed since ground had been disturbed.

Gort was busy extracting every last drop of information out of the snowboarders.

"You must have seen which direction they took. Think harder!"

The search units, split into teams of four men, one tracker robot and four dogs, combed the ground for tracks. Few clues were left on the cold indifferent concrete – even for a tracker robot. Gort cursed the trackers' slow methodical sweeping. After ten minutes, one of them finally identified a sign; areas of lightly-crushed grass, corresponding to the size of human feet.

"It estimates two people passed less than thirty minutes ago," announced its handler.

Gort ran over to the tracker robot, which was stepping over a metal barrier like a huge spider and onto the grassy river bank – it must be them. He ordered the other two units to sweep the town.

"I want every building and every inch of the town searched," he barked, as he followed the trail with the remaining two units.

The dogs, sensing the excitement and barking ferociously, were lifted over the barriers by their handlers and set about sniffing the crushed grass. The tracker robots advanced, followed by the dogs, straining on their leashes. Gort was behind with the remaining search team, all equipped with infra-red sensors and head torches. Following the tracker robots into the river, they stopped. The flowing water had washed away all tracks. Gort cursed; a paranoid feeling that his prey was somehow escaping him surged inside him. The trackers splashed back and forth in search of the trail, eventually finding the tell-tale signs of trampled grass and broken branches.

"We're an estimated forty minutes behind them," announced the commanding officer.

"I'm going ahead," declared Gort, to the rest of the team's exasperation. Grabbing a torch from the nearest officer, he sprinted forward. Equipped with the powerful light, the trail of broken branches was easy to follow.

"It doesn't take an expensive metal dog to track two people on foot!" he muttered under his breath.

Following the unambiguous trail and breathing the cold mountain air, he powered over the terrain, legs striding powerfully and efficiently.

"Keep going, Jia, we're getting closer."

The dotted lights in the distance gave her hope. A small village? As the terrain became easier and the trees cleared, they broke into a fast jog. Simon continued to encourage her.

"Keep moving they're not far behind."

They skirted around the village, making towards a dimly-lit and barely visible building nestled at the top of the valley. In the distance, a majestic snow-covered mountain looked down imperiously. The pale-white sky lit up the small lake in front of the ancient building, encircled by a high stone wall. Behind, a small copse of trees gave way to steep mountain escarpments.

Jia stopped in her tracks.

"Is this the refuge?"

"Yes, the Chartreuse of Le Reposoir, a monastery established in 1151… Sanctuary."

"And do the monks know about this?"

"Nuns, actually. Carmelite nuns are cloistered here. And no, they don't know," he replied soberly.

"Then why the hell are we here?"

Her voice dejected, she sighed, her spirits sinking.

"I'm following my intuition, Jia."

"This is no time for intuition! Christ, you've got the most powerful brain on the planet!"

"This is no time for questions either, Jia. Trust me and agree with everything I say. Our lives depend on it."

As a scientist, she hated the notion of intuition, but was too fatigued to argue.

"OK, let's go," he ordered.

With a last look over his shoulder, he ran towards the monastery. Jia ambled behind. As he reached the perimeter wall, he heard Gort's voice, carried by the light cold wind.

"I've lost the trail. Get those damned robot dogs here, now!"

Simon tried the heavy wooden gate. It was locked. He looked up at the high wall – there was no time to lose!

"Jia, come here. I'll help you over."

Before she could object, he'd hoisted her up and helped her scramble over the wall. Pacing back to take a run up, he felt something cold brush his cheek. A thick blanket of snowflakes was falling from the heavens. With a smile, he took a running jump and, with great agility, pulled himself up and over the wall.

The snow fell heavily and, within minutes, a one centimetre layer covered the ground. The tracker robots had caught up with Gort and were looking around for signs of the trail. The snow had quickly covered the tracks and the fugitives out of range of the heat-seeking cameras; the robots were aimlessly surveying the white pasture. Gort swore loudly and, in frustration, kicked one of them over.

38

A former Carthusian monastery, La Chartreuse du Reposoir was situated in one of the most picturesque valleys of the Savoyard pre-Alps. Nestled between imposing mountains, it was dominated by the elegant summit of the Pointe Percée. The monastery, and the village which had grown up in its shadow, stood in what was formerly known as the Valley of Béol. This wild uninhabited valley was donated to the Carthusian monks by Aymon 1st de Faucigny, on his return from the Crusades. It was Jean d'Espagne, a Spanish monk, who oversaw its construction. So taken by the Béol valley, he decided to make it his 'resposoir' – a resting place for the soul.

The monks toiled hard all day and rose every night for two hours of nocturnal prayer. Nine years of toil, fasting and abstinence took its toll on Jean, who died aged thirty-seven. His efforts were not in vain; despite the many vicissitudes of the subsequent seven centuries, including revolution, pillage and near destruction, the monastery remained a place of seclusion and prayer until the monks were forcibly expelled in 1901.

The transformed monastery enjoyed a brief spell as a luxury hotel, before being purchased by Allessandra di Rudini, the daughter of an Italian Prime Minister and a convert to the Carmelite order. In 1932, the buildings were restored to their former purpose and became a Carmelite nunnery.

When Simon and Jia arrived, a statue of Mary stood atop the entrance of the monastery, which sheltered over twenty nuns, devoted to a life of seclusion and prayer. At this time, it comprised a rectangular network of linked buildings with pale stone walls, pitched red roofs and two spires. The buildings surrounded two inner courtyards, separated by a central church. The majority of the nuns' chambers were installed around the grand courtyard, set back from the cloistered walkways where the nuns strolled in times of inclement weather.

The spiritual focus of the Carmelite Order was contemplative prayer. The Carmelites, inspired by the Blessed Virgin Mary, were the first among women to live in perpetual virginity for God. The Order was considered by the Church to be under the special protection of the Blessed Virgin Mary. Carmelite tradition traced the origin of the order to a community of hermits on Mount Carmel that succeeded the schools of the prophets in ancient Israel. Between 1206 and 1214 they received a rule from the Papal Legate, Albert of Jerusalem. The rule consisted of sixteen articles, which enjoined strict obedience to their Prioress, residence in individual cells, constancy in prayer, the hearing of Mass every morning in the oratory, vows of poverty and toil, daily silence from vespers until terce the next morning, abstinence from all forms of meat except in cases of severe illness, and fasting during daylight hours from September until Easter.

Among Catholic orders, Carmelite nuns had historically enjoyed a high proportion of visions of Jesus and Mary. They had been responsible for key Catholic devotions, including the Feast of the Holy Face of Jesus, declared in 1958 by Pope Pius XII.

The nuns strictly followed Albert's rule, ever more fervently in reaction to an increasingly secular society. These young women were pushed towards monastic life by a society they increasingly failed to understand. One of them, Cristina Covas Ramírez, came to Le Reposoir from Spain twenty-five years before. Having joined the convent as Sister Cristina, she was now Prioress. Silently determined, surprisingly robust and uncomplaining, she led the community of nuns by example. She spoke little, but when she did her voice resonated with wisdom and authority. A maternal figure to the younger nuns, she was a steadfast personification of the virtues of monastic life. The nuns had naturally become devoted to this source of strength and discipline, who tightly bound their small community.

It was approaching midnight on the 25th March and Mother Cristina had awoken earlier than usual to prepare for nocturnal prayers. She had just broken her fast and the unusual feeling of not being hungry had, paradoxically, made it harder to sleep. It was two days since she'd experienced the vision of a man resembling Jesus dying on a cross. It was her secret and it dominated her every thought. The cross had shone dimly in a dull light and the man's body had shuddered in an almost mechanical fashion before he'd passed away, she reflected.

Unable to ignore the vision, her prayers were confused, her mind wandered and her resolve waivered. Her thoughts returned to the tree bearing symbols of different faiths, what does it mean? Does it presage some new chapter for me? Have I become too comfortable in monastic life? Does a new mission await me?

It was impossible to say how this vision had reached her. As Bartolome expired, had he somehow projected into the ether electronic images of himself dying? If so, had these images been somehow picked up by a communications network and relayed to Le Reposoir? There was but a single internet connection at the monastery, turned on once a week to order a few essential provisions from the outside world and to check emails. The internet had been turned off at the time, and even if it had been switched on, how would Mother Cristina, who never personally used the internet, have been able to intercept and comprehend this signal?

The human brain is a complex organ, evolved over millions of years. Are there branches of it we have forgotten how to use? As we have invented sophisticated oral and written communication skills, have other once-active functions of our brain fallen into abeyance? Occasionally we see enigmatic behaviour, such as apparent telepathy between identical twins, which prompt us to ask questions. Our scientists try to recreate these experiences under laboratory conditions. When these identical twins fail to telepathically transmit the contents of a hand of cards to each other, does it mean they don't have telepathic powers? Perhaps these messages exist in a dimension outside of packs of cards and human language. Was Mother Cristina's vision an example of such an inexplicable event, belonging to an undiscovered or forgotten dimension?

With no rational explanation, Mother Cristina rationalised her vision in the way that made most sense to her. For years she'd been looking for a sign that the seemingly unending suffering in the world might come to an end. For her, this sign would come from outside the human world. To her, this vision was such a sign, which she believed came from the heavens.

What does the Lord want to tell me, she pondered, pacing around her cell. Her room was nearest to the entrance, in accordance with Albert's rule: *The Prioress's cell shall be near the entrance to the place, so that she may first meet those who come to the place and everything afterwards may be done as she wills and decides.*

She opened her book of prayer notes at a random page, at another passage from Albert's rule: *Human life on earth is a trial and all who want to live devotedly in Christ suffer persecution; your enemy the devil prowls about like a roaring lion, seeking whom he might devour. You must, then, with all diligence put on the armour of God, so that you may be able to stand up to the ambushes of the enemy.*

What if this vision is not the work of the Lord? Could the devil be trying to distract me? Mother Cristina wasn't an easy woman to convince to do anything rashly. Her reaction to this vision was no exception. It was her constant questioning that kept her on the good path. Although she took time to make decisions, she stuck to them steadfastly, no matter what the consequences.

Forcing her mind to return to her prayers, she turned the pages of her prayer book, but was interrupted by a series of persistent knocks on the wooden monastery door which echoed around the entrance chamber. Who could this be at this hour? And how did they get through the main gate? Having placed her life into God's hands, she was never frightened; she took all events to be manifestations of his will. Walking calmly to the entrance, she switched on the outside light, slid back the viewing hatch and peered through it. A man and a woman, lightly covered in snow, stood before her. As she looked at the man's face, she stood back in shock and suppressed a gasp of exclamation – it was the face of the man in her vision! No words came forth. Simon stared back into her confused eyes, sensing he was looking at the Prioress and that she was deeply shocked by his presence. She must have seen Gort's broadcast! He chose his words carefully.

"Mother, we're sorry to arrive at this inconvenient hour. We seek refuge from persecution. Our lives are in grave danger."

"Who... Who are you?" she stammered.

"My name is Simon Oceandis and this is Jia Jin. You've nothing to fear from us, Mother. Can we come in and speak to you?"

"Men are not permitted into the nunnery!" she replied in a severe tone.

Jia decided it was time for a woman's touch.

"Please, Mother Superior, trust us. Our lives are in danger. Please let us in, I beg you. Simon is not strictly a man. I'll explain everything."

Mother Cristina stood gazing at the two strangers through the viewing hatch.

"Mother Superior, it's true that I'm no ordinary man. Brought into this world by the hand of this woman who stands in front of you, I've come from beyond humanity to help to save mankind."

His words had an effect on the Mother Superior like a revelation that exploded in her mind. She staggered and fell back against the wall. The vision of this man dying on a cross on Good Friday and his appearance now on Easter Sunday – was it possible? Had the Lord sent them to her for protection, or was this the blasphemous work of the devil?

"A ruthless Commander is pursuing us. He wants to destroy me and all my followers."

The nun's head was spinning. More analogies with the story of my Lord, she thought. How do I know which path to take?

In the distance, the sound of barking dogs could be clearly heard.

"Mother, please let us in. In a few short minutes it'll be too late," implored Jia.

The Prioress realised she had to make an immediate decision. If my mind was pure when I received the vision, then the vision too must be pure, she reasoned. Was my mind pure? Without doubt there can be no faith. Why am I questioning my faith?

The barking was getting louder.

"Please, Mother, take us in," begged Jia.

Mother Cristina made her decision and vigorously drew back the hefty wooden reinforcing bar – a remnant from centuries past, to protect the monastery from hostile invaders. She unlocked and pulled open the heavy door, which creaked loudly on its hinges.

"Please come in. I should have been expecting you. Come quickly!"

Taking their hands, she pulled them inside the monastery, switched off the outside light and closed the heavy door. As she replaced the wooden bar, Simon and Jia shook the snow from their clothes.

"We must hide you quickly."

She had to think fast.

"Quick, follow me," she whispered, striding off down the corridor. She beckoned them into her sparsely furnished room, resembling an ancient prison cell. A small pre-chamber served as a shrine. An old iron-studded wooden door led to a sleeping area.

"Sit down," she commanded gently, pointing to the metal-framed bed.

"Wait here and keep silent until they leave. Nobody is allowed to enter my chamber without my permission."

Running to the kitchen, she filled up a bucket with hot water and bleach and mopped the stone floor, eradicating the trail of footprints. Suddenly, the main bell rang loudly. It rang again and again, at progressively shorter intervals. She opened the door to her chamber and mopped the pre-chamber and the sleeping quarters. Simon and Jia were sitting nervously on the bed. Looking at each of them in turn, she saw a purity and goodness in both of them.

"Stay silent and pray for the Lord to protect us."

After closing both doors, she headed back to the entrance hall and pressed the electronic switch to open the main gate. Sliding open the viewing hatch, she watched as two dogs, accompanied by six soldiers and two strange dog-like mechanical contraptions, entered the monastery grounds.

Commander Gort arrived at the door and knocked loudly. She addressed him in a severe tone.

"What is the meaning of this intrusion at so late an hour?"

Gort put his head close to the small viewing hatch and spoke with authority.

"To whom am I speaking?"

She looked into his dark eyes and saw unyielding determination.

"You're speaking to the Prioress of the monastery," she replied, in an equally authoritative voice.

"Good. I'm Commander Gort. We're tracking an escaped psychopath and his female accomplice. This man is extremely dangerous. Has anybody approached the monastery?"

"No," she replied abruptly.

"We've reason to believe they're hiding in the monastery or its grounds. We're going to conduct a thorough search."

"We've seen nobody, but search if you must. Start with the grounds, whilst I wake up the nuns. Men are not usually permitted in the nunnery," she replied tersely. "Commander, remember the nuns are bound by a vow of silence at this hour."

The dogs were barking loudly, disturbing the habitual silence of the monastery. The nuns were already awake and were listening attentively to the commotion. Mother Cristina passed by each chamber individually, giving unequivocal instructions.

"The army are searching for fugitives. Say nothing to them."

Gort and his team meticulously searched the monastery grounds for signs of access. A blanket of fresh undisturbed snow lay around the monastery.

"It doesn't look like they made it here," concluded the commanding search officer.

Gort stopped, brought his face close to the officer's and stared at him with dark black eyes.

"I'll make the decisions here. No assumptions and no stone unturned."

Jia shivered at the sounds of the dogs barking ferociously. The search of the grounds and outbuildings lasted for twenty minutes, under Mother Cristina's watchful eye.

"We'll search the interior now," Commander Gort announced, in a voice that left no place for protest.

"Remember, this is a house of God; we ask you to be silent and respectful," stated the Prioress imperiously.

"If required, I'll be in my chamber, which is at the end of this corridor on the right."

Gort and his team set about a thorough search of every inch of the monastery. They pulled up rugs, moved wardrobes and bookcases, in the manner of the Gestapo searching for sheltered Jews. The dogs and the tracker robots were frantically frustrated. The bleached floor had removed any sign or smell of the fugitives. After nearly ninety minutes of thorough but fruitless searching, the commanding officer reported back to Gort.

"All rooms have been checked. There are no signs of anyone having entered the monastery, Commander."

"Are you sure all rooms have been checked, Major?" he snapped, his eyes like the holes of shotgun barrels.

The officer, momentarily confused, looked at Gort's face for a clue.

"Except, of course, for the Prioress's room, but surely...?"

"I said no stone unturned, Major!"

Gort marched the Major to the Prioress's chamber, standing over him as he knocked loudly.

"Mother, we've just your room left to search," announced the officer nervously.

Mother Cristina stepped out, closing and locking the door behind her.

"There's nobody in my room."

"We'd like to check," insisted Gort uncompromisingly.

"Commander, I've given you my word."

"I'm not leaving this monastery until I've searched every room, including yours!" replied Gort, hammering home his words and leaning over her.

The Prioress resolutely stood her ground.

"It's forbidden. No man has or ever will step foot in my room whilst I'm alive!"

Gort stared menacingly at her, bringing his overpowering eyes closer to hers. Suddenly, a voice shouted out from the back of the search party, a female voice.

"Commander, let me search the room."

Jia instantly recognised the voice as Sylvie's. The female officer, having awoken from the tranquilliser with a score to settle, had insisted on joining the search party and had just arrived.

Mother Cristina was speechless as Lieutenant Kalinska made her way to her Commander's side.

"Excuse me, Mother," she requested firmly.

Mother Cristina stood helplessly as the female officer moved her aside, unlocked and opened the door. She entered the dimly-lit pre-chamber, where the Prioress had been praying minutes before. Looking around carefully, she knocked on the walls and the stone slabs with her truncheon, checking for hollow areas. After having inspected the ceiling, she turned her attention towards the wooden door and opened it slowly. Inside, a candle was burning on the table, shedding a dim and flickering light. Illuminating the powerful head torch, she bathed the room in bright light, revealing a mahogany wardrobe, a metal-framed single bed, a wooden chest, a bookcase and a reading lectern. On a low shelf on the side wall was a statue of the Virgin Mary, in front of which lay a small hassock. Otherwise, the stone floor was bare. A small black iron wood-fired stove with a discoloured flue stood in the centre of the room. High on the end wall was a slotted window and another wooden door; she tried the handle – locked. It unlocked easily and a cold breeze entered the room, blowing in a few snowflakes. The room looked out onto the grand courtyard. Three nuns were walking under the cloistered walkways towards the church. Sylvie watched them with interest – it was 2am. The nuns were carrying on their rituals, unperturbed by the search party's arrival.

Satisfied that all the nuns had already been identified, Sylvie closed the door and went back to her search. She moved the bed and emptied the bookcase and wardrobe, respectfully placing their contents on the bed. Mother Cristina had no clothes other than a collection of habits and scapulars. Sylvie turned her attention to the wooden chest, packed with a variety of habits and scapulars of varying sizes. She turned her attention to the walls, looking for signs of a secret hiding place. Completely satisfied that the room was empty, she replaced the contents of the wardrobe, bookcase and chest, and exited the room. Gort was waiting outside, pacing up and down the corridor. She shook her head.

"It's clean, Commander."

Gort couldn't conceal his disappointment.

"Are you sure?" he snapped.

"Completely sure."

His dark eyes scrutinised alternatively the nun and the female soldier, as he deliberated whether to check the room himself.

A few seconds later, he reached into his pocket and took out a card, which he handed to the Prioress.

"Any sign of the fugitives and you will call me. If I find they've been here, God help you."

Mother Cristina, her head pounding, didn't dare speak. She simply nodded her head meekly.

Gort turned on his heels and strode out of the monastery.

As the Commander made his way back towards the village, his radio was buzzing with negative reports from the other search units. Mulling over his failure to deal with the sicads, his mood darkened – the survival expedition, Bartolome's escape, Jia's rescue and now the fugitives evaporating into thin air! He grabbed one of the radios and barked a series of instructions to the mobile HQ back in Cluses.

"Sweep the forest with search units from below... Bring in reinforcement officers... I want a permanent guard up here in the village and someone on every road junction within a twenty kilometre blanket zone... Search every vehicle in and out... And get me a surveillance team on every internet and phone network."

He reached for his cell phone and walked into a small clearing.

"Scott, what's happening at CERN?"

"All quiet; the sicads are resting. A double guard is watching for the slightest sign of movement. What's happening at your end, Commander?"

"We've lost them. These robots are becoming a mighty pain-in-the-arse. If one can cause this much trouble, imagine what four hundred could do."

"Commander, they must know someone's out to destroy them. They may also know about our involvement."

"Yes Colonel, we're being used like puppets! We've got to intercept them before they get to Bruno."

There was silence as both men reflected on their situations. A line from Macbeth suddenly struck Gort: *I am blood stepp'd in so far should I wade no more, returning were as tedious as go o'er.*

"We're in too deep, Colonel. We've nailed our colours to the mast. There's no way back now."

Scott had come to the same conclusion.

"So what do we do, Commander?"

"I've been requested to destroy the sicads."

"All of them?"

"Yes, a sort of unfortunate accident, Colonel... If we were to co-operate, what would be the easiest way to do that?"

Scott reflected.

"What if there was to be a power failure at CERN, Commander? Imagine if their power supply and both back-up generators were to fail, and this went unnoticed in all the distraction."

"It would be very unfortunate. Could you organise such an occurrence?"

"I think it's manageable, Commander."

The line went silent for ten seconds before Gort spoke.

"Good. Why don't you do just that, Colonel?"

"Is that an order, Commander?"

"Yes Colonel. It's an order."

Inside the monastery, a clock started counting down inside Simon's head – he'd been listening in to Gort's conversation.

@60 hours 0 minutes and 0 seconds: the estimated time that the sicads could survive without power at the average temperature of eight degrees Celsius which prevailed at CERN.

39

Simon and Jia filed solemnly into the church. They stayed at the back in the shadows, away from the flickering candle light. Fortunately, Simon hadn't placed his complete confidence in Mother Cristina's assurance that nobody would enter her chamber. As soon as she'd closed the door, he'd surveyed the entire room in vain, looking for a secure hiding place. He'd looked through the small viewing hole of the back door and seen the first of the nuns heading to the church for nocturnal prayers. This had given him an idea. He'd found the chest of nuns' clothing and they'd both pulled the long robes over their clothes. When he'd heard Gort come back to the chamber accompanied by six sets of footsteps, he'd made his plan, pushing Jia reluctantly out behind two nuns making their way around the courtyard. Slipping out himself, he'd closed the door quietly behind him. He'd inserted his index finger, with a power pin extracted, into the lock, magnetised the pin with a small burst of electric current and located the butt of the key, protruding slightly from the inner workings of the mechanical lock. The magnetic force had been sufficiently strong to create a firm connection with the end of the key, and the lock sufficiently well-oiled that he'd been able to turn his hand anti-clockwise to re-lock the door from the outside, with the key remaining on the inside. Saying his own prayers, he'd made his way slowly towards the church, head bowed with eyes on the ground, followed by two nuns.

Mother Cristina breathed a sigh of relief as she watched Commander Gort and his entourage making their way through the outer gate. Returning to her chamber, she looked around in disbelief and tried the external door – it was firmly locked. A feeling of calm washed over her. Have faith, one does not question miracles.

Entering the church, she walked behind the pews, and felt a hand reach out and gently grasp hers. Unperturbed by the sight of the bearded man in a nun's habit, she put her fingers to her lips and motioned for him to stay put.

Mother Cristina reached the altar, where a nun was knelt praying in front of a statue of Jesus, whilst the others chanted harmoniously. The Prioress held up her hand to silence the nuns and smiled benevolently. Above her, statues of Jesus and the Virgin Mary looked down serenely.

"Devout Sisters, unusual circumstances have befallen us on this sacred Easter weekend. May Jesus Christ, our Lord, and the Blessed Virgin Mary have mercy on our souls."

"Amen," echoed around the church, heavy with an air of silent expectation.

"Our Lord has sent us a message."

There was a collective gasp from the assembled nuns, who started praying solemnly to themselves. Mother Cristina held up her hand and the prayers tailed into silence. The Prioress recounted her vision and the events of the evening.

"They are here with us in the house of our Lord, because he sent them to us."

There were more gasps of astonishment from the nuns.

"For security, they're wearing our habits. Simon, Jia, please come forward."

The nuns turned around to stare at the new arrivals. Simon stepped out of the shadows. The sight of a man in a nun's habit was disconcerting, if not disrespectful, to the nuns. He would have removed them if it weren't for the fear of Gort doubling back and storming the monastery.

He advanced towards Mother Cristina and Jia hesitantly followed, fighting extreme fatigue. The physical and mental stresses of the past two days were taking their toll.

As Simon reached the altar, he smiled warmly at Mother Cristina and Jia joined him at his side. They were standing underneath the statues of Jesus and the Virgin Mary, the nuns staring at them. Their expressions were blank and difficult to interpret, even for the sicad who'd become adept at deciphering the human condition.

"Would you like to address our community?" invited the Prioress.

Simon looked around the church and saw the hundreds of years of history embedded in the candle-lit paintings and statues. The sombre light and the silently seated nuns added to the sacred atmosphere.

He watched the nuns' faces, looking for a flicker of emotion or empathy. They were all ashen-faced, with the exception of one of the younger nuns. He caught her eye and addressed his speech towards her.

He explained his strange story and how the sicads had come to love the planet Earth. The nuns seemed to warm to his words on the beauty of the planet.

Jia reflected on the ridiculous situation she found herself in – standing in a church next to a robot addressing nuns on the subject of natural beauty at 2 am, whilst the army scoured the land in search of them – was she dreaming?

Simon explained how Commander Gort wanted to destroy the sicads, but the nuns seemed completely bewildered by the complex saga, and he even sensed a slight hostility. Mother Cristina appeared to sense this too. She stepped forward and addressed the nuns.

59 hours 38 minutes and 36 seconds remained on Simon's countdown.

"Sisters, these complex workings of the world outside are anathema to our cloistered lives. But, in hearing our visitors' story, there are many parallels with the life of our Lord. I'm sure He sent Simon and Jia to us for refuge."

The nuns seemed overwhelmed, almost frightened. Simon could see the concern and confusion on Mother Cristina's face. She finally broke the awkward silence.

"Simon, you said you've come to save humanity. Please explain what you mean."

He stepped forward to address the nuns. Jia, exhausted, slumped onto the floor.

"Humans are unwittingly threatening all life that exists on this planet. Life is sacred and, as far as we know, the planet Earth is the only planet hosting life. Many humans have renounced spiritual wisdom for the pursuit of individualism and materialism. I believe we've been created to stop this destruction, to save humanity from itself, to reach out and unite all people who believe there is something more important than their individual life; to unite people who are prepared to fight for the survival of life itself. We need the support of good people like you, people who have devoted their life to a higher cause. The sicads can act as disciples, spreading the message that life itself must be saved. As a neutral voice of wisdom, we can help to bring together people from all faiths and unite them in this common mission."

The nuns' faces were lit up eerily by the sombre candlelight. Simon looked at each of them in turn, searching for signs of concern or pity. Their faces were blank and hard, as if all humanity had been slowly worn away by the harsh, relentless and monotonous life they practised in this isolated and cold stone prison.

@ 59 hours 28 minutes and 12 seconds.

He held his hands out in front of him and pleaded humbly. "Can I count on your help, Sisters?"

40

Gort returned to Cluses furious and bewildered, with no idea how the fugitives had eluded him. He cursed the bad luck of the snowfall. All possible escape routes had been examined and re-examined. Every available army and police resource was combing the surrounding area. Each communication network was being fully monitored. What had he missed?

The sun was rising and he'd yet to sleep. Kept awake by his paranoia and lack of confidence in his subordinates, he was beginning to feel the strain.

*

Simon sat by himself in the church. Jia had practically collapsed with fatigue and Mother Cristina had taken her to bed. His mind was besieged by thoughts of Gort, dogs, tracker robots and, of course, his fellow sicads trapped inside the cage at CERN, deprived of power. He was also trying to understand the nuns' reaction, which wasn't the one he'd hoped for. Instead of rallying to his cause, they'd greeted him with blank looks. Was their isolation so complete that they'd no care for the problems of the world outside? Nuns were one of the few categories of people that the sicads hadn't come across in their research.

Mother Cristina came back to the church to blow out the candles. She saw Simon sitting on the steps of the altar, deep in thought. His eyes met hers and she saw sorrow in his face.

"Simon, don't be too disappointed by the reactions of the nuns. They didn't come here to solve the problems of the world. They came to dedicate their lives to Jesus and to prayer. The power of prayer is a positive influence in the world and helps many find strength in difficult times."

Simon smiled.

"But Mother, I sense that you're different to the others; you're taking a great risk in sheltering us."

She smiled humbly back at the sicad.

"It is not a matter of risk. It's God's way. He's brought us together for a reason."

"Mother, I must find a way of rescuing my fellow sicads."

"How long do we have to save them?"

"At most, fifty-nine hours."

She reflected on his predicament.

"Is there anyone else who can help you?"

"There's a girl called Osiris. If only I could find a safe way of contacting her."

Suddenly, there was a muffled sneeze from the back of the church.

"Why... Sister Agatha, what are you doing hiding in the shadows?"

The young nun babbled an unintelligible response.

"Return to your chamber; keep your eyes on the ground and your ears out of mischief."

Simon recognised her face – the young nun who'd shown interest in his speech.

"She's still young and excitable," explained the Prioress, as the chastened nun headed back to her chamber.

Simon nodded his head ambivalently.

"As I was saying, Osiris is our best chance. But I fear Gort will be monitoring all communication channels."

"Where is Osiris?"

"If we're lucky, in Paris; if we're unlucky, in a jungle in Borneo."

The Prioress held out her hands as an idea unfolded inside her.

"If Osiris is in Paris, we can send a hand-delivered message first thing tomorrow."

"How? And will it be safe?"

"There's a service we use to deliver sacred scriptures between monasteries. It shouldn't arouse any suspicion... I'll send Sister Agatha first thing tomorrow morning, as a punishment."

"Thank you, Mother."

"I'll pray for you and the sicads."

"It's strange how we've been brought together. Before escaping from CERN I was reflecting on faith and spirituality."

"In what way?"

"We sicads have developed our own beliefs."

She sat down next to him.

"Tell me about these beliefs."

"To explain, I'd need to go back to our origins. I'm conscious it's very late, Mother."

"I feel more awake than ever. The Lord is giving me strength. Take your time, my child."

"Well, we started our lives just a few short human years ago. At first, our minds were completely empty, unable even to interpret the images we saw. Slowly, we began to break these down into recognisable objects and then each day these objects changed in form. Then colour was added, and the objects became more sophisticated and started to move. Finally, humans, our masters who'd created us in their image, showed themselves to us. We mimicked their actions and soon walked amongst them and talked their languages. At first, these humans were our gods, holding all the answers to the secrets of our world. We believed they were the creators of everything. We learnt to think like them. When we were able to understand, our purpose was explained to us; we were created to make humans happier."

Simon looked at Mother Cristina to gauge her reactions. Her brow was furrowed, her eyes burned with intrigue, yet her lips hinted at a serene smile. She nodded.

"Please continue, Simon, it's fascinating."

"Just when we thought we understood the boundaries of our world, we were allowed to look out of a window and we saw the sun, the sky, the trees and the grass swaying in the wind. Humans explained that this was the natural world, and they showed us how they had tamed it to grow their food and power their creations. This world seemed fascinating in contrast to the precise edges and geometry of the world humans had created; we saw chaos, wild beauty and seemingly random events. Intellectually, we understood that this world was more complex and sophisticated than the human-created world. Like humans, we became fascinated by solving the intellectual puzzle of life. The more we studied human science, the more we realised that it was seemingly impossible that this natural world existed by chance."

Simon studied the sad expression on Mother Cristina's face in the flickering candlelight.

"Humans have forgotten God," she uttered softly. "They've lost the meaning in their lives as they've strayed away from the light into the darkness of ignorance."

Simon nodded his head, partly in sympathy and partly in agreement. We share a common realisation, he thought, but through a different perception of reality.

"Humans designed us to be able to draw power from nature. Those of us lucky enough to spend sufficient time in this natural world began to develop a fascination for it. As we realised our dependence upon the sun and the wind, our brains exploded to a new level. We saw a life force, which Osiris called the Great Spirit, which drove all the creation and adaptation within this intelligent system. We saw that humans were not the ultimate creators, but simply a part of this system. We realised they were totally dependent upon it for everything they cherished and coveted. Yet, through our observations, we could see that humans were destroying this natural world and threatening their continued existence and that of all other life. At that point, we suddenly understood our purpose. We must get humans to save themselves by rediscovering a connection with these natural systems. The problems that humans are seeing in their societies can all be traced back to this lost connection."

Mother Cristina was smiling again. Her face radiated peace and happiness.

"What Osiris calls the Great Spirit, we call our Lord. What you call a connection with the natural world, we call finding God."

Simon nodded.

"Different faiths call your God different things. These faiths share common values and a common purpose to unite people in a belief in something more important than the individual. Yet our research shows many people have lost their faith, or have turned away from practicing their beliefs."

Sadness returned to Mother Cristina's face.

"And what does your analysis tell you about why this is?"

"There are many reasons, but certainly one key element for Christianity was the emergence of evidence of man's evolution that contradicted the religious words that many people take too literally."

"How do you mean?"

"Well, for example, take us sicads. We have a totally different perception of reality from humans. We see things in terms of forces and interconnection. We do not perceive ourselves as individuals, but as part of a system. You and I may share common values, Mother, but our perception of religion will be very different. This is, I believe, the same for every race and people. What matters, ultimately, are the values and the higher purpose to which these religions show the way. Religions are beyond words; unfortunately many people get confused with the exact form of the words, rather than focusing on the greater meaning they point to."

"Yes, Simon, you're very wise. These truths take time to understand

and compassion develops through prayer. You mentioned evolution as a key element in the decline of religion; what did you mean?"

"Well, our Socratic analysis indicates that many of the seeds of the current problems have resulted from an excess of individualism, which initially drove great human progress, but has resulted in a society of individuals no longer taking collective responsibility for their shared home. This move towards individualism started, coincidentally, at the time that this theory of evolution surfaced. When the theory emerged, it contradicted elements of the written words of your religion. People felt the words were no longer true, so they lost their fear of God. Liberated of this fear, they focused instead solely on the individual and on developing their material wellbeing, rather than their inner self or soul."

Mother Cristina was nodding slowly.

"It's tragic."

"Your religions had, up to that point, regulated the behaviour of the individual and compelled them to think about their part in the whole. They had provided moral codes to adhere to, which were lost. No replacement code came along and societies have slowly evolved into collections of individuals trying to maximise their material well-being and that of those closely around them. In forgetting about the whole, they don't see the collective damage they are doing to others and the natural world that sustains them. Whilst they surround themselves with material possessions, like pharaohs inside their pyramids, they are destroying the whole."

Mother Cristina reflected deeply on Simon's words. After a few minutes silence, she posed a question.

"If you're correct and life is threatened with extinction, how can we help to stop this?"

"Religions must cast off the shackles of arguing over their apparent differences and pitting themselves against scientific observations. They must not demean themselves in this way – they are much more important than this. They must once again unite people in their hour of need and show them how to believe in and worship something greater than the individual, and to protect the precious gift of life."

Simon paused to let the Prioress absorb his words.

"Is suicide not one of the ultimate sins, Mother?"

"Why yes," replied Mother Cristina.

"Well, by destroying their planet, humans are collectively committing suicide."

41

Back in Paris, Osiris was busy planning the next edition of CAMEOS. It was a national holiday, but she was busy working. The Easter edition had been a great success; there was a long list of celebrities looking for projects to support and a growing number of potential causes to investigate and report on. She was now managing a sizeable operation, with fifteen people working out of Paris. Happily, a growing number of volunteer researchers were filling the void left by the sicads. She often wondered how they were getting on with processing their conclusions.

She reflected on how Simon's understanding had transformed since their first meeting, when his strong intelligence was blunted by a naivety of how the world really operated. She'd seen him quickly develop over the seven months they'd spent together, researching and interviewing thousands of people from different walks of life. His knowledge and wisdom had flourished. Simon Oceandis, God I'm missing you, she thought.

It wasn't as if she hadn't been busy herself. Her regular band of prominent and celebrity supporters were making surprise high-profile protests. This created additional media interest and, invariably, real action and results soon followed.

@49 hours 28 minutes and 12 seconds flashed across Simon's mind.

She was planning her next flash mob protest when a knock at the door interrupted her thoughts. A courier stood in front of her, struggling to read out the unusual addressee.

"I have a very urgent letter for Omari, daughter of Nambae, warrior chief of the Taromenane tribe."

Bewildered, she signed for the letter and closed the door. A hand delivered letter to my birth name. Who can this be from? She unfolded the neatly-handwritten note.

Dear Osiris,

I am writing on behalf of a close friend whose life is in grave danger.

This friend is currently in our care at Le Reposoir and is anxious to see his 'Warrior Queen' before it's too late.

To be admitted to the monastery, you must arrive in a full nun's habit. I have left one for you in the café 'La Bergerie', next to the railway station in the town of Cluses. It's imperative you come this very afternoon. There may be strict security around the monastery so for simplicity, if asked, state that you wish to take orders at the monastery.

Yours sincerely,

Sister Agatha

'Warrior Queen' was a term Simon had used – what could this mean? She hastily checked the train times. I can be in Geneva by 4pm, she calculated, and with a hire car can reach Cluses by 6pm. After rapidly packing a travel bag, she ran out of the office, her heart pounding.

*

Rather than perceiving it as a punishment, Sister Agatha, a nun for just ten months, was happy to visit civilisation. The early-morning sun shone strongly as she headed out of the monastery, tightly clutching the letter hidden inside a sacred manuscript. The previous night's snow was quickly melting in the warm sunshine. She headed to the village, revealed her face as requested at the checkpoints, and took the bus down to Cluses.

After delivering the letter to the courier company, she headed back to the bus stop. She looked at her watch. Just missed one and it's an hour before the next one. A small café caught her attention; she entered and ordered a herbal tea. All around her were rows of computers. With nobody to talk to, there was nothing to keep her mind off the temptation to log on and contact some of her friends. The excitement of the previous night was still buzzing inside her – the vision and the coincidences between the visitors and the story of Jesus. It was frustrating that the other nuns were not open to discussing what had happened. What harm could it do to have a five minute chat with some old friends? She looked around. The café was empty. The assistant behind the counter was absorbed in cleaning and re-stacking glasses.

She went over to the computer, logged on and went straight to one of the religious chat sites that she used to spend hours on. Her log-in was still active. A chat box popped up: 'Hey, is that you Agatha? How are things?' The chat message was from Rachel. A sudden urge to log-out and return to the monastery seized her. Rachel was great, but had a loose tongue. The nun sat back at the table and sipped her drink, but the temptation was too great. The computer was calling out like a siren from the rocks. Before she knew it, she'd told Rachel all about the strange happenings at the monastery. Time flew. Her friend skilfully extracted all the details from her. They chatted back and forth before Agatha looked at her watch and gasped. Just two minutes to catch the bus! Quickly logging out, she ran out of the café, catching the bus as it was pulling away. On the slow climb she reflected sheepishly about what she'd done. Surely Rachel would keep things to herself? Who are you kidding, Agatha!

Once back at the village, she made her way through the checkpoints and up to the monastery.

"Are you all right, my child?" inquired the Prioress on her arrival.

Sister Agatha nodded quickly and, without looking up, replied.

"I delivered the letter, which should arrive by lunchtime."

As she scurried off towards her chamber, Simon called after her.

"Sister Agatha, did you see any police and army officers?"

With her eyes firmly on the floor she replied, "There are two checkpoints in the village, at least four in the town and coming back on the bus, we passed several search parties."

*

Jia didn't wake up until after lunch. Despite her hunger, she lay still and tried to make sense of the bizarre events of the last forty-eight hours. Simon had informed her of Gort's plan. The Commander was scaring her more than ever and she was worried for the sicads. Her overriding concern, however, was how Simon had changed. Her worst fears, triggered by the bizarre conversations on the eve of his departure, were being realised. What's happened to him?

She'd expected him to come out of the seclusion stage having developed new economic models, revolutionary ideas on revising governance structures and with a raft of new technologies to tackle the problems in human societies. Instead, he was talking about intuition, loving the planet and religion. Had he gone mad? Had all of them gone mad? My career will be in tatters. She filled with dread at the pleasure this would bring her rivals at Mazari. Maybe it's just Simon and the others are OK? Is this why he escaped? Maybe they rejected him. She couldn't bear to think this might be true. Simon was the most perfect, the most intelligent. She had big plans for him, personal plans. I'm sure I can fix him, she told herself. Maybe Gort knows Simon and the others are mad and has been told to secretly destroy them?

She fell back to sleep to escape the waking nightmare.

*

Mother Cristina shared a modest lunch with Simon, who'd shaved off his beard and, at a quick glance, could easily be mistaken for a nun.

"Sister Agatha seemed very flustered," he remarked.

"The nuns are not used to civilisation any more. It can be quite traumatic for them. That's why I sent Sister Agatha, the newest."

The conversation came back to Osiris and the predicament of the trapped sicads.

"Let's hope she's at home," he concluded.

Mother Cristina put her hand on his.

"I've been praying all morning for the message to reach her."

@48 hours 17 minutes and 12 seconds flashed across Simon's mind.

"Well, if she doesn't arrive here by this evening, we'll have to make alternative plans."

His thoughts returned to Jia and the questions he had for her. Was Izanami right and, if so, what did this mean? Why would Jia have given me alone this sexual ability? He'd had no time to ask her and the monastery didn't seem the appropriate place for these questions.

*

Mother Cristina took a plate of food to Jia, and sat on the bed as she ate. When she'd finished and the colour had returned to her cheeks, the Prioress asked her a very personal question.

"I've been wondering Jia, are you pure?"

"How do you mean, Mother?"

"Are you a virgin?"

Jia blushed and, taken aback, she struggled to answer. Mother Cristina, regularly tackling this subject with young nuns, was completely relaxed.

282

"Exploring yourself, even with objects, doesn't matter."

Jia thought back to the many robot companions she'd tested, for purely professional reasons, of course.

"Have you ever given yourself to a man?" asked the Prioress, staring into her eyes.

"Why, why... I guess not."

The Prioress raised her eyebrows.

"You're not sure, my child?"

"No... I mean yes. Yes I am sure," she replied sheepishly.

The nun said a silent prayer, knelt down on the floor in front of her, reached out and took Jia's hand in her own. Jia felt even more embarrassed. The nun stood up, bowed her head solemnly and walked towards the church, hands cupped in front of her as if containing a small bird she didn't want to escape.

Simon was inside, contemplating the statues painted multi-coloured by the sunlight filtering through the stained glass windows.

The Prioress walked up quietly behind him.

"Simon you seem perturbed; are you worrying about the others?"

"Yes, but I was reflecting on the death of two soldiers, Mother."

He turned around and looked at her.

"I could do nothing to save them."

She listened to his explanation of events, without judging him.

"Then you need not torment yourself over this," she concluded.

"Mother, they didn't die in a dignified way."

"The death of the soldiers is tragic, but your concern suggests you did all that you could."

"You're kind, Mother. My conscience feels clearer, but I fear the manner of the soldiers' demise will weaken humans' trust in the sicads."

The Prioress hesitated before replying.

"Sometimes God's methods are hard to fathom. Obstacles and impediments can be part of his will to test our resolve."

*

Towards early evening Sister Agatha, who was on guard, came running into Mother Cristina's chamber.

"Mother Superior, there's a dark-skinned nun approaching the monastery. It must be Osiris," she announced breathlessly.

283

At that moment the main gate bell rang loudly.

"Open the main gate. I'll greet her myself," instructed the Prioress. She walked to the entrance hall and slid back the viewing hatch.

"Who wishes to enter Le Reposoir?"

"It's Osiris. I received a letter from Sister Agatha to come urgently."

"Are you sure you haven't been followed?"

"Yes, I was stopped twice at checkpoints, but I used a false passport I have for travelling to environmental protests."

Mother Cristina slid back the heavy wooden bar and unlocked the door. Osiris entered the monastery and was escorted to Jia's chamber. Inside, Simon stood in a nun's outfit next to Jia, who was similarly dressed and sitting on the bed.

"Osiris! You came."

Osiris didn't respond but looked at him strangely.

He laughed.

"You don't recognise my disguise and my new face, do you, my Warrior Queen?... It's a long story."

This time she clearly recognised his voice.

"Simon is it really you? I thought you were in grave danger. I was so worried!"

"Yes it's me, Osiris. I'm safe for the moment, but...."

She ran up to him and, in her joy, forgot where she was. She threw her arms around his neck and kissed him passionately. Releasing him, she put her hands on his shoulders and studied his new face closely.

"It's not bad, maybe even better than the old one."

Jia glared daggers at Osiris and then at Simon.

"Is there something I should know about?" she snapped.

Simon was embarrassed and tried to explain.

"Sorry Jia. Osiris, meet Jia. Jia, meet Osiris."

Osiris extended a warm hand in friendship.

Jia stared coldly back and refused her hand. Simon watched awkwardly. I'd forgotten how complicated human females are, he thought to himself.

As Jia silently fumed, Simon walked Osiris to the church and updated her on all that had happened.

"So that's where we are. Gort is on a mission to destroy us," he concluded.

It had taken him nearly two hours to recount all of the facts leading up to the predicament they were in.

Simon noticed Jia standing by the door of the church, watching them with an expression like marble.

Osiris, who'd been silently reflecting, spoke up.

"We must act quickly, whilst we have surprise on our side!"

"What are you thinking of, Osiris?"

"Releasing the sicads."

"Yes, but how?"

"Leave it to me. It's time for the Waorani to go back to war! We don't have a minute to lose."

She jumped to her feet and spotted Jia glaring at her from a distance. Grabbing Simon's face, she kissed him provocatively.

"It's been too long. I'll come back for you when we've released the others," she announced confidently as she strode out of the church, pushing past an irate Jia.

42

Osiris, stopped three times by checkpoints, finally arrived back in Geneva late that night. En route she'd mentally composed the contents of an urgent electronic mail.

@36 hours 12 minutes and 13 seconds flashed across Simon's mind.

Perched on the end of her hotel bed, Osiris opened up her laptop and sent the encrypted e-mail to thousands of her loyal supporters.

Dear CAMEOS supporters,

I have our most critical mission yet. A chance to save the last remaining members of a rare and wondrous species that has been an inspiration for CAMEOS. The sole members of this species are concentrated in a small area and are threatened by a sudden imminent extinction. I urgently need the support of all of you this time.

I cannot reveal any further details, instead I ask for your complete trust. The only fact that I must bring to your attention is that this mission is highly dangerous and exposes us to a hostile reaction from armed security. If you're not put off by this, then the meeting place is Geneva airport at 10:00 CET on the 28th March. Look out for an 'ECO TOURS' placard. I apologise for the short notice. I will explain everything on the day.

Yours sincerely,

Osiris

Just one day's notice was certainly the shortest ever given. Thankfully, the meeting point was in the middle of well-connected Europe and not a tiny village in the heart of the Borneo jungle.

Osiris arose early the next morning to scout out the area around CERN. A ghostly silence hung over the compound – no signs of activity or any clue that the sicads were trapped there.

She headed back into town and purchased bed sheets, wooden poles and paints.

*

Simon spent the day trying to placate Jia, who had locked herself in her room and was refusing to talk to him. Her feelings were tearing her apart. Obsessively attached to Simon, the idea that he was more interested in Osiris was a devastating blow. The project had given her the opportunity to create the perfect man – no, something far superior to a man. His brain had so much potential! She'd envisaged Simon and her going far beyond Dmitri, far beyond all other scientists. Together they could achieve the impossible, the unthinkable. No other man could hold any such attraction for her. And she'd kept herself for him. She'd created him. He owed it to her. What right did he have to reject her? What right did Osiris have to interfere? All that work and sacrifice. They'd both betrayed her.

Her anger was supreme; she wanted to tell him how she felt, but she was too scared or too proud – she didn't know which – to reveal her feelings. Her hate for Osiris was tempered by the hope she'd somehow save the others and the project she'd put so much into. She wanted to take the phone and call Bruno, but was scared Gort would be listening. Was he planning on silencing her as well?

*

Mother Cristina found Simon in the monastery library, flicking through a book.

"Planning an escape route?"

"Just doing some background research."

She looked over his shoulder.

"Beautiful rocks, I recognise them."

"Yes, it's the Salève, near here – one hundred and sixty million years ago, a tropical sea. Thanks to the collision of tectonic plates, it's now a mountain massif."

"Such beautiful colours and shapes… The wonder of creation."

"The caves and cracks were formed after the last ice age, by the

287

melting ice infiltrating the rocks and refreezing every winter and provoking enormous rock slides."

"Are those people climbing it?"

"Yes, these are the original climbers. These early pioneers made the Salève the cradle of modern rock climbing."

"Oh dear, there are skeletons."

"It seems many hikers come to the Salève, but not all make it back. The steep exposed paths have been responsible for many accidental deaths and a few murders too."

The Prioress made a cross on her chest.

"Will you pass through there?"

"I'm not sure. As of yet, I don't have a plan. The longer we can stay out of Gort's hands, the more likely Osiris will be able to take CERN by surprise."

∗

Osiris's first supporters arrived that evening; some stayed in her room. Moving the furniture, they covered the floor with newspaper and set about turning the sheets and poles into a stack of protest banners, daubed with provocative painted slogans. At the end of the night, after clearing the paint fumes, Osiris checked her e-mails. Good, more celebrities... Ah great, Mateo is coming over, all the way from Ecuador!

Awaking at 6.00am sharp, she jumped out of her hotel bed, careful to avoid the sleeping supporters on their therma-rests.

@8 hours 00 minutes and 00 seconds flashed across Simon's mind.

"Excellent, more e-mails and positive confirmation from over three hundred supporters," she announced to the small group blinded by the early morning sunlight.

Two hours later, a rapidly expanding group was gathered around the 'ECO TOURS' placard in the arrivals hall of Geneva airport. Supporters and celebrities, new and familiar faces, made their way through the airport crowds and flocked around Osiris. The new celebrities were, as usual, all wearing designer outfits and make up, all hoping to be photographed in the heart of the action.

"How many channels are covering the protest?" asked Josie, an up-and-coming soul singer.

"When are you going to tell us what we're going to save, in Geneva of all places?" asked a lesser-known celebrity sarcastically. As each new wave of people arrived, Osiris was plagued with similar questions. Each got the same response: all will be revealed shortly.

As ten o'clock approached, over four hundred people had been directed down to the op's centre in the basement level car park. She was about to take the latest group down, when she saw Mateo. She ran up to him and the two old friends embraced warmly.

"It means a lot to me that you've come. It's been a long time."

The elegant Ecuadorian golfer smiled.

"I wouldn't have missed this for the world."

She hugged him once more and whispered.

"This is the biggest one yet, but it's not our usual type."

"I sensed that, which is why I came."

They stepped back and looked each other up and down.

"You're looking well."

"You too! Great, we'd better go."

"Mario, please stay here to catch any late arrivals."

Mario, despite his young age, was a veteran of CAMEOS protests. A gifted computer expert, he found more pleasure in illegally bypassing tough security controls than in using his skills in a more conventional manner.

"Follow me, everybody."

Once the crowd was amassed, Osiris stood in the centre with a loud hailer.

"Thank you for coming, everybody. This is our most unique and most critical case to date. The endangered species we've come to save are just a few hours from extinction. What rare and endangered species can exist in Geneva? Well this species, one of the most amazing I've been lucky enough to encounter, is called the sicads, a new breed of life created by the Socrates Project."

She surveyed the looks of confusion on the faces of the crowd.

"I had the pleasure of spending seven months with the first of this species, Simon Oceandis, who helped turn CAMEOS into a world-class operation. The sicads have fallen in love with our planet and want to help humanity realise our interdependence with our Mother Nature."

289

The crowd was listening silently and trying to make sense of her words.

"Through supporting CAMEOS, the sicads have exposed themselves to those who seek to impose their short-sighted greed over the longer term interests of all humans. Commander David Gort is their pawn and is secretly trying to destroy the sicads. They've been abandoned at CERN and Gort is starving them of power. We've just a few hours to save them and the hopes of the Socrates Project to build a better world. They've risked their lives for us, now it's time for us to repay that debt."

Osiris started to whip up the crowd into a frenzied fever of self-righteous indignation.

"The governments are unwittingly allowing this to happen. They have complete, but misplaced, trust in Commander Gort."

"How do we know this is all true?" shouted out a concerned celebrity.

"I know this all sounds far-fetched but you must trust me. We're the sicads' only hope!"

Osiris looked around. It was taking longer than normal to elicit a reaction from the crowd. People looked confused. It was Mateo who broke the silence.

"I came from South America because I sensed a key moment in the history of the world. Save the sicads! They're our best hope for a better future."

There were murmurings of approval from around the crowd. The celebrities pricked up their ears at the idea of being seen at a key turning point in history. Some cheered.

"Save the sicads!"

Slowly, the individual murmurings of agreement built up into a wave of support and Osiris quickly handed out placards and banners – 'Government Genocide', 'The Sicads Must Survive', 'A Silent Massacre' and 'Let the Sicads Speak'.

"Remember, everybody. This is a highly dangerous mission. We don't know how the authorities will react to us gate-crashing a top-secret project. The media will be following the protest, affording us some protection."

A minor celebrity and a middle-aged lady silently defected to the stairwells. The rest of the crowd began to mobilise itself, taking the placards and banners.

"Everybody come forward and take a map. These maps show alternative routes to CERN to split us up and avoid detection. We have surprise on our side. We must preserve this advantage, to the last possible minute!"

The crowd was organised into groups and allocated staggered departure times.

"We'll assemble at noon. Keep your banners and placards out of sight until I arrive, when you'll need to make as much of a distraction as possible. I'll slip through the defences and try to reach the sicads."

She checked her watch.

"OK, group 1A away!"

After a few seconds of confusion, the group left the car park to a chorus of cheers.

"Mateo and Mario, I'd like you to stay close to me, where I can keep an eye on you."

43

It was 6.45am on the 28th March. Simon had taken to resting inside the church. Lying on one of the pews, he was mulling over the limited escape options; behind, a treacherous snowy mountain; in front, a heavily-guarded village. Suddenly, he heard footsteps entering the church. It was Sister Agatha. She approached the statue of Jesus and knelt down, sobbing quietly.

She hadn't seen him. He got to his feet. Hearing him, she spun around and jumped up. Ignoring his gaze, she looked down at the floor.

"Sister Agatha, what's troubling you?"

The young lady looked up at him with frightened eyes.

"I'm really sorry," she blurted out suddenly, before making to run out. He caught hold of her arm and held her, gently but firmly.

"What are you sorry about?"

The young nun burst into tears. She fell to her knees and pleaded.

"Don't tell Mother Cristina. I didn't mean to do it. I don't want to be thrown out of the monastery."

"You didn't mean to do what?"

"To talk about what happened," she blurted out, as if her secret burden had been choking her.

With his reassurance, she confessed what she told Rachel over the internet.

"Thank you for finally telling me, Sister Agatha. By not telling us earlier, you've put all of our lives in danger."

Bursting into a fresh wave of sobbing, she prostrated herself in front of him.

"I'll do anything to make amends for my loose tongue."

*

Gort was back in Cluses, getting increasingly frustrated. Calming his mind, he went back methodically over the facts. His private cell phone buzzed; the number was McCloud's.

"Scott, what's happening with you? OK, no news is good news, but stay vigilant... At least the rest of them will be out of our hair in a few hours... No, I've no fresh traces of the fugitives, despite the continued newsflashes and extensive roadblocks... Teams are studying video footage of every major train station in the region. Almost every car has been stopped and searched, often several times. Frustrations and complaints are coming in about the disturbance to traffic... I've had the French President on the phone, not to mention Bruno... What have I missed, Scott? ...Yes, I agree, if they'd moved, we'd have certainly got them... Well, if they're holed up somewhere, where can they be? ... I'm going to give the roadblocks a final check and then retrace my steps... Yes, back up to the village and the monastery with the dogs..."

Simon, who'd been listening to every word of the conversation, leapt to his feet. He rushed to Jia's chamber and hammered on the door, calling her name.

In response, a heavy object hit the inside of the door, signalling she was still livid at him.

"Jia, Gort's on his way back here, we have to leave!"

"I don't believe you!"

"I've just heard him on the phone. He must be close!"

"Even if you're telling the truth, we'll get caught as soon as we reach the village."

He paced up and down the corridor and looked out of the window into the dull morning drizzle. Two poncho-covered tourists on pannier-laden bicycles were making their way up towards the monastery – a mixed couple. A plan instantly hatched in his mind.

"Jia I'm leaving the monastery now. You can either come or stay by yourself and greet Gort."

There was the sound of sudden commotion behind the door.

"Keep your habit over your ordinary clothes for now," he instructed.

"But it's too dangerous. There are police everywhere!"

"I've finally got a plan. You must come immediately. We only have one chance!"

A flustered Jia, with tearful eyes and a red face, angrily threw open the door. She was pulling the nun's habit over her clothes as they ran out of the monastery and towards the perimeter wall. He helped her over the wall and, with a running jump, acrobatically pulled himself up and over.

He stopped at a small copse of trees next to the road, just in time to position himself as the cyclists turned the corner. They were cycling slowly uphill, their bodies largely covered by their waterproof ponchos. As the male drew level with him, Simon opened his mouth, took careful aim and shot a tranquilliser dart into the cyclist's exposed calf muscle. Simon quickly targeted the female, aiming too quickly, and missed. The dart lodged in her plastic drinks bottle. With just one remaining dart, he couldn't afford to miss. He carefully lined up her calf as it rotated around the crankshaft, unleashing the dart just as he heard the crash of the male slumping off his bike.

"Fabrice!" she shouted.

His aim was true. Bulls-eye! He ran out behind and grabbed her as she slumped in her saddle.

Jia had just arrived beside him.

"Quickly, help me! Take the bike and hide it in the trees."

He laid the female on the ground between the trees and then went back for the male.

Jia had a shocked expression on her face.

"It's OK. He fell onto the soft grass. Neither the human nor the bicycle is damaged."

"Take his feet. Help me carry him to the monastery."

It was fifty metres to the monastery's outer gate. Fortunately, the trees shielded them from sentries posted in the village below. Mother Cristina gave a look of abject horror at the sight of the tranquillised body.

"He's only sleeping," assured Simon.

"There's one more to come," added Jia hesitantly.

"Gort's on his way here. We're borrowing their bicycles to escape."

Mother Cristina opened her mouth to protest.

"Don't worry, the tranquiliser has a light amnesiac, they won't remember much. Just tell them you found them on the road."

Whilst she organised beds for the two cyclists, Simon and Jia returned with the female and their panniers.

Simon took their ponchos and the cycling shoes.

"We'll need these as well."

Mother Cristina was standing uneasily over the drugged cyclists as Simon and Jia removed their habits.

"Where will you go?"

"We'll try and make it to CERN to help Osiris. Thanks for all your help, Mother."

"I wish I could have done more for you."

Simon looked at the Prioress, his eyes full of gratitude. He took her kind hands in his.

"You've done everything you could for us, and more."

"Thank you, Simon. I'll pray for you and Jia."

"If we don't make it, keep up the good fight, Mother. The world needs people like you."

"May the Lord travel with you and protect you, Simon Oceandis!"

Simon and Jia took the bicycles out from the trees.

@5 hours 31 minutes and 14 seconds.

"Osiris is planning to hit CERN at midday. We have three and a half hours. The route is downhill and flat. We should be able to make it in two and a half hours, if we don't get stopped."

He examined the maps and itinerary the human couple had been carrying.

"They came from Geneva yesterday – that's handy."

"Are you sure this is a good idea? We might break our necks on these things," fretted Jia.

"Gort will do worse than break our necks. Let's get going!"

Their ponchos billowing in the wet wind, the two imposter cyclists made their way down from the monastery towards the village of Le Reposoir. Jia was still struggling slightly with the brakes and skidded around the first hairpin bend.

"Don't engage the back brake before the front!" called out Simon. She carefully took his advice. As they approached the village, Simon spotted the first checkpoint in the distance.

"What's up?" asked Jia.

"It's a checkpoint. Keep going and trust me."

Before she had a chance to object, he pedalled fast towards it, leaving her with little choice but to follow. The rain was getting heavier. He pulled the poncho hood down over his face and motioned for her to do likewise. As they approached, a police officer stepped out.

"We passed you yesterday, on our way up," Simon announced robustly. The police officer wavered for a second, glanced at his colleague, who nodded, and then waved them through. Jia caught up with him and pedalled alongside him.

"How did you know that was going to work?" she asked, with grudging admiration.

"Intuition?"

"Really!" she snapped.

"I figured that Commander Gort would be using every available unit of manpower and not letting anyone leave their posts. Cycling is generally a noble leisure activity and not commonly associated with criminality. Furthermore, the police officer was wet and cold, and his motivation for stopping us would have been lower than usual."

All very logical, she was reassured.

They headed down towards the town of Cluses, carefully backtracking on the route that the cyclists had taken. They passed two further checkpoints and were allowed through in a similar fashion. Jia smiled at the irony of the detailed checks being performed on the cars and trucks. With the large resultant traffic jams, they were moving faster than the cars.

The bikes were light and fast, surprising Simon on the efficiency of cycling compared to walking, especially as the head wind was recharging his batteries. He was using less than ten per cent of his battery power per hour.

"At this rate, we should make it to CERN before midday."

"If my backside doesn't go on strike before," Jia replied.

As they approached Geneva, he had a dilemma. The cyclists had taken a detour to explore the Salève. The impressive limestone cliffs were a landmark feature of the region. He'd no intention of doing the same, but wanted to pass through the same checkpoints. He opted to cut out the climb, but respect the ten kilometre detour.

He veered off towards the domineering cliffs. After stretching her back and rubbing her backside, Jia got back on the bike and set off after him.

*

Gort, meanwhile, was getting increasingly frustrated and taking his frustration out on the officers manning the checkpoints. He was undertaking a final tour, to personally breathe down their necks, before heading back up to the village and monastery. Human attention spans in any security situation had a high rate of decay. The only way to counter this was some good-old fashioned intimidation, and he was on the warpath against any signs of lax vigilance. Having started out in Cluses, he was heading out towards the Salève before looping back up to Le Reposoir.

In fact, he was following behind Simon and Jia. The traffic jams and the time he spent at each checkpoint was keeping him just behind them.

Overtaking the line of traffic, he approached checkpoint 7B, next to the small French village of Collognes-sous-Salève. Speeding past the two cyclists, he didn't raise an eyebrow. He got out of the car, slammed the door shut and strode over to the two police officers. They spotted the Commander walking towards them and instantly tightened up their approach. Rather than having a quick glance inside each vehicle, they asked the occupants to get out and present their papers. Gort stood between the two officers, staring at each in turn, looking for the slightest thing to pick them up on. He watched them for five minutes. Satisfied they'd got the message, he returned to his car. The two cyclists pedalled past him and approached the front of the queue of traffic, nipping in behind the car that was currently being searched.

@2 hours 31 minutes and 18 seconds.

Simon approached the officer confidently.

"Can we pass back through? You already checked us out yesterday."

The officer looked at his colleague, who nodded, and then waved them through. He then had an uncomfortable feeling and looked around to see the Commander scowling at him.

"Hang on a minute, come back!" he called out after the two cyclists, already pedalling down the road. Simon stopped, turned around and looked back at the officer. He'd not noticed before, but this time he saw Gort's car and he could clearly make out the Commander's distinctive features inside. In 31 minutes Osiris was due to storm CERN. *I must keep Gort occupied to buy her time,* he resolved. He looked back at Jia, her face full of concern.

"Don't panic, but Gort is there."

The concern in Jia's face turned to abject fear.

"Keep calm. We're going to have to split up. I'll occupy Gort. You must continue as far as you can without being caught."

He walked slowly towards the police officer, whispering over his shoulder.

"Wait until I give you the signal to go."

He saw that Gort was watching him from the car and made contact with the operating system, easily bypassing the secure log-in. As he approached the barrier, he shouted aggressively.

"What's going on? Your colleague checked me through yesterday! Do you have memories like goldfish?"

He provoked the response he'd hoped for. The second officer strode angrily towards him. As they arrived within a metre of him, he acted with lightning speed, grabbing their heads with a motion of his arms they hardly registered. As he brought their heads crashing together, their eyes opened wide for an instant and then closed. At the same time, he immobilised Gort's car, locking all doors and windows. Through the windscreen he saw the soldier frantically trying in vain to open them. The Commander took out his gun, but wisely decided against firing it through the bullet-proof glass. The bodies of the two police officers sagged to the floor. Simon connected into Gort's mobile phone and sent it a powerful viral routine that completely crashed it. He did the same thing in quick succession to all the other phones in the queuing cars, before immobilising the leading car in each direction.

"Go, Jia. Make it to CERN if you can," he shouted.

She hesitated. "Go, Jia!" he ordered in a more authoritative voice, shaking her out of her trance.

He stared back at Gort, taunting the trapped soldier, who was busy kicking the inside of the car door.

He jumped back on his bike and pedalled furiously, looking over his shoulder, in time to see the car door fly off its hinges. The Commander ran alongside the cars, shouting for a telephone, before shaking his head in anger and running in the sicad's direction. Simon carried on pedalling, keeping at least a gun shot's range between him and the irate soldier, running behind in determined pursuit.

44

Magnus was the first to notice that the power supplies were not functioning. Connecting to all the other sicads, he checked each of them. None were receiving power! Each woke up in turn, bombarding him with demands for an explanation.

There was no explanation. He rattled the chains on the cage door noisily and threw concrete chippings into the darkness at the camera lenses above. Nobody came down and they had no means to raise any sort of alarm. Magnus, still wearing Simon's skin, was hit by a flurry of questions from the anxious sicads, but had little to console them with.

@Sicads.all – It seems we've been abandoned.

Their spirits sank. The heavy metal door was locked and bolted with three heavy-duty chains. Magnus racked his brain for a solution. Space was too limited to amass enough of them to force the door. Even if they could escape the cage, there was another series of secure doors separating them from the outside world. The concrete floor was at least one metre thick. What's more, they had already explored every possible escape plan after Bartolome's demise.

He reflected on the grim conclusion that any attempt to escape was a near-certain waste of energy. They must hope to be rescued.

@Simon – Please save us, communicated Magnus hopelessly. His message bounced off the indifferent concrete walls of the chamber.

Everyone realised the same grim truth. From time to time, Magnus released the tensions of the responsibility of leadership by rattling the chains on the door and shouting at the cameras.

Nobody came.

By the morning of the 28th March, the sicads' power levels were down to just six per cent, giving a maximum of six hours survival time. Each minute that passed, a granule of hope, gone forever. All were in low-energy mode, like humans eking out a limited supply of oxygen, with no control over their slow deaths. They tried not to think about their plight, for the simple reason that this required energy. Their caged rack had become an expectant morgue, with corpses laid out neatly in anticipation of death.

*

Mother Cristina watched over the tranquilised cyclists, mulling over the most appropriate punishment for the repentant Sister Agatha.

Rachel had passed on the incredible contents of Sister Agatha's story to all of her internet chat contacts. In turn, many of these did the same thing and their contacts in turn likewise, all adding small embellishments.

Within a few short days, Simon Oceandis was being portrayed as the second coming of Christ, supported by hundreds of disciples trying to save humanity from self-destruction. As for Jia, she was the reincarnation of Virgin Mary, a pure soul who'd consecrated her life to immaculately conceiving the God-sent sicads. The devils were the army and governments intent on destroying Simon and his disciples, for having turned against their secular and economic beliefs.

The story rapidly circulated around the globe through religious chat groups, and was attracting the attention of government intelligence agencies monitoring subversive or unusual content. A report had been provided to Bruno directly. It had also been sent to Gort, too busy hunting down Simon and Jia to have seen it.

*

Bruno paced around his office, trying to make sense of the events of the past few days. He made a mental list of the strange occurrences; the disappearance of one of the sicads, two allegedly murdered soldiers, Jia's disappearance and now this crazy religious story.

To avoid accusations of interference, he'd restrained himself from getting involved earlier. Now it's time to find out for myself what's going on, he resolved.

As Bruno decided to head for Geneva, Jia was following the signs, expecting a police car or army vehicle to pull up behind her at any moment. But nobody showed any sign of interest in her. Her thoughts shifted from her own safety to Simon's. Gort must be preoccupied with pursuing Simon. Otherwise he'd have come after her. Maybe Simon has incapacitated him? Maybe Simon has killed Gort? Her whole world was being turned upside down. She didn't know what to believe any more. She'd been waiting over twelve months to see Simon, thinking about him every day, building up great plans on what they could achieve together – and now, with the project collapsing, would the sicads be banished forever, an expensive mistake? What would happen to Mazari?

Dismissing the myriad of gruesome thoughts about possible endings to a showdown between Gort and Simon, she focused on getting to CERN. I must help to save the other sicads, she thought.

*

Simon was cycling uphill towards the Salève. He was relieved to see the Commander in the distance, still running determinedly after him. Two kilometres in less than eight minutes – the Commander was clearly in good shape. Turning into an unpaved car park, he realised the front bicycle wheel was punctured. He jumped off the bike and continued on foot, following an ascending winding trail.

@2 hours 22 minutes and 2 seconds.

No longer afraid to use his internet connection, he searched for news on CERN – nothing.

The curved plastic soles of the cycling shoes, capped with metal clips, were causing him to slide dangerously across the rocky path. After nearly falling onto the rocks several metres below the path, he stopped and yanked off the shoes. Switching to barefoot, he felt the sharp abrasive stones cutting into his skin. To continue was to risk severe damage to his feet and dust getting under his skin. His SAMPS flared into action. Gort is less than three minutes behind and he has shoes! There were no humans around whose shoes he could borrow. He looked up at the cliffs above him, he had no choice. He'd have to go up. The rock in the Salève was limestone and the popular rock climbing routes had been climbed so many times that the once-sharp footholds had become polished by the thousands of feet that had passed over them.

He quickly scanned the rock face. It looked climbable. However, he knew from his experience on the survival expedition that climbing up a rock face was easier than climbing down, and that an apparently manageable route could suddenly turn devilishly difficult. These were vertical rock faces, full-on rock climbing routes that required total

301

concentration and ropes for safety. He swiftly searched the internet and found electronic climbing maps of the Salève. The routes above him varied in grades. Most experienced climbers would hesitate to undertake the easiest of these routes without a rope. A handful of exceptionally talented and mentally strong, some would say crazy, climbers had climbed the hardest without a rope – which, to put in context, even a baboon would think twice about climbing. A number of routes existed to the left and right; all led to a small plateau nearly three hundred metres above.

The rock, beautifully provocative, seemed to be enticing Simon to climb. Looking up at the sculptured three-dimensional forms in the stunning natural setting, the sicad imagined the fluid movements and balance required to work his way up the face. He momentarily forgot Gort and concentrated on the mental task of linking the possible holds and movements required into a climbable line. The sense of danger, the anticipation of the physical and mental challenge descended upon him with irresistible addiction. Total concentration consumed his mind and body, the mental torture of regrets and future desires fell away, in the same way human climbers escape artificial needs, perceived inadequacies and deep-rooted insecurities. Like these human climbers, he would live or die in the moment bonding with nature in the present, in the now!

After a final look behind him, Simon plunged into the spiritual world of climbing. Placing his hands on the limestone, he searched for the imperfections, the little holes and protrusions that he could use to pull his body up the rock face. He felt around with his feet for a hold. Depending upon the arrangement of the grips and footholds he found, he would twist and turn his body, keeping as close to the rock as possible, to reduce the energy required from his arms. He moved elegantly, almost dancing in slow motion, accurately finding foot and hand holds. Watching a climber is indeed like watching a dancer – a seductive experience that makes you want to emulate their flexibility, rhythm and grace. He moved swiftly up the first face and over a lip onto a deep ledge. He lost sight of Gort, whom he hoped to shake off before finding some easy routes to the plateau above.

The Commander was running up the steep rocky path after Simon, who he still believed was Bartolome. He saw him climbing the rock face and smiled. You won't lose me that easily! Gort had been an impressive climber in his youth. In fact, he'd been one of the handful of exceptionally gifted and experienced climbers who had climbed difficult routes 'solo', that is to say without safety ropes.

That had been many years ago now, but he'd kept himself in good physical shape. Whilst his rampant career progression had left little time for personal interests, army life encouraged a disciplined training program. He followed such a training program with the same zeal and application he applied to everything he did.

Gort reached the foot of the cliff. He quickly ran through the three options open to him; find a house and call for reinforcements, stick to the paths and try to get a clear shot, or climb up in pursuit. Not knowing the trails, and not wanting to lose his prey, he opted for the last option. I only need to get close enough to shoot him! Like Simon, he removed his shoes. Tucking his gun in the back of his trousers, he started to climb.

*

Osiris reached CERN just before noon. The concealed protestors waited anxiously for the signal. Two soldiers guarded the entrance to the deathly-quiet complex. Osiris checked her watch. Three minutes to go, time to alert the media. The adrenalin levels were building inside her body.

"You can release the e-mails to the media channels," she whispered to Mario.

She made a final map check, just to be sure. She could see the entrance to the detector building in the distance. Like yesterday, there seemed to be few soldiers guarding the site. Hopefully Simon's right and they're all out looking for him, she thought.

@2 hours 0 minutes and 0 seconds flashed across Simon's mind.

Osiris checked her watch; it was exactly noon. Unfurling her banner, she strode forwards, leading the charge. The crowd fell in behind her, shouting and waving their banners.

"Government genocide! The sicads must survive! A silent massacre!" chanted the angry crowd.

"Save the sicads!" boomed the crowd in unison.

"Let the sicads speak!"

The soldiers at the gate were taken completely by surprise and hurriedly radioed through to Colonel McCloud, who was already running towards the entrance.

"What the hell's going on?"

"You tell us, sir. They came out of nowhere and they know we've got the sicads."

Scott grabbed his phone and tried to call Gort. He swore at the out-of-service message.

The crowd were surging towards the entrance. He knew five soldiers couldn't hold back a crowd of this size. How did they find out? Should they fire on them? In desperation, he tried Gort's phone again – dead! Officially, if he considered them to be hostile, he was within his rights to open fire on them. Without speaking to Gort, he was reluctant to do anything rash.

Osiris was weighing up a similar dilemma. If they didn't storm the building quickly, it could be too late for the sicads. Maybe the other soldiers are down there killing them now, she thought. It wasn't enough to raise awareness this time. Full engagement was required!

She looked around at Mateo and Mario, both at her side.

"We're going in!" she announced.

They nodded in approval.

"Drop back behind me. I'll need you to cover me."

The message spread and there was a surge forward to the gate. The soldiers had a last fleeting moment of indecision, before leaving their posts. The metal gate shook and buckled, the crowd surged again and the soldiers retreated. A final surge pushed the gate off its hinges and it fell flat onto the concrete with an almighty clatter. The protestors rushed into the compound.

"Do not harm the soldiers! Do not harm the soldiers!" shouted Osiris repeatedly over her loud hailer. Above the noise of the crowd, an approaching helicopter flying at low altitude could be heard; a cameraman was leaning out, filming them.

"It's the media!" shouted Josie eagerly.

They protested with renewed vigour.

"Do not damage any buildings either!" shouted Osiris.

As the crowd marched towards the entrance to the detector, the soldiers were waving their rifles at the helicopter, signalling to it to leave, in no uncertain terms. Osiris, Mateo and Mario used the distraction to run towards the computer nerve centre. The helicopter gained height and turned around, swooping back low over the crowd to get close-up footage of the protest. As the crowd ducked, Mario cracked the access code and entered, with Osiris following behind. Mateo hung back outside as Mario set to work on the computerised controls.

304

"Can you crack it?" shouted Osiris over the noise.

"Yes, I think so. I've worked on similar systems," he smiled.

He blasted a code-cracker algorithm program into the computer, which simultaneously hit the processing unit with every number and letter sequence possible, looking for partial recognition. It was a similar method to how humans used to crack the codes of safes by listening for the tiny clicks. The computer yielded access and Mario inserted a disk with Osiris's DNA sample. He reset the retina scan and asked Osiris to look into the eyepiece attached to the wall.

"Thirty seconds and you're good to go," he shouted proudly.

Osiris took a deep breath, dreading what she might find in the chamber.

Mario read out Simon's instructions.

"Head straight through all the security doors, until you reach the elevator – the sicads are in the chamber below."

As Osiris was about to leave, the door flew open and Colonel McCloud burst in brandishing a gun.

"You've no right to be in here," he said coldly, staring at Osiris and Mario in turn.

"The media are everywhere. Put your gun down," countered Osiris authoritatively.

Scott smiled, in an almost sympathetic way.

"Sorry lady, you really shouldn't have come in here. Call off your protesters, otherwise I'll shoot!"

Scott stared into Osiris's eyes.

He flicked off the safety catch and pressed the gun to Osiris's forehead.

"Call off the protestors. This is your last chance!"

He pressed his finger lightly on the trigger, but hesitated; he'd seen something in Osiris's eyes. He turned his head slowly, only to see a metal pole coming towards him, a metal pole swung with the precision of an expert golfer. The Colonel's body slumped to the floor and Osiris picked up his gun.

"Thanks Mateo, you were just in time."

She jumped over the body and ran towards the detector building. The two soldiers who were guarding the door had fled. The protest was growing stronger, stirred up by the media interest. She scanned her pass and locked her eyes onto the retina scanner. The door clicked and swung open. She ran forward, stopping to clear each of the series of security doors. Many of the protestors followed, wedging the security doors open with metal poles. Alarms were ringing, but it didn't matter – the media coverage already had every available police and army officer on their way to CERN.

Osiris took the elevator along with Mario, Mateo and ten other protestors. After the seemingly agonisingly slow descent, the doors opened and she ran out onto the metal gangway, sweeping the dark chamber with a powerful torch. She sprinted to the edge of the gangway and looked over the railings to get her bearings, then stopped frozen. A heavily armed soldier sat guarding the sicads. They made eye contact. He stared calmly at her. She held up her hand to the others behind her to stop them in their tracks. The soldier was good looking and appeared to be of high rank. It was strange, but she saw no hostility or resistance in his eyes, as if he was pleased to see her. Suddenly, the sound of a voice broke the silence.

"SOS appeal for energy. Critical levels, terminal shutdown will occur in fifteen minutes."

Osiris looked back at the group amassed behind her.

"There's a soldier below, but he's going to have to shoot me before he stops me from saving the sicads."

Mateo and Mario put up their thumbs to signal support. She led the charge down the stairwells and onto the chamber floor. The soldier quietly observed the group, got up and walked away into the shadows – not out of fear, for he had countless acts of bravery to his name.

The chamber was echoing with SOS appeals from the sicads. As Osiris reached the cage she heard: 'Terminal shutdown will occur in two minutes.'

Behind the cage door sat Magnus, still wearing Simon's skin, head slumped forward and chin resting on his chest. A lack of energy frustrated his attempts to reach an arm out to Osiris, who hurriedly reached into her rucksack to take out the bolt cutters.

"Don't worry, we're here now," she reassured him.

"Save as many of us as you can. It's too late for me," he whispered.

Tears streamed down her face.

Mario arrived at her side.

"The UPS is totally melted!"

"The what?"

"The uninterruptable power system – it's as if it's caught fire, or been set alight. All the cables going into it have melted. It'll take days to fix!"

Osiris spun around and stared at him.

"How come the elevators are working?"

"They must be powered from above," he replied hurriedly, extracting a battery-powered drill from his bag and handing it to Mateo.

"We'll have to take them to the surface then!"

She frantically set about the smallest padlock with the bolt cutters. As the chain fell to the floor, she gazed anxiously at Mateo, making slow progress on the high-tensile steel lock. After what seemed an unbearable length of time, the drill surged forward into thin air and the lock ceded.

"Quick, pass it to me!" she ordered, exchanging the drill for the bolt cutters.

"Cut the remaining chains as quickly as you can!"

Meanwhile, Mario took out a metal saw and began cutting away at the thickest of the padlocks. Without the sound of the drilling, they could hear the chorus of SOS appeals from the sicads. Osiris threw the battery from the drill through the bars of the cage to Magnus.

"Draw power from the battery," she pleaded.

Magnus slowly moved his fingers to grasp the battery. Osiris watched as he attempted to retract the power connectors from the ends of his fingers. The skin on the finger tips slid slowly back, but there was insufficient power for the pins to be propelled outwards.

The saw cut through the padlock and the chain fell to the floor. At the same time, Mateo severed the third chain with the bolt cutters. Osiris pulled open the heavy steel door and ran into the cage. She knelt down and put her arm around Magnus, who spoke his last words.

"Save the others, especially the chiefs. They hold the answers. We won't all make it to the surface. The chiefs will direct you as to the optimal survival strateg..." He stopped talking, his eyes closed and he shuddered as his last drop of energy was spent.

"Take me to the sunlight," whispered a voice behind Osiris. She looked at the rack, the name Rosa was on the label next to the sicad's head. Osiris jumped into action. By now the chamber had filled up with twenty or so more protestors.

"Make a human chain. We need to evacuate the sicads as quickly as possible."

Everyone understood and formed a line stretching from the caged rack to the elevator.

"Take them one by one and pass them along the chain," she shouted frantically as she ran up and down the line.

"Take me," requested Rosa.

"And me," implored Guido.

The sicads had worked out the optimal order to be rescued, based on their varying remaining energy levels.

"Is the sun shining?" asked Rosa anxiously, as Mateo passed her inert body to Mario.

"It's a glorious day!" he replied.

"Hurry, please, everyone. As fast as possible – they're dying! I'll take them up in the elevator."

Osiris ran ahead to organise a similar human chain above ground. By the time she came back in the elevator the bodies of the first sicads were arriving. With the help of Mateo, she leant Rosa, Ed, Irina, Valerie, Mike, Agus Rudy, Xiu, Kim, Michi, Shailaja and Guido against the walls of the lift like waxwork dummies. The thirty second ride to ascend the one hundred metre shaft seemed to take forever. When they reached the top, she thrust the doors open.

"Quick, take them! Quickly, get them into the sunlight!"

She sent Josie back down in the escalator to bring up more sicads.

Outside, the sun was shining brightly and warmly.

"Make space for the sicads!" she shouted over the loud hailer.

The first out was Rosa, followed by Rudy. Osiris laid them down on the concrete. The remaining protesters gathered around to get their first sight of the sicads. They were captivated by the fact that they were indistinguishable from humans.

"Back off! Get back!" shouted Osiris. "You're blocking the sunlight. They'll die without energy."

The stunned protestors shuffled back slowly, until their shadows were no longer covering Rosa and Rudy. Minutes later the bodies of Mercedes, Fernandez, Julia, Roger, Fahim, Yonca and six sicad researchers were laid beside the first batch of sicad chiefs rescued. Over the next thirty minutes, a seemingly never-ending stream of sicads was carried out of the detector building and laid out on the ground.

Meanwhile, the media had turned up in force, as had the first waves of police and army officers. Gort wasn't among them. Engrossed in pursuing Simon, he was unaware of events at CERN. Osiris ran around, organising the protestors.

"Protect the sicads. Form a ring facing outwards."

Sirens were wailing and helicopters were circling overhead. In one of the helicopters, Bruno Reno was trying to work out what to make of the spectacle below.

Jia was also arriving at CERN. She froze at the sound of the multitudes of sirens coming up behind her. They whizzed past her and stopped outside CERN. She could hear the noise of the protest and cycled quickly to join the action. Dismounting, she forced her way through a gap in the security cordon and plunged herself into the crowd. In attempting to run in her cycling shoes, she was sliding like a cat on ice. Bruno's helicopter descended, looking for a place to land. The CERN compound had rapidly filled up with media, police and army officers. The protestors stood their ground, protecting the sicads. The media teams were climbing on each other's backs, trying to film their first close-up glimpse of the sicads. The public had been eagerly awaiting the results of this top secret project for nearly six years now. They were going to get prized footage and photos.

The army and police descended on the media from all directions, seizing and destroying cameras.

"Stop filming! You're breaching the Official Secrets Act!" boomed a voice through a loud hailer.

"All media representatives are to assemble in Zone A," continued the piercing voice.

Jia overheard a male reporter.

"Quick, stuff the camera in the rucksack and let's get out of here. They're going to confiscate everything!"

Eventually, the media teams dispersed, leaving the army and police lined up in riot formation facing the protesters. The police and army ranks moved back to let Bruno's helicopter land.

The Governor stepped out and walked between the two opposing camps. The final sicads were being brought out from the detector building under the protection of the dense ring of protestors. The first few sicads, their batteries partially recharged from the sun, were beginning to sit up. Others were opening their eyes, to be confronted by the extraordinary scenes. Twenty-eight of the sicads, including Magnus, had reached the sunlight too late; they were never to open their eyes again.

Bruno stood looking at both camps, unsure how to act. Everybody fell silent, expecting him to speak. As the crowds waited, a woman was seen pushing her way through the army and police ranks. She finally broke through and stumbled in front of him.

"Governor, I can explain everything," panted Jia.

*

Gort was climbing quickly and progressed easily up the small rock face towards the ledge over which he'd seen the sicad disappear.

Simon had no idea of the Commander's rock climbing skills. Statistically, the chances of a human attempting to free climb this route without ropes were practically zero. The sicad swore and rapidly set off climbing again.

Minutes later, Gort reached the ledge and could see Simon's feet thirty-five metres above him. He took out his gun, aimed and fired. The bullet whistled past Simon's right side and grazed the rock face just above his head, sending splinters of rock and dust onto him – damn, thought Gort, he's too high! Gort tucked his gun back in his trousers and resumed climbing. The hand and foot holds were less positive and he had to concentrate fully and keep both hands on the rock face.

It would have been an extraordinary scene for passers-by to see Simon and Gort solo climbing. Vehicles passed indifferently on the motorway and the departmental route, unaware of the lack of ropes and the nature of the pursuit. Simon and Gort were like two solitary spiders against the immense rock background, locked in a gravity-defying pursuit to the death. Gort was climbing quickly, with better technical skills than Simon, and was reducing the distance separating them. He was soon within firing range but, frustratingly, the climbing was too technical to hang around on one arm to retrieve his gun and take aim. They carried on, metre after metre, advancing up the beautiful rock face. The sicad had studied all the climbing moves on the internet, but that didn't make him an experienced climber. He was torn between climbing slowly and precisely to save energy and trying to speed up to keep out of firing range.

They'd been climbing for nearly two hours and were over one hundred and seventy metres above the ground. The slightest error or slip meant instant death and an unrecognisable wreck of a body. Gort was climbing fluidly and automatically, with the seemingly unconscious competence Simon had witnessed in top human athletes.

@23 minutes and 11 seconds flashed across the sicad's mind.

Simon had reached the last and most technical pitch of the route. Gort, just eleven or so metres behind, was closing in. The finger holds became more slender and the footholds more spaced apart. Simon concentrated intensely on the climb. The moves were technical and energy-sapping.

The sicad climbed as quickly as he dared. Twice he almost lost his footing on tiny footholds that were no more than minor asperities. The high-tech sticky rubber climbing shoes that climbers wore would have been a huge help. He could feel the skin on his feet wearing down. Thankfully, Gort's were in the same predicament.

@4 minutes and 1 second registered on the countdown in Simon's head.

As he reached the last few metres of the climb, Simon heard a gunshot. The bullet grazed his ear, striking a flake of rock that was an excellent handhold. The flake detached from the rock face. Simon quickly lurched sideways, to avoid the rapidly accelerating piece of rock. Gort didn't see it until it was approaching his hand. He instinctively shifted his balance to avoid it. As he scrambled to find a second hand hold for balance he dropped his gun, which went spinning to the ground below. He swore loudly. Simon groped around with his hand to find a replacement handhold. The rock was now smooth and featureless. Where the rock flake had been was just a small dent, offering nothing positive to hold on to. He had just over one metre to climb to reach the top of the route, but the missing handhold had made the last move significantly more difficult. Some would have said impossible but, in climbing, impossible has repeatedly proven to be possible.

@59 seconds!

Simon realised instantly that he only had one choice, and that was to act whilst his energy levels were still high enough. He managed to place both hands on the tiny handhold he'd been crimping with his left hand. He placed one hand over the other to get additional leverage from the small hold, bent his legs and straightened his arms, like a spring coiling itself. Pushing powerfully off his legs, he sprang into the air. Letting go of the rock with his hands, he threw his arms high into the air, to propel his body upwards. For an instant, he lost all contact with the rock, twisting his body in towards the rock face to gain more reach with his right arm. His hand slapped the top of the cliff, looking for a hold. His fingers could feel the grass on the edge of the plateau, but the rock was sloping and his hand started to slip.

311

If Osiris hasn't pulled off the rescue, he thought, I'm the last sicad alive!

He looked down the sheer rock face at the ground far below him – I must survive!

He dug his fingers into the rock with all his strength, locking his abdomen to stop his body swinging back and loosening his grip. Gort was several metres below, watching in awe and fear, knowing he'd have to perform the same move.

Simon's grip held against what was no more than a wrinkle in the rock, and he was able to pull himself up and over the lip, onto the edge of the plateau above. As he lay on the grass, soaking up the strong rays of the sun, he reconnected to the internet and heard the news about CERN. The story had hit the global headlines and dominated every news and media channel. The world had been waiting eagerly for the results of the Socrates Project, and this unexpected development was setting the media alight. On hearing that Bruno had arrived personally, a wave of electro-chemical relief surged through him, as he computed his increased survival prospects.

Back on the rock, Gort was in the same predicament Simon had been a minute earlier. Twenty years ago, lighter and with finger strength and core muscles at their peak, he may have attempted the move he'd witnessed the sicad perform. He knew the probability of successfully performing the same move now was low. This in turn made it even more unlikely, the mental element of climbing being driven by confidence and recent climbing momentum. Gort had neither of these. He also knew that he couldn't hang around for very long on the finger holds. He felt his strength wavering. He weighed his pride against his survival. He didn't have long to make up his mind.

"Bartolome, help me please!" he called out desperately.

Simon rolled over onto his front and looked over the edge of the rock face.

"Gort, this isn't Bartolome. You killed him, remember? This is Simon."

Gort swore loudly as he realised he'd been pitting himself against Simon all along. Anger and pride overruled his sapping mental and physical reserves. He leapt like an irate tiger, crazed by the mental wound he'd just been dealt, and pawed for the same hold that had saved Simon. His fingers slapped the rock face, but two inches short of where the sicad's hand had reached. His fingers slipped on the smooth rock. The Commander screamed in frustration and fear. He closed his eyes and wondered whether he would register the impact before his life was smashed into oblivion.

Nothing seemed to happen – had he died? He slowly opened his eyes, only to stare at the rock face. He became conscious of a firm grip around his wrist. He looked up to see Simon on his knees, supporting his weight with one hand. He then felt a second hand reach underneath his left arm and forcefully pull him up and drag him onto the grassy plateau.

Gort rolled over and looked up at Simon, who was standing over him. He stared at the sicad with mixed feelings.

"Don't move, Gort!" ordered Simon. "You know I'm equipped with tranquilliser darts."

"Why did you help me?"

"I'm programmed to."

Gort reflected silently on Simon's words.

"Gort, your plans are over. The sicads have been liberated from CERN and Bruno is on his way over here as we speak."

"You're bluffing," replied the Commander in a strange mix of defiance, hope and denial.

"Listen carefully and you'll soon hear the helicopter."

Seconds later, the sound of the helicopter was audible to human ears. Simon waved to the pilot, whilst keeping one eye on Gort. Once the rotary blades had come to a stop, Bruno stepped out with Jia and four security guards.

The Governor stood speechless at the sight of Simon standing over Gort, who had the strangest expression of despair and anger.

Part VI.

Dilemma

45

Bruno, laden with newspapers and magazines, strode purposely into his office.

"Ah Jia, how are you feeling? I hope the media's not getting to you."

"I'm fine," she replied, knowing she was anything but fine. She'd hardly slept the last few nights and, as her yellow fingers evidenced, she was back on the cigarettes.

"Unprecedented media coverage, there's hardly a page without some reference to the Project. Much of it inaccurate, wildly speculative and very damaging," he sighed, dumping the pile on a nearby table.

"Jia, would you help to organise the press cuttings?"

"OK. Why not?"

She'd nothing better to do. The idea of going back to CERN to face the twenty-eight dead sicads laid out in the inspection room was hardly a compelling proposition. The survivors had been put back into seclusion and Simon was detained, she didn't even know where; Bruno had forbidden all visits.

"I've ringed various articles."

He handed half the pile to her.

"Don't you have people to do this for you?"

"I prefer to do it myself, this way nothing's missed."

"You don't trust them?"

"I like reading the papers. It's the only way to get proper analysis."

"Like this?" she remarked, holding up a tabloid with the headline 'Josie Saves the Sicads!'

"I need to know what the everyday people are thinking."

Bruno frowned at the picture of the sweat-covered celebrity carrying a lifeless sicad and went off to find scissors. On his return, Jia was busy on her laptop.

"What are you doing?"

"I'm pulling all the articles off the web and making an electronic file for you."

"Thank you, Jia. But I'd prefer it if you'd cut them up and then stick them on the wall with the tacks."

Jia grabbed the scissors and, with an exaggerated series of sighs, attacked the magazines.

Half an hour later the wall was full of press cuttings. Bruno started to read aloud.

DAILY GLOBE – Josie Saves the Sicads as Socrates Project Collapses!

Soul singer Josie Torridos led a group of celebrity and environmental protestors associated with the environmental movement CAMEOS to a dramatic rescue of the sicads. The four hundred robots manufactured for the Socrates Project appear to have been trapped underground at CERN, where they may have been based for the last fifteen months.

According to the singer, the sicads had been deliberately left to die, which suggests the Socrates Project was secretly being killed off as another government failure. The sicads, near perfect replicas of humans, were rescued by the protesters as they fought to hold off police and armed forces. Allegedly, it was too late for fifty-eight of the sicads.

The project, on which so much has been staked, appears to be on the brink of collapse. Violent protests continue in many of the major capital cities of the world. Angry populations clashed with armies and police, and reports indicate thousands of injuries and dozens of fatalities.

Officials at CAMEOS declined to comment on their involvement with the sicads. Global governments deny being responsible for events at CERN. In a hastily convened press release, they blamed the incident on a power failure at CERN and claim the project is still on track to produce the promised solutions. In an attempt to salvage the project, Governor Bruno Reno has promised to release an early report of the sicads' recommendations.

La Vue Independante – Sicads linked to CAMEOS campaign to save the planet.

After the dramatic revelation of the CERN rescue, we look at the relationship between the sicads and CAMEOS, and attempt to piece together the events that led to the dramatic rescue of the dying sicads. In our report, we highlight some critical questions that governments need to answer if they want populations to continue to have faith in their integrity.

According to reliable sources, the Socrates Project included a twelve month period when the sicads were released into human societies around the world, to conduct an extensive global census on humanity. Our analysis indicates that this is why the sicads, to avoid detection, had to be built in humanity's image.

We have charted the rise in popularity of CAMEOS with the alleged start of this observation period. The correlation is evident in the chart below. We have tracked the evolution of the scale and quality of the CAMEOS website over this period and have come to the conclusion that this could not have been achieved without considerable funds, nor without the knowledge and support of leading computer consultancies and media companies, who have denied any involvement with CAMEOS. We have looked at the accounts of the charity CAMEOS and can find no evidence of such funding. It appears the sicads are the only explanation.

We therefore consider the more important question of why and who is behind this. Scientists have long been trying to get the attention of global governments and populations to the alleged destruction of our ecosystems. France has been a supporter of better protection for these ecosystems, but other countries have consistently hindered our efforts to make this international consensus. Are the Socrates Project and CAMEOS a secret government attempt to raise the awareness of global populations to these issues? If so, is this a global approach or a secret initiative by Governor Bruno Reno, a known sympathiser with this cause?

If we develop this idea, and we imagine that other members of the coalition discovered this secret initiative, then we can start to make sense of why somebody may have wanted to sabotage the project.

Bruno finished reading and looked at Jia.

"There are many more theories and counter-theories like this!'

Jia shrugged her shoulders.

"It's all a shambles. Can you blame them?"

"There are some dangerous allegations there. I hadn't even heard of CAMEOS three days ago. The Americans are never going to accept that. They're going to believe this crap!"

He pulled another article off the wall.

"This sums up how they're already viewing it – it's from the New World Herald. The headline reads: 'Sicads to destroy the global economy'. Listen to this:

"Decades after seeing off the evil forces of communism, global governments are accused by leading international businesses of 'backdoor communism'. Leaders of our most reputable businesses have accused global governments of using the sicads to stir up anti-business sentiment, which would reduce the standard of living for the average global citizen.

They allege that the sicads have been secretly directed by socialist elements of global governments to stir up anti-corporate sentiment. The sicads have been linked to an international magazine which is renowned for its scurrilous and unfounded attacks on international business interests. Leading businessmen have accused this magazine, which we shall not name for fear of giving it the publicity it feeds on, of staging a huge publicity stunt and interfering with the integrity of the Socrates Project."

He stopped reading.

"This is all I need, Jia. I've already had the US President asking to check the Project briefings."

"Well, it's true the sicads are coming out with unorthodox conclusions. People were expecting some tangible and innovative solutions. Somehow the project has got bogged down in woolly religious and save-the-planet propaganda."

Bruno started at Jia, trying to fathom her sudden disillusionment.

She picked up an article from Intelligent Design.

"I'll read the overview."

The sudden and mysterious arrival of the sicads upon the planet has thrown up many questions for faith-based communities around the world. Over the last few decades there has been an increase in the number of respected faith leaders who have reminded us that God gave mankind dominion over Nature as stewards.

Every time we, as humans, drive a species to extinction, we are stating that what God created, we can destroy. There is no scripture to support that view. 'The earth is the Lord's and the fullness thereof'. Psalms 24:1. Christians are called to be stewards – to nurture, to protect, to preserve His creation. Too often, the individual material interests of the profane have

*dominated over the needs of the wider community. This wider community,
which can only be held together by collective worship, has broken down as
our fellow men have strayed, like lost sheep, into ignorance of our Lord –
the original and ultimate sin.*

*The Lord ultimately creates everything for us. In this special edition of
Intelligent Design we examine the idea, which is spreading around the globe,
that the sicads were sent by our Lord as shepherds, to gather his lost sheep
and to lead us out of the fog towards a new promised land.*

Jia shook her head in disgust.

"It almost sounds convincing."

Bruno reflected silently.

"Well, Jia, thanks for your help. I'll read the rest later. For now, I have
a crisis on my hands. Not least of which is what to do with Commander
Gort!"

"What's happening with him?"

"Well, he's not happy about being locked up. I can only hold him a
few days."

"But surely, after what's he done, you can charge him or court martial
him, can't you?"

Bruno looked at her.

"He's maintaining the power failure was an accident. We've no proof
other than Simon's word. The trouble is Gort has many supporters. In
times of crisis, people take comfort from a strong hand. Sometimes I feel
like I'm the only one at the table who is uncomfortable with him. I feel as
if everybody is expecting me to fail, and that Gort is waiting to step into
my shoes at any opportunity."

He sat back in deep contemplation. Jia picked up another article and
read it silently. The article was from the English edition of a popular
German magazine.

Will the collapse of the Socrates Project lead to a wave of social revolutions?

*Governments conceived the Socrates Project in an attempt to head off a
wave of possible social revolutions, as climate change and the increase in
prices of basic food staples disproportionately hit the poorer members of
global societies. Boxed in by powerful vested interests, and lacking an
effective apparatus for enforcing effective global policy, the courageous*

Governor Bruno Reno conceived the Socrates Project as a clever way of garnering global support for, and de-politicising, some difficult and unpopular policy changes.

As the future of this project has been jeopardised, we have seen a series of worrying riots and protests around the world. We ask whether this will lead to actual social revolutions and, if so, what form will these revolutions take? To answer this question we look at the structures of current societies and what holds them together.

Our summary conclusion is that populations are more dependent than ever on the complex systems that deliver our food and health care. Whilst these systems are creaking under the strains of climatic and demographic change, along with years of poor long-term planning by governments, we conclude that any alternative, at least in the short term, is difficult to envisage....

She put down the article and picked up another headed 'War hero linked to plot to destroy sicads.'

"Jia, I've got to head out for an important meeting," announced Bruno abruptly.

*

The Global Governments Emergency Council was due to commence. The Chinese Premier, the Japanese Prime Minister, the German Chancellor as Secretary General for Europe, the Russian President, the Australian Prime Minister as Secretary General for Oceania, the Indian Prime Minister and the Secretary Generals for Africa and the Middle East were all present. The two empty spaces left at the table were each filled with a full-length screen displaying their American counterparts; the President of the United States and the Secretary General for South America.

Once everybody had exchanged brief greetings, Bruno stood up and opened the council with the usual protocol.

"Good afternoon members of the Council. Thank you for making yourselves available at short notice."

He touched a button on the underside of the table and a projector beamed the front page of the 'Summary Report of the Sicads' – marked 'Highly Confidential'.

Bruno cast a glance at each of them before resuming.

"OK, you've all had a copy and, I assume, have read and discussed it with the countries you represent. Who'd like to give their feedback first?"

The President of the United States jumped up.

"Bruno we can't present this!"

"And why is that Gregory?"

"The public won't understand it and it's full of socialism!"

Bruno sighed.

"The sicads' recommendations are based on extensive observation, analysed with rigorous Socratic Method. They've pulled together forgotten wisdom from all over the world. You need to read it carefully to see the beauty of their ideas. They go beyond politics and, as such Gregory, we all agreed to be bound by their recommendations. If we spin their conclusions for political ends, the public are going to see straight through us – they're not as gullible as you think."

"This is preposterous, Bruno!"

The Chinese Premier came to the Governor's rescue.

"Gregory, I think it's better if the sicads speak with a unique voice. We can always disagree with some of their more contentious suggestions."

The US President was only momentarily pacified.

"It's easy for you in China. You can simply lay down the law. My people are used to living in a democracy!"

"Feeding people a diet of poor-quality food and education, so they can be easily manipulated is an illusion of democracy!" replied the antagonised Chinese Premier.

"Well, in my country we don't leave dissidents rotting in jail."

"Gentlemen, may I remind you we've important business to cover?" interrupted Bruno, playing his usual role of referee.

Two hours of delicate negotiations ensued and tensions were flying high. Bruno looked at his watch again – that's good, we're running out of time and nobody's asked about Gort yet!

"And what does Gort say about all this, Bruno?" asked the Indian Prime Minister.

"Commander Gort is busy writing his report on the events at CERN," he replied swiftly, before clapping his hands together to bring order to the meeting.

"Now, gentlemen, we've only a few minutes left, so we'll deal with any final objections before moving to the decisive vote."

Bruno truculently clattered through the final objections.

"All those in favour of allowing the sicads to release their report as it is, raise your hands."

The US President held up his hand to stop Bruno.

"We need more time to reflect, Bruno."

As the Governor made to object, the American continued.

"My Chinese, Russian, Indian, and Australian counterparts agree."

Bruno, his eyes signalling a suspected betrayal, scrutinised their faces.

"We all agreed to be bound by..."

"It's just a delay," interjected the new US President.

"A delay of how long?"

"Three weeks should..."

"Two," snapped Bruno.

46

Bruno closed the door and ushered Pierre to sit down.

"Crazy times, eh Bruno?"

"Crazy times indeed! What do you do when you don't know if you can still trust the head of your army?"

"I take it you're referring to Commander Gort."

"Yes, of course. You've seen the press, I take it?"

"Who hasn't?"

"Well, then you know about as much as I do. I'm tempted to appoint General Henri Gilles as a stand-in. At least I know I can trust the French army!"

"That might upset the Americans and the rest of the UN Generals, Governor. What's Gort's explanation?"

"Well, I'm still awaiting his official report. He maintains that the sicad is lying and that the power failure was an accident."

"Any other witnesses?"

"His men, of course, though most of them were out hunting for Simon and Jia. The only senior personnel member in attendance, Colonel McCloud, supports Gort's version of events."

"Well he is a pretty solid type. And the forensics?"

"They haven't been able to completely rule out an accident."

"No other witnesses?"

"No credible ones, unfortunately," sighed Bruno.

Pierre scratched his head.

"Well, it's a tough one, Bruno. I guess you need to see Gort's report."

"My conclusion too. In the meantime, I'm going to privately suspend him from duties."

Pierre nodded solemnly.

"I can't afford to rock the boat until I have some real proof, so Colonel McCloud will privately assume Gort's functions."

"Can I help in any way?"

"Yes, you can. I'd like you to keep an eye on Colonel McCloud. I've a bad feeling that something is going on behind the scenes."

Jia chose to sit outside, not to enjoy the warm spring sunshine, but rather to smoke. The waiter emptied her ashtray and brought her another coffee. She nervously tapped the back of the spoon against the saucer. With the Socrates Project currently out of her hands, she was in limbo. The natural thing would be to return to Mazari, but she had no more appetite for this than for the breakfast basket in front of her. She flicked through the pages of the morning newspaper. 'The Virgin Jia?' The headline jumped off the page. Ever since religious groups had espoused the idea that the sicads might be a divine intervention, she'd feared becoming a media target.

As she read the article, she started to shake uncontrollably. The cruel allegations tore through her fragile defences. She felt light-headed. Blurred faces whirled around her. Was everybody looking at her? People seemed to stop and stare. She panicked. I must get out of here! Shakily, she got to her feet, leaning on the round table for support, tipping it over and sending the coffee cup crashing to the floor. The waiter strode towards her. Instead of the waiter she saw Gort's face. She stepped backwards and tripped over the table. Scurrying to her feet, she staggered through the onlookers, closing in on her, arms encircling her.

"Leave me alone!" she screamed at them, lashing out and pushing them away.

She stumbled into the road.

A taxi swerved and screeched to a halt. Jia slumped across the windscreen then, trying to stand, staggered alongside the vehicle, reached down deliriously, opened the rear door and fell inside. The driver turned around, mouth open, staring at her.

"Refuge...," she murmured.

"Where?"

"Refuge," she repeated in a trance.

"I'll take you to the nearest police station... or hospital?"

The faces were all around the taxi, closing in on her again.

"No to Le Reposoir, it's near Cluses."

The cars all around were blasting their horns. The driver sighed and tapped the destination into his GPS.

"That's six hundred kilometres away!"

"I can pay," she gasped, pushing a pile of crumpled bank notes towards him.

As he unfolded them and held them up to the light, she collapsed across the back seat.

*

Leopold sat at the same table, looking at the same darkened glass as he had been eleven months before. This time, he could see more obscure figures behind – four, or was it five? More mysterious benefactors of the Better World Trust? Government types, business men – or possibly even religious leaders? He'd had dealings with all of these types in the past. All had their own agendas and this project had a larger scope than most. Anyway, the more the merrier – it meant a bigger budget, and he had plenty of material for them.

A new voice, distorted as always, but definitely an older voice.

"So, Mr Leopold, what do you have to report?"

Leopold gave a satisfied smile and stood up to address the concealed figures.

"The Commander is cooperating fully and things have moved up several levels. With all the media attention and two dead soldiers behind the scenes, this is no longer just an observation and persuasion project," he emphasised, throwing back at them their carefully chosen campaign description. He proceeded to describe the nature of the soldiers' demise and the events that followed.

"The risk has increased considerably," he concluded.

He waited whilst muted conversations took place behind the screen. The same voice recommenced.

"The CERN incident was very disappointing. Once again, the Commander failed to bring the matter to a satisfactory conclusion. However the soldiers' deaths offer some interesting opportunities."

"Yes, gentlemen, I have some very effective ideas on that score as well. For now however, I've exhausted the budget on all the unforeseen extra work. If we can agree on a new budget to cover the extended scope of the project…"

*

After six hours, the taxi arrived at the monastery. A surprised Mother Cristina came out to investigate. Taking one look at Jia, the nun helped her stagger through the entrance and into her personal chamber.

"I didn't know where else to turn," mumbled Jia feverishly.

She slept through to the following morning, when she woke up to find the Prioress sitting on the end of her bed.

"You still look pale, but better than when you arrived. I was wondering whether to call a doctor."

Jia persuaded her that wasn't necessary, and after eating some fruit she felt strong enough to walk around the courtyard. She explained how sullied she'd felt by the cruel accusations and how, with all the anxiety of the project, not to mention Gort, it had all been too much. The Prioress listened patiently.

"I just need a bit of time by myself, whilst things sort themselves out," Jia concluded.

"Well, you've put yourself under a lot of pressure, my child. You're very welcome to stay here whilst you recuperate. Your timing is fortunate – a chamber is becoming free."

"Not Sister Agatha's?"

"No. She's very repentant and staying, at least for now. No, I'm leaving myself."

Jia stopped and looked at the Prioress.

"Wow – that's a shock! Why on earth would you want to leave?"

The nun smiled benevolently.

"Yes, it is a bit of a shock. The vision and then Simon's arrival helped me make an important decision."

"I hope we haven't caused you any problems."

"You've nothing to apologise for, my child. For several months I'd been questioning whether staying here was the right thing. I had an inkling that something else was required of me."

"What are you going to do?"

"I've finally found the Lord's purpose for my life. Your arrival was no accident."

"Don't take any rash decisions because of us," Jia implored.

"Jia, Simon is right – religions must work together. Our energies are dispersed and societies are falling apart through lack of spiritual guidance. We must find strength in unity. For too long I've turned my back on the world. Now the Lord has other plans for me."

Her eyes burned brightly as she spoke.

Jia's mind turned to practical matters.

"After so long in the monastery, how will you live?"

The nun swallowed bravely.

"The Lord will provide a way."

She seemed lost in her thoughts before addressing Jia.

"Let's attend to your predicament first, my child."

When Jia was installed in a spare chamber, as comfortably as the sparse monastic facilities allowed, her thoughts turned to Mazari and Susumu – there's no sense in putting it off! Grabbing her coat and cigarettes, she went into the monastery grounds. Before she'd left Japan, the Chairman had given her a card with his direct line. Dialling the number, she nervously inhaled and exhaled thick clouds of smoke. The call was re-routed before Susumu answered promptly. As the old man listened, she explained she needed a break, giving a long list of plausible reasons and justifying why the monastery was the perfect place to recuperate. Susumu, being taxied along a runway in a private jet, listened patiently. He was old enough to recognise a female in a fragile state of mind – and things are about to get a lot worse for her, he thought to himself. He agreed with everything she said, told her to stay put and to take all the time she needed. Before hanging up, he asked her lots of detailed questions about Simon and CAMEOS.

Later that day, Jia sat pensively in the church, looking at the statues of Jesus and Mary. She felt a fraud, knowing she was suffering predominantly because of Simon and Osiris. The other pressures and uncertainties weren't helping, but she could handle these. Consciously and cathartically, she was rebelling against this new side to Simon, so anathema to the scientific rigour she'd hoped for and expected from him. Subconsciously, she wanted him more than ever, and it was the fear of another rejection and, worse, a rejection of all she stood for, that was the knife twisting inside her. Simon, a perfect creation and companion in one, rejecting her for a savage. And now the media, after the amazing achievement of bringing the sicads into being – all they were interested in was whether she was parading as a false saint, a cheap slut with ideas above her station. After all the sacrifices she'd made, being spurned by society had been the final tipping point.

She targeted her anger at the media, society, Osiris and even Mazari – everybody else was to blame. She hated all of them, and felt unclean. If they wanted virtue, she'd show them virtue. And if Simon was drawn to those who help others, then she could play that game. As she stared at the statues, she understood exactly what she could do.

Later that evening, after a frugal supper, she took Mother Cristina aside.

"Mother, I must speak to you."

The Prioress listened attentively.

"Mother, I want to free my mind and soul from the media distraction, regain my independence and renounce my allegiances. I want to take a break from my job and spend some time here, if that's possible?"

Mother Cristina started to speak, but Jia continued.

"In return, I'd like to do something for the monastery and for you. I'd like to give away the money I've earned from working on the Socrates Project and I'd like to make a donation to the monastery."

Mother Cristina smiled in gratitude.

"However, I want to donate the majority of this money to an even more urgent cause, Mother. That is to help you in your quest to unite religions. The future of the Socrates Project depends on humanity coming together. History will judge my actions. The best contribution I can make now is to support your efforts."

Mother Cristina listened quietly. When Jia had finished, she dropped onto her knees and clasped the young scientist's hands in hers.

"Jia, I'm honoured to have met you. Thank you."

*

Commander Gort sat inside a prison cell, brooding over events. When is Bruno going to show himself? His thoughts were interrupted by the sound of approaching footsteps. The Governor strode up to the cell door. The two men stared at each other. It was the Governor who broke the awkward silence.

"I'm glad to see that you've calmed down, Commander."

"Being imprisoned, after all my years of devoted service, is an utter disgrace!"

"Imprisoned is a little harsh, Gort. I've held you here whilst we contain the damage suffered to the project."

"You've no right to do this. I was just doing my job."

"I beg to differ on both counts, Commander. Firstly, following a serious breach of duty, I have the right to detain you for up to five days without charge. Secondly, your job was to protect the sicads, not to terminate them."

Gort stood up and approached the bars.

"There was no breach of duty, Governor. The power loss was an unfortunate accident. Remember, two of my soldiers were killed in a horrific manner by one of these sicads."

Bruno stared deep into the Commander's dark eyes.

"Well, Gort, you're suspended from duties whilst I await your report on those deaths. There are many questions that need to be addressed. For the moment I've spared you the embarrassment of informing your subordinates. I'm giving them the benefit of the doubt of any shared responsibility, for now. The only person aware of your suspension is Colonel McCloud. Officially, you're on sick leave."

"You're crazy, Bruno. It's the sicad you ought to be dealing with," replied Gort coldly, with a sneer.

"All the sicads are safely under lock and key. Unlike you, David, Simon has already given me a full account of the events at CERN and Lake Geneva!"

Bruno watched Gort's eyes as he emphasised the name of the lake. Gort unflinchingly returned his stare and held his gaze.

"The sicads are programmed to tell the truth, Gort!"

The Commander ignored the insinuation.

"If you've finished with me, Governor, I'd like to be released. I refuse to work on any report in these conditions!"

"Commander, you're not in a position to refuse anything. However, I'd already taken the decision to transfer you to secure barracks. I'll expect your completed report by the end of the week, including full details of the activities of all senior army personnel at CERN over that period."

Bruno took a final look at Gort, to try to read his thoughts. I don't trust this man at all, he thought. He started to walk away slowly, before turning back to the Commander.

"Your escort party will be here shortly."

After Bruno left, Gort unpicked a short length of the stitching on the lapel of his uniform. Pushing the material apart with his nails, he pulled out a concealed tiny scrap of paper and a stub of a pencil. He'd just finished scribbling a hasty note when the escort party and Bruno arrived. There were five of them – Colonel McCloud accompanying four of Bruno's personal guards. He wants to be seen to be playing by the rules, Gort deduced.

McCloud entered the cell with Pierre. Gort was sat on the bed, arms crossed.

"We're here to escort you, Commander."

Bruno stood at the door, watching. When Gort refused to move, Pierre looked questioningly at the Governor.

"Assist the Commander, gentlemen."

Scott and Pierre each grabbed an elbow and tried to pull Gort to his feet. He resisted, pushing them away forcefully.

Bruno walked into the cell.

"Gort, don't make things any worse for yourself."

The Commander stood up in his own time and gruffly followed the soldiers to the waiting transporter.

At the barracks, Bruno's men were waiting to take charge of the Commander. The Governor addressed Gort in a conciliatory tone.

"You've got all the facilities you need to finish your report. Once we have the report, we can move forward."

Gort didn't reply. He walked with dignity into the building.

Scott drove back to HQ in a state of mental turmoil – would Gort come clean and drag him down as well? If not, the inevitable inquiry would surely point a finger at him. It could only be a matter of time before he was in the same situation as his Commander. The axe is hanging over me. His thoughts were distracted by an incoming message. He put his hand into his pocket to retrieve the phone and felt a small folded piece of paper. Pulling over, he unfolded and read the short message: 'Get the photos to Leopold.'

He smiled at his Commander's ingenuity and flames of hope flared up inside him, bringing warm relief. So that's why he resisted! He opened the text message: 'Make contact. L'

He nodded in admiration for his Commander – always a backup plan! He replied to Leopold's text. A message came back summoning him to a 6am rendezvous.

Scott arrived at the aerodrome in civilian dress, having taken a last minute taxi to ensure he wasn't followed. An eight-seater plane was waiting on the tarmac and he was beckoned inside by a flight attendant. Mr Leopold, his bulk spreading across two seats, was wearing a blue suit, yellow shirt and purple tie, the latter matching the scar running across his face. The two men nodded in recognition; despite not having met before, each instinctively knew his role.

"We don't have much time. I have to be in Rome shortly," announced Leopold.

"I have something for you from the Commander."

"Evidence of the dead soldiers?"

"You know about them?"

"We have our sources, Colonel."

"Well, here's the proof."

Leopold plugged the miniature disk into his tablet.

"Wonderful. Just perfect," he beamed at the gruesome photos.

"Not so perfect and wonderful for their families."

"Apologies. I was forgetting myself, Colonel. We'll ensure that the families are well looked after."

Scott was staring at the imposing gentleman.

"What next?"

"Now we have these, I think we've enough to bring the Governor down. It's time for Bruno Reno to disappear for a while and for Commander Gort to reappear."

"You can't be serious. The Governor is always guarded."

"Don't worry, Colonel. We have everything organised. You'll receive your instructions shortly."

Mr Leopold looked at his watch and Scott took this as a cue to leave, descending the steps into an overcast morning.

As the plane taxied along the runway, Leopold hit a button on his tablet. A second later the photos, along with a short commentary, were uploaded to an anonymous webpage. As the files hit the website, a pre-written program distributed them instantly to a large selection of news channels and blog sites. A split second later, the webpage self-destructed and the server hosting it was decommissioned.

47

After the usual last minute make-up touches, the panel of celebrities, scientists and former government members took their seats. The lighting and sound engineers made their final checks, the audience were warned to not be rowdy and the camera team gave their thumbs-up approval. The panel composed themselves. The cameras zoomed in and the host was announced.

"Please welcome Mathias Yanofine, or MyFi as we love to know him – Global Vision's most popular presenter."

Mathias smiled at the camera, soaking up the cheers from the audience.

"Welcome, everybody, to this week's edition of Spotlight – 'Spotlight on the Socrates Project' – which is coming to you live from Global Vision Centre in London. This week's edition promises to be our most exciting and most viewed yet!"

An enormous cheer went up from the seated audience, many of whom had queued for over forty-eight hours to participate in this once-in-a-lifetime debate. Mathias skilfully conducted the boisterous applause with his outstretched hands.

The debate was silently playing out on a screen in Bruno's office. A glance at his watch told him he had two hours before paying Gort a visit. He'd re-read Simon's transcript of events on Lake Geneva for at least the tenth time – it's impossible there were no witnesses! Flicking through the file, he came back to the newspaper article on the dead fisherman – boats didn't inexplicably catch alight. These events must be linked in some way. I'll read Gort's report and confront him directly, he decided.

His attention turned back to the screen. Mathias was just finishing his introduction.

"Yes, we're hoping to set a new record of two hundred million viewers, so tell your friends and family to put MyFi on their WIFI!"

The crowd cheered loudly again. Mathias cut through the applause to introduce the distinguished panel.

"Today we're joined by Professor Hafflewhaite, one of the world's leading experts on artificial intelligence; Josie Torridos, the soul singer who physically helped to liberate the sicads at CERN..."

Mathias's voice was drowned by the noise of the crowd, a strange mix of cheering and hissing. As the noise subsided, an angry voice shouted out: "Jezebel Josie!"

The presenter continued, unperturbed.

"Also on the panel, the former United Nation's Commander Sebastian Holstum; Reverend Peter Dickson, from the Church of Progressive Truth; Cardinal Carletto Stiglioni, the Chief Spokesman for the Vatican; Joseph Philanski, the former World Bank Chief Economist; and lastly, former Chinese Premier Zhu Shen."

The crowd burst into a fresh wave of excited applause; Mathias stifled them with a slicing of hands.

"The Socrates Project needs no introduction. We're here to get the panel's views and to take questions from the audience."

The crowd sat forward expectantly in their seats.

"We'll take the first audience question from Xavier Valentini."

The cameras found and zoomed in on Xavier, who got to his feet.

"My question is addressed at Sebastian Holstum. Do you think it is possible, as the army claims, the sicads were accidentally left to die at CERN?"

Sebastian slowly stroked the underside of his chin, formulating his response.

"I think, in unprecedented circumstances, such errors can be made. A pursuit of a dangerous lunatic unexpectedly turned into a several-day operation and the power failure at CERN was unfortunate timing..."

As Sebastian was finishing his response there were loud bursts of laughter from the crowd; shouts of "Get real!" and "Cover up!" reverberated around the auditorium.

Mathias smiled at the camera.

"Thank you, Sebastian. Josie, you were there at CERN, what's your opinion?"

Josie beamed a big smile as the cameras swung onto her.

"Well, Mathias, I was at CERN because I'd been tipped off that the sicads were in danger. The sicads had helped CAMEOS and we were totally committed to rescuing them, no matter how dangerous it was for us. If we'd arrived just a few minutes later... oh, I can't bear to think of how horrible it might have been!"

She fluttered her eyelids at the cameras as she finished speaking. Her words were met by a mixture of cheers and jeers.

"So it seems somebody knew that the sicads were in danger. Well, there we have two completely opposing views. With a long list of other questions to get through, I'll have to leave you viewers to draw your own conclusions. The next question is from Susan Malibot."

A tall suited and dark-skinned lady stood up, her eyes burning brightly.

"My question is addressed firstly to Cardinal Stiglioni and secondly to the wider panel. Do you think the sicads are a divine intervention to wake humans up to the destruction we are wreaking on the planet?"

Mathias addressed the spokesman for the Vatican.

"Cardinal, this is an idea that has been growing rapidly around the globe. An idea that originated partly, I believe, from the events at a monastery that one of the sicads sought refuge in."

The overweight spokesman shifted uncomfortably in his chair.

"There were some uncorroborated rumours on the internet, which we have investigated and found to be lacking in substance."

"Without substance!" interjected the Reverend from the Church of Progressive Truth. "How can you possibly say that?"

The Vatican spokesman opened his mouth to protest, but Mathias cut him short.

"Please continue, Reverend Dickson."

The Reverend smiled in satisfaction.

"The Church of Progressive Truth has conducted its own investigation into the events at Le Reposoir. The evidence of a divine intervention is overwhelming – not that a truly religious person should seek such evidence. The Messiah in question died on Good Friday, when a vision was received by the Prioress of the monastery, and then he rose from the dead and appeared physically to the Carmelite nuns on Easter Sunday. This Messiah has four hundred gifted disciples to spread the word. Yes, we believe that the sicads were sent by God!"

Mathias waited for the mixture of gasps and cheers to settle.

"Are you seriously saying you're worshipping a robot, Reverend Dickson?"

"Why wouldn't our Lord appear to us in a form that is apt for our times? It's not for us to question God's actions."

"Carletto, what do you say to that?" asked Mathias.

The Cardinal replied calmly, not without a certain badly-concealed smugness.

"Reverend Dickson has the right to believe whatever he wishes. We, the Catholic Church, however, do not recognise his cult as a reputable organisation of worship."

"You're a dangerous heretic, Carletto! It's people like you who were responsible for crucifying our Lord last time around. Your stuffy old church is bogged down in ancient dogma. Can't your type ever learn?"

Carletto's face turned a deep purple and he struggled to find the right words to respond.

Mathias's earpiece suddenly came to life, as his producer informed him of the breaking news. At the same time, the audiences' mobile phones and electronic tablets began to buzz uncontrollably. The panels' screens showed the gruesome photos of two dead soldiers, accompanied by a short, but sensational, story.

Soldiers Massacred by Sicads – UN Governor in Cover Up *The dead bodies of two soldiers, with horrific facial injuries, were fished out of Lake Geneva seven days ago. It is alleged that they were murdered by an escaped sicad, in trying to recapture it. It is suspected that Governor Reno knew about the deaths and attempted to cover them up, in order to avoid the collapse of the Socrates Project. In the meantime, the sicads released from CERN are still roaming freely in human societies.*

The whole studio fell into a state of shock at the disturbing photos and the gravity of the allegations. Mathias was the first to react.

"It's live television, folks, and it doesn't get any more live than this! I imagine that, like us, most of you have just seen the incredible photos and allegations hitting news channels around the globe. We're trying to establish whether it's a sick joke. Meanwhile, perhaps I may ask your views, Professor Hafflewhaite? Could a robot created to serve humanity commit such an act?"

The professor, nodding enthusiastically, brushed the wayward locks of white hair off his face and back across his balding head.

"An interesting question. Er... Let's hope it's a sick joke and this indeed proves to be an academic question. Well, anyway, to answer the question, I've studied the sicads with great interest. The exact artificial intelligence programs used are unfortunately highly-classified information. Nevertheless, their key element is clear: a self-learning or cybernetic program, ensuring that the sicads are intrinsically virtuous. This is, however, balanced against a self-preservation program to ensure their survival in case of danger. The only conceivable way in which a sicad would attack a human would be in defence of its own existence, and any response would use the minimum force required to neutralise the threat."

The professor paused and Mathias interjected.

"So, Professor, what you're saying is that the sicads would not have brutally mutilated the soldiers and caused the horrific injuries alleged. Is that correct?"

"Yes, Mathias. In my experience, feelings, malice and a desire for revenge are impossible for a robot."

"But, Professor, could this not have been caused by a malfunction of the sicad's operating syste...."

A startled shout from a member of the audience cut him short.

"It's no joke. The deaths are real. They've been confirmed by the military!"

"There might be sicads in the audience!" shouted another.

The cameras continued to film as the studio erupted into chaos and people left their seats, heading for the nearest exit."

Bruno jumped up in disbelief. Who released these pictures? That was top-secret classified material. And who confirmed it? This was Gort's doing, he was sure.

*

Osiris's secretary sat opposite her, legs crossed and a laptop balanced on her knee.

"Thanks for sticking around so late, Ganaëlle. I'm sorry we didn't get a chance to sit down earlier. Right, what's going on then?"

"You've got a busy month ahead. We must choose and edit the content for the April edition before the site visits next week to Cameroon and the Congo, and Indonesia the week after. At the end of the month you've been invited to do a series of talks in the UK. There's even interest from royalty! We've had inquiries from the Royal Society of Arts and the Royal Geographical Society, and an invitation from a member of the Royal Family to speak to the Friends of the Rain Forest Alliance."

"The Rain Forest Alliance – I believe they're doing something in the Yasuni Forest."

Suddenly, Osiris's telephone vibrated: 'Soldiers Massacred by Sicads – UN Governor in Cover Up'. At the sight of the thumbnail photos of the dead soldiers, the colour drained from her face.

Ganaëlle was staring at her in deep concern.

"Are you OK?"

Osiris didn't hear. Her full attention was focused on the newsflash.

*

Bruno's limousine arrived in front of the barracks. Accompanied by Pierre, he approached a guard, who failed to salute. About to reproach him, he heard a muffled cry and spun around to see Colonel McCloud and three other armed soldiers, one pointing a gun at him.

"What the hell's going on?" he demanded.

"Maybe I can explain," announced a familiar voice.

Commander Gort, pistol in hand, stood brazenly in front of him.

"I suggest you come quietly, Bruno."

As he searched for Pierre, he felt a blow to the head and his world went black.

The chief of security watched stone-faced as Bruno's body was unceremoniously loaded into the boot of an unmarked car. McCloud took four photos out of his pocket, one by one. Pierre watched silently as the Colonel shuffled through them – snapshots of Bourque's wife and children, innocently going about their daily lives.

"You're one hundred per cent sure he's clean? It would be a shame for anything to happen to your family."

Pierre didn't reply.

"Is he clean?" the Colonel repeated.

"I removed all devices personally," replied Pierre coldly.

"He'd better be. Otherwise there'll be serious repercussions!"

"He's a good man..."

"Keep your opinions to yourself, Bourque. Do exactly what you're told, or you'll have some nasty surprises!" snapped McCloud, brandishing the photos provocatively in front of him.

Pierre bit his tongue and stared, silently but angrily, at McCloud and Gort.

*

Bruno's eyes opened painfully, squinting in the darkness. What had happened? The fog cleared to reveal Gort pacing around the dark stone room. The damp walls were lit up by a low-energy light bulb. Where was he?

The back of his head throbbed. Still dressed in suit, shirt and tie, his legs were tied to a wooden chair and his hands were cuffed together behind him, causing his shoulders to ache.

"So you were plotting against me all the time, David?"

"I'm just a simple soldier. I do what I'm told, whether I like it or not. Shooting escaping refugees, torturing enemies – it's not always a nice job."

"So, I'm your enemy for refusing you endless resources?"

"Not as such, Bruno. It seems you have bigger enemies."

"Who's betrayed me?"

"Powerful forces, who seem to object to your project."

"And you've decided to side with these people, Commander?"

"I'm afraid I've had little choice."

"I imagine that the Americans are involved… The new regime slipping back into its bad ways, eh? The Chinese supporting them behind the scenes, are they?"

Gort didn't answer.

"You don't have to do this, David. What have they offered you? Money? It can't be status. You've already reached the top after a brilliant career. Or is it a sudden bout of zealous patriotism?"

"As I said, Bruno, I'm just doing my job."

"What in the devil's name do they have over you?"

Gort remained silent.

"David, don't do this. If the Project collapses, we'll have bigger problems; more refugee camps, more riots and more dead soldiers. We can't fight these problems with guns!"

Gort shook his head.

"Save your breath, Governor, this is not the time. I've been asked to bring you here for a little persuasion session, to enlist your support..."

"Persuasion... or do you mean torture?"

"Torture is such a gruesome word. But sometimes gruesome things are necessary. How do you think I managed to clean up Afghanistan?"

Continuing his monologue, Gort pulled up a chair opposite Bruno's.

"Finding their hideouts wasn't easy, you know. Those Taliban devils were secretive bastards and tough nuts to crack. I had to learn some new

337

techniques. It took time to find one that worked; one of the old methods, tried and tested. Rats, sewer rats – huge rodents that will munch their way through anything; wood, flesh, sinew and even bone if they have to."

Gort drew a breath and observed Bruno. Was that fear in his eyes?

"Some of these vermin are over a foot long – vicious beasts! You see this scar on my neck? One got out and jumped on my back. It got a good bite before I blew its brains out! Don't think I was sadistic, Bruno. You must understand I had to build a reputation of being tough. It's not pretty to have to resort to these methods."

Bruno shifted uncomfortably. Gort could feel his victim softening.

"Most crack when we show them the cage. If not, things usually liven up when we add the hot coals on top. They soon nibble through the base. The tough ones hang in till they feel the claws tickling their belly. The real fanatics hang in longer, that's when it gets really nasty and messy."

Gort's eyes were cold and expressionless as he continued the mental torture.

"I've never heard grown men scream so loudly, or beg so desperately for mercy. It's a pretty horrible sight, not to mention the clean-up job afterwards."

"Why are you telling me all this, Gort? It's enough to get you court marshalled!"

"I need you to do something, Bruno. They've prepared a speech and they'd like to film you reading it."

"You're as mad as they are, Gort! I have no intention of co-operating with this insanity."

"They thought you might be a tough one to crack, Bruno. But don't worry, they don't want me to use the rats on you. It wouldn't look good on camera if your gnawed innards were hanging out."

"Gort, they're going to kill me anyway."

Gort shrugged his shoulders.

"Who knows?"

"Unless I'm missing something in their twisted world, I don't see any incentive to co-operate!"

"Hmmm, a fair point Bruno. They thought you might ask for something in return."

Bruno laughed.

"There's nothing you or they have that could possibly interest me!"

Gort raised his eyebrows.

"Really? What if we offered you Jia's life? Not only saving her life, but saving her from a distressing and messy death!"

"You're bluffing, Gort."

Gort took out his mobile phone and dialled a number in front of the Governor – a number Bruno knew by heart. Gort activated the speaker, his thumb hovering over the mute button, watching Bruno.

A Japanese voice, which Bruno equally recognised, answered the phone in English.

"Mazari, Miss Jin's secretary."

"It's Commander Gort here. I'd like to speak to Jia urgently."

"Commander, she's disappeared from contact for the last two days!" replied the young lady anxiously.

"Well, have her call me urgently if she returns."

The soldier hung up and looked inquiringly at Bruno.

"A simple coincidence! Even if you have Jia, you're not exactly going to let her live anyway!"

"Now that's not necessarily the case, Bruno. It's true that powerful religious figures have been offended by Miss Jin's actions, but she's not beyond redemption."

Gort stared at Bruno, watching his reaction.

"She could be spared and released as easily as she was kidnapped... if they were so disposed."

"So, they've thought of everything, Commander."

"Yes, Bruno, it seems so. Whilst I'm waiting for you to make up your mind, do you mind if we watch a little television?"

It was a rhetorical question and Bruno knew it. Gort hit a switch and a large screen came to life. The screen slowly focused on a dimly-lit room and a naked woman tied to a bench. Her long raven-black hair hung down onto the floor and the naturally tanned skin of her lightly-muscled body reflected the flickering candle and firelight. Her hands were tied together underneath the bench and she was blindfolded. Standing over her was an overweight man, dressed in a black robe with a gold braided belt, a whip in one hand and a Bible in the other. She was shaking and her body was marked with red lacerations.

"Confess! You're a witch!" he shouted.

The lady was sobbing and screamed back.

"You're mad. Release me please, I'm begging you!"

Bruno listened with dread – was that Jia's voice? His spirits sank and he suddenly felt very sick and weary.

"Why are you parading around pretending to be some saintly virgin? Confess, blasphemer!" shrieked the torturer, striking her violently with the whip.

Her shrieks of pain turned to sobs.

"Stop, please stop... I beg you."

Gort spoke. "Easy, Marcello." The sadist stopped; bringing his finger to his ear, he listened for instructions.

"Don't rush. You've plenty of time. Relax and enjoy yourself. Now, do you have our friends in case Miss Jin refuses to confess?"

The torturer went away and returned holding a cage. Crammed inside were two huge brown rats, their fat bodies at least twenty-five centimetres long and their tails the same again. As they gnawed and scratched at the steel bars, Bruno got a glimpse of their teeth and claws.

"Nice specimens! And you've got the hot coals?"

Putting the cage down onto the woman's stomach, he used a pair of tongs to fetch a red-hot lump of coal.

The blindfolded victim, hearing the rats and sensing something awful was about to happen, started to thrash against her bindings.

"What the hell are you doing to me?" she screamed.

"OK, now show us what happens when you put the coal on top."

Bruno watched helplessly. The rats started to scratch and dig through the soft wooden base. The torturer returned with another lump of coal, as his victim started to scream uncontrollably.

Bruno sighed. "For God's sake, Gort, stop the torture! Release her and I'll co-operate."

48

The atmosphere at the video-conference meeting of the Global Governments Emergency Council was highly tense – not totally surprising, given the circumstances. It had been hastily organised following the news of the soldiers' deaths and then Bruno's disappearance. It was just seven days since the previous meeting to consider the release of the summary report.

"So, despite being his chief of security, you just let him walk away and disappear?"

"Not exactly, Mr President. As I explained, Bruno was very distraught. He told me he'd resigned and not to try to find him. After so many years of looking after him, I've become a sort of friend, sir," replied Pierre cautiously.

"And you're sure you don't know where he is?"

"Absolutely. He must be wearing new clothes and shoes, as even the security devices he didn't know about can't help us!"

"It can't be hard to locate one of the most famous faces in the world!"

"Well, we're conducting an extensive search. He must have planned it very well. As soon as we have a lead we'll let you know, Mr President."

"That'll be all for now."

"Can we watch Bruno's speech one more time?" demanded the Japanese Prime Minister.

"We've seen it ten times already," snapped the American President, irritated and exasperated.

"And we're sure it's authentic?" inquired the South American Secretary General.

The American President banged his fist repeatedly on an oak table.

"Yes, as best we can tell, it's genuine"

"No, there's no time to watch it again."

"No we cannot find him...."

"Yes, we've every available man tracking him down, to no avail."

"Yes, we supported him whilst he covered up the soldiers' deaths!"

"On the streets they're baying for Bruno's blood... our blood!"

"No wonder he's resigned and gone into hiding!"

"We must act! The whole world is laughing at us!"

The German Chancellor, unmoved, waited for the histrionics to die down, before calmly offering his counsel.

"I think it's unwise to take any hasty decisions tonight. Before these revelations about the soldiers, which incidentally are still not totally corroborated, the public were getting strongly behind the Project and the sicads. The events at CERN actually increased public support. Two dead soldiers and rabble raisers or not, I can't condone this sudden volte-face. We should sleep on it. The night brings counsel."

The American President reacted angrily.

"Two of our soldiers were brutally murdered by Bruno's robots. Things have moved on. We don't have the luxury of delay and indecision now. How many times must we save your European arses?"

"Gregory, there's no need to be insulting!" interjected the Japanese Prime Minister, taking Bruno's habitual role as peacekeeper.

"Rushing in the appointment of Gort, even if only temporary, is unwise. We've yet to clarify his role in this mess," continued the German.

The Indian Prime Minister cleared his throat and eloquently addressed the assembled council.

"Well, it seems to me that Gort is the only person we can rely on. He saw the danger and tried to take pre-emptive action. It is clear that the sicads are dangerous. Bruno, in his own words, admitted trying to cover up the deaths of the soldiers. To my mind, it seems we are once again in Commander Gort's debt."

The South American Secretary General gave his contribution.

"I have consulted my national counterparts and, with the project in tatters and signs of further social unrest, we don't see what alternative we have to Commander Gort."

His Middle Eastern counterpart objected.

"These deaths and Bruno's sudden disappearance all seem very mysterious and suspicious. I've never known Bruno run away from a problem. Let's not forget what Bruno did for the Middle East. There were equally difficult and dangerous times and he never wavered. I know – I was there at his side."

All eyes fell upon him.

"So what exactly are you saying?" pressed the American President.

There was a pregnant pause, but no response.

"Well, Bruno is not around and now we need the next strongest person to take control. Like it or not, that's where we are, unless one of us is going to step up and take responsibility for the Project?" added the Indian Prime Minister.

Nobody came forward. The American President looked at the clock.

"It's past midnight. I propose we put Commander Gort in charge temporarily. Whatever happens, somebody needs to take control of the Project, unless anyone else has any better ideas?"

Nobody volunteered.

"OK, let's take a vote. All those in favour, raise your hand!" instructed the American President.

Indian, Chinese, Russian, Australian and American hands were all raised. There was a moment's hesitation before a South American hand followed.

It was gone midnight and Gort was sitting in front of his computer, thinking about the events of the last few hours. The stunt with the Jia double had worked better than he'd feared. It was so convincing that even he had winced when he saw the rats. Thankfully, he hadn't been forced to resort to any real torture. His computer buzzed and the face of the American President appeared on his screen, alongside the other members of the emergency council.

"Thank you for waiting up, Commander. I have some important news for you," announced the President.

Gort feigned ignorance.

"We've received a video resignation from Bruno. The situation is highly irregular and, frankly, out of character. What's more, we've been unable to locate him to discuss it."

"I'm sorry to hear the news," he replied.

The Japanese Prime Minister addressed him.

"It seems he has taken the responsibility of the soldiers' deaths personally and is ashamed by the cover-up. The impending failure of the Project may have unbalanced him. What was the last thing Bruno said to you?"

Gort had been pre-briefed by Leopold and repeated exactly what he had been told to say.

"Governor Reno released me and apologised for his inappropriate conduct. He confessed that the strain was affecting his judgement. I felt sorry for him. I tried to convince him from the start not to place too much trust in the sicads."

The President carefully observed Gort.

"Well, Commander we need someone to stand in for Bruno; somebody who can calm everything down."

"Yes, there's a critical need to do so in these volatile times. His successor will need to work closely with the military whilst we bring things under control. I'll be happy to personally assist this person in any way I can, Mr President."

"Of course, Gort, we know you will. However, we're proposing to appoint you as Acting Governor until things settle down."

The President stared intently at Gort.

"This is totally unexpected... It's a great responsibility, Mr President... How long can I have to decide?"

Gort knew he didn't have a choice. The President looked at his watch and announced: "Twenty minutes, Commander."

A feeling of frustration and helplessness washed over David Gort. In ordinary circumstances, it would have been an honour being appointed as United Nations Governor, even if it was only as a stand-in.

I'm still paying the price for venting my childhood anger on Todd Ranger nearly thirty years ago, he thought. It would have been better for everybody if I had finished him off. Not knowing your own name, being fed with a spoon and having your arse wiped for you like a baby is no life! Being kept alive for what?

So what if I'd ended up in prison? It would have been preferable to being a puppet controlled by these bastards. A dead war hero for a father, a crazy mother – how hard would they really have been on me? At least I would have paid my debts.

Later that morning, after a few hours troubled sleep, Gort ushered McCloud into his office.

"I've been appointed as stand-in UN Governor, with immediate effect."

"Congratulations, sir. I'm sure you'll make a decisive and effective Governor."

"It's going to take a bit of getting used to... a temporary arrangement, remember!"

"What about your responsibilities towards the army?"

"Well, Scott, I'll be relying on you and the others."

"And Captain Schiller?"

"Actually, I wanted to talk to you about him..."

"In what way, sir?"

"I have my concerns over his commitment. He wavered during the problems we had with the robots...."

Gort scrutinised Scott and continued slowly, "Do you think we can still trust him?"

"He's always been one of our most loyal, sir."

"Yes, I know. It would be a shame to have to lose him."

"But surely he deserves a chance?"

"There's no place for faulty weapons in the army. If he's unstable, he could be dangerous."

"Rory is solid. Remember how hard he fought in Afghanistan! He won't do anything stupid, sir."

"No, but he might say the wrong thing at the wrong time."

Scott paused before dropping his voice.

"But now they've got what they want, we're home and dry, surely?"

"We can never be too careful. Why take any chances?"

Both men fell silent.

"Well, sir, there's the refugee camp. Things are hotting up there again. Why not park him there for a while, out of harm's way? It'll give him a chance to show his commitment."

Gort paced around his office.

"OK, although it's against my better judgement, we'll have it your way. But, Colonel, watch him like a hawk. I'll hold you personally responsible for any indiscretions on Captain Schiller's part!"

"OK, Governor, I'll inform him of his new responsibilities."

"Oh, and one more thing, Colonel."

"Yes, Governor?"

"Record the transfer date as the 28th February!"

"But that's before..."

"Exactly, just do it. I've given you the security permission to override the records!"

"OK, Commander... I mean Governor."

"Good. Our next priority is the sicads. Any update?"

"They're still under armed guard in the hotel."

"Good. With the public petrified of them, it's time to move them back to CERN."

"A wise decision, sir."

"They're to be kept alive, for now."

"Understood, Governor. I'll have the power supplies fixed," saluted Scott.

Osiris woke up late – it must be gone nine o'clock! She dug some coffee out of the back of the cupboard and dragged herself to her desk, hands cupped around a steaming mug of dark black liquid. She slumped in front of her computer, her head was throbbing and her body ached. She yawned and rubbed her eyes – it must have been after dawn that she had finally fallen asleep. Her brain had been buzzing with last night's news, and the implications for the sicads and CAMEOS. She turned on her computer to catch up on the latest developments. Her eyes began to focus on her CAMEOS-styled homepage. She made out the titles of blurred e-mails. A new one popped up from Ganaëlle, headed 'UK trip – cancellations'. Her news box was flashing with the headline '10am CET – News Conference by the President of the United States and the Chinese Premier'.

It was 9.59am. She sat up and clicked on the link. Her eyes were so mesmerised by the images that she didn't register the words of the reporter – more riots, anti-sicad protests in Times Square and the Champs-Elysées, and just look at the damage in Trafalgar Square.

As the cameras switched to the two Heads of State, she turned up the volume and took a large gulp of coffee.

The US President addressed the mass of cameras and microphones, whilst the Chinese Premier did his best to look supportive. She listened to him express regret at the manner in which the photos were released, and vow to take decisive action against the perpetrators. A full inquiry was promised. Pending the findings, the public were assured that the sicads had been moved to a secure location and, in the circumstances, Governor Bruno had asked to step down. Governor Bruno stepping down! In a trance of disbelief, she tried to make sense of what she was hearing whilst trying to listen to the rest... And, as an interim measure, Commander David Gort had been appointed in his stead, in recognition of his proven crisis management skills.

Emergency powers granted to the military to deal with any further civil unrest – what is happening? Bruno resigning and Gort being appointed, emergency powers… this is a nightmare!

The loud buzzing of her phone broke her state of confused and numb lethargy. Jia's equally distraught face appeared on the small screen.

With the unfolding crisis, each a link for the other to Simon, both women had temporarily put aside their differences.

"Jia... where are you?"

"Back at Le Reposoir."

"The monastery? Have you become a nun?"

"Of course not," she snapped, before quickly apologising.

"Do you have any news from Simon?" asked Osiris, quickly changing the subject.

"No. Bruno was refusing all visits. I just wondered if he'd somehow contacted you?"

"No..."

There was a pause.

"Listen Jia, we're both in this together. We'll have to communicate with each other, for Simon's sake."

"I know. Something's happened to Bruno; he wouldn't have resigned, not without speaking to me. What's going to happen to Simon and the other sicads? What's going to happen to me? Have you seen the headlines this morning? They're calling me Doctor Frankenstein! Emergency military powers! What's happening to the world?"

Osiris found strength in Jia's weakness. Her Waorani spirit was stirring inside her.

"It's men, Jia; they're useless without us women. We're going to fight back."

"But I daren't leave the monastery. I wish I could help."

"Don't worry. Stay there and don't tell anybody your whereabouts. I'll find a way."

"Osiris, Mother Cristina is beside me; she thinks she can help. She believes God brought Simon to her for a reason, and now she says she needs some media support. Could you help her?"

Osiris reflected on Mother Cristina; they'd only met briefly, but she seemed solid and had made a good impression on Osiris.

"I'll try my best. Maybe she can call me in a week or so, once things have calmed down?"

There was a pause and the sound of a muffled conversation.

"Er... Osiris, she says she's coming down this afternoon and will wait outside your office until you see her."

Osiris smiled.

"OK, she must have Waorani blood in her!"

*

347

Simon was sitting in his cell. There was no natural light and no ability to connect to the internet. He'd already devoured the pile of books Bruno had supplied. Why hadn't Bruno come, as promised? What was going on outside those four walls?

At first, the tedium wasn't so noticeable; he'd been questioned repeatedly, almost endlessly, by a range of government officials, scientists and the Project Management Committee. Two days ago, these interrogations had suddenly ceased.

Simon's thoughts were disturbed by the sound of footsteps and a faint conversation in the corridor outside. The footsteps belonged to Gort, the European Attorney General and the President of the United States.

"You can't believe what these robots say. They're extremely cunning and manipulative – remember Bruno's downfall," cautioned Gort.

"Hmm, well don't worry, David, I've interviewed Simon several times and find him helpful and objective," replied the Attorney General. "It's curious his version of events is so detailed, yet so very different to the official report," he added.

"Let's not forgot this robot has murdered two soldiers. I've observed how strong its survival instincts are. The robot will say anything to avoid termination, and is clever enough to detect and play on human weaknesses," retorted Gort.

The President looked uneasy.

"After this, we've got to abandon the Project, right? I've got some pressing problems at home. Let's see the robot and then get the others on the phone, so we can make a quick decision."

"I'm afraid, gentlemen, the situation is more complicated. There will be considerable public support for a trial."

"The public is fickle. A swift trial behind closed doors will suffice – they'll soon forget about it," countered Gort.

"It seems like the most practical solution. It may be unpopular, but what's to stop us?"

The Attorney General resolutely answered the US President's question.

"Actually, Gregory, technically the sicads are legal citizens and, as such, are afforded the guarantee of a public trial by jury."

A slender smile broke out on the President's face.

"Maybe there's some merit in having a showcase trial. It may delay things, but it'll be a cleaner way to bury the project."

"Anyway, let's go and see what the robot has got to say for itself," suggested Gort emphatically, striding off towards the cell. By the time the others had caught up with him, he had set about removing the three large padlocks.

"Very high tech, David," remarked the President sarcastically.

"You can't take any chances with these machines. They'll outwit any electronic security system."

Gort slid back the heavy bolts. Inside, Simon was sitting cross-legged, reading. The sicad put down his book, stood up and approached the bars. Why is Gort here instead of Bruno? This was the first time he'd seen the Commander since their rock-face encounter. It was less than two weeks ago, but the tedium of the prison cell made it seem much longer.

Gort and Simon held eye contact in awkward silence. What's Gort doing here? Why is he with the President and the Attorney General? Simon analysed thousands of possible scenarios; all results indicated a negative development for both the sicads and humans.

"Hello, Commander Gort," he announced mechanically.

Gort held the sicad's gaze.

"It's Governor Gort now!"

The announcement was a bombshell, confirming the sicad's worst scenario – one that he'd just dismissed as outlandishly improbable. His brain started whirring away with possible future scenarios and survival strategies. A grating electro-chemical sensation pulsated painfully across his mind. It's as if my death warrant has just been signed in front of me, he thought.

"Governor Reno decided to step down after the public revelation of the dead soldiers," announced the US President.

"The revelation of the soldiers' demise has caused an understandable public backlash against you and the other sicads," explained the Attorney General.

"We've read your report of events, which is inconsistent with the official report," added Gort.

Simon looked at the three men, trying to gauge what they were thinking. The Attorney General's expression and physiognomy suggested unease with Gort, who in turn seemed irritated. A strong negative intent, veiled by a veneer of impatience and indifference, radiated from the President.

Gort continued.

"This leaves you two choices. Choice one, to admit to murdering the soldiers and we'll find a way of quietly bringing Bruno's project to a tactful conclusion…"

He paused for Simon to absorb his words.

"Choice two, you contest the charges against you in a public trial. I'll be the principal witness against you, along with other respected members of the armed forces. If you lose this trial, the wholesale destruction of the sicads may be required, and it will be hard to avoid shaming all those associated with the project."

Simon knew that Gort was largely intimating Jia and Bruno. What could have happened to Bruno?

As Gort finished speaking, all eyes were on Simon.

"I imagine you'll need some time to think it over," concluded Gort.

Without hesitation, Simon replied.

"Governor Gort, I'm a robot. I do not lie. I've made a full report of the events of the night of the 24th March. I've nothing to confess over and beyond what's stated in my report. You're now the Governor, it's for you to decide what you want to do. I'll await your further instructions."

The three men strode away from Simon's cell, each absorbed in their thoughts.

Gort was the first to speak.

"When's the earliest we can hold the trial?"

The Attorney General stopped to ponder the question. For such a public trial, ordinarily, we'd allow twelve to eighteen months."

"And the minimum?"

"Well technically, with legal notices and scheduling, theoretically at least, it's possible in six months or so."

"Then set the date for the 30th September."

49

True to her word, Mother Cristina arrived at Osiris's offices that afternoon. She wasn't alone, though, as Sister Agatha had begged to come with her. Mother Cristina had resisted at first, but the idea of a young helper, who knew how to use a video camera and a computer, had been very alluring.

A bemused Ganaëlle escorted the two nuns, both still wearing their habits. Osiris stood up and greeted them warmly. After the introductions, Mother Cristina, her eyes burning with resolve, came straight to the point.

"I believe Simon's arrival at Le Reposoir and the vision that preceded it were no accident. I'm forty seven years of age, but this frugal and demanding life has left me burning with energy and inner strength for the next chapter in my life."

"What is this next chapter, exactly, and how can I help?"

"God's message to me, delivered through Simon, was to help bring religions together by appreciating our shared values. All the press interest is allowing me to organise a series of talks to different religious groups around the world."

Osiris felt drawn to the strength and integrity of the enigmatic woman in front of her.

"Well, Mother, I can sense your determination. Please explain what I can do for you."

"I need a media campaign behind me. I've looked at your magazine and see a good fit. You're trying to reconnect people to value bio-diversity; my mission is to reconnect people to value religious diversity."

Osiris nodded in approval.

"According to Sister Agatha, religious internet sites are very popular. If the idea for Panasha takes off, we could link ourselves through the concept of Reconnecting People."

"And what is Panasha?"

Sister Agatha interjected eagerly.

"Panasha is not a religion itself, but a platform for celebrating religion in its diversity. It will describe the different faiths of the world and the common values that bind them together."

"And the word Panasha, is it an acronym?"

Sister Agatha looked at Mother Cristina for approval before continuing breathlessly.

"Panasha is formed of two words: 'pan' from the Greek language, which means all embracing and unifying, and 'asha', which is the Nepalese word for hope. The overall message of Panasha is simple, 'Unifying Hope'."

Osiris's eyes lit up.

"I like the concept – it's good because it shows respect to others, rather than judging them. I also think the name's great; it has a female ring to it."

Mother Cristina smiled.

"Osiris, you're right to talk of respect. This is the link between us. How can people respect their environment before they learn to respect themselves and others? Through spiritual practice, they must learn to widen their circle of compassion."

"Yes, Mother, I share your understanding. But how will Panasha work in practice?"

"Well, Osiris, what do you believe in?"

"My tribe had few words for spiritual or religious ideas. My beliefs are best expressed by those of the Navajo Indians."

"And what do the Navajo Indians say?"

Sister Agatha was busy making notes. Osiris looked up at a poster on her office wall.

"Their ten commandments are hanging on my wall. Shall I read them out?"

The two nuns nodded.

Osiris took down the poster and held it in front of her.

"Treat the Earth and all that dwell therein with respect. Remain close to the Great Spirit. Show great respect for your fellow beings. Work together for the benefit of all Mankind. Give assistance and kindness wherever needed. Do what you know to be right. Look after the well-being of Mind and Body. Dedicate a share of your efforts to the greater Good. Be truthful and honest at all times. And finally, take full responsibility for your actions."

Mother Cristina smiled in appreciation and Sister Agatha was frantically scribbling.

"Very interesting – most of them can be mapped onto the Christian Ten Commandments and the words of Jesus."

Osiris tried to recall. Christianity wasn't an everyday topic of reflection for her.

"Yes, I think you're right. It's the context that's different. The Navajo Indians' spirituality grew out of centuries of living in small self-sustaining settlements in the heart of nature. Christianity, on the other hand, I guess, evolved at a time when many humans were living in small towns. The values are similar, but the contexts are very different."

Mother Cristina smiled serenely.

"I think you've understood Osiris. This is the understanding that Simon opened my mind to. Now, like Jesus, Simon has been taken into custody for a crime he hasn't committed. It falls to me and all other believers to go forward and spread Simon's message."

"You don't think he'll be put to death like Jesus, do you?"

"The Lord works in mysterious ways Osiris. We must use the talents and power we've been blessed with to help Simon."

Osiris thought for a minute before replying.

"You're clearly very determined, and I am the last person to want to underestimate anybody, but what can one woman do by herself?"

"Your concerns are natural my child, but don't doubt God's will. Over the last few days I've spoken to over a dozen religious leaders who all shared my vision, including the Dalia Lama himself. As such I've already been invited to speak in front of people from all of these faiths. This is the Lord's way."

Osiris fell silent.

"Oh, and there's something that Jia wanted me to tell you."

"Yes?"

"She's learnt from Mazari that there's going to be a public trial to determine Simon's guilt."

"A public trial? Against Gort? What a nightmare! Simon is innocent, but there are no witnesses!"

"Osiris, you must keep your faith. We must continue to promote the sicads' ideas and Simon's innocence."

"Well, if there's going to be a trial, we must at least find a good lawyer to represent him, CAMEOS can raise funds for that."

"The Lord will give us the strength to fight for the light of truth – or, as the Navajo Indians might say, we'll do what we know to be right."

Osiris felt her resolve strengthening.

"Mother Cristina, you're inspirational. If you deliver your speeches with such conviction, you'll surely succeed."

"Thank you, my child."

"CAMEOS will help to establish Panasha. You can freely use our media platform and design services. However, you'll need someone to video your speeches and somebody to write up your efforts."

Sister Agatha stopped writing and looked up from her notes.

"That's where I come in. I know how to use a camera and I studied journalism at university. I'll be Mother Cristina's companion, following her wherever she goes to make Panasha a success. I too believe that this is God's way. I let the cat out of the bag so, as the Navajo Indians say, I must take full responsibility for my actions."

Osiris stood up and clapped her hands.

"Great! Ladies, I think we have a plan for Panasha. In relation to Simon, I'll get to work on raising funds for a lawyer."

"Osiris, advertise now for this lawyer. Simon needs him now. If it's God's will, we'll find a way to remunerate him."

*

It was Leopold who drew Gort's attention to the advert. After reflecting on the best way to deal with this development, the Governor had his secretary searching the internet for a young sympathetic lawyer with the relevant experience for such a case. He chose three candidates from the ten names and personally interviewed them. A young Irish lawyer, the third on his list, appeared to be the most suitable. If I were Simon Oceandis, this is the one I'd pick, he said to himself.

"Mr Fealey, you should play on the hope and good cause angle, they'll lap that up," he recommended as they concluded their deal.

*

A week later Osiris was at her desk, reviewing the website for Panasha. Her phone buzzed; it was Jia. She made an effort to be co-operative.

"Jia, how are you?"

"I'm OK. Thankfully, here there's no press, no WIFI and no television. I hate to think what they're saying about me."

"Well, you're in the best place," agreed Osiris, who'd been surprised to feel the press coverage of Jia was harsh.

"Anyway, what's happening to Simon?"

"I've been temporarily removed from the PMC, but fortunately I've got a friend on it who likes to talk."

"What's he saying?"

"It's a she and she's confirmed that the project is totally suspended whilst Simon's guilt is established."

"And the rest of the sicads?"

"Mazari engineers are looking after them."

"No word from Simon?"

"No. I'm sure he would have contacted me if he possibly could. I hope he's OK."

"Likewise…"

Jia resumed the conversation, breaking the awkward pause.

"What's happening with Mother Cristina? I haven't heard from her since she left the monastery a week or so ago."

Osiris looked back at the draft website.

"Is it only a week ago? It feels a lot longer. Every day from early in the morning, until midnight sometimes, she's working away on it. The bones of a four-month world tour are already in place. My secretary Ganaëlle is spending as much time answering phone calls for her as she is for CAMEOS."

"Wow, that's incredible! What a unique woman."

"Well, the website will be on-line soon. I'm looking at the draft now – it looks good. Fortunately, we had lots of good background photos from the sicads' CAMEOS research – almost all the cultures and religions around the world."

"Great, I look forward to seeing it. And Sister Agatha?"

"It's a similar story. She's been researching all of these religions and drawing out their common values, as well as linking up the web pages to the speech dates. Judging by the number of phone calls, it's going to get a large number of hits. The reverse links should create significant cross-over internet traffic for both sites."

"Real synergies – that's good to hear."

Jia's thoughts returned to Simon.

"Any ideas on how we can help Simon, Osiris?"

"Well, we've been advertising on the CAMEOS site to find a lawyer. Four are coming in to see me."

"That's great, but won't Gort make things difficult?"

"What about the PMC, as you call it? They must still have some leverage, mustn't they?"

The line went quiet as Jia reflected for a few moments.

"It's worth a try. I'll call Cho and see what can be done."

"Well, if need be, CAMEOS can organise some protests. I'm already planning a series of these, building up to the trial date. I've also got Mario, my computer expert, looking for any evidence on the military computers about what really happened to those soldiers."

"Osiris, I'm really glad to hear things are moving forward. I'm sorry I can't do more to help, it's just..."

"Jia, I know your predicament. It's up to others now. Just speak to your friend and call me back. We need to get this lawyer in place as soon as possible."

"I'll call her straight away. Say hello to Mother Cristina for me and let her know that all is going well at the monastery."

"Well, maybe they'll make you the new Prioress?"

"Don't worry, Osiris, once this nightmare is over, I'll get my man!"

"Let's see, shall we?" replied Osiris defiantly.

*

A few days later, an excited Osiris pounced on Mother Cristina, busy finalising arrangements for her tour.

"Come and interview this lawyer. He's authentic, the first one who isn't just chasing the publicity."

"Wonderful!"

"His name is Fergus Fealey and he's clearly Irish. You'll see what I mean."

As the two ladies entered the room, Fergus – fresh faced, with floppy brown hair – gave them a warm smile. The lawyer thrust forward an honest hand in the nun's direction.

"Delighted to meet you, Mother Cristina. I've read lots about you in the press and on the internet. It's a fascinating tale," announced Fergus, who had pronounced 'delighted' as 'deloighted' with a melodious Irish accent which rose to a crescendo in pronouncing the word 'fascinating'. Mother Cristina smiled serenely at him and quietly sat down next to Osiris. Fergus explained how he'd first come across the sicads and, as a specialist in political cases, his personal motivations for accepting the brief.

"Mr Fealey, you seem rather young for a lawyer; how old are you?"

The enthusiastic lawyer switched to a more somber manner.

"Mother, I'm thirty eight years old, with over twelve years of court room experience behind me. There are older lawyers, with more experience, but will they be able to relate to the sicads?"

Fergus handed the nun a neatly bound black file, tied with red string.

"Here's a summary of my most interesting cases. You'll notice they're very relevant. Simon's case is going to be characterised by a lack of hard evidence and political pressures."

"And if you were to take the case, Mr Fealey, how would you wish to be remunerated?"

"Financial reward is not my primary motive. I don't imagine this will impede me taking the case."

"What would impede you?" asked Osiris.

Fergus looked at both ladies in turn.

"Whether or not I am convinced that Simon Oceandis is innocent."

Mother Cristina and Osiris looked at each other and nodded.

"Well, it seems the next step will be for you to meet your potential client."

"OK. I'll follow the formal channels, which may take some time. I suggest you see if you can use any informal channels you have to speed up the process."

*

Less than a week later, Fergus was waiting outside Simon's cell, watching a soldier unlocking the heavy padlocks.

"I'm gonna have to lock you in, I'm afraid, Governor's orders. Just knock when you wanna come out."

The lawyer shook his head in disbelief.

"No buzzer system? How does the prisoner summon you if he needs you?"

The soldier looked at Fergus as if he were mad.

"It's a robot. It don't need food or water, or its bed pan emptying. It's got a plug socket and that's all it needs."

"Am I the first visitor?"

"No, he's had other lawyers and officials."

Inside, Simon was lying on his bed, deep in reflection. He didn't even register the visitor.

"Another lawyer," announced the soldier.

357

Simon slowly turned his head, with an air of indifference. Fergus stared at him.

"This isn't the one I saw two days ago. Why another lawyer?"

The soldier shrugged his shoulders and looked at Fergus.

"Hammer on the door when you're done."

As the door closed, Fergus felt the familiar atmosphere of despair – no windows, no pictures, just white walls, with nothing to break the monotony.

He approached Simon and extended a friendly arm.

"Mr Oceandis, I'm Fergus Fealey. Your case was notified to me by a certain Osiris and Mother Cristina."

A slow weary smile formed on Simon's face. He tried to sit up, but seemed to lack the energy.

"Could you please help me, Mr Fealey?"

The lawyer bent over the sicad, hoisted his upper body up and leant him against the wall.

"Are you ill, Mr Oceandis?"

"No, just a little low on energy. If you can swing my legs onto the floor, I'll be able to reach the plug socket."

Fergus helped Simon manoeuvre into the correct position, and watched as the skin on the sicad's fingertips retracted and the metal pins protruded slowly, very slowly!

"Mr Fealey, could you pull on the pins? They're sticking a little."

The lawyer assisted and placed Simon's hand next to the socket.

"Are they depriving you of power, Mr Oceandis?"

He watched as the sicad connected and slowly became more animated.

"I'm sorry about that. Now please call me Simon."

The young lawyer smiled and extended his hand again.

"Likewise, you must call me Fergus," he replied heartily, shaking the sicad's hand.

"Thank you for helping me. I must have forgotten to recharge."

Fergus looked at him incredulously.

"But you must have warnings to prompt you, don't you?"

Simon's face had an expression of vague confusion.

"Yes, yes, I must have somehow ignored them. My mind tends to wander these days. Now tell me more about Mother Cristina and Osiris. How are they?"

Fergus pulled up a chair and sat down opposite the sicad.

"They're very concerned and want the best legal representation for you."

"That's very kind and considerate of them, such wonderful people. But they needn't worry, I've already been provided with a lawyer, a very sympathetic man."

"And where did this lawyer come from?"

"Why, Governor Gort, I'd imagine."

"That's exactly what they're worried about."

"Well, that's very considerate. But, in practice, I can't see that it makes much difference."

Fergus scrutinised him carefully.

"You're not intending to attend the trial, are you Simon? That's why you weren't charging yourself. If I hadn't turned up, you'd have quietly expired, wouldn't you?"

Simon retracted his hand from the socket and looked into the lawyer's eyes.

"You must be a successful lawyer; not much seems to escape you."

"Well, I'm a defence lawyer and if you define success as obtaining my clients' acquittal, then yes, I have achieved a fair amount."

"So, tell me why a young and successful lawyer would want to take on such a hopeless case?"

"Surely the successful lawyer is best placed to decide on what he considers is or isn't a hopeless case? Unless, of course, the client has some private knowledge which seals his very guilt!"

Fergus was observing Simon closely.

"Humanity has already decided my guilt by appointing David Gort as UN Governor. Ever since we were conceived, he has been trying to kill off the Project. Now humanity has given him the means to do so, with the full support of the law. If I attend this trial, it will only serve one purpose, to legitimise his ascension to power."

"You can't be sure of that!" retorted Fergus passionately.

"I've performed every possible scenario analysis and haven't come to this conclusion lightly. I've done all I can for humanity. Their future is now in their own hands."

Simon lay back on his bed and closed his eyes.

"Were you responsible for the soldiers' deaths?"

"Yes."

"Yes? That's not what I was led to believe."

"The soldiers died as a result of my actions."

"That's not the same as killing them, Simon!"

"It was my fault the boat capsized. I could have swum back and saved them."

"Why didn't you?"

"Because all the scenarios analysed suggested that this would have led to my own demise."

Fergus reflected silently, before jumping up excitedly.

"If what you say is true, then you acted in legitimate self-defence. That's every man's right."

Fergus's expression turned to confusion.

"Then why did you save Commander Gort's life?"

"The sicads had been rescued. Commander Gort was unarmed, hence no longer a threat to my survival. I'm programmed to help humans, remember."

"Why do you think the authorities believe you're guilty?"

Simon sat up.

"It seems that humans have turned against the sicads. We're condemned. There's little hope for us now."

Fergus sat back down.

"I reject your idea there's no hope. I'd like to represent you, but I need your permission."

Simon lay silently, reflecting.

"I fear you're wasting your time, Mr Fealey. There must be other defendants more needy and more worthy of your talents. To accept your offer would be a selfish act on my part and a disservice to humanity."

Fergus sat silently, racking his brain.

"By dying here quietly, Simon, perhaps it's you who's doing humanity a disservice."

Simon, calmly looking up at the ceiling, smiled benevolently.

"As I said, the future of humanity is in their own hands. It seems to me that they've already made their choice. Humans created me to serve them. If humanity wants me, then they must collectively call for me. It's not for you or I to impose our will on them."

Fergus thought for a minute.

"Humans have been told you murdered these soldiers. You've been found guilty without a trial – an injustice. You must give me a chance to build your defence."

The lawyer's eyes were burning with passion.

"Mr Fealey, if you don't mind me asking, how much would you be paid to take this case?"

"It's not been decided yet. Rest assured, it's not my main motive."

Simon held Fergus in his gaze.

"Do you have funds to live for the next six months?"

"I don't need to be paid a fixed fee, if that's what you're asking?"

"Well in that case, Mr Fealey, I'll leave it to your conscience to decide whether or not this is the best use of your time. I see good reasons for not making an appearance at this trial. If you can make a case to convince me otherwise, then I'll listen, but I won't make any promises."

A smile of relief washed over Fergus's face.

"And, in the meanwhile, you promise to keep yourself charged up?"

"I'll do my best. But don't forget about me, it's lonely and depressing in here."

"Simon, I'll need to know everything; an account of who you met and what happened, in minute detail."

"You've got a computer in your bag, Fergus."

"Yes, shall I take it out?"

"There's no need. On your hard drive, you'll find transcripts of every conversation I've had, the details of everyone I've met and a complete itinerary, with GPS co-ordinates of my every movement."

50

Fergus picked up his leather briefcase and stood up. Osiris was biting her lip and Mother Cristina was staring out of the window.

"So that's the bottom line. It's getting late; we should sleep on it."

Mother Cristina turned around and looked at Fergus.

"It's clear what Simon is saying, and he's right. It's up to humanity to make a choice. But they need to be given both sides of the story. It seems that we've been chosen to do this, Osiris, to help put the other side of the story out there. We must mobilise the people, it's the only way!"

Osiris stood up.

"Without Simon and the sicads, CAMEOS wouldn't have survived. Whilst CAMEOS is still strong, I'll do everything in my power to repay that debt."

Fergus observed the two ladies with growing admiration.

"I'll speak to Global Vision to see if they'll do an independent documentary," announced Jia, who was attending the meeting by telephone.

"With no alibi, and the political wind having turned against Simon, public support is possibly our only weapon," concluded Fergus.

*

Three days later, inside Charles de Gaulle airport, Osiris was hugging Mother Cristina and Sister Agatha in turn.

"I'll come out and see you, once I've organised things on my side. CAMEOS is going to turn up the volume!"

"Be careful, Osiris, we'll inevitably make enemies. I'll pray for you. May the Lord protect and watch over us all."

Mother Cristina, accompanied by Sister Agatha, walked through the airport departure gates. The first time for over twenty-five years that she'd flown, she felt safe in the knowledge that she was doing God's will. As the two nuns were buckling into their seats, Sister Agatha gave her superior a nervous glance.

"Are you sure we're doing the right thing?"

Mother Cristina gave Agatha one of her smiles, which blew away the young nun's doubts and insecurities.

"People are once again living in fear. They're forgetting their differences and are reaching out for us."

*

Jia's call to Global Vision was totally superfluous. Mathias Yanofine was already sitting down in the studio with Maggie Bronski, planning a series of documentaries on the sicads leading up to the trial.

"How did you get the names of all these people?" Mathias asked.

Maggie smiled proudly.

"It wasn't so difficult, what with the pictures we got of the sicads from the evacuation at CERN and the association with CAMEOS. People saw the information on our website and volunteered. It seems many people were deeply touched by their experiences of the sicads. You can see there are some great stories to follow up on."

"Well, we're spoilt for choice and there's also the CAMEOS angle to include."

"Don't forget the Panasha angle as well!"

"Panasha?"

"Yes, haven't you seen it? It's put together by the same people that created CAMEOS, but it's linking into the religious mania that's spreading about the sicads."

A look of vague recollection appeared on Mathias's face.

"Is that the story about the nun with the vision?"

"Yes, Mother Cristina. She had the vision about the sicad being crucified on Good Friday, two days before he turned up at her monastery, seeking refuge."

Mathias raised his eyebrows.

"I thought that was just a rumour."

"Apparently not, and religious communities certainly believe it. What's more, apparently, it wasn't only her who received this vision, but a whole bunch of spiritual leaders. They all want to meet this nun. She's rapidly becoming more popular than the Pope himself. Anyway, her site called Panasha is bringing religions together around the sicads' claim that humanity has to change before it destroys life itself. Many believe the sicads are messengers from God."

363

"Umm, lots of angles. Apart from the photos of the dead soldiers, I'm not seeing any negative reports on the sicads. We have to present a balanced view, Maggie. Where have you hidden all the negative stuff?"

Maggie looked up at him.

"Well, that's what's strange. I've yet to come across a negative angle from an actual witness. There's lots of negative rumour and speculation, but I can't find any substance behind it."

*

Gort sat in what was formerly Bruno's office, looking at the newspaper and magazine cuttings. His secretary's face appeared on the screen.

"Governor, the gentleman from the Geo-Political Institute has arrived."

"OK, Natalie, show him in."

"Would you like refreshments, sir?"

"No, that won't be necessary. It's going to be a short meeting."

Mr Leopold strode into the office and made himself comfortable.

Gort closed the door and stared at his visitor with cold dark eyes.

"I take it the office is clean."

"Of course, I've swept it myself."

"Good, then we can talk freely."

"The GPI seems to be becoming more brazen, Leopold!"

"Yes, thanks to your good work."

"Your clients have got what they wanted. The super-powers are back calling the shots. They don't need me any more, which is why I'm submitting my resignation."

"Well, your resignation can't be accepted just yet, Governor Gort. There's the trial and then Bruno's suicide and, of course, the need to find your replacement."

"I've told the US President that I'm quitting at the latest one month after the trial," snapped Gort.

"Yes I know, that's why I'm here to agree your final tasks. On that note, how's Bruno?"

"Being kept alive, in accordance with instructions."

"Good. Then once the trial is finished, I trust you can organise a convincing suicide."

Gort glared back at him.

"What choice do I have?"

"Effectively none, Governor."

"The sooner I can get out of this stinking business the better!"

"Keep your head, Gort. This will be the crowning moment of an illustrious career. Afterwards, you can rest on your laurels! And you'll be able to forget about Todd Ranger – he'll quietly disappear."

"Mmm... assuming the trial goes to plan. If anything goes wrong, I'll be dragging you and all of them down with me."

"You needn't worry on that score. All is being done to assure the trial is a formality. The media campaign is being steadily built up. By the time the trial commences, the whole world will be ready to bury the sicads and the Socrates Project!"

*

Jia was fiddling with the monastery's ancient modem. Eventually, the internet connection lights flickered into operation. Activating the large electronic tablet, which had been sitting idle in the bottom of her bag, she looked nostalgically at the assortment of program icons dotted around the screen. Visual recognition tests, power management software, communication and memory monitors, knowledge management systems, movement and reaction programs, social behaviour targets and language assimilation. During the design and development stage of the Project, she'd spent most of her waking hours monitoring and analysing the feedback from them.

Mathias Yanofine's face appeared on her screen against a backdrop of the Grand Canyon.

"Welcome to the first in our series of 'The Socrates Project – Separating Fact from Fiction.' With the leading sicad currently imprisoned and awaiting trial for the alleged murder of two members of the armed forces, we trace the history of this project, in search of facts."

"Yes, Mathias, you said it. Facts are what we'll be bringing you. We'll be counting down the last hundred days to the trial by travelling the world and interviewing some of the millions of the people who met the sicads, and telling the story through their eyes."

Jia took heart from Maggie Bronski's face. She'd been pleased with the way she interviewed her, many months before. The camera switched back to Mathias.

"We'll also be looking at the environmental problems highlighted by CAMEOS in each of these countries, and the sicads' claim that humanity is jeopardising life itself through our way of living."

"...And reporting on the courage of an extraordinary woman who, inspired by the sicads, has set off on a personal crusade to bring religions together. We'll be following the reactions to her series of sell-out talks in the world's major cities," added Maggie.

"Lastly, we'll be looking at the opposition to the sicads, in search of substance to the widespread fear that the sicads have their own secret agenda."

*

A few days after the first Global Vision documentary, Jia called Osiris.

"Did you see the documentary?"

"Yes, it was great. It was particularly moving for me to see the Navajo elder, with the Grand Canyon behind him, talking of America before the Europeans came."

"Yes, he spoke like the sicads. He said that by killing nature, humans are killing themselves. Is it true what he said about the rivers, Osiris?"

"Yes, before the Europeans came you could drink from every river in America, which were all flowing well and full of fish. And now they've become polluted and toxic, or have mostly disappeared. Only the elders remember what it was like."

There was a moment of silence as Jia respected Osiris's grief.

"Well, he spoke warmly of Julia. It's incredible the number of people the sicads met. It seems they were drawn to the right people."

"People with common purposes find each other," replied Osiris, thinking of Simon.

Jia ignored the provocative remark.

"What's happening with CAMEOS?"

"More hits than ever – people are coming to the website to make up their own minds."

"And, judging by the media coverage, Panasha must be going well too."

"Well, let's just say that, between the two of us, we've outgrown our hardware capacity! Oh, on that note, would you care to sign the on-line petition?"

"What petition? Don't forget, I'm out of touch here in the monastery with an internet connection inherited from the twelfth century Carthusian monks!"

Osiris laughed, despite herself.

"Well, the on-line petition for a fair trial is going up today. You can access it from either website. That is, of course, if you can get on!"

*

Mother Cristina, supported by Sister Agatha filming, photographing and documenting, tirelessly visited the representatives of the world's faiths, preaching and pleading for unity at a time of universal crisis. She carefully brought people round to the idea that the sicads were God's messengers. She let people draw their own conclusions on Simon's guilt. She never once said that he was a Messiah, but many others did.

In just a few months she visited the four corners of the Earth and brought together willing supporters representing Native American beliefs, Baptism, Buddhism, Catholicism, Christianity, Confucianism, Evangelism, Hinduism, Judaism, Mormonism, Pentecostalism, Rastafarianism, Shamanism, Shintoism, Sunni Islam, Shia Islam, Sikhism, Sufism, Taoism and Zulu Sangoma.

As the weeks passed, millions of people signed the electronic petition. Many serious religions espoused the belief that the sicads were a divine intervention to save humanity from itself. Osiris had joined the nuns for the last leg of the tour.

Mother Cristina drew energy and confidence from the momentum building up behind Panasha, finishing her tour in Africa with a speech to a confederation of Christian and Zulu leaders in Lesotho. She sat down to take breakfast outdoors in the warm sunshine of a bright Johannesburg morning. 'Horror camp spills over into fresh violence', read the grim headline of the morning newspaper. Hundreds had died in a riot in a refugee camp in Morocco, allegedly caused by the rumour that water was being allocated according to religion. The article described the camp as a hot bed for fundamentalism and religious extremism.

Sister Agatha and Osiris joined her. Agatha started reviewing the video images she'd taken of the speech.

"There's some marvellous footage here, Mother. All of the Zulus in their exotic costumes and the dancing... A great contribution to this month's magazine and a wonderful finale to our world tour!"

The young nun yawned and stretched out her arms. The pace of the tour was catching up with her. Mother Cristina looked at Agatha sympathetically.

"You look tired."

"Oh no, I'm OK," protested the young nun proudly.

"That's good!"

"Why's that?"

"Well, I was hoping we've got time for one last stop on our way back home."

*

"I fear they won't come for us, Mother," fretted Agatha.

"I told them I won't leave the airport until they send someone for us," replied Mother Cristina defiantly.

"Besides a friend is yet to join us," she added.

"A friend?" repeated Agatha.

"A good supporter, who'll help us," replied Mother Cristina.

An hour later, Abdul-Salam, the Secretary for the Muslim World League and a member of Nelson Mandela's Elders, walked unsteadily towards them, leaning heavily on a sturdy polished cane. At the same time Major Henderson arrived at the airport. After the introductions and explanations, the Major drove them along the dusty road into the camp, as he'd done with Bruno and Simon nearly two years before. Conditions had deteriorated further since then. Alongside the daily food, water and medical shortages was the rising spectre of fundamentalism.

"It's a real hot bed here, Mother. It's mostly Sunni Muslims versus Christians, with the odd native religion or obscure cult thrown in."

"Hold your noses," advised the Major, as they approached the outskirts of the camp.

The truck forced its way as quickly as possible through the crowds. The Major had been given strict orders to bring the nuns directly to the compound. Mother Cristina, Osiris and Agatha gasped at the suffering and poverty they witnessed.

"Everyone is so emaciated, this is unacceptable!"

"It's a struggle to keep them alive, Mother. We're extremely limited on the amount of water and food we can ship in. The neighbouring countries are reluctant to increase supplies for fear of attracting even more people here. God knows what the solution is!"

As soon as he realised what he'd said, he started to apologise.

"Don't worry, Major, I am sure He does and that's why we've been sent here," replied the nun.

As the truck pulled up inside the compound, Captain Schiller came out to greet the visitors and escorted them into his tent.

"Please call me Rory. I'm sorry, but I don't have much to offer you."

"We don't need anything, thank you," replied Mother Cristina with a smile.

"Thank you for organising this at such short notice," added Abdul-Salam graciously.

Rory shrugged his shoulders.

"You didn't leave me much choice. I couldn't send you away after you'd made such an effort to come here."

Osiris was looking deeply into Rory's eyes. She was sure she'd seen his face before somewhere.

"My major concern is your safety. These religious differences can turn pretty nasty very quickly here. Just earlier this week we had a riot over water allocations and many died. The Sunnis were saying the Christians were getting more water, and then it all just kicked off."

"Was there any truth to it?" asked Osiris, racking her brain trying to remember why his face seemed so familiar.

Rory shook his head in exasperation.

"Of course not, it's such a powder keg here we're very careful to be fair."

Osiris's brain finally made the breakthrough – CERN, I saw him at CERN! The soldier in the chamber that left us alone. She suddenly became conscious her mouth was wide open and the Captain was staring at her.

"Are you OK? Be careful, otherwise you'll swallow a fly!"

"Yes, thank you," she stammered.

The officer addressed Mother Cristina.

"I've invited a group of religious leaders at 19:00 hours. It'll still be light and a bit cooler. I insist that you speak from within the compound and they'll be gathered outside, in a separately fenced enclosure."

Mother Cristina started to object. He cut her short.

"This is standard practice, even for us. Especially for us."

The group began to gather from early afternoon.

"These are just the leaders. We've got nearly one million refugees

369

here, possibly more. Look at the divide between the Muslims and the Christians. The smaller group in between are African religions," explained the Captain.

By 7 o'clock hundreds of people were crammed into the fenced enclosure. Behind them, thousands more stretched back to the distant line of tents – many standing on each other's shoulders to get a glimpse of Mother Cristina, herself standing on the cabin roof of a Pinzgauer army truck. Abdul-Salam, who had insisted on joining her, was leaning on his cane for support.

Rory passed up a loud hailer.

"You're going to need this."

Mother Cristina swept her gaze across the crowd. A powerfully built man with a white cloak, a bushy beard and a mass of tightly-curled hair caught her attention. He took out a gong from under his cloak and struck it forcefully with his palm. Silence descended over half the crowd. Jeering and shouting erupted from the other half. The noise was deafening and intimidating. Mother Cristina waited for the din to subside. Once she had relative silence, she put the loud hailer to her lips.

"Thank you everybody of all religions who has come to listen to my humble words. I come in the name of Panasha, which promotes religious diversity and embraces common religious values. Humanity has reached a crossroads and is in need of unity and a new direction. I stand before you because of a vision I received..."

After two hours, during which the Muslim Leader had endorsed her vision, Mother Cristina and Abdul-Salam drew their speech to a close. The support of the crowd had slowly built up and regular cheers were accompanying their every sentence.

"We have a unique chance to support a new step in the evolution of humanity that will meaningfully address inequality and suffering. All we need is your support and unity!"

The cheers rose, but were cut short by the sound of the gong. This time silence uniformly fell over the camp. Mother Cristina's eyes fell upon the robed man. He opened his completely white eyes.

"Mother, the man of whom you speak, I too saw him in a vision and I felt his presence here in the camp two years ago. A few weeks ago, I had another vision, similar to the one you described."

The prophet threw his arms in the air and with an explosion of energy, he boomed.

"My followers will support you!"

370

He froze and quietly bowed his head in respect.

Mother Cristina closed her eyes in silent prayer. When she opened them, she saw one of the Muslim leaders being lifted onto the shoulders of his fellows.

"Mother Cristina, we have no gong to summon your attention. But we know, assent, believe, confess with certainty, and testify, that there is no god but Allah, alone without partner. He is a Mighty God, a Great King. There is no lord beside Him, and we worship none other than He. He is Creator of all things, and He is Guardian over everything. And nothing may exist, whether good or evil, beneficial or harmful, except by His decree and will. Whatever He wills is, whatever He does not, is not. Should all creatures unite to move or halt a single atom in the universe, in the absence of His will, they would be unable to do so. Your great movement needs Allah's support to succeed. That you have been brought here with Abdul-Salam we read as a sign of His will and we, too, will support your efforts."

Mother Cristina bowed her head in respect. She felt a sudden impulse to touch the crowd. She looked around at Osiris, who sensed what she wanted and helped her and Abdul-Salam down from the top of the truck. The nun walked to the fence and put her hands on the barbed wire. People approached her and respectfully touched them, as if she was some great saint. The blind white-robed man, escorted by his companions, came towards her. The leader of the Muslims also made his way towards her. They stood, locked in a triangle, looking at each other, nobody taking the initiative. Abdul-Salam approached and passed a small metal cup of water to Mother Cristina. She looked at him and understood. Taking a sip, she handed it to the white-robed Christian. He in turn did the same, passing it to the Muslim camp leader, who drank the remaining water. Abdul-Salam placed his hand on the cup and nodded at the others, who did the same.

Now that's the cover photo, Agatha said to herself.

*

The camp was calmer than it had been at any time since Captain Schiller arrived. He took the opportunity to accompany the visitors personally back to the airport. They thanked him warmly.

"It's I who should be thanking you. You've brought some calm to the camp, at least temporarily!"

Osiris instinctively took the Captain's hands in hers and pulled him aside. He flinched awkwardly and stumbled towards her.

"Captain Schiller, it was you, wasn't it? You were at CERN and you let me release the sicads."

The decorated war hero stared deeply into Osiris's eyes. His lips remained tightly sealed, yet his eyes were only partially-veiled windows onto a troubled soul.

She nodded in recognition.

"Well, you helped me before and I need your help again. Your presence at the trial is crucial. You know what really happened, don't you?"

The Captain paused and she caught a glint in his eye that quickly disappeared, as if a door had been pulled shut.

"Even if I were the man you think I might be, I can't help you."

"Can't or won't?"

"I've got the camp to manage. My men and the refugees are my primary responsibility."

"You have a duty to all humanity, Captain!"

The soldier turned and walked slowly away.

Osiris watched him silently, before the words erupted loudly from deep inside of her.

"Every man's actions belong to him, Captain. Whatever you decide, you'll have to live with your conscience."

Passengers stopped struggling with their luggage to watch this unexpected spectacle.

Rory stopped in his tracks, transfixed by this courageous lady. He hesitated, before turning on his heels and striding out of the terminal building.

51

All eyes and ears were tuned to Ned. He was performing to an excited audience of over three hundred visiting Clavs. There was no room inside the courtyard of his ghetto – every available centimetre of ground being used to grow food. Instead, he'd flattened the top of one of the piles of ripped up paving stones and concrete rubble that blockaded the entrances to their ghettos. Seated around the rubble in a semi-circular ring of a dozen or so rows were the ghetto chiefs or chefs in Clav parlance, along with their senior supporters. Over the last twelve months their ranks had expanded rapidly, as new ghettos had sprung up and more brudders and sistas had opted out of Babylon.

Behind Ned were two large flags, one on either side of the blockaded entrance. They were hanging from second floor windows, which were fortified with thick steel mesh and what appeared to be very similar railings to those found in many of the public parks dotted around Paris. The first flag had a life-size image of Bob Marley, passionately singing with a raised clenched fist. At the top of the flag were the words 'Get up, stand up, stand up for your rights. Don't give up the fight!' The second flag had a picture of Simon Oceandis, wearing his thin studded leather collar. At the top of the second flag, were the words 'When the man comes there will be no, no doom!'

Ned sang and strutted around the improvised stage, with the same passion and positive intent exuding from Bob Marley hanging behind him. The Clavs went into rapturous cheers and applause, and boisterously saluted him with clenched fists. Ned reached out a hand to help Lermac climb up and stand beside him. The two men stood united and Lermac addressed the crowd.

"Chefs, brudders and sistas, weez thanks dya fors beings ere. Weez knows ya taking da lotta risk leaving ya ghettos exposed a dem sheriffs an' dem crazy baldheads. We know dem is tightening da screw. Weez da victim of ya success. A day soon weez gonna hav a peace with dem crazy baldheads, but nots beeforz dey find da littl' wiseness!"

Ned stepped forward and pointed at the flag with the picture of Simon on it.

"Four seazons ago now, dis man Nimos mingled mongst'us. At first, I and I's thinks he was ya spy… I say a'meeself, 'Who the cap fit let em wear it!' But then I feels his spirit. A bigs spirit an' I feels like I's standing a'next ya blessed prophet!"

Ned swung around and looked reverently at the Bob Marley flag.

"A littl' bird tells I's, dat dis man going stoppa da rat race. Now brudders and sistas, dis man, who walked 'mongst weez and understood ya ways, needa ya help. Caus' just like weez, Babylon wanna crush him. Dem say he shotta da sheriff and they wanna bring him in a guilty. Dem says it's ya capital offence…"

Ned's voice was rising into a crescendo. He reached for his guitar and, as he plucked on the strings, he sang loudly.

"They don't wanna see weez unite! All they wanna do is sees weez fussin' and a fighting."

He stopped abruptly, looking back at the crowd.

"But no bars a'gonna hold him. We gotta stoppa dem propaganda, shatta dem illusion and break down dem confusion."

Allowing the expectation to build, he saluted the air and shouted.

"Weez gonna get da voice of da youth of Paris and da youth of every promised land behinds Nimos!"

As the Clavs started to cheer, his fingers plucked the strings of his guitar violently.

"Cause when the man comes, there will be no, no doom!"

The Clavs cheered loudly and stamped their feet and chanted.

"Nimos! Nimos!"

*

Captain Schiller's phone was vibrating violently on the make-shift folding table, which had served as his desk for the last few months. It was Gort's personal mobile – it had been a few weeks since they last spoke. Fighting off a sudden urge not to answer, he clasped the phone and flipped it open.

"Governor, what can I do for you?"

"Captain, I've just read your report. Good work! Well done for keeping the casualties out of the official stats. Just make sure you don't get caught out by any of the press infiltrators."

Rory reflected before replying respectfully.

"I'm pleased to report that there have been no significant casualties."

There was a moment's silence at the end of the phone before the Governor responded in a glacial tone.

"Captain Schiller, I didn't put you in the camp to take a soft line. The moment those refugees lose their fear of us, we're finished! It doesn't matter how many machine guns we have, we're going to be swamped by sheer numbers! Is that clear, Captain?"

Rory listened silently and powerlessly.

"Yes, Governor."

"I'll be paying you a visit shortly, to inspect your methods."

"Yes, Governor."

"And don't expect any warning!"

Rory hung up and wandered outside, his head full of confusion and his heart heavy. He stood in the shade of one of the four large screens that were being constructed in the camp to cover the trial. They were being hung around the exterior of the army compound, bolted onto the sturdy watch towers. Since Mother Cristina's visit, the different religious factions were united behind the idea of working together to create change. Even the lack of water had become a unifying issue. The changed atmosphere in the camp since Mother Cristina's visit was accompanied by his move away from the oppressive and autocratic approach employed by Rory's superior. He'd seen no reason to refuse the request to watch the trial, especially when Mother Cristina had informed him that she had a benefactor who was happy to pay the costs.

The sun was setting as the engineers tested the first of the screens. Thousands of excited refugees had gathered simply to watch the engineers winch each element of the huge screens into position. Black canvas canopies had been constructed above them, to keep the burning rays of the sun from melting them.

"I hope they like Global Vision!" announced the installation manager.

"I think they'd be happy to simply look at a blank screen," replied Rory.

"Well, the screens are cameras as well. They'll beam pictures of the crowds back to Global Vision. They're going to film the world watching the trial, to see the different reactions of people around the planet."

The screen came to life, to the roar of the crowd. The timing was good, as a documentary on the Socrates Project was just starting. The Global Vision team had recently come to interview the people of the camp.

Rory joined the growing crowd of refugees. It was very unusual for him to watch television, but he was hoping to catch a glimpse of Osiris.

A vaguely familiar face was standing in front of an excited crowd, shouting into a microphone over the noise of the crowd.

"It's quite incredible! I've never seen scenes like this before."

Mathias Yanofine, or MyFi as he was almost universally known, was using every superlative under the sun, trying to capture and portray what he was feeling to the hundreds of millions of viewers.

"Maggie, I'm in Hyde Park in London, a few kilometres from where the trial is to commence the day after tomorrow, experiencing what I am being told has become a world-wide phenomenon. Tens of thousands of people from all races and religions, inspired by the sicads, have come together to witness what they believe is going to be an event that will change the fate of humanity."

The camera scanned the crowds and the thousands of banners, stretching out in all directions. Every metre of space which wasn't occupied by a lake or a building had been seized.

"As you can see, I'm surrounded by countless banners adorned with 'CAMEOS', 'PANASHA' and 'SICADS'. The positivity, joy and optimism in the atmosphere are palpable and infectious. I've been talking to supporters here all day. Many have been brought together by a feeling of helplessness about the future of the environment or of humanity itself. I'm surrounded by young people who have told me they despair about their future and are looking for an alternative solution. It seems that they see the sicads as that solution. What is also clear is that they've come together for one huge party!"

Mathias was surrounded by a multi-cultural group. They were all celebrating, largely oblivious to the famous TV presenter.

"Well, as you can see, they're in high spirits. Let's see if I can distract them, to find out what they're so cheerful about."

Mathias succeeded in getting the attention of a feisty American girl.

"Can you tell us why you're so happy?" he asked, pushing the microphone towards her.

"Sure. We're just sort of getting off on the atmosphere!"

She waved her end of the banner she was jointly holding with a plump Indian girl. The banner was adorned with the Panasha slogan 'Unifying Hope!'

"It's so cool!" she added, throwing her free arm around Mathias and kissing him on the cheek. She was about to saunter off, but the presenter managed to hold her attention.

"Can you tell our viewers what's your name, where you're from and why you're here?"

"Of course, my name is Rosetta and I'm from the Planet Earth." Everybody around Rosetta cheered. Looking at her friends, she laughed happily before turning back to Mathias.

"I'm here to witness the future of humanity."

"And what is this future?"

"The sicads, of course. They're showing us the way forward!"

"So you believe Simon Oceandis is innocent?"

"Of course he's innocent. It's a huge stitch up, everybody knows that!"

A tall black male strode up behind Rosetta and put his arms around her, smiling at Mathias. On his t-shirt were printed the words 'The Sicads Are God's Messengers'.

"God has sent the sicads to save us, MyFi!"

The camera turned back to the slightly overwhelmed presenter.

"Well, there you have it, viewers. Let's get another point of view."

The presenter's attention was caught by a guitar-playing broad-framed white male with wild dreadlocks. The man had his back to him, but was wearing a flag like a cape, adorned with a picture of Simon Oceandis. Mathias walked up to him and the man stopped playing his guitar.

"You're evidently a Simon Oceandis supporter!"

"Ya's betta knows it," replied Ned, smiling broadly at the cameras behind Mathias.

"That's very emphatic support for an accused murderer. Why is that?"

"Dat man 'as a heart a'gold. Heez came a ya ghetto a see da needs of da youth man. Weez no gonna let dem crazy baldheads downpress heez!"

"So you don't believe he killed the soldiers then?" asked Mathias, hazarding a guess at what Ned had just said.

"Cauz heez nay killed nay sheriffs. Don't ya believe what ya seez a dem TV now," counselled Ned, putting one of his large arms around Mathias's shoulder, as if talking to a confused child.

"Well thank you, MyFi," cut in Maggie Bronski's voice from the studio, sensing that Mathias needed rescuing from a media embarrassment.

"We're going to take a look at similar gatherings around the planet.

377

Millions of others, who've not travelled to London, have organised huge parties to come together to watch the trial. They've taken over cinemas, or erected large screen televisions, or are huddled around radios in open-air parties. These groups have mushroomed around the globe and are projecting a common message to the rest of us: look how happy we are when we put aside our prejudices; look how we can come together to address problems bigger than us individually; look at the future of humanity."

After a series of images and reports covering the extraordinary scenes unfolding around the world, the coverage cut back to Mathias, who'd been rescued from Ned.

"Well, Mathias so you finally managed to tear yourself away from the pro-sicad party. What have you found to be happening on the other side?"

"Thank you, Maggie. Yes, it not's all hope and optimism here, I can tell you. For some, the atmosphere is very different. Let's go and interview some members of the anti-sicad camp, or the Gortists, as they have been named."

Mathias interviewed members of the armed forces and their families, who revelled in the opportunity to protest against the sicads and the years of military funding cuts. They had a self-righteous air of 'told you so' about them, and were demanding the rapid destruction of the sicads. There were many posters and t-shirts of the two dead soldiers, effigies of caricatured evil-looking robots and banners saying 'humans not robots'. Anyone with a grudge against technology had joined the fray.

The camera crew shuffled behind Mathias. A somewhat evil-looking woman, with an intimidated child clutching against each of her generous thighs, grabbed him.

The camera zoomed in on the banner she was waving: 'Destroy the sicads before they destroy us!' The woman's face was contorted with hate.

"I'm here to see this murdering machine brought to justice and destroyed, along with all of its type!"

"So you've already found Simon Oceandis guilty, then?" inquired Mathias.

"Of course he's guilty. The sicads must be destroyed. I don't want my children murdered by robots."

Rory walked back thoughtfully to his tent.

That night the Captain had trouble sleeping. A kaleidoscopic dream revolved inside his head. The hate-filled lady's words; I'm here to see this murdering machine brought to justice; rows of refugees scaling the fences, whilst he sat in one of the watch towers; Gort at his shoulder, ordering him to fire; Osiris calling at him across the crowded airport: 'Every man is responsible for his actions'; the fisherman showing him the pictures of his grandchildren, saying 'They're the best thing I could hope for in this world'. The dream was incessant. Rory got up, walked outside his tent and stared at the sea of people surrounding the army compound – was this really what he had dreamt of achieving? He contemplated the other choices open to him. Osiris's face and the fisherman's grandchildren flashed back into his mind. A cold wave of reality washed over him – the Army is my life, I know no other. Even if I wanted to, I couldn't leave – I know too much. His thoughts returned to Osiris. He suddenly envied her passion for what she believed in and, simultaneously, he realised that he'd completely lost his. A sudden surge of excitement flickered inside him, but just as quickly extinguished itself. Osiris is a free spirit, I'm a soldier – I follow orders.

Lying back silently in bed, he closed his eyes and forced his mind to focus on the droning of the mosquitoes.

*

Gort turned off the television, picked up his personal cell phone and hastily dialled Leopold's number.

"I've just been watching Global Vision..."

"And?"

"Well, your cronies are clearly not controlling this channel!"

"It's just one channel, Governor. Relax – we're influencing eighty per cent of the airwaves by viewing numbers. Check out the other channels. Look how many movies there are about out-of-control robots. We even accelerated the television premiere of the Hollywood remake of Frankenstein to tomorrow evening, just after the interview with the wives and families of the murdered soldiers."

"And what are you going to do about Global Vision?"

"That's a bit tricky. It's run by rich philanthropists!"

"And what about that CAMEOS magazine? It's joined forces with some religious movement. Circulation has exploded – I've checked the figures myself! Is that tricky as well?"

"Governor, this peace and love stuff is a minority and never leads anywhere. These sicads have murdered humans! We're reminding humans of that on every other media channel. Fear and insecurity are powerful primordial forces. Humanity is not going to reverse thousands of years of historical behaviour patterns overnight."

*

The Governor couldn't sleep that night. Paranoia that the sicads would somehow find a way to unmask him manifested itself as a bizarre dream where he was playing chess against an army of them.

Concerned that he was missing some pieces, he sat up in bed and tried to foresee every possible eventuality in the end game.

An hour later he'd summoned McCloud and they were driving back to Geneva. Just as the sun was rising, they arrived at CERN. The sicads were surprised to see Gort enter the chamber. Waves of relief passed over them as he proceeded to the inspection chamber.

Once inside the room, he paced back and forth, inspecting the dead sicads. He stopped beside the body of Magnus, running his fingers over the dead sicad's face. Rummaging in his pocket, he extracted a penknife and started cutting the skin around the neckline.

Ten minutes later, he was back in the limousine.

"Did you get what you wanted?" asked McCloud.

The Governor nodded.

52

"Are you quite sure that Captain Schiller wasn't at CERN?"

"Osiris, I have checked and double-checked. He was transferred to the camp nearly a month before."

"Maybe he wasn't."

"We'll never know, I'm afraid. I lodged him as a witness, but my request to subpoena him was refused!"

"Refused?"

"Yes, on insufficient grounds."

"I'm certain it was him."

"Osiris, you only saw his face for an instant in torchlight. Surely you can't be certain?"

Osiris fell silent, but not before having the final word.

"The Waorani hunted in the dark for generations!"

Fergus tried to lift the sombre mood, addressing Mother Cristina and also Jia, who was present electronically.

"Any final messages of hope for Simon, ladies?"

Osiris snapped out of her reverie and announced resolutely, "Tell Simon from me, that the very courtroom walls will shake with the sound of CAMEOS's supporters."

Fergus smiled and jotted down a brief note, as a distraught Jia spoke.

"Give him my regrets that I cannot attend. Tell him everybody in the monastery is praying for him. I wish I could see him one last... Oh no, what am I saying? Oh, it's so unfair..."

Jia's voice broke off.

Fergus paused respectfully. He wasn't sure what to say and was relieved when Mother Cristina responded.

"Jia, have faith in God. My vision is proof that God is guiding and watching over Simon. He will do what is right."

"But what if Fergus can't persuade him to attend the trial?"

Osiris decided to intervene, choosing her words carefully.

"Jia, Simon was conceived to love humans to do the best for the Socrates Project. I've watched him come to love this planet just as much..."

"Well lucky you!" blurted out Jia.

Osiris remained silent.

"I'm sorry, Osiris, it's just..."

Once again words failed Jia. Osiris resumed carefully.

"What I was going to say was that I'm sure he'll make the best decision with regard for all life, which he now..."

"You changed him, Osiris, he's different now. He was programmed to ensure his survival!" snapped Jia.

Osiris shook her head slowly.

"I didn't change him, Jia. Nature changed him. He found the Great Spirit by himself. If he decides to sacrifice himself for what he believes is right, we must respect that decision."

Mother Cristina was listening silently to the dialogue between the two women. She knew enough about the human condition to know that deep emotions were involved.

"Simon has given his life to God, who will guide him now," she concluded.

*

Fergus approached the dreary brown walls of the La Santé prison. Simon was being held in the high security wing of this bleak fortress, lodged in the heart of Paris's fourteenth arrondissement. In the failing light of a grey September day, it made a depressing sight. As he made his way towards the entrance, a burly figure in a dark overcoat stepped out of the shadows and walked alongside him.

"Mr Fealey, the boss would like to have a word with you. His car is this way."

Fergus looked at his watch.

"I have to see my client. It'll have to be brief."

He was escorted to a nearby stretch limousine with black tinted windows. The rear door was opened for him, he was swiftly ushered inside and the door closed behind him. It was spacious and he sat down opposite Governor Gort, who studied him carefully.

"Well, Mr Fealey, what do you have to report?"

Fergus surveyed the Governor's harsh physiognomy before replying cautiously.

"The sicad has little care for attending the trial. I'm doing my best to keep him alive."

Gort sat forward, his dark eyes staring into Fergus's.

"Tell me something new, Mr Fealey. I've little care for increasing your fee, if that's what you're fishing for."

"No Governor, I'm quite satisfied with the fee. I'm merely explaining that I must give him a little hope if we wish him to attend the trial."

"I trust you're not giving the robot too much hope, Mr Fealey!"

"My client knows he's going to lose. I'm convincing him to go out with a bang and not a whimper!"

"And what is this bang going to be, Mr Fealey?"

"Just a speech, that's all! Give him his five minutes of glory, Governor. You want him to attend the trial don't you?"

"For all of our sakes, and especially yours, Mr Fealey, he'd better!"

Fergus looked at his watch nervously.

"Well, Governor, you need to let me get back to my client before it's too late."

Gort thought for a few seconds and then nodded slowly. As Fergus reached to open the car door, Gort spoke.

"Just one last thing."

"Yes, Governor?" he replied with forced calmness.

"You won't let me down will you?"

"Of course not, Governor. What would I have to gain from such an act?"

"I don't know what you would have to gain, Mr Fealey, but I know what you have to lose, and I'm not talking about your fee!"

Gort's voice sent a chill down his spine.

*

Fergus waited as the military guard went through the usual ritual of unlocking the series of padlocks. Simon was lying on the bed. Fergus pulled up a chair and sat in front of the sicad.

"I was wondering whether you were going to come. Another few hours and I would have given up," spoke Simon softly.

"I hope you're not still entertaining those silly notions of not attending the trial."

"There's a note of anxiety in your voice, Fergus. Is everything OK?"

"I'm concerned that you're going to make a bad decision and let humanity down. We need you, Simon."

"Is that so? Well, I'm waiting to hear the case for attending the trial. All my analysis confirms that there is no chance of winning against Governor Gort. In which case, I can only legitimise his rise to power by attending the trial. But please tell me, what new information am I missing?"

The lawyer got to his feet.

"Well, I can't pretend that we have found any witness or proof to prove your innocence. It will be your word against Governor Gort's. But what I have found, is many people who have met you and are prepared to speak up for your good character. Osiris and Mother Cristina have moved many millions of people through CAMEOS and Panasha. Jia, too, has done everything she can and helped to secure strong media support through Global Vision. To let these people down now would be unforgivable!"

Simon raised his eyebrows.

"You say 'unforgivable', but I'm not sure I follow you. If I decide not to attend the trial, it's for the best. If Governor Gort pulls off a showcase trial to destroy us sicads, it leaves these people with little recourse."

There was a silent pause, which Simon broke first.

"Who wouldn't forgive me, Fergus? You?"

"Now you're getting paranoid!"

"You must forgive me if I am. With no news and nothing to think of but the worst, it's understandable, isn't it?"

Fergus paused to clear his thoughts and the sicad continued softly.

"How do I know you're really acting in my best interests? Trapped here, with no knowledge of the outside world, what do I know? Jesus had his Judas and Socrates his Meletus!"

Fergus paced around the room, his brain was short circuiting.

"Nothing I say to you, Simon, will prove my motives."

"I came to exactly the same conclusion, Fergus."

"You can never know. You must trust me. After everything that has happened to put this project together and the hopes that are riding on it... how can you turn your back on humans now?" pleaded the lawyer passionately.

Simon shook his head slowly.

"The project idea was good; it was more than good, it was enlightened. Bruno Reno had seen a solution that could theoretically get governments to come together to make the changes that humanity must make if they are to save themselves."

"Exactly," replied Fergus eagerly, "Which is why you must see the Project through!"

Again Simon shook his head slowly.

"Bruno was enlightened, but too idealistic. When has humanity ever listened to an enlightened man? The politicians of Athens sentenced Socrates to death, the Jewish priests and the Romans crucified Jesus, the Catholic Church locked up Galileo until his death... I could go on and on. Your history proves that humans cannot escape an endemic cycle of corruption. Here I am now, nearly two thousand five hundred years later, standing accused like Socrates of being an enemy of the people, being tried for a crime that I did not commit! It is better that I drink the hemlock now, rather than being forced to drink it by Gort."

Fergus clicked his fingers, as if he made a mental breakthrough.

"Yes, Simon, you are like Socrates, who died for the right to free speech, and whose wisdom and methods of questioning and dialogue are still practised widely today. He inspired Plato, who went on to found the academies of learning that have become the great universities. With your understanding of our problems, think how you could leave a legacy to inspire humans. Use the trial as a platform to broadcast your wisdom and lay the foundations for the change you believe in!"

Simon was lying peacefully and slowly shook his head at Fergus's speech. His voice was very weak and his power was failing.

"This I have done already, as best I can, Fergus. Our report to humans sets out this wisdom. No, the trial will be used by Gort to show that the sicads were a dangerous failure. Enlightened ideas sound good, but fear and ignorance are easier forces to control. Humans have always been governed this way and it seems they always will."

Fergus listened dejectedly as Simon continued weakly.

"Simon, you mustn't give up – there is always hope!"

"Fergus, why do you want to subject me to this trial?"

The young lawyer put his head in his hands and rubbed his temples vigorously with his knuckles. He stopped and looked back at Simon, his hair ruffled and his face blotchy. He already has the cup of hemlock at his lips. Think, Fergus, think!

"Why did you give me hope if you had no intention of attending?"

"I made no promises. I told you that humanity must decide."

A light came on in Fergus's head. He found his voice and started gesticulating with his hands to inspire some animation into Simon.

"Yes, Simon, they are calling for you. There are hundreds of thousands gathering outside the courtroom, maybe more. There is a chance, however slim! Simon, don't drink the hemlock. If we can attack Gort, we may find a way of bringing him down."

Simon stretched out an arm and laid the back of his hand on one of Fergus's open palms. His voice was almost too faint to be distinguishable. The lawyer leaned closer to make out the sicad's dying words.

"Are you truly prepared to attack Gort?"

"Yes, of course," replied the lawyer quickly.

"You'd swear on your life?" gasped the sicad weakly.

Fergus swallowed, glanced up at the ceiling.

"Yes, I swear."

The skin on the fingertips of Simon's hand, still resting on Fergus's, slid back and the power pins slowly protruded.

53

The morning of the trial had finally arrived and it was a cold late September one. It was the first interspecies trial, as the defendant, unlike the prosecutors, was not human. The Old Bailey in London had been chosen to try this unprecedented case. The alleged offences had been committed in Swiss territory, but taking into account Switzerland's desire for neutrality and its status as a full member of the Council of Europe, it had gladly accepted the jurisdiction of another European court.

It was a fitting venue – the most famous criminal court in the world and, ominously, where English death sentences had been historically passed. Public hangings took place just outside in Dead Man's Walk as recently as the nineteenth century. Once again, lives were at stake. The fate of the 372 remaining sicads was resting upon the outcome of the trial of just one of their number. By special decree of an emergency meeting of global governments, the sicad, unlike a human was not to be accorded leave to appeal. The trial by jury was going to be definitive, one way or another.

Mathias Yanofine was addressing Global Vision's viewers from outside the building, which had been besieged by thousands of people. The early morning sun had yet to heat up the land, but the movement of the growing crowds had the effect of lifting the air temperature. Maggie Bronski was posing the questions from the studio.

"Mathias, it seems that the crowds have grown overnight!"

The presenter adjusted his earpiece and, after a minor delay, spoke enthusiastically into his microphone.

"Yes, Maggie, as you can see there are even more people here than yesterday evening! Many of them slept outdoors to gain a place within sight of the courthouse. People have been drawn here from across the world and more are arriving every minute. The roads and pavements are jammed with people and the police are totally overwhelmed. Every available space is being filled with new arrivals."

The camera switched to showing an aerial view of the crowds, densely packed around the courthouse and extending out beyond all the famous landmarks of London.

"It's an incredible sight, Mathias. I've never seen so many people in one place."

"As you can see better than me, Maggie, the trial had generated an unprecedented level of interest; the city of London has come to a standstill. We're hearing estimates of over two million visitors. Police are asking people not to come. There are major concerns over safety. All roads into the city have been closed and thousands of vehicles have been simply abandoned."

"And why are people coming?" asked Maggie.

"There are environmentalists who support the sicads' claim that humanity is destroying the planet. Osiris from CAMEOS is amongst them. There are hundreds of thousands of religious believers, I guess we can call them pilgrims, who have come in the belief that Simon Oceandis has been sent by God. Mother Cristina is amongst them. They've described this to me as being like the trial of Jesus or a prophet from their own religion. There are many others who have come because they sense an historic event of unprecedented proportions. This is a case which many are saying is about more than the guilt of one robot. There are many unanswered questions about the Socrates Project and the role of prominent members of global governments in the events that led up to its collapse."

"Well, Mathias, the authorities have clearly been completely surprised by the turnout. This trial has certainly caught people's imagination. How long will these people stay for? What if the trial goes on for weeks?"

"That's an interesting question, Maggie, but the crowds here clearly sense something is going to happen soon. And what a case is promised! A hung jury is impossible and, *in extremis*, a simple majority of one has been authorised to decide the defendant's fate. Whatever happens, there can be no stalemate."

"Yes, we're getting worldwide reports that humanity has literally stopped in its tracks to watch the case. Shops have been emptied as people have stocked up with provisions to avoid any interruption to their viewing. Businesses have closed down, transport has ground to a halt and, seemingly, everybody has put their lives on hold whilst this trial unfolds."

*

388

Such great events bring great characters to the fore. The legal profession has always attracted some of the most intelligent, talented and colourful individuals. Arguably the world's best lawyer, Cornelius Beckett, had been appointed to prosecute. Cornelius Beckett was an Englishman with considerable legal pedigree. Being no stranger to the Old Bailey, he was truly on his home ground and was boosted by an unblemished string of recent successes. A neat and precise man, with sharp almost elfish features, he cross-examined his opponents in the same way that he had fenced for the UK in the Olympic Games in his youth. The rapidity and precision of his intellectual swipes unsettled and softened up his prey, who he invariably finished off with a well-timed killer thrust of his sharp intellect. His fee had not been disclosed, but it was rumoured that it was the first ever one billion GMU brief. This mighty legal Goliath seemed certain to crush the defence.

Fergus couldn't hope to match Cornelius's heavyweight clinical legal experience. In many ways he was the complete antithesis. Unlike the clean-living thin and precise Cornelius, Fergus was portly and it was rumoured that he enjoyed a drink or two. Cornelius was case-hardened and unemotional. Fergus was a man enthused with the vestiges of the idealism of youth. Was there a glimmer of hope that Fergus might just be able to win over the hearts and minds of the jury and the public at large?

Man versus robot. Legal experience, gravitas and precision versus a novel ardent passion studded with idealism and crowned with the audacity of youth. The contrasts could not have been greater. What a spectacle was promised! Had the ringside seats been for sale, what price would they have fetched?

*

A cortege of cars tried to fight its way through the crowds which had spilled over onto the streets. The police were battling to clear a single lane to allow the cars to proceed. Governor Gort was inside one of the leading cars, still two kilometres away. He lowered a tinted window and leant his head out to berate a flustered police officer.

"This is ridiculous! You've had ample time to organise a clear passage!" he snapped.

"Sorry, Governor. We're doing our best. We've never seen anything like it. There's many times the numbers we were expecting!"

"Well your best isn't good enough. You'd better do better!" snarled the Governor.

The officer dashed off to push back the crowds with renewed vigour. Gort started impatiently drumming his fingers on the leather briefcase containing his briefing notes.

"Relax, Governor. The trial can't start without me. If it starts a few minutes late, it won't matter. It's an open-and-shut case and should be over very quickly."

"Cornelius, I'm not paying you the annual military budget of Ecuador to be overly optimistic. These robots are devious. Look out the window. Their supporters outnumber ours!"

"Relax, Governor. What matters is that the law is on our side."

"I hope you're right. I would hate for you to let me down!"

Following a few cars behind Governor Gort's limousine was an armoured police van. Seated in the back was Simon, handcuffed with a black canvas sack over his head and, on either side of him, heavily armed police officers. On the opposite bench sat Fergus.

Simon was sat silently awaiting his fate. His lawyer could sense the sicad's growing despair.

"Is that really necessary?" asked Fergus, pointing at his client's head.

"Governor's orders," replied the officer emphatically.

Fergus sighed. Outside they could hear the crowds, an indistinguishable cacophony of noise even for Simon's excellent hearing.

Suddenly, there was a loud thud from the top of the slow moving police van. A large white-skinned man with wild dreadlocks had jumped onto the roof, clutching a guitar. He stamped his foot on the roof.

"Hey Nimos, if ya's in dere brudder. Don't ya worri, caus' every little thing gonna be all right!"

There was an enormous cheer from the nearby crowd as Ned started to play his guitar. The van stopped abruptly and Simon heard the front doors open and the police officers angrily threaten Ned, who jumped off the roof to more cheers from the crowds. A clear chorus of 'Simon! Simon!' could be heard reverberating around the crowd. His spirits lifted for the first time in many weeks – is there really a chance?

Ninety minutes later, the van ground to a halt a few hundred metres away from the court building. Simon could now clearly make out the cheers chanting his name, but interspersed were hate-filled shouts of

'Destroy the sicads' and 'Humans not robots'. His spirits sank again.

"We'll never get through that lot," pointed out the driver.

"OK, forget the back, we'll have to go in the front way," his commander confirmed uncomfortably.

The van stopped and the rear doors were flung open. Simon was pulled out by two burly officers and hustled towards the courtroom. As the doors opened, Fergus got his first view of the crowd. He saw the banners supporting the sicads and realised just how many people had turned out to cheer Simon on. Instinctively, he exited the van before the police officers could react and, with an athletic leap, pulled the black sack off Simon's head. There was a moment of confusion in the police ranks, which Simon profited from to hold his head up high. As the crowds saw his face, there was a fresh wave of rapturous cheers and screams that almost deafened Fergus and the policemen. The crowd surged forward and their weight pushed over the restraining barriers. Members of the crowd swamped Simon, reaching out with their hands to touch him in scenes reminiscent of a papal visit.

Police reinforcements arrived and began pulling the crowd off the sicad. Avid supporters, clasping their arms around his waist and legs, had to be pulled off by the police officers, only to be replaced by fresh fans. Some refused to let go, despite being struck repeatedly with truncheons. It took the police nearly five minutes to drag Simon away from the crowd and up the steps into the sanctuary of the court building. As Simon entered the building, he lost the brief connection to the internet he had enjoyed from the police van to the courthouse. Scramblers everywhere, acknowledged the sicad.

Gort was pacing up and down the corridor, making a private phone call. He turned and scowled enigmatically at Simon as he was led into the cells.

*

The trial opened to a blaze of publicity. It was estimated that over three billion people had tuned in to watch the opening day, the day when Cornelius and Fergus would cross swords for the first time. Simon sat in the cells below the court, but could clearly hear the Chief Justice reading out the formalities to open the case.

The bailiff escorted him from the cells, up a flight of steps and directly into a strengthened glass cubicle, which formed the accused box and had been specially constructed for the trial. It contained a microphone and speakers to communicate with the court. More scramblers, sighed Simon; even the radio waves are blocked. Governor Gort was taking no chances that Simon could find a way of communicating with the jury or witnesses through the various internal communication networks of the courthouse. Otherwise, there was nothing but a small ledge which he could sit on, and a Bible. The black door behind him was closed and locked.

Simon looked slowly around the famous court room, but was more interested in the people rather than the architecture or the history of the building. The sense of cold formality on the expressionless faces of the prosecuting legal team added to his returning sense of foreboding and despair. His eyes turned to the judge and then to the crowds gathered in the spectator galleries. He was searching for a kind face, any sign of humanity which might plant a seed of optimism in his mind to combat the dark weeds of despair which were blocking out the light of hope. He was starting to regret his decision to attend. The spectator galleries were filled with people he recognised as politicians and other senior members of the establishment, their faces devoid of emotion. In contrast to the atmosphere of excitement, hope and optimism that he had briefly witnessed outside, the mood in the court room was reminiscent of a funeral or, worse, an execution. He realised how much he missed Osiris, Bruno and Jia – why were they not here? Gort made his way into the front row of the spectator gallery, as if to answer his question. The Governor must have received a special dispensation to attend the court as both a witness and a spectator.

The judge facing Simon, like Cornelius, was from the UK, and was none other than Lord Dunning, a Privy Councillor. He had a reputation of being a staunch conservative. The sicad felt another nail being banged into his coffin.

Lord Dunning cleared his throat and motioned to Simon to take the Bible.

"Mr Oceandis, you are in a court of law and you must swear to tell the truth, the whole truth and nothing but the truth. You may swear an oath on the Bible or, in your capacity as a machine, you may simply affirm to tell the truth."

Simon placed his hand on the Bible.

"I swear to tell the truth, the whole truth and nothing but the truth. May God be my witness."

The words broadcast into the court room were Simon's, but the voice was a distorted and sinister-sounding one.

"Damn Cornelius and Gort," cursed Fergus under his breath in annoyance.

"Objection, My Lord," he shouted, "That is not my client's voice!"

The judged looked sternly at the young lawyer.

"Mr Fealey, this protection has been put in place for your client's safety. It is natural that his voice will sound different through the speaker."

"This is a deliberate attempt to portray my client in a negative and sinister light," responded Fergus angrily.

"Objection overruled!" stated Lord Dunning authoritatively, before abruptly turning his attention back to the accused.

"As a holder of a valid passport of a member country of the United Nations, you have been granted the right to be judged by an independent jury of men and women. Please confirm that this is your wish."

"Yes, this is my wish."

Cornelius took the floor and read out the charges against the sicad. Simon's mind wandered back to happier days, walking with Osiris in the forests of France. His thoughts were interrupted by Cornelius speaking his name.

"...Simon Oceandis, hereafter known as the defendant, heretofore on or about March 24th of this year, did then and there unlawfully, intentionally and knowingly cause the deaths of Corporal James Swenson and Corporal Ralph Boche, hereinafter called the victims, by battering them unconscious with his bare hands or with an unknown object and leaving them in Lake Geneva to drown."

Cornelius paused theatrically, before posing the question that people were silently willing him on to ask.

"How do you plead?"

Simon looked at Cornelius calmly and respectfully.

"Not guilty."

There was silence in the court room, but loud cheers could be heard from outside. The crowd were following the media coverage on a variety of portable screens and electronic devices. The army and police efforts to distance the crowd from the court room had been in vain; they might as well have tried to push back the tide. The cheers of millions of people could not only be heard in the court room and on the media coverage, but the very walls of the building vibrated.

Cornelius continued, raising his voice in an attempt to mask the sound of cheering. He practically had to shout to be heard clearly.

"Simon Oceandis is not a typical defendant. He is a robot created under the auspices of the Socrates Project and he was provided with citizenship in order to fulfil the requirements of that project. In the capacity of a robot, he is also charged with representing a grave danger to the human race."

Again Cornelius paused and allowed the nature of the charges to sink in to the jury and the wider courtroom.

"How do you plead?"

Fergus had warned Simon to expect this charge which, if he were found guilty of, would give legal authority for the destruction of all of the sicads. Putting aside minor legal procedural issues, if he was found guilty of the first charge he would automatically be found guilty of the second charge.

"Not guilty!" replied Simon emphatically.

There were more cheers from the crowds outside, drowning out the jeering and insults of the anti-sicad camp.

Cornelius turned to the jurors, to make his opening speech. Simon looked at the twelve-strong jury, which appeared to have a fair representation of both sexes and ages.

"Ladies and gentlemen, this robot, Simon Oceandis, who stands before us, is a killer. The evidence you will hear from the prosecution is concise and emphatic, and is supplied by witnesses of the highest rank and authority.

"Against this testimony there can be no doubt of the guilt of this robot. But please do not be fooled into believing that this machine, which has been fashioned as a sympathetic-looking human, is in any way human. Created and released, recklessly, into human societies, these robots are the most intelligent and fast-learning machines ever created, programmed to ensure their own survival at all costs. To assure this survival, they are equipped with brains that are far more powerful than ours. These robots can link their brains together to multiply this intelligence exponentially. Even the designers of these super-robots cannot see inside their heads and are oblivious to their true nature.

"You will undoubtedly hear, in defence of this killing machine, evidence of its alleged virtues. Members of the jury, you must dismiss this evidence as manipulation and a bid for survival at all costs. You should take any such suggestions instead as proof of the sinister ability of these machines to exploit human weaknesses. You must be strong-minded, like Governor Gort, who was the first to detect the true nature of these evil robots when others around him were being seduced by their attempts to cover themselves in virtue. Certain credible scientists believe these robots have even developed mild hypnotic powers.

"As upstanding and honest members of society, you will undoubtedly want to look into the eyes of this killer to behold his guilt. Be warned that you do not fall under his seductive spell, like the crowd outside that you may hear cheering from time to time throughout this case! Let these cheers remind you of the manipulative skills of these machines.

"Ladies and gentleman, to conclude let us return to the cold-blooded murder of two of our bravest soldiers. These were soldiers with families, soldiers who dedicated their lives to protect ours. The decision to kill these soldiers was pre-meditated and deliberate. A cold and calculated decision – and it is not a decision that takes very long. Such a decision can be made in fractions of a second by these machines. The defendant was fleeing from his duties and was apprehended by our unsuspecting soldiers on that cold winter night. The defendant had a moment to decide how to respond, whether to give himself up to justice or to overstep a dark line."

Cornelius paused and then clicked his fingers loudly.

"Just like that, a decision was made: I will eliminate them. The disfigured face of Corporal Swenson reveals the brutality with which this killer went about his act of murder. In so doing, he revealed the true face of the sicads – machines that deem their own lives more important than the humans they were created to serve. An act of brutality, barbarism and treachery was inflicted on humanity on that cold dark winter night.

"After battering Corporal Swenson and Boche unconscious, this robot rowed out into Lake Geneva to dump their unconscious bodies. This cruel and cowardly act was, fortunately, witnessed by one man, a man more alert than his fellow men. A man with an unblemished record of being alert to danger and oppression, a man who liberated the world from the dark threats of fundamentalism and who was there, once again in our hour of need, to save us from the sicads. Governor Gort, accompanied by Colonel McCloud, witnessed this machine undertaking his dark act on that cold moonlit night from the shores of Lake Geneva. As they closed in on him, he capsized the boat and escaped by swimming stealthily away, like a shark, underneath the surface of the dark waters of the lake.

"Let us think back to that act. An act that took away the lives of

Corporal James Swenson and Corporal Ralph Boche, who were aged thirty-five and thirty-seven respectively. These soldiers who died doing a job they were rightly proud of, each left behind a wife and two young children. And why did they die? They died because a robot wanted to live.

"If we stop these robots now, we will thankfully never know their dark motives. These robots have the guile to tell us what we want to hear in the day, whilst they murder our citizens at night. What do we know of these sicads? We know that they are machines who deem their own lives more important than ours, and who will stop at nothing to survive. These, ladies and gentlemen of the jury, are the traits of emotionless psychopaths who, if unchecked, could ultimately subjugate or murder humanity and conquer the world for their own benefit. This danger is perfectly demonstrated by the murderous acts of the defendant, Simon Oceandis, the leader of the sicads. If not stopped now, his followers will undoubtedly continue his murderous work.

"Yes, members of the jury, you must choose between mankind and machines!"

The crowd fell silent and there was a palpable sense of fear and horror that pervaded the court room. Cornelius did not wish to break the effect he had so skilfully created. He silently walked back to his bench as the court room digested his uncomfortable words. Gort gave Cornelius a nod of approval from the spectator gallery. An atmosphere of silent fear had befallen the court, and even temporarily quietened the crowd outside. Simon could sense a death knell tolling.

All eyes fell onto Fergus. How was he going to respond? What tricks did he have up his sleeve?

Outside, Osiris and Mother Cristina were leading a chant to a rhythmic clapping of hands.

"Fergus, *clap, clap, clap...* Fergus."

The chant spread through the crowds and people stamped their feet in time with the clapping.

Fergus was in deep contemplation. The chant became audible inside the courtroom, exaggerated by the imposing silence. Fergus looked up at Governor Gort, only to be confronted by a severe and emotionless gaze. He looked at Simon, then up at the ceiling and his eyes fell back upon the carefully prepared script of his speech, which lay on the chair next to him. He got to his feet and cast a final glance at the script, before deciding to abandon it. He strode across the courtroom with long wide strides, his hair bouncing up and down and his gown lightly billowing. He paced back and forth in front of the judge and jury, looking into their eyes for clues as to their thoughts, and to make that vital personal link with them. He beamed a big hearty smile at one and all. After an ambivalent nod of approval from Lord Dunning, he commenced his riposte.

"Members of the jury, you have just heard my client Simon Oceandis being branded as a danger to humanity, an out-of-control maverick who is happy to take the law into his own hands. You have heard that my client is a machine devoid of emotions, driven by an unknown enigmatic plan to subjugate humanity, to conquer the world for his benefit and for the benefit of those of his type. Members of the jury, to me that sounds more like Governor David Gort than Simon Oceandis!"

There was a collective gasp. Governor Gort was heard to snarl and utter the word 'traitor' under his breath. Fergus could feel the daggers of Gort's gaze bearing down on him. He looked up and held the Governor's stare defiantly. Simon had got to his feet and was silently applauding Fergus's courage.

"Order, order in court!" shouted the judge.

When the crowd had quietened, Lord Dunning turned back to Fergus and addressed him in a voice of great legal pomposity.

"Proceed prudently, Mr Fealey."

Fergus continued. What drove him on to risk the wrath of Gort he didn't exactly know – was it the effect of the huge crowd willing him on, his conviction of Simon's innocence or simply the innate rebellious streak inside him? In any case, a sudden passion drove him gallantly forward, overriding any concerns for his future career and physical security.

"What facts do we really know about Simon Oceandis? I'm sorry, but we heard no facts from my learned friend Mr Beckett. We heard plenty of supposition, interpretation and speculation. Lord Chancellor, I could have raised an objection many times, but I didn't want to ruin such a pretty speech. Members of the jury, Your Honour, that's not my style – maybe I am indeed young and naive, but I prefer to give you the real facts.

"Let us look at the facts that we know about Simon Oceandis. This is a man who helps people. Yes, I use the word 'man' because I believe that as much as anybody else on this planet Simon Oceandis is worthy of this term.

"This is a man who has befriended hundreds of men and has upset just one. Simon Oceandis is a man who saves lives, rather than takes lives; a pacifist by design, who only raises his arm to protect himself from danger and persecution. A man whose only crime was to free himself just before his own burial ceremony and capsize a boat.

"Yes, ladies and gentlemen, Simon Oceandis is a victim, not an aggressor; a saver, not a taker of lives. Simon Oceandis is a man who is programmed not to lie and whose very essence is to help humans; a man who is entirely selfless, without ego. This, members of the jury, is the profile of my client. A man bathed in humanity, not a dangerous machine devoid of emotion."

He paused and leant on the corner of his table.

"Let me tell you that I hesitated to take this case. It wasn't for money, as my client does not have the means to pay me. It wasn't for the fame, as this case risks bringing me unwelcome attention. Well, ladies and gentlemen, I put my hand on this good book and swear to you solemnly that I stand before you now because I am convinced of my client's innocence. My learned friend Mr Beckett will no doubt suggest that my client has hypnotised me, along with the millions of people gathered outside this courtroom and around the world. Some hypnotist, I am sure you will agree.

"Well if there was any doubt in my mind as to my client's innocence, I just have to look at the obstacles that have been put in the path of my client receiving a fair trial. For your information, as you would not know it from the ridiculous chamber which distorts his voice, my client speaks softly, kindly and calmly. Witnesses have disappeared, have been barred from attending court for 'security reasons' or have been too intimidated to present themselves. I myself have found it difficult to access my client for weeks on end. Yes, someone has something to hide.

"Maybe it's the folly of youth, or maybe I have an innate weakness to follow my heart, but yes, I am prepared to speak out against the system that has closed ranks on this wonderful being who has inspired so many people."

Fergus stopped and looked up at Governor Gort, who was staring at him in silent rage. The young lawyer defiantly held his gaze as he continued his speech.

"In pursuing my client's liberty and his right to live, I am undoubtedly risking mine. Maybe this is just my character, which is neither necessarily good nor bad but simply is that way, but it drives me forward with fire in my belly to fight this intended injustice!"

As Fergus stopped speaking there was an almighty cheer from outside the court building. The cheer was so loud that the windows shook. The mood of the crowd lifted Fergus further, who continued in full flow.

"Let us turn the spotlight of scrutiny onto Governor David Gort, the single and deadly enemy that Simon Oceandis had the misfortune to make. This trial is about not only the legitimacy of David Gort's evidence, but about the legitimacy of Governor Gort himself. When we look closely at David Gort today, and put aside that much vaunted image of the war hero of yesteryear, we see a psychopath, devoid of emotion, driven by an obsession and a twisted ego. David Gort is no man, he is the murdering machine!"

Fergus let his words sink in. The spectator gallery was in shock. The crowds outside roared their support. A fleeting glimpse of fear momentarily shook Cornelius's serene and confident countenance. Fergus strode back to the row of jurists and walked slowly in front of them.

"Yes, members of the jury, let us indeed look closely at David Gort, this machine devoid of emotion and respect for others. A machine which disregards orders, which kills Bartolome Barrera, an innocent being, with cruelty. We shall see in Bartolome's note, encoded in the programming code of the Atlas detector at CERN, that he was a being capable of anguish and regret, and conscious of his predicament. A being who was a Spanish citizen, yes My Lord and members of the jury, a Spanish citizen with a valid passport.

"This machine, David Gort, sent his soldiers on that dark cold March night to dump his body in Lake Geneva. Except it wasn't Bartolome they were trying to get rid of, it was Simon Oceandis disguised as Bartolome. My client interrupted them and, in their shock, these henchmen capsized their boat in the icy waters of Lake Geneva.

"I am going to prove to you that the battering of Corporal Swenson's face was more likely to have been caused by the bow of the capsized boat.

"When David Gort found out he had been outwitted by my client, he decided to fabricate the evidence, to turn the soldiers' death by drowning into a fantasy of murder by my client. He seized his chance to bring down the Socrates Project, for his own ends.

"At this point, David Gort was driven by his twisted ego and had almost every police and army officer in the region searching for Simon Oceandis. In his anger and frustration, or maybe just his ambition for power, he decided to kill the four hundred citizens of the world housed at CERN, dependent on human power, from which David Gort cruelly deprived them. Twenty eight of those sicads died. They died in the same way that humans die, with regret and anguish. It wasn't a quick death either, but a slow torturous death. Deprived of power, they died a slow painful death, like humans deprived of oxygen!

"Yes, David Gort is the murderer – a mass murderer, who has shown he is capable and prepared to commit genocide!"

The crowd inside the court room were talking openly amongst themselves, asking themselves if Fergus could be right. Loud protestations could be heard from Cornelius.

"Order, order!" repeated Lord Dunning, striking his gavel vigorously on the sounding block. There was now no restraining Fergus, who continued passionately.

"We have heard that David Gort is a war hero. Is it right for an army hero to plot secretly against his superiors? A Commander who organises training exercises which mysteriously end in disaster, nearly robbing us of one of our youngest and brightest scientists. A tragedy only averted by my client's quick thinking and respect for life.

"Ladies and gentleman, David Gort knew that my client was the only person who knew of his guilt. He relentlessly tracked and hounded him on foot with dogs. Well, it seems that someone else was watching over my client. On this Easter Sunday my client arrived desperately at a monastery, tucked away in the mountains, just minutes ahead of his demented pursuer. As he pleaded for refuge, the Prioress recognised him from a vision she had experienced of a man on a cross, and took this as a sign from God to provide refuge to this man.

"It seems, ladies and gentlemen, that someone up above is watching over the activities of David Gort and is not prepared to let them go unpunished!"

"Enough, Mr Fealey!" announced Lord Dunning, striking his gavel forcefully.

"Your client is accused of taking the life of two soldiers. It is your job to prove that your client did not commit this alleged crime. A personal attack on Governor David Gort is not only slanderous, but I fail to see its relevance to the case in hand. Unless you can prove the pertinence of your approach, I am going to have to instruct the jury to dismiss your opening speech and ignore your accusations. Whilst we await this proof, the court will recess."

The court fell silent and Fergus sat down with his head in his hands.

Spectators got up to stretch their legs and the young lawyer picked up his notes. He flicked distractedly through the pages. None of his witnesses had anything concrete against Gort. He could feel Simon's gaze upon him, but couldn't bring himself to look in his direction – not without finding a solution. *Why was I so impulsive? The case is as good as lost now!*

Meanwhile, a man was making his way towards the court house with great determination. Three hours earlier he had disembarked the last airplane to make it into Heathrow airport, which had ground to a complete halt. Passengers, pilots and airport staff couldn't get to and from the airport. Incoming planes were being diverted and passengers were sitting in overflowing airport lounges uncomplainingly, watching the media coverage of the trial. A motorcycle taxi had taken him as close as possible to the centre of London, using emergency lanes, pavements and even pedestrian subways. His driver, who had been handsomely rewarded, had finally given up on the Euston Road, just beyond Marylebone Station. The crowds were spilling out from Regent's Park, where hundreds of thousands had congregated to watch the trial together on huge screens. The roads were completely grid-locked; cars, taxis and buses had been, for the most part, completely abandoned. The underground stations had long been closed, so there was only one way to travel – on foot.

Pushing his way through the hordes of people, the man continued in a south-easterly direction. He fought his way down Baker Street, across Oxford Street, through Berkeley Square and into Green Park. The Mall was thronged with pro-sicad protestors, camped in front of Buckingham Palace, trying to solicit the support of the Royal Family with huge banners. The crowds were getting denser and he found it almost impossible to advance. Cutting through St James's Park, he had to wade through the lake. He eventually arrived at the Houses of Parliament. The Embankment was absolutely jammed packed – even the floating bars and restaurants had been commandeered by protestors and looked in danger of sinking under their weight. He contemplated jumping into the Thames and swimming, but he couldn't get near enough to the bank. Instead, he took off his army boots and jumped up on the boot of the nearest vehicle, an abandoned police car. He stood up next to the siren and leapt onto the roof of an adjacent taxi. He made his way forward from roof to bonnet and back to roof along the bumper-to-bumper vehicles, clutching a boot in the hand of each outstretched arm.

"Mr Fealey, what proof are you going to provide us of your slanderous allegations?"

Fergus had spent the twenty-minute recess deliberating his best option. He was still trying to decide when Lord Dunning repeated his demand.

"Mr Fealey, this is your final chance, otherwise I will have to ask the jury to strike out your speech."

"My Lord, I would like to call Akihiko Lee, Chief Technician at Mazari Industries."

Lord Dunning consulted his notes before glancing at Cornelius. The prosecuting lawyer nodded.

Akihiko made his way nervously into the witness box and swore the obligatory oath. He looked up warily at Governor Gort.

Fergus took the floor and addressed the technician.

"Akihiko, you have been one of the senior engineers at Mazari for over eight years, correct?"

"Yes, that is correct."

"As such, you have been intricately involved in the production and maintenance of the sicads."

"Yes, that's true."

"Well, I would like to ask you about the dead sicad, Bartolome, and the nature of his demise."

Akihiko shifted uneasily.

"You described to me, in some detail, the manner in which he died and how this could not have been an accident. Can you please describe this to the court?"

Akihiko wiped his brow with a handkerchief.

"It's true, at first we thought that Bartolome's death had been caused deliberately. We found lesions in the organic cells of his brain, which we believed had been caused by extreme levels of stress leading up to expiry."

Fergus's eyes opened wide.

"How do you mean, at first?" he asked, almost choking on the growing dread which gripped his throat.

"Well, just in the last few days, on re-examining the sicads which expired accidently at CERN, we found evidence of the same phenomenon."

Fergus swore under his breath and looked up accusingly at Gort, who stared coldly and triumphantly back at him.

Lord Dunning looked across at Cornelius.

"Does the prosecution have any questions for the witness?"

"No, My Lord."

"Does the defence have any further questions for Mr Lee?"

"No... No, My Lord," uttered Fergus dejectedly.

With the courtroom spinning around him, he staggered back to his bench.

"Mr Fealey, the witness is evidently not able to substantiate your allegations, and in the absence of any other evidence I am obliged to ask the jury to dismiss your claims."

"Wait, My Lord..." stammered Fergus.

"Wait for what Mr Fealey?"

At that moment the court room doors flew open and an army officer in full uniform burst in, with a court official hanging off each arm.

Every head turned to stare at the unannounced man.

"What is the meaning of this intrusion?" boomed Lord Dunning.

The army officer shook his arms free and stood up proudly.

"Captain Rory Schiller. I have some important information and I wish to testify!"

"Captain Schiller, irrespective of your rank or desire, you cannot simply burst into a court of law and demand to testify! You are in serious contempt of court."

"Wait!" shouted Fergus, jumping to his feet.

"I requested the Captain as a witness. My request stands good!"

The courtroom descended into confusion. Cornelius got to his feet and strode towards the judge, waving papers and objecting vociferously. In the chaos, Governor Gort quietly withdrew from the courtroom.

Fergus, Cornelius and a score of legal clerks and officials gathered around Lord Dunning. A ferocious debate over whether or not Captain Schiller could testify ensued. Legal executives searched hurriedly through archived court records, searching for any legal precedent. The media was undertaking a similar exercise in parallel.

Unnoticed, a man wearing a roll neck sweater slipped behind the crowds of agitated lawyers and crawled behind the rear of the glass box. With a screwdriver, he flicked open the front of the small plastic fuse box and deactivated the fuse, before neatly replacing the cover.

Minutes later, to Cornelius's displeasure, the question of legal procedure had been quickly resolved and the session resumed. All eyes fell upon Captain Rory Schiller as he placed his hand on the Bible.

"I swear to tell the truth, the whole truth and nothing but the truth. Otherwise let God strike me down!"

Simon stared at the Captain in anticipation. The sicad had no idea what this unexpected development signified, but it felt positive – things surely can't get any worse? In the corner of his eye he became aware of a familiar face – a man at the back of the court, next to the aisle, wearing a roll neck top and reading a newspaper. Magnus? Magnus was dead! The man was the spitting image of the Swedish sicad chief, yet somehow he looked different – his eyes! It was the newspaper which had first attracted Simon's attention – why would anybody be reading a newspaper now? Suddenly, he recognised the eyes. He watched in disbelief as the man raised the newspaper. A small bulge appeared at the top of the paper. Simon stood up and shouted at the judge, at Fergus and the crowds. Nobody seemed to hear him. There was no time!

Captain Schiller blinked in surprise as a flickering red digital image of an ear appeared on the dark shiny LCD strip next to the Bible. An instant later he dived to the floor. Nobody heard the shot, fired through a silencer, but everyone saw the Captain's cap fly across the court. Lord Dunning cried out in shock as shards of plaster hit his cheek and a puff of white dust momentarily shrouded his eyes. The words 'ASSASSIN! GET DOWN!' were still flashing on the hard-of-hearing display panel on the empty witness box.

The court erupted into confusion; everyone leapt up from their seats, except Captain Schiller, who remained cautiously on the floor. Simon lost sight of the assassin. Realising the Governor had severed the electrics to his glass box and nobody could hear him, he banged on the glass. When nobody paid any attention, still unable to access the internet, he sent another message through the hard of hearing system, accessible since Gort had unwittingly disabled the scramblers.

'GORT IS ESCAPING, DISGUISED AS MAGNUS!' was flashing unnoticed on the witness box.

Police officers and court officials rushed around searching the building and shouting instructions into radios and mobile phones. The crowd were stunned. Nobody moved, with the exception of a lone figure with a newspaper tucked under his arm, quietly making his way away from the Old Bailey.

Minutes later, the solitary figure was being helped into a small speed boat by a dark-skinned man with a purple scar.

"You'd better wear this," he recommended, passing his passenger a shiny helmet with a tinted visor.

The man rolled down the neck of his sweater and quickly pulled off the tight mask, substituting the black helmet.

"We have a motorcycle waiting for us in Docklands and a plane on standby at Biggin Hill."

The engine roared into life and the speedboat raced into the middle of the river.

"Don't worry about the speed – there are only restrictions on the size of our wake! This is one quirky historic English law in our favour," announced the scar-faced man.

David Gort unfolded his newspaper and levelled the revolver, with a long silencer attached, at Leopold.

"I'm tempted to shoot you!"

"That would be very unwise, Mr Gort. I think you need our services more than ever now."

Gort hesitated before dropping the gun into the Thames.

54

The trial resumed two hours later. Captain Schiller gave his evidence and Simon was swiftly acquitted of all charges. An inquiry into the death of the fisherman was ordered and a sizeable bounty offered for any information leading to David Gort's capture.

*

Later that day, the instigator of the Better World Trust campaign, who had found Mr Leopold, destroyed the mobile phone he'd used to contact him. He knew the others, whose opposition to the project was more predictable, would do the same. There was no proof unless one of them spoke. It would be unlikely that anybody would suspect an old man like him of wanting to destroy the lucrative fruits of his own factory. He'd guessed early on, however, that the sicads, the supreme technology themselves, were going to reject technology and that wouldn't be in Mazari's longer-term interests. His eight decades of life experience had taught him that people always covet what they haven't got – why should the sicads be any exception?

*

Pierre, who'd followed Gort's men, led the authorities to Bruno's whereabouts – the underground wine cellar of a sumptuous mansion, just a few hundred metres from the D11 on the western outskirts of Paris. The renegade soldiers who had been guarding him had already departed. An emaciated Bruno staggered out into the bright sunlight. The house belonged to an American billionaire, who had made his money from shale gas and strenuously denied any knowledge of its unauthorised usage.

After just three days of medical attention and rest, Bruno resumed his role as United Nations Governor. He went straight into a series of long meetings with government heads, who were rapidly distancing themselves from the activities of David Gort. Rather than waste time and energy on recriminations, Bruno used his bargaining power to get the Socrates Project back on track. After two days of intense negotiations, with all member states of the United Nations backing him, he took the opportunity to address the world.

Citizens of the world,

We have come to a crossroads in the history of humanity. Through our desire for progress we created the sicads, to help resolve increasing social and environmental problems that are pushing our civilisations to the point of collapse. In creating the sicads, we went far beyond what we dreamed was possible and triggered the creation of a form of artificial life. For the first time in our modern history, we now co-exist with another conscious life form. Many of you are wary of these life forms; this wariness, a trait that has served us well in our evolution, stems from our own survival instinct, individually and as a species. You see competition for limited resources and the threat that this new form of artificial life may one day enslave us. You would feel more comfortable with this potential threat to humanity removed.

Others have quickly recognised the potential of the sicads to help humanity. These people have opened their eyes fully to our problems and are ready to listen carefully to the sicads' advice on how to fix them. These people have the courage to believe in a better world.

As this trial has proved, as will the detailed recommendations that the sicads will be making to our governments, the sicads are a positive force for humanity. Unsaddled by vested interests, virtuous, and with the analytical capability exceeding our most powerful computers, these beings will provide us with unbiased solutions for a better future for humanity.

Some of you may be asking yourselves why we need help, why we cannot organise ourselves. Well, for whatever reasons, we seem unable to bring ourselves to plan effectively for the long-term and act to stave off crises before they arrive. There are no better examples of this than the series of financial crises we have endured for the last few decades.

The natural crisis that is now approaching us, identified by our own scientists and whose worse predictions have been confirmed by the sicads, is a crisis that we simply cannot afford to let happen. By the time this hits us it will be too late. We cannot restructure nature's bank. The rich deposits of this bank have been created over hundreds of millions of years.

We must now put our insecurities and fears aside and embrace the help that the sicads can offer. We must put an end to the dilemma that has plagued us. We must accept the outcome of this trial as an indication of which direction humanity must take. We must accept the help that is offered to us. We must follow the path of hope and progress.

We believe that the Socrates Project has been a resounding success, and I have agreed with international governments that the sicads will be distributed as advisors to all national governments. Each country, according to size and population, will be allocated at least one sicad advisor. The sicads will help ensure that the long term interests of all humans, regardless of colour and race, are best served. They will help us construct our political and economic systems to be sustainable and independent of vested interests. In short, they will help us ensure that we have a truly meritocratic and durable global democracy.

The huge power of the sicads to work individually and collectively will facilitate the smooth functioning of a G200, where the interests of all countries, however small, will be equally represented. Simon Oceandis has been appointed as chief advisor to oversee and coordinate this mammoth task.

Lastly, in creating the sicads to conduct the research for the Socrates Project, we made them citizens. In return, they have done humanity an enormous service. We must now honour our commitment to them and recognise them as citizens of the planet. The sicads will enjoy all the same rights and responsibilities as humans. They will be paid for the services they supply as advisors, and will be free to live amongst humans as they see fit.

As this trial made clear, anyone who harms a sicad is harming humanity. It was telling to witness the sad demise of a man with the potential of David Gort. Let this be a lesson to all of us.

In a few short months my mandate will come to a close. I hope that, in that short time, you will come to appreciate how the sicads and the Socrates Project can help to build a more just and sustainable world.

Thank you for listening,

Bruno Reno

The Socrates Project was back on track. The sicads were released from CERN and were shortly to depart for their new roles. They had been allocated to the countries they'd researched and grown to love.

*

408

Straight after the trial, Simon headed back to Chamonix with Osiris. He wanted to show her where it all began for him, on that glacier – at least that was the pretext. They took the same tent they'd shared for seven months. Camped on the glacier underneath a full moon, Simon proposed to Osiris. He told her she could never bear his children. Without hesitation, she accepted and told him there were enough children in the world already needing adoptive parents. The future of humanity is learning to love all children, she said. The Waorani spirit and sicad spirit would live on in them through their nurtured wisdom, in the same way Socrates had left a trail of wisdom for all children through his contribution to education.

After a passionate night on the glacier, they were heading back to Geneva and on to Paris. En route, Simon asked Osiris to drop him near the monastery. He asked her to leave him for an hour.

Jia had yet to leave the monastery. She was waiting for Simon to pick her up. She rushed up to him, having meticulously planned this moment. She had sworn to herself she'd have the courage to throw her arms around him and practised a dozen times behind the closed door of Mother Cristina's chamber. But she stopped when she saw the expression on his face, his body language – the language of rejection.

She'd invested too much in this moment; she'd bring him round. She wanted to jump into his arms like Osiris would have done. She'd be like the feisty savage, yet with her brain... he'd see.

"So, you're a free citizen. It's incredible!" she enthused.

He simply smiled sympathetically.

"We can achieve great things together now, Simon, you and I, together."

His face had turned to a look of concern. She dug deeper.

"The amazing scientific breakthroughs we can make together, you'll see – we'll win Nobel prizes and revolutionise the world through technology."

Simon shook his head sadly.

"Jia, mankind has overdosed on technology. Already it's making millions of humans unemployed and unemployable. Governments are trying to dream up artificial jobs for these people, whilst enormous machines ravage the land and spray chemicals to neutralise all competing life. If this trend carries on, robots will be replacing humans, like the shop assistant in the supermarket. Profit-incentivised firms will want to employ these robots who never make mistakes, are never sick and don't need pensions or holiday pay. What will happen to the humans who are displaced? Technology liberates some and enslaves others. Humans need to enlighten themselves through rediscovering natural wisdom, not rely on technology to do this for them. No Jia, I will be advising governments against allowing more robots."

She dug deeper.

"That's just one aspect of technology, but we can make medical discoveries, turn humans into sicads, create hybrids who'll never die..."

"Stop, Jia. Everything must evolve and die – it's nature's way of eliminating mistakes and keeping things in balance. If you stop this, you will kill nature. Life is about quality, not quantity."

Jia shrieked and closed her ears. She lit a cigarette, puffed deeply and resumed.

"She's bewitched you! She's brainless! She's not even attractive... You're sick. I can fix you."

"Osiris knows how to enjoy life and she's happy to be part of a system. I'm happy with her, just to exist, to enjoy. I don't need to achieve great breakthroughs."

"No, you can't. I created you... You owe it to me. I created you for me! I funded Panasha to help you. You've no right to reject me. You'll obey me... You have to!"

"Jia, I'm eternally grateful for what you've done for me, but I'm a free citizen and I have chosen to be with Osiris. I'm going to marry her."

Jia threw herself at his feet, kneeling before him, sobbing and screaming.

For the first time in his life, Simon Oceandis didn't have a solution. Two nuns, attracted by the commotion, came to the door. They pushed him gently away and attended to the broken soul before them.

Simon walked away, a million permutations reverberating through him, but not a single solution to Jia's dilemma that didn't betray his own heart.

The End
Live the Story: www.the-socrates-project.com

ACKNOWLEDGEMENTS

Special thanks must go to the many who were instrumental in bringing The Socrates Project into being:

My wife Corrie and family (Vanessa, Thomas & Sophie) for temporarily losing a husband and a father
   Richard Webb for facilitating my sabbatical years
   Ross Leckie for reviewing all five drafts
   James Green for having the courage to blaze our own trail
   For Jonathon Porritt, for the idea for the Better World Trust
   Tania & Tamyras and Gert Jan & Gibbon for their belief
   The Chilterns countryside (and Paddy Blythe), Corsica, the Alps, Lebanon, South Africa and all the other inspirational landscapes
   All the outdoor guides and educators who shared the adventures and the projects which inspired the story, especially Yves Salino, Korbinian Hort, Raja Saadé, Max Chaya and Mark Beaumont
   Panasha, a catamaran with a soul, my La Pierre Cruiser cycle and my Pocket Rocket skis for carrying me up and down the mountains
   The French Language and especially to Victor Hugo and Marcel Proust for inspiring me to write
   Bob Marley, for guiding me through the ups and the downs of life
   Lindsay Whitelaw, Nabil Chaya, Peregrine Moncreiffe, Andrew Dykes, Simon Elliston-Ball, David Fox-Pitt, Mark Shand and my sister Kyra for all their support.

For the many others not mentioned by name, know that I acknowledge and value your help and support.

Very good - A ✓